A School Mistress at War

Eileen Ramsay grew up in Dumfriesshire. After graduation she went to Washington D.C. where she taught in private schools for some years before moving to California with her Scottish husband. There, she raised two sons, finished her Masters Degree, fell in love with Mexico, and published her first short stories and a Regency novel. The family returned to Scotland, where Eileen continued to teach and write and to serve – at different times – on the committees of the Society of Authors in Scotland, the Scottish Association of Writers and the Romantic Novelists' Association. In 2004, her novel *Someday, Somewhere* was shortlisted for the Romantic Novel of the Year award.

For more information, visit www.eileenramsay.co.uk

A School
Mistress
at War

Eileen Ramsay

ZAFFRE

First published in Great Britain in 1995
by Little, Brown as *The Dominie's Lassie*
This edition published in Great Britain in 2021 by
ZAFFRE
An imprint of Bonnier Books UK
4th Floor, Victoria House, Bloomsbury Square, London,
England, WC1B 4DA
Owned by Bonnier Books
Sveavägen 56, Stockholm, Sweden

A CIP catalogue record for this book is
available from the British Library.

ISBN: 978–1–785–76226–0

Also available as an ebook and audiobook

1 3 5 7 9 10 8 6 4 2

Typeset by IDSUK (Data Connection) Ltd
Printed and bound by Clays Ltd, Elcograf S.p.A.

Zaffre is an imprint of Bonnier Books UK
www.bonnierbooks.co.uk

For Colin and Alistair
With a big much love

1

KIRSTY COULD BARELY CONTAIN HERSELF. Father was the dearest man in the world, and the cleverest, but if he didn't tell her what the Board had said in that letter, she would, she would . . .

'Jessie, my dear, if I might have a generous bowl of your excellent soup?'

'Father,' groaned Kirsty. He was deliberately being provoking, trying to sound like something out of a novel by Dickens. John Robertson, headmaster of the small country school, always read all official letters quietly before drawing his chair into the table and smiling at his wife and daughter, but this letter, Kirsty knew, just had to refer to her and therefore should be treated differently – and immediately.

'John,' said Mother reprovingly but, as always, she smiled when she looked at her husband.

'Oh, are you two ladies interested in hearing what was in my communication from the Board?' He unfolded his large linen napkin and solemnly spread it across the knees of his second-best suit before taking pity on their curiosity. 'Why, naturally they said that Miss Christine Robertson could be employed as a pupil teacher.'

Kirsty jumped up and threw her arms around her father and then danced across and hugged her mother, almost covering the pair of them with hot soup. She was going to be a pupil teacher. That frightening body called the Board had allowed it, and now she could help him officially. Oh, was it not about time?

'Immediately?' she said. 'Do I start tomorrow, and may I put my hair up? It would be better, wouldn't it, Mother?'

'No.'

'Yes.'

Her parents spoke together and they all laughed.

'Your father first,' said Jessie Robertson.

'Miss Christine Robertson is to start at the beginning of the next session, and at the truly magnificent sum of five pounds per annum.' He smiled to soften his daughter's disappointment. 'It's only another three weeks, Kirsty. You can wait three weeks.'

Three weeks! It was an age, and she was bored to tears with being a pupil: she was cleverer by far than any of these farm children. Conveniently Miss Cameron forgot that she alone of the children never missed school through working on the surrounding farms. But besides, only today there had been seventy-one pupils in a one-room school and she had already waited five months for permission to become part of his staff; his only staff, if you didn't count Jessie, who, being a married woman, was graciously permitted to teach sewing to the girls. The embroidery taught at the little country school was of the highest standard – but of what use to farm children, Kirsty could not imagine. Still, the two hours weekly, from three to four on Mondays and Thursdays, were much enjoyed by the girls and the small payment did help to eke out John's meagre salary.

'They call what they pay your mother an emolument, Kirsty,' John had said when he and his daughter had discussed her proposition that, now she had reached the age of fourteen, she might be hired as a pupil teacher until she was old enough to sit the scholarship examinations for the university. 'Is that not,' he went on, 'a splendid word to wrap up a few shillings in? Why, I do believe it's bigger than the sum itself.'

'And naturally you must put your hair up, Kirsty,' said Jessie now as she watched her daughter prance around the room, 'and I shall make you a new dress, and with a longer skirt as befits a working woman.'

'With an apron, Jessie. Kirsty is only fourteen years old. We do not want her aged before her time.'

Mother and daughter smiled at one another but said nothing. There would be an apron all right, but it would still be a dress that told the world that Christine Robertson was embarking on a career.

After tea John went back into the school to correct exercises and, after helping her mother clear up, Kirsty wandered outside into the garden. It was a riot of spring flowers and already neat rows of vegetables were thrusting themselves importantly from the ground. She walked among them, bending every now and again to remove a weed that had had the audacity to show its sinful head. When schoolwork permitted, John Robertson could be found in his garden. He said that he enjoyed the hard physical labour after the mental torture of trying to fill young – mostly unwilling – minds with the three Rs.

'Kirsty.'

She looked up from her weeds with a smile that transformed her face, had she but known it, from little girl to blossoming woman.

'Jamie, oh, Jamie, where have you been? You've not been at school for weeks.'

Jamie Cameron was thirteen years old, almost a year younger than Kirsty, and from their first day together at the small country school he had been her rival and her dearest friend. She looked at him now, too pale, much too thin. His long, badly cut hair lifted from his forehead in the gentle evening air as they talked, and Kirsty saw the bruise his hair had tried to hide and felt the pain of the blow that had caused it.

'I think that could poetically be described as a noble brow,' John Robertson had said once when talking to a school inspector who had laughed at his plans for the ragged urchin before them. 'This laddie might well have more brains than either of us. With a modicum of care and affection and an education, I vow the lad could go anywhere.'

Where was he going? Kirsty thought now as she looked at her friend.

'Ach, spring's too busy a time on a fairm, Kirsty,' Jamie excused his truancy. 'I dinna ken when I'll get back, but I brocht the Dominie's book. Could he let me have another by the same fella? Grand stories.'

He handed her a thick leather-bound volume and she looked at the title as she took it, one of her father's most precious possessions. How he must value Jamie to allow the treasured volume from his sight.

'*Hard Times*.' Clever as she was, she hadn't yet read it, hadn't wanted to. Dickens was too . . . too gloomy. A sombre choice for a farm lad.

'I'll ask Father for another book for you, Jamie. Are you sure you want another Dickens? Maybe something from Sir Walter Scott?'

He smiled. 'Will he let me hae the lend of another book, Kirsty? I'll no' be back till winter, if at all.'

Kirsty decided not to remind him that he had missed most of the winter months too, and surely there was nothing to do on a farm in the cold dark days? 'I'm sure he will,' was all she said. 'Come on in. Father's in the schoolroom – he'd love to see you.'

'I cannae bide,' said the boy cautiously, but already moving with her towards the school. 'M'faither'll miss me. I should be in ma bed. We're up at three these mornings.'

'Heavens, what on earth do you do at that time of the morning? Surely cows and things are still asleep?'

John Robertson rose from the desk where he had been labouring over the exercises, and his smile showed his pleasure at the sight of his young visitor. 'Jamie. You've come for another book.' He ignored the boy's truancy. 'I suppose we won't see you in school until the winter now?'

'I'll be fourteen by November, Dominie. I've maybe had my last lesson.'

'Would it help if I spoke to your father, Jamie? Maybe he needs reminding that there's a fine mind in that haystack of a head of yours and that, unlike turnips, it needs nurturing?'

The fear on the boy's face was answer enough.

'It doesn't take a fine mind to plant tatties, Mr Robertson,' said he, trying hard to remember the standard English words that warred with his Angus dialect.

'Your father's employer is a good man, lad, with his own son off to a fine school. Perhaps . . .?'

'Father.' Kirsty, tired of being completely ignored, interrupted. 'Jamie likes Dickens, but I thought something not quite so intense.'

'My daughter prefers mainly happy endings to her stories, Jamie.' John looked at the title page of the book the boy had returned. 'I think something stirring, perhaps Sir Walter . . . a medieval adventure, or no, wait . . .'

From the shelf behind his table he lifted down a slim volume. 'Poetry, lad. All the greats are here, and if you learn them off as you read them, you will always have beauty in your head.'

Jamie took the book reverently and opened the pages at random. 'There's beautiful words of my own in my head, Dominie, not near so great as these, but I like fine to hear them now and then.'

His thin cheeks coloured at his own audacity and with a stifled 'Thank you' he went from the room, taking the little book with him.

Kirsty and her father looked after him.

'It's an unjust world, Kirsty,' sighed John. 'That laddie has more ability than you and me put together, but he'll die at the handle of a plough with his beautiful words still in his head, not out there for the world to console itself with.'

Kirsty bridled a little at her father's seeming criticism. She was cleverer than Jamie Cameron. She always beat him in tests – well, almost always.

'You could talk to Balcundrum, Father. Did you see the bruise on Jamie's head?'

'It's the bruises I can't see that bother me, lass. Damn it, to have a son like that and . . .' He pulled himself together. 'Come, Kirsty, your mother will be looking for you. Were you not to attempt some stitches before bed? And something tells me that there is a bolt of cloth put by just in case Miss Christine was acceptable to the Board. I know you ladies and your wiles: a tuck here, a tuck there, and what starts out as a simple frock becomes a fine gown. Off you go. I must try to make some sense of the Supplementary Class essays before I come through for supper.'

Kirsty moved to the door that connected schoolroom and living room. Her brown curls bounced on her shoulders and a devil lurked in her brown eyes as she turned to smile at her father.

'Jamie will not be the first unlettered farm lad to write poetry, Father. Was not Robert Burns a farmer?'

'Ach, come back a minute, Kirsty, if you can tear yourself away from your sewing,' said John wryly. Kirsty was more his daughter than Jessie's; she would never happily spend time sewing. He waited until his daughter had seated herself at a desk, looking, had she but known it, more child than teacher.

'My intellect tells me that Scotland's national bard was a fine poet, but my upbringing drummed into me that Lallans is the language of the peasant classes. Can you try to understand, lass, that it is therefore to be avoided by those who are themselves scarcely a step from the peasantry.' He stood up and walked around the small room as if to better emphasize what he had to say. 'What fine people your grandparents were, Kirsty. Did I not go to the university on the shoulders of their sacrifices? Then there was your Uncle Chay, my brother, who happily, proudly even, worked day in, day out for his bright laddie. They wanted me to better myself, to be able to mix in any society.'

Kirsty looked up at him, her eyes shining. 'Grampa told me that the day you became a teacher was the greatest day of their lives.'

'Yes, indeed.' John's thoughts went to his mother who, worn out by toil and too many pregnancies, had not lived to see her only grandchild, or to see her son become master of a one-room school. He could never say such things to a young girl, of course.

'For your grandma it was enough that I was educated, but it was she who encouraged me to adopt the language of my books as a natural one. "I dinnae want ye ever to be ashamed o' yer faither nor me, John," she used to say, "but God's seen fit tae gie ye a brain and yer faither an' me wants fer you to use it. An' Chay tae. Is he no' longing fer the day he can say, ma brither's a dominie?"'

'And now you are the Dominie, the teacher.'

'Yes, and can you understand that every class contains my parents and my brother, who never had my advantages? Their sacrifices will be repaid. Every child who passes through my hands will receive the best that I can give them, especially you, my wee Kirsty.' He looked at the young girl, at her shining, loving eyes, at her tumbled brown curls, and with a little trepidation he noted the determined little chin. Kirsty would fight for what she wanted: he hoped the battle would not be too onerous. When she was a little older he intended her to go on to Edinburgh University. Now she was saying that she was perfectly content to become a pupil teacher and to qualify here in his classroom, but he feared that she was thinking only of him. There were sometimes over seventy children on the register, but with illness, which was common, and the need of many families for their able-bodied children to work, there were often fewer than twenty pupils in the classroom. It was difficult, therefore, to persuade the Board that a second teacher was necessary, though it was due to John Robertson's care and ability that many of the children were allowed to come to school at all.

'Schooling's no' for the likes of us,' was the attitude of many itinerant farmworkers, but when they stayed in this little corner of Angus near the town of Arbroath they heard of the skill and ability of the local Dominie, and they registered at least their younger children. Such had been the experience of Jamie Cameron. He had been sent to the school when he was too young to be of any help at home, and when his mother was told that the lad was bright she had taken the news back in awe to her husband, who had been singularly unimpressed. Jamie had been in attendance regularly until he was seven. After that he had helped out with chores or minding his even younger brothers and sisters in order to free his mother to do a man's work.

But young Kirsty Robertson was not thinking of her schoolfellow's problems as she returned with a toss of her brown curls to the little living room where her mother was already unrolling a bolt of blue cloth. In her exchange with her father, Kirsty had temporarily forgotten Jamie, and for now she was interested only in her mother's plans for the new dress.

'See, Kirsty, I will make a pale blue collar and blue cuffs which we can interchange with white ones for variety and to save the material. It's lovely, isn't it? Then we will have a white apron to please Father, and a pale blue one, and perhaps for Sundays and special days I might find some lace. We'll see.'

'And no more pigtails. I am Miss Robertson from now on. Oh, Mother, show me how to put up my hair. There's too much, surely, to sit securely on my head.'

'You must anchor it with pins,' said Jessie, gathering her daughter's curls and holding them on top of her little head. 'Your hair, like your pupils, will require discipline.'

'You sound just like a schoolmarm,' said Kirsty, throwing her arms exuberantly around her mother and hugging her. 'Just think,' she continued as she dropped into an armchair and began to pick at a loose thread on one of the beautifully embroidered covers, 'the Board is going to let me help Father. He'll have to let me help with marking now, Mother, and I can prepare lessons for the little ones and hear them read while Father does mathematics and science with the older ones, and then at night, when he's finished his logbooks, he'll have time to read or to sing or to work in his garden if it pleases him.'

'Don't unpick that butterfly unless you are prepared to replace it with another one,' said Jessie mildly. 'Here, find me a blue thread and I shall mend it.'

'No, I can manage a repair. I'll stitch this loose end in while you cut the pattern for my dress.'

They worked together companionably until John returned from the school.

'And where is the fine seam you were to try tonight, Miss Pupil Teacher?' he asked as he bent over his daughter to kiss her good night.

'There, Father.' Kirsty pointed to the delicate butterfly that hovered over an exotic bloom on the chair arm. 'I worked on that.' True enough; but it was rather a stretching of the complete truth.

She ignored her mother's reproving look and blew her a kiss. 'Don't strain your eyes with sewing, Mother. The new pupil teacher promises to help you with the easy bits: the bits that don't show.'

Upstairs in her little room under the eaves, she stood for a while holding up her hair and admiring the picture she presented in the mirror. 'Good day, Miss Robertson,' she bowed to her reflection. 'We, the Board, have been told that never in the history of Angus education has there been such a pupil teacher as yourself. We have decided, there-fore, to go against every tenet we have been taught to hold dear, and to offer you, a woman – and here she stopped to contemplate the enormity of what she was saying – the Rectorship of the Arbroath Academy.'

The very idea of a woman head teacher was so over-whelming that Kirsty found herself unable to continue with her posturing and went to the window. Down there in the valley was the magnificent Georgian mansion of Balcundrum Farm, and just behind it but still visible from her window was the tiny tied cottage where Jamie and his family lived.

'Oh, it's an unjust world, Jamie lad. Here's me with a room to myself and you sharing with five brothers and sisters, and me with a new dress and your sisters in my cast-off petticoats.' For a moment Kirsty allowed herself to realize that she enjoyed her privileges: she loved her little room with its simple privacy and she took clean clothes and good food as her natural right. Was she not the Dominie's lassie? Then as she remembered the bruise on Jamie's thin face, her better self surfaced. 'Ask your father to let you stay at the school. Ask him, Jamie, ask him.'

But Jamie did not hear and he did not ask.

2

THE NEW TERM STARTED AND the Dominie had a pupil teacher, his daughter Christine. Many of the older children were missing and John Robertson knew he would not see most of them until after the potatoes had been harvested in October or November. He must stop grieving over them and give himself up to the task of teaching the ones he had. He looked at the children sitting scribbling on their slates or laboriously deciphering the words in their readers. There they sat, girls on one side of the room – the side nearer the fire – and the boys carefully segregated on the other.

The spring was still wet and had been cold, but many of his pupils had no shoes and some were without overcoats: possibly another reason for their non-attendance in the winter. He must think of something different for them to do. He stood up and immediately the room was quite silent. Gentle though he was, when the Dominie spoke it was an unwise child who did not listen.

'Children,' he began, 'raise your hands if you come up Pansy Lane to school in the mornings.' He counted a score of hands of varying degrees of cleanness. 'Good. And how many walk from the direction of the valley? Ah, good. Everyone, therefore, passes meadows of wild flowers on his or her way to school.' He stopped and looked smilingly at their expectant faces. 'Tomorrow we will have drawing from still life for all the classes' – again he paused, sure of his audience and their reaction – 'and the prettiest arrangements will be taken to the town to the Infirmary to cheer the lives of the patients there. Miss Robertson will accompany the winners. In the meantime Netta Spink will wash her hands before Mrs Robertson comes to take sewing.'

He sat down again amid an excited murmuring from the little ones who would merely be cautioned if they spoke too long and too loudly. The older pupils contented themselves with conspiratorial smiles at one another, except for the embarrassed and hapless Netta who went outside to scrub her hands.

'We must find a list of the flowers among our library books,' Kirsty told her little ones, who had no seats and sat tumbled together like a litter on the floor at her feet, 'for I am sure Mr Robertson will want to see that we have learned something in our nature studies.'

The school library was woefully inadequate, being, apart from some weighty biblical texts and some ponderous classics, almost non-existent.

'The Dominie has a book, Miss,' began one little girl hesitantly.

'Which book, Cissie?' asked Kirsty cheerily, for children in 1908 were not usually encouraged to contribute to any discussion.

'Oor Jamie says the Dominie's got books aboot everything.' It was Cissie Cameron, Jamie's sister. How Kirsty longed to ask for news of her friend.

Seeing that bold Cissie was not punished for her audacity, another spoke proudly. 'My grannie kens the names of the flooers, Miss.'

Kirsty smiled at her small pupil. 'Good, then you must ask your grannie to write the names down for you and to describe the flower. It need not be a big boy or girl who wins tomorrow. If our drawings are the very best that we can do, Mr Robertson will judge them fairly.'

A large tear was rolling down the face of Tam Grant, the little boy whose grandmother knew the wild flowers.

'Why, Tam dear, what's the matter?' asked Kirsty when the tear was followed by sobs, loud enough to cause the Dominie to turn his head to their corner of the room.

'My grannie cannae write, Miss. There's naebody in oor hoose writes.'

Kirsty was furious with herself. How could she have been so stupid!

'My brither will write them for her, Tam, and draw wee pictures tae.' It was Cissie who comforted her friend. 'There's naethin' oor Jamie cannae do.'

'Cissie's right, Tam. Jamie will write the words for you and I will read them to you tomorrow. Are you and Cissie going to pick flowers together?'

'Aye, Miss,' said Cissie. 'Baith oor faithers are hae jobs at Balcundrum and we walk tae school thegither. I take care of Tam. He's only wee.'

Kirsty smiled to herself, for Cissie Cameron was smaller than Tam even though she was almost two years older. Like her brother and the other Cameron children who were in the schoolroom, young Cissie was undernourished. Like her brother, she was also intelligent.

'Well, we must attend to our reading. Look at the chart I have prepared, and everybody read after me.'

The children's voices went on and automatically Kirsty corrected their hesitant pronunciation. Her mind was on Jamie Cameron, who was doing a man's job while he wrote poetry in his head. Wasn't that what he had hinted the last time she had seen him? The wonderful words in his head were his own, were they not?

'Miss Robertson, I would ask you to try to instil some appreciation of the words they are reading into the minds of the children in your care.' Her father had come up behind her and was listening to the droning of the small bees while their teacher's attention was clearly elsewhere. 'Should a poem by Wordsworth and a recipe for a cough linctus be delivered in the selfsame tone? No? Good. Then have young Jock read again. Now that he has the words, let him have also some pleasure in the task.'

Kirsty accepted the rebuke and turned her full attention to injecting some feeling into the oral reading of the children. They were so shy, they reminded her of calves grazing in the fields around the school. They would stand for a moment looking around them with big, wide eyes, and then they would turn and flee whenever an imagined danger threatened.

'Good, Cissie,' she said when the girl had solemnly finished her piece. 'Your reading is really beginning to sound very nice. Are you helping Tam with his ABCs?'

'Aye, and I've learned him to write his name, Miss.' Cissie looked at her young teacher to see how her confidence was received.

Kirsty thought quickly about correcting this grammatical error and decided against it. 'Show me, Tam.' And Tam, tongue firmly stuck out to help his concentration, scratched 'TAM' on his slate.

Kirsty enthusiastically praised his effort and, flushed with hard work and sweet praise, Tam sat at her feet.

'We have worked hard today, children,' said Kirsty, gathering up the primers and her charts, 'and already here is Mrs Robertson with her sewing boxes. Now, remember the flowers and your list of words, Cissie. I should like at least one infant to accompany me to the Infirmary tomorrow.'

When the school bell announced to the waiting farms that school was over for the day, Kirsty was exhausted. Teaching, and it seemed somehow the teaching of reading, was unbelievably tiring. The infants were all at different stages. Some were as young as five and others as old as eight, and sometimes a five-year-old had as much experience of education as the eight-year-olds. The itinerant or travelling children were the hardest to teach because there were great gaps in their education. Sometimes, if they were very lucky, there were schools near all the farms where their parents worked, but sometimes there would be months when no schooling at all was available.

'We must plug the gaps as best we can, Kirsty,' consoled John when his daughter confided in him. 'And if we can make education a pleasant experience, then the children will be eager to attend the schools in the various areas where their fathers work. Clever ones like wee Cissie will be fine. It's the slower ones like wee Tam and Jock, poor laddies, whom we have to worry about. They can't keep what they have learned from Friday to Monday, never mind from season to season. Our job is to accept them where they are and do the best we can with the material the good Lord has seen fit to give them.'

'I'm sorry I wasn't attending when they were reading this afternoon. It was just that Cissie mentioned Jamie and I felt sad and wondered what he was doing.'

'Planting barley today, I should imagine,' said her father drily.

'Oh, Father, you know I didn't mean literally. I was just thinking that he is as clever as I am.' She blushed and hung her head as his gentle eyes quizzed her. 'Well, I know you think he is cleverer, but I don't see how you can prove it.' She rushed on before he could speak. 'I know he would be so patient with the children, and here am I, the pupil teacher, and he is working on a farm. If I wasn't your daughter I would never have been given the job.'

'You were given the opportunity because of your education, Kirsty, not because you are the Dominie's lassie. Jamie, poor lad, doesn't have the knowledge that you have. He can read and write, but he knows nothing of mathematics or Latin or Greek, and the only history or geography he knows comes out of the books he reads. And how many books does he read in a year? A book of poetry between now and winter will not make him a teacher, lass.'

'His father should be forced to send him to school.'

'Jamie is only one of thousands. Don't waste your energy worrying about him, but concentrate on doing your best for his brothers and sisters.'

Kirsty said nothing, for she knew well that no one worried more about the bright children he could not reach than John Robertson. She had read his logbooks: the books he filled in every night when he had dismissed the children.

March 19th, 1908. Today Matthew Scroggie was given permission to leave school because of family necessity. I said 'Goodbye' to this boy with a heavy heart for since his first day in this school, Matthew Scroggie has shown by his diligence, ability and demeanour that he is capable of benefiting from the highest education. A great loss to all.

Oh, yes, John Robertson did not easily dismiss from his mind or heart the children whom he taught.

'Mrs Robertson says if you twa dinnae come fer yer tea noo, ye'll get naethin.'

'Thank you, Angus.' John looked up at the school janitor. 'We'll thankfully leave the rest to you.'

'Did Father tell you we are to have a drawing from life lesson tomorrow, Mother?' asked Kirsty later as she washed the dishes after their meal. 'They are to pick wild flowers.

We will hear the children in the lane hours before school, I should imagine.'

Jessie Robertson looked at her husband as he sat reading by the window. 'What a lovely idea, John. And who is to judge your competition?'

He looked up in surprise. 'I hadn't considered an outside judge. It's nothing great, not like the annual exhibition of your sewing, my dear.'

Kirsty turned with a swirl of blue skirts. 'Mother's right. It would be so exciting for the children. Now, who could we find at such short notice?'

'The Colonel,' suggested Kirsty and her mother together, and when John looked doubtful, Kirsty set herself to assuring him. 'He takes his responsibility as laird seriously, Father. He is interested in the children, and if they are to decimate his wild flowers he might as well see them in their jam jars.'

John looked at his silver pocket watch, but he was already rising to his feet. 'It's nearly nine o'clock. No time to be calling on a man.'

'He'll be at his dinner,' said Kirsty, hurrying into the hall for her father's hat. 'The gentry eat later than plain folk. No doubt he will invite you to coffee, and if there are ladies there, you must remember their dresses and their jewels to tell us about.'

'Make sure you are in bed before I return, Miss. Dresses and jewels, indeed! Have I taught you nothing of what is truly valuable?' was his parting shot as he left the house for his mile-long walk to the home of Colonel Granville-Baker, a small thirteenth-century castle which the English Colonel had bought and set himself to restoring on his return from the Boer War.

Kirsty and her mother watched his tall figure as he walked off down the road until he disappeared from sight.

'Has Father not become very thin this year, Mother?' asked Kirsty. 'He works too hard. Perhaps I was wrong to suggest the Colonel.'

'No, no, you were quite right, and if Colonel Granville-Baker is at home, he will offer your father some refreshment. He is a true gentleman. And then, the walk in the lovely evening air will do John good. He spends too long over his books. Now, you must take yourself off to bed before he returns. You have a longer walk than to the castle before you tomorrow.'

'Oh, Mother, it's hardly five miles to Arbroath,' said Kirsty lightly. Her healthy young body relished the idea of a long walk to the hospital and back and, in her brand-new position, she relished the thought of being seen: C. Robertson, Pupil Teacher, in charge of the children. 'The children will be overjoyed to be released from lessons and, just think, I shall be being paid for taking a walk. We should have such lessons every day.'

Kirsty dawdled over her preparations for bed and, since her bedroom lay at the back of the house, even left her door open in the hope of hearing her father return. He smiled quietly to his wife when they closed it on their sleeping daughter after midnight, for John had found the Colonel at home, and not only had he been offered brandy and coffee as they chatted, but he had been driven home by the Colonel's chauffeur. How Kirsty would have enjoyed seeing that!

He relived it for her in the morning, but a motor car did not hold the same fascination as London dresses.

'I regret, for your sake, that I did not see Lady Sybill Granville-Baker, Kirsty. She was in the drawing room, where I believe she sits for a while after dinner. The Colonel's son was at home though; a charming young man, a student at Sandhurst, the Military College, you know.'

Kirsty had no interest in students at Sandhurst. Colonel Granville-Baker's son might be the man in the moon for all the chance Miss Kirsty Robertson had of seeing him.

When John vigorously tolled the school bell at precisely nine o'clock, he did it in the very ears of most of his students. For once there were few stragglers in the lanes that led to the little school. The children, their faces rosy from exertion, were already massed in the small playground. Almost everyone, boys and girls alike, carried huge straggling bunches of flowers, and most had a jar in which to arrange them.

'Put your flowers here in the shade,' ordered John, 'and when we are ready we will come for them.'

The day progressed. Attendance. Bible study. Dictation for the older ones, prepared by John and given by Kirsty while the Dominie examined the little ones in their retention of number facts. He stood towering over them, his gown making him seem even taller, but few faces registered any fear. His delight in Jock's awareness that two times eight did indeed make sixteen was as great as Jock's own.

And now there should be the dreaded parsing and analysis which had to be the Dominie's favourite since he did it every spare minute, but eyes darting from the slates where they were transcribing Miss Robertson's dictation could see no sentences with innumerable and terrifying clauses. Perhaps they were on the back. The Maister was leaving the wee ones: he was moving to the board, he would swing it round to reveal the sentences . . . There was the release of a collective sigh. He was standing before it waiting while Miss Robertson finished.

'Children, we will adjourn for five minutes to refresh ourselves. Each child will visit the conveniences.' His dark eyes dwelt for a moment on Tam. 'When I ring the bell you will bring in your flowers, arrange them artistically and commence drawing. This afternoon we are to have an honoured guest. Colonel Granville-Baker has kindly agreed to judge your arrangements. I know he will not be greeted by dirty hands or jammy faces.'

He finished by giving some of the older children the responsibility for seeing that the younger ones did not disgrace the school or their illustrious guest. Kirsty smiled to herself as she pictured the harsh scrubbing of little faces that would go on in the school lavatory in the dinner hour.

After dinner the children stood in rows before their flowers, waiting breathlessly. There was the sound of a motor car. They would see it: they would actually be able to see the exciting machine close up when they went out to bid goodbye to the Colonel. Kirsty stood with the children while her father greeted his guest. She was almost as excited as they were.

John followed Colonel Granville-Baker into the room and then behind him came the most beautiful creature Kirsty had ever seen. Hugh Granville-Baker was a very handsome young man. He stooped to enter the classroom and then straightened up and looked at Kirsty with blue eyes that were sparkling with suppressed merriment. His clothes had that mixture of carelessness and good tailoring that can only be worn well by the self-assured.

'Christine.' Her father's voice alerted her to the fact that not only was she staring at the slender, dark-haired apparition as avidly as eleven-year-old Netta, but that she was ignoring the Colonel's outstretched hand. She coloured furiously and desperately sought to recover her poise. He would be laughing at her; she just knew he would.

But Hugh's eyes registered only friendliness. 'Miss Robertson,' he said, and shook her hand.

She almost pulled her hand away. He had to have felt it, whatever it was that had shot from her fingers up her arm and across her shoulder to the very point of her small breast. She could hardly breathe. Father would be furious. Oh, dear God in Heaven, what was happening to her?

No one noticed, and certainly not Hugh. Already he was wandering around chatting to the children. If he thought their unsophisticated arrangements amusing, his feelings did not show.

'Miss, Miss.' A horrified whisper from her side, a small hand tugging at her arm. 'Tam's peed.'

The excitement of a visit from not one but two deities had been too much for small Tam's control, but Kirsty welcomed the interruption.

'Wipe up the puddle, Cissie, and I'll take him outside.'

She stood with the sobbing child looking out over the fields and felt the early-summer breeze cool her hot face.

'It's all right, Tam. Mr Robertson will understand.'

How blue the sea was today, more blue surely than she had ever seen it. *Mr Robertson will understand.* It was she who would not understand. Something had happened and she was changed for ever. She knew it. She heard her mind whispering his name: Hugh. Had there ever been a more noble name? Hugh. Her lips formed the syllable and blew it away across the fields to the sea.

'The Dominie's looking for you, Miss.'

Kirsty started, hoping the boy had not heard. 'Yes, yes, I'm coming. Tam, you stand here in the sun till you dry. Mrs Robertson will get you clean drawers when the Colonel has gone.'

Inside the schoolroom the competition was over. The proud winners stood before their jars, Netta holding a large blue rosette, lovingly stitched the night before by Mrs Robertson, to show that she had won first place. She was bursting with pride, and indeed she had made something very special of her flowers and a marmalade jar. Wee Cissie had won the Infants' section for her flowers, which to Kirsty, and no doubt to the judges, looked as if they had been pulled protesting from the ground and dumped in what she called a 'jeelie jar'. Mrs Robertson had promised a smaller rosette for Cissie and the other prize-winners.

'Colonel Granville-Baker has done us the honour of accepting an invitation to a cup of tea, Kirsty. The children may have an afternoon playtime. Now run ben the house and help your mother.'

Kirsty was well used to important visitors. They were so far from town that all their guests were invited into the little Schoolhouse for some refreshment, but never ever had her heart sung while she loaded the immaculate tablecloth with their best plates full of her mother's delicate biscuits and cakes.

Hugh was a hearty eater and did justice to the tea. He was also very polite, and chatted first with his hostess and then with her daughter.

'And do you like being a pupil teacher, Miss Robertson? I must admit that I had not thought you old enough.'

'I am almost fifteen,' she insisted, 'and could have been helping Father for months if only the Board had allowed it.' Oh, heavens, her unbridled tongue. The Colonel was president of that august body.

But Hugh went on, 'And how do you become a real teacher?'

She looked at him. His face was serious; it seemed that he really wanted to know.

'I must study with Father, and that is easy because he is the cleverest and kindest teacher in the world, and then I will have classes in the evenings in Arbroath, although I'm sure I already know everything they will want to teach me.' She blushed furiously. How conceited that had sounded. 'I mean,' she said desperately, 'I have had the benefit of Father's personal tuition. One day I hope to attend the university in Edinburgh, although I could become certificated by passing exams.'

'Good heavens, you terrify me, a bluestocking,' but his eyes were twinkling and she laughed with him.

'Father tells me you are a student too, Mr Granville-Baker,' said Kirsty, boldly grasping the horns of her first conversation with a man other than her father or the local minister.

'Indeed, but none of my fellow students has to stand outside to dry,' he laughed, and Kirsty blushed to the roots of her hair. He had seen Tam's fall from grace. No doubt the Colonel had too . . . and Father.

'Oh, poor Tam,' she said. 'He is still standing outside.'

'Shall we rescue him? Come.'

Their elders were deep in conversation as they slipped out and watched the excited children still milling around in the playground. Tam stood in the same place, thumb in mouth, rocking back and forth, almost asleep.

'Tam, you're dry now,' whispered Kirsty. 'Go and play.'

The child darted a look at her and the magnificent male creature beside her and then ran off to join the other boys hanging over the school railings while they examined the even more magnificent motor car. At the appearance of his employer's son, the chauffeur had begun ostentatiously to rub the dust from its great gleaming sides.

'I have an idea,' said Hugh laughingly. 'We must chauffeur the winners to the hospital, poor little beggars – and their beautiful young teacher, too,' he added, eyeing

Kirsty appraisingly so that she blushed. It was one thing to stand at her mirror and decide that she really was a very attractive young woman, and then quite another to have to deal with seeing the same message in the eyes of a personable young man. 'Excuse me a second. I'll talk to Father.'

He rushed off and a few minutes later the Dominie appeared with the Colonel beside him. As usual, the children lined up quietly when they saw him.

'Children,' he said, 'I have a wonderful surprise for the winners.' There was an excited twitching from the assembled children. 'Colonel Granville-Baker is going to allow the six winners to drive with him in his beautiful machine as far as the entrance to the castle driving sweep.'

The children could not contain their exhilaration and an excited buzzing broke out. The Dominie held up his hand. Again there was quiet.

'Let us have three rousing cheers for the Colonel and Mr Granville-Baker.'

Had ever three such loud cheers been heard in the whole of Angus as the children expressed their pleasure at the happiness of the day! If they were not winners and therefore not allowed the privilege of being driven in a motor car, each one now knew someone who was about to achieve such sophistication. Was the Colonel not the most wonderful man in the world, and his son and his driver and even their own Dominie? They cheered them-selves hoarse.

The odd procession set off, only the chauffeur looking disapproving. He had not lovingly polished his car for the benefit of the country's riff-raff. The Colonel sat majesti-cally in front; Kirsty and the children squeezed into the back seat while Hugh perched himself on the back, his long legs hanging over the side, heedless of the dust clinging to his polished shoes and immaculately creased trousers. Several other children walked beside the car as it gathered some speed, and hurried it on its way with more cheers and loving touches of its elegant sides. There was no con-versation, and all too soon the castle gates were reached and Hugh jumped off to open the door.

'Goodbye, Miss Robertson. I wish we might drive you all the way, but the walk is supposed to be good for the children.'

He was holding her hand. She was more conscious of him than she had ever been of anyone else in her entire life as she smiled at him.

'Goodbye, Mr Granville-Baker.' She wanted to cry. There was an empty feeling in the pit of her stomach where a moment ago there had been such joy.

'Children, wave to the Colonel,' she said, and the assorted group stood watching the car as it progressed up the long drive to the castle. She hoped Hugh would turn to catch a last glimpse of their waving hands, but he did not and somehow she knew that they were completely dismissed from his mind. His visit to the school had been but a small incident in his busy life. He was the son of the laird. One day he would own the castle and all the farms around, and it would be his duty to show interest in the people who worked his fields. But he had called her beautiful. He had laughed with her as if, for a moment, they were equals, and Kirsty Robertson would never be the same again.

3

THE INFIRMARY IN 1908 WAS a pleasant building situated on a hill, which awarded its ambulatory patients a magnificent view of the sea. Bearing their offerings, the majority of which had lost most of their water and not a few of their petals, the children led their young teacher to it. Were they aware that, although she had chatted and laughed with them as they had walked along the country road, part of her had been reliving and reliving the afternoon?

He had called her beautiful. Had he been teasing? Father called her his beautiful princess sometimes, but that was Father, who found few faults with those he loved and was inclined to exaggerate their good points. Did he not do the same with the children to encourage them to further effort?

'Splendid, Daisy, splendid,' he would say, looking at some grubby offering, and next day the work would be a little neater and a little cleaner.

How beautiful Hugh was. His face was similar to the faces of some of the statues in Father's Greek textbooks:

exquisite, closely moulded and yet sensuous; and the eyes, those sparkling blue eyes that had smiled and danced all afternoon with happiness and merriment, not amusement, never amusement. She had thought his clothes very fine, too, so unlike Father's sober black and, alas, rather shiny suit. She had wanted to touch the arm of his sleeve, merely to feel the quality of that fine material.

'What is the meaning of this disgraceful disturbance?'

Matron! Had Mother not warned her? Keep the children very quiet: find the matron – she runs the hospital – and ask her if they might visit a children's ward or perhaps one of those wards for women. Kirsty's heart skipped a beat. How awful if they were thrown out in disgrace because she had not controlled the children's exuberance. She forced her Prince Charming from her mind and set herself nervously to pacify the justifiably enraged woman out of her temper.

'Do forgive the children,' she pleaded after she had introduced herself and explained both the purpose of their visit and why there had been no time to send a letter of request to the hospital. 'Many of them have never been to Arbroath before and they are so excited. I should have had them in better control and I promise that they will be so good in the wards, if, of course, you allow us to give your patients these flowers.'

Who was this poised young woman who was talking? Not Christine Robertson, pupil teacher, almost fifteen years old and until this very afternoon shy of her own shadow. That was, of course, before she had grown up, before a deity had called her beautiful.

Matron looked at them. Could anyone have resisted the flushed little faces beaming up at her, offering her their jam jars? Was there the hint of a smile on that grim, tight-lipped face?

'Well, keep them quiet as mice, Miss Robertson, there are sick people here. You may visit Wards One and Three. Mr Harris may be in Ward Three. He is our senior consultant and is not to be disturbed.'

As they walked down the polished corridor, Cissy's grubby little hand slipped into Kirsty's, and she squeezed it reassuringly. They would certainly avoid the *consultant*. The nurses on Ward Three greeted them in delight and put Netta's jar of flowers on a table by the window. The arrangement looked even more beautiful with the blue sky and the sea beyond creating a perfect backdrop. Kirsty was excited. Just by chance Netta and her teachers had found her talent.

'We're very proud of Netta,' she told the women in the iron beds.

'I should say so,' said a deep voice behind them. 'Quite a beautiful arrangement. You must apprentice yourself to a good florist, young Netta.'

He had come into the ward behind them and from the attendant pack of students and nurses who buzzed around but one step behind, Kirsty – and the children – realized that this must be the 'consultant', who was under no circumstances to be disturbed. She prepared to gather up her charges.

'Don't go,' he said. 'This is a lovely interlude for our ladies, and your teacher is to be congratulated for his foresight.'

'Miss Robertson's the Dominie's lassie, Mister,' piped up Cissie boldly, but once again clinging to Kirsty's hand, 'and she's a teacher too.'

He looked down at Kirsty and smiled. 'Your pardon, Miss Robertson.'

Why, he was not so frightening after all, but better to be wary. 'We have quite finished . . .' oh, heavens, how did one address a consultant? '. . . sir.' Better not ask him if the children might use the conveniences. 'We were told we could visit Ward One. Come children, quietly.'

Clutching her dignity to her as tightly as she found she was clutching Cissie's hand, Kirsty fled.

They did not see the consultant or the matron again, but a nurse rather grudgingly allowed them to use the toilet.

'This is not for the convenience of visitors. You should have gone before you came,' she said, but since Kirsty and her charges all understood this rather strange request, they used the facilities offered as quickly as they could and soon found themselves out on the road again.

'Oh, children,' said Kirsty as they walked back, 'was there ever such a day?'

Mr Robertson was so pleased by the success of their art lesson that he announced an annual competition. The children were delighted. Another milestone in their young lives: something to which they could look forward, like the Angus Fair or the New Year's holiday. To complete their happiness a gift arrived the day after the competition, when everyone was struggling with the dreaded parsing and analysis that they had been spared the day before. A box was delivered by the Colonel's very superior chauffeur, who once again appeared ill-used at the idea of being a mere delivery boy, and to a country school full of the children of farm labourers.

The Dominie opened the box amid the excited rustling of his charges, who squirmed with ecstasy as he wrestled with the wrappings.

'Oh, how beautiful, and how very generous,' he said as he held aloft an exquisite silver vase. 'The Colonel thinks your flower arrangement was worthy of such a receptacle, Netta.'

There was a cheer and then a barely stifled groan as their Dominie showed them that pleasure is almost always associated with pain. 'When we have finished our grammar lesson, we will attempt a letter of thanks to the Colonel. The best one, when it is neatly and correctly rewritten, will be delivered by myself.'

Kirsty watched the children as they worked: four children together at an uncomfortable wooden bench. There were four inkwells set at equal distances along the edges of the lids, and some of the desks also had slates carved into the tops. Neat one-inch squares were permanently etched on these slates, on which generations of farm children had learned to write neatly and legibly. Kirsty monitored her class, but her mind was elsewhere. Father intended to return to the castle. He would see Hu ... Mr Granville-Baker. Could she, dare she, offer to deliver the letter? No, he would not allow her to journey so far the very day after her long walk to the hospital. She must prove that such an undertaking was nothing, that she had barely realized the distance, that she felt she could have walked even the road to Dundee (over ten miles in the opposite direction) without flinching.

As it happened, the letter was not to be delivered until the next day, for the struggling authors' standards fell far below those of their headmaster, and it would not leave the classroom until handwriting, together with the sentiments expressed and the punctuation and sentence structure, were all perfect. In the end, Netta was chosen to write to the Colonel. She was the oldest girl, she had won the competition, and although her first effort at the thank-you letter could never have been sent, by the time she had cried over her mistakes and rewritten it several times, it was passable.

'Pathetic,' decided the Dominie in the privacy of his own living room. "Dear Colonel, Thank you for the nice

vase as it will be very useful, us not having one before."
Hardly great literature.'

Jessie looked up from her stitching of rosettes. 'I'm sure
you managed to make it a little more interesting, dear, and
as it is, it does convey the message neatly. I'm sure you will
help her . . . brush it up a little.'

'Perhaps I should have chosen one of the boys. Several
of them are more intelligent than Netta. I would like the
Colonel to see the best of the children.'

'He will see that they can write a proper letter. He knows
they are simple country children but well taught.'

He shrugged aside her remark almost angrily. 'You
don't understand, my dear. I had hoped that Netta might
shine before the Colonel, that he might think her worth
employing.'

'Kirsty says the doctor at the hospital suggested that
Netta apprentice herself to a good florist,' smiled Jessie over
the blue thread she was biting off. 'We would never have
thought of such a job for the likes of Netta. Would it not be
a better future than domestic service, even in a castle?'

'I could make enquiries, I suppose, and see the girl's
parents too.' John stopped his pacing and turned to his
wife. 'A pity that we have never been wealthy enough to
hire the services of a florist, my dear, or even to be num-
bered among their customers, but I shall seek one out to
offer Netta's services.'

'Only if she wants it, John,' smiled Jessie, who a moment before had been extolling the merits of such a career for John's pupil, 'and if her parents agree. The winning arrangement may merely have been a fluke after all. Take her with you to deliver the letter. Take Kirsty, too, for propriety's sake, and in this way Netta can see the castle, which she may find infinitely more exciting than a florist's shop.'

Kirsty could hardly believe it. Without having to ask, an opportunity to see Hugh was being given her. She would wear her lace collar and the white apron; she could tie it very tightly to accentuate her neat waistline. If only she possessed one shop-bought dress! Hugh's mother, a titled lady in her own right, and all her guests, would always be magnificently gowned. Hugh must spend his life surrounded by attractive young women. But he had called her beautiful.

'He must have been teasing,' she told her mirror angrily as she savagely brushed her hair until it took on a life of its own and danced around her head in undisciplined flight.

All the effort was for nothing. A superior servant met them at the door. Apparently the family were not at home, and he took the letter and closed the heavy wooden doors. They were left standing in the courtyard which, out of the sun, was cold and unwelcoming. Above them the castle stood square and uncompromising, and quietly the little group turned to go back through the outer gates. John took the opportunity to deliver a history lesson.

'See, Netta, the castle well stands here in the forecourt. It still provides a good supply of fresh drinking water. In times of trouble the animals would have been brought in here, the outer gates would have been closed, and the occupants could defend themselves from their superior position.'

'My mum would grow some nice flowers in that water pot,' said Netta. 'They'd be a right treat against all that old iron,' said she, dismissing the work of a master craftsman.

'Not a historian, our Netta,' said John to his daughter after the girl had left them at the much inferior iron gate to the Schoolhouse and had run across the fields to the small damp cottage that was home to her, her parents, an elderly grandmother and several brothers and sisters.

'But she sees objects in terms of flowers, Father. Can you imagine? Should Netta go into service at the castle, there would be window boxes full of wild flowers on all those stark windows. Better than guns, you must admit.'

'Neither is appropriate to that castle, even in the twentieth century, Kirsty. Now off to bed. Tomorrow evening your classes begin in Arbroath. I wish I could afford a bicycle for you.'

Kirsty dismissed his worry lightly. 'I'm strong and healthy. The walk to town is nothing. I'll look forward to it after a day in the classroom.'

But John was thinking of the winter months, which would be dark and probably wet and cold. He would meet her, of course, after each class, but still such long walks after a full day's work would take their toll. He could count on her mother to keep her well nourished; that, at least, was something.

The classes were a revelation to Kirsty, and she opened up in the atmosphere of learning like a flower opening to the sun. Not that the content of the instruction taxed her intellectually: she had, as she had rather vainly told Hugh, been required to do much more as her father's senior and brightest student. The pupil teachers did no Latin or Greek; they did not wrestle with higher mathematics. Kirsty, who had been so well taught, relaxed and, although she did her homework assiduously, she looked on the classes as more of a social occasion. Crammed into a classroom at Keptie Primary School were almost fifty pupil teachers from all areas of the town and the surrounding villages, and almost everyone was her own age or older.

On her first night she hurried into the toilets to tidy her hair after the walk – it would never do to appear in front of strangers with her hair all over the place – and almost bumped into another girl who stood just before the door as if debating whether or not to go to class or to stay in the lavatory.

'Gosh, I'm sorry! I almost slammed you with the door. Are you all right?'

'You missed me,' said the girl, 'and it would have been my own fault anyway. It's just that every year I get more and more feart . . . scared.'

'What of?' asked Kirsty anxiously. 'Are the lessons hard?'

'Aye. No. I've managed twice . . . just, to pass. This year, I'll fail, I just know it.'

Kirsty studied the girl, seeing someone who would probably face life with a perpetually frightened expression, and her soft heart melted.

'Come on, it can't be that bad. You've passed two years. Think of me: I'm only just starting.'

They introduced themselves and went into the classroom to join the other students. After the two-hour class, they walked out together.

'I'll never pass these exams he was talking about,' moaned Meg Stewart. 'Maybe I should stop now and work with my father' – she saw Kirsty's questioning look – 'gutting fish. I'll never remember all that Shakespeare, and I'm not good at writing essays. Never been one of my family a teacher before.'

'But you want to be one?'

'Oh, more than anything. I love babies, and being clean and not smelling of fish.'

If Kirsty thought these hardly compelling reasons for embracing a lifetime in education, she did not say so. 'I'll help you if you like,' she said instead.

And thus began a friendship that was to last for the rest of their lives.

'Look,' said Kirsty, 'here's my father come to walk me home.' She introduced him to her new friend proudly, her heart brimming over with love. 'Father,' she scolded, 'you didn't need to meet me. It's such a fine night. This is Miss Stewart, who is also a pupil teacher. We are going to work together on our homework tasks. We are to study Julius Caesar' – she paused to allow them to appreciate together that the Noblest Roman had been well and truly studied by Miss Robertson over two years before and thus held no terrors – 'and we are to write an essay. May I ask Meg to tea on Saturday, Father?'

'An excellent idea. Will we have the pleasure of seeing you on Saturday, Miss Stewart?'

Meg dropped a quick curtsey by way of acceptance and stammered her thanks.

'Kirsty will walk out to meet you. Assure your parents that we will walk you home safely.'

'Oh, no need, sir. One of my brothers will do that, but thank you. Thank you very much, and you too, Kirsty. Until Saturday.'

'Meg's father is a fisherman, Father, and she wants to be a teacher because she loves babies and teachers don't smell of fish.'

'Meg does, only a little, and so, my dear, do you.'

They laughed together and walked home, the first of many nights, in all seasons and in all weathers. The classes could not be missed. There was no transport between the town and the village, and so Kirsty walked and John walked out to meet her in the summer. In the winter he accompanied her and waited in a cold, unheated classroom, preparing his own lessons or marking his children's work, until Kirsty was ready for the walk home. They were hours of togetherness and love that Kirsty was to treasure.

Every Saturday for two years the girls met in the little Schoolhouse, or, when Jessie was assured that no harm would befall her only chick, in the fisherman's cottage at Meg's home near the sea. After the shabby gentility of the Schoolhouse, Meg's home was a revelation. The floor of the front room – or *but* of the *but 'n' ben*, as the houses were called – was lined with waxcloth on which were placed a few washable rag rugs and several wooden stools, painted black or brown and all paint-grained. Meg's grandfather was one of the village's most admired grainers, and it was on these stools that the sheilers sat when they were setting the lines. The Stewarts were a large, happy family: parents, nine children – some, thankfully, already married and with families of their own – and even an aged grandparent. He had been not a fisherman but a whaler, and he would hold the younger children spellbound with his stories of the dangers and wonders of the sea and his visits to Eskimos on days so cold that icicles hung from the beards of the white men.

Kirsty thought him a marvel herself, but Meg would dismiss him affectionately. 'Wash your mooth wi' soap, Grandfather. That whale was half as lang the day afore yesterday!'

On occasional Saturday mornings during term-time, the girls had classes in town or sometimes – to Meg, the dreaded – examinations. She struggled with the very idea of a written test while Kirsty soared through, almost always at the top of the class, and once even at the top of all the students in Scotland. She could hardly wait to be old enough to go on to the university in Edinburgh. Meg became a certificated teacher in the autumn of 1910 and was awarded a post in the Brothock Parochial School.

'I'll miss you at classes, Meg,' said Kirsty, 'but I'm so glad you got Brothock. You deserve such a nice place-ment, and with a good headmaster you will do well.'

'Sixty-one infants, Kirsty. Can you imagine all those babies in one room? But the infants' mistress is so good, gentle but firm, and she says they have enough primers for all, so that's a blessing. In some schools, they must take turns with the books. How can they learn to read with one primer between three?'

In their new-found experience and authority, they discussed the difficulties of teaching and learning in the manner of certificated teachers with twenty years' experience until it was time for Kirsty to walk home.

'Our Tam will walk you home if you wait a bit.' Meg laughed and Kirsty laughed with her. Two of Meg's unmarried brothers vied with each other for the privilege of walking sedately by her side on the road to Aberannoch and the Schoolhouse. They were handsome lads, and no sixteen-year-old girl would mind being seen with either of them, but if one was at home and therefore free to accompany Kirsty, it was usually because he had spent the morning gutting fish and quite often she wished the country road somewhat wider.

'I'd best not wait this evening. It looks like rain and Father will come out with his umbrella.' She frowned for a second, but then shook off the nagging worry. 'How happy he'll be to know of your placement.'

John too had helped to coach Meg through her exams and would be justifiably pleased with her success.

'Faither's . . . no, I must say Father, like you, now that I am really Miss Stewart,' said Meg. 'Father has a lovely halibut all ready for your mother. Caught this morning, so you'll enjoy it for your tea.'

This also had become a welcome part of many Saturdays: fresh fish would be given by Meg and, in time, Mrs Robertson would return the favour in the form of a pot of her newly made raspberry jam, or vegetables freshly gathered from the large Schoolhouse garden.

Kirsty began her walk home, the halibut coolly wrapped in leaves and paper in a basket and Tam, the tall young fisher laddie, at her side. Alex was the quieter of Meg's two unmarried brothers and conversation with him was always a problem. Kirsty sometimes wondered why he fought for the dubious privilege of walking her home, for he said very little. His brother Tam, however, used the walks as a chance to air all his thoughts, and many seemed to Kirsty quite radical, about politics and government. Tam had even talked of a time when women should have a share in the running of their own lives, and tonight he was painting a vision of a world in which everyone, rich and poor, men and women – even the unmarried – would vote for their elected officials, when the rains came down.

'And don't you say as that's what the good Lord thinks o' my idees, Miss Kirsty,' laughed Tam as they began to run. The village was in sight and there was no shelter, not so much as a bush between them and the downpour.

It was Tam who saw John. He was slumped against the hedge by the side of the road, half in and half out of the ditch running with icy water.

Kirsty screamed and threw herself down beside her father. 'What's wrong, what's wrong?' she cried. 'Tam, he doesn't answer me.' Futilely she shook her father's wet shoulder, desperately trying to turn him over. 'Father, answer me!' But the heart of her already knew that he would never speak to her again.

Tam was beside her and gently he turned John over.

'Wheist, lass. He's jist hid a turn o' some kind. Rin an' warn yer mam an' I'll fetch him hame.'

Tam lifted the inert form of the Dominie and began to hurry, as if John's weight was no burden at all to his strong young arms, and, after looking once more on the loved face so white and still, Kirsty picked up her skirts and began to run. Breathless she reached Millhill Farm and, unable to go further, stopped to catch her breath and to relieve the hand that seemed to be gripping her ribs in their fashionable cage of stays.

'Gawd A'mighty, Kirsty lassie! Whit's tae dae?' It was the farmer from Balcundrum and he looked back along the road. 'Has somebody frichted you?'

She gasped out her story and he half carried, half dragged her towards the farmhouse. 'I'll get the horse and cairt. We'll hae him warm in his ain bed in nae time.'

And so he did. Kirsty, who had spent many hours of childhood watching the huge gentle beast that worked the farm, could not believe such an animal could move so quickly. She shook off the comforting hand of Bessie, the farmer's wife, who offered her warmth and hot drinks by the fire, and was soon, or so it seemed, perched miles above the ground watching but not seeing the muscles ripple over the Clydesdale's massive brown haunches. On another journey she would have been terrified of the glimpse of ground that showed through a small gap in the floor of the cart, but today she could think of nothing but her father.

There was no end to the farmer's goodness. They met Tam hurrying along, his burden still and lifeless in his arms, and when they had brought John to the little Schoolhouse and carried him to his bed, they went to fetch the doctor. Kirsty, banned from the room while her mother undressed her husband, stayed with clenched hands by the window and prayed. But her prayers went unanswered. Before the doctor arrived there was a wail from the bedroom and Kirsty hurried in to find Jessie lying almost on top of her husband as if her life could somehow pass to him.

'Mother, leave him. Come, sit here by the bed and wait till the doctor comes.' But it took the combined strength of both fisherman and farmer to force Jessie from the lifeless body. John Robertson had been dead before he reached his home: his heart, never strong and weakened yet more by years of overwork and strain, had simply refused to keep on working.

It was several days before Kirsty had time to consider all the terrible consequences of her father's death. Jessie had become the child and had to be consoled, to be held for hours until she sobbed herself into an exhausted sleep, to be coaxed to eat, 'just a few bites, Mother, for his dear sake'. There was the funeral to arrange and their single living relative to be informed – John's brother, Uncle Chay. The Board too had to be advised of the vacancy at Aberannoch School. It was Kirsty who arranged to walk to Arbroath to buy the mourning blacks, and who was again heartened by the friendship of their farmer neighbours, who always stopped their work in the fields to take her in the horse and trap.

'I saw yer faither walkin' ev'ry nicht, Kirsty lass – hail, rain, sun or snaw. I shoulda lifted him then and he'd maybe be alive the day.'

No sense in screaming, 'You *should*, you *should*.' John would never have expected another man to stop his work or leave his warm fireside. It was unrealistic, but she was still angry and glad to have someone to blame.

'Father loved the walk – such a change from the classroom,' she said quietly. 'It was sitting waiting for me all those hours that weakened his heart.' That part at least was true. Who was to comfort Kirsty?

Jamie came first: a changed Jamie, tall and brown and strong from his hours in the fields. He carried some beautiful autumn leaves to cheer her. 'He was a guid man, Kirsty. I'll remember him all ma life,' he said as he turned to go.

'Wait, Jamie, wait. His books. Of course, he would want you to have his books.' That was when she first realized that she and her mother would have to leave the Schoolhouse: the books would have to go. Where, dear Lord, where were they to live? She bit back the panic as she pulled some volumes from the shelves; she needed to concentrate on the present for now.

The stiff white envelope with the embossed letters on the flap came the next day. For a moment she did not recognize the crest: H.G.B.

> *My dear Miss Robertson,*
>
> *Father has informed me of your sad loss. Please convey my deepest condolences to your mother and accept them for yourself. If I can help in any way, please do not hesitate to count me among your friends.*
>
> *Yours, etc.*
> *Hugh G.B.*

How kind. How very kind . . . But Kirsty's heart was too numb to leap with joy. She put the letter in a drawer and it was thrown away when they cleared the house.

4

CHAY ROBERTSON ARRIVED JUST IN time for the funeral. He was unlike his brother in appearance but like him in everything that mattered.

'I've no' got much, Kirsty lass,' he said, 'but you're aye welcome to it. There's naebody left on yer mither's side noo, and only me on John's. I've thocht it all oot on the way, and if you and Jessie was tae share ma mither's room, I could tak the wee one John and me used tae have. I'd be richt honoured tae have the caring for ye both.'

Kirsty was deeply touched. All his life this old man – for that was what he was, even though he could not yet be fifty years of age – had laboured for others. First for his brother, then his parents, and now he was prepared to take them and to have them live with him, new burdens. As far as she knew he had seen her, his niece, only twice in sixteen years.

'I'll talk to Mother, Uncle Chay.' A home, they had a home, even though it was only a farm labourer's cottage.

Well, there were others who had less. Now was not the time to ask if there was a school within walking or cycling distance. It would be a waste of all John's dreams if she could not finish her training.

The day of the funeral was crisp and clear. Was it better to see the countryside lying coldly beautiful as it welcomed its son, or would it have been better to have had driving rain hiding one's grief while it echoed one's thoughts? The small church was filled with mourners, present and past pupils, many in tears, and local farmers and their wives. There was no one from the castle. The Colonel and his son were on active duty and Lady Sybill was not in residence. Kirsty did not even notice their absence.

It was the minister who voiced the problem.

'Your mother is too grief-stricken to think, Kirsty, but you know a new teacher will have to be found.'

Kirsty looked at him out of dull eyes. 'My father's brother, my Uncle Chay, has offered us a home, Reverend. We'll move as soon as the Board finds someone.'

'Even if you were qualified, you are a woman and we couldn't have you in charge, Kirsty. We've arranged that a teacher from Arbroath come in, in a temporary capacity while the post is advertised. He'll start tomorrow. The question is, lass – do you want to exchange positions with him, more or less?'

Kirsty's heart soared. Oh, how could she feel so happy standing almost at the very grave of her father, but her first thought was, 'I don't have to give up teaching.'

The minister could hardly have been unaware of her feelings. 'I'll stay behind after the other mourners have gone, Kirsty, and we'll talk. It's a pity the Colonel is abroad, but the rest of the Board are aware of your predicament and we won't throw you and your mother out into the street.'

In the event it was Kirsty and her uncle who talked with the minister. Jessie had been unable to hide her grief and immediately the mourners had returned to the Schoolhouse for the traditional tea, Balcundrum's wife had taken control and put her to bed.

'There's jist the tea tae make,' she said before she closed the door on Jessie's grief, 'and the whisky tae hand roon – and Balcundrum'll dae mair than a guid job of that, lass. You make the tea, keep yerself busy.'

Kirsty did, and when all the mourners were eating and drinking she made up a tray and went in to her mother. The farmer's wife was still sitting by the bed.

'How is she, Mrs Lovett?'

Farmers in the area were usually known by the name of their farm and so the farmer himself was Balcundrum: his wife was either called simply Balcundrum's wife or Mistress Lovett, her proper name.

'Sleeping, lass.'

'I'll stay with her in case she wakes. She's never been alone before.'

Mrs Lovett rose, her best black silk creaking with age as she did so. 'Well, I'll away ben and hae a cup of tea – she was aye a grand baker – but I ken the meenister wants a word.' She looked down at Jessie lying still and white against the whiter pillows. 'Whit help yer mam will be, I don't know.' At the door she paused again. 'I'll come back when they're leaving, lassie.'

Kirsty looked up and managed to smile. 'Thank you, Mrs Lovett,' and then she sat down beside the bed and watched her mother. Vaguely she was aware of voices in the front room, sad and solemn, with occasional suppressed laughter. The tea grew cold beside her. She wasn't thirsty or hungry; she hardly noticed the darkness.

'Sleep's the best thing for her, lassie.' It was Mrs Lovett. 'You should have come ben.'

Stiffly Kirsty rose. She couldn't tell her there had been thinking to do, plans to make.

'You've been very kind.'

'Ach, lassie. She'd hae done the same for me.'

At last Uncle Chay closed the door behind the departing mourners. 'That was a grand send-off, Reverend,' he said, 'and your words were much appreciated. Are ye here tae tell my sister-in-law when she has tae be oot? Kirsty'll tell ye, they're welcome tae come hame wi' me.'

'It's good that they have a home, but I know John Robertson would have wanted Kirsty to continue with her studies. That's what you want too, isn't it, Kirsty?'

'Yes, but I don't see how it can be managed.' How could it, how *could* it? She had gone over and over the problem in her head. Where could she live if she were to stay in Arbroath? How would her mother fare if she were to be moved from her home without even the company of her daughter? She couldn't do it. She had to take care of her.

'The Mr Brown who is coming here is at present assistant teacher at Burnside Primary.' The minister was speaking. 'The headmaster of Burnside is willing to take you and another pupil teacher from Auchmithie in exchange for Mr Brown. Buchanan is a splendid Dominie. You will be well taught, and the experience will be excellent. It's the biggest primary in Arbroath.'

She was to continue with her dream: she would become a teacher. 'I have nowhere to live.'

'You will live with the Buchanans. The Schoolhouse is very big – they have no family of their own and Mrs Buchanan is always happy to board the pupil teachers. A Miss McNeil lodges with them already, and so you will have young company of your own age. She's a quiet lassie.'

It all seemed so easy, and Kirsty wanted to grasp the opportunity. There was no chance now of university, but she could continue, she could become a teacher.

'And Mother?'

'Your mother will live with me, Kirsty lass,' put in Uncle Chay. I'll get a lassie from the parish to come in and bide tae help her and . . . well, make it proper, if you ken whit I mean, Meenister.'

'I'll be glad to help there.' The minister rose. 'Naturally, Mr Brown would like to move in while he's teacher here, Kirsty. We can give you a week. Will that be sufficient?'

Kirsty nodded. She couldn't speak. A week. It was all so awful, so real. In a week they would be gone from their home. At last she faced the bitter truth that nothing would ever be the same again.

The week passed relentlessly, as does all resented time. Kirsty helped with sorting and packing. John's few clothes were given to the minister for distribution among the poor, and the books she had not forced on Jamie were packed with the furniture to be taken to Uncle Chay's cottage. Jessie roused herself from her grief to help.

'I can't believe he's gone, Kirsty,' she explained almost apologetically. 'If he'd been ill, maybe I could manage better. It's as if my mind's in a fog and I can't think or see clearly.'

Uncle Chay walked in with Kirsty to see her new school. It was a massive sandstone building with staircases on either side and a huge front door that the children were not allowed to use in any circumstance whatsoever. The noise from the playground, where it seemed as if hundreds of children were running and shouting, was reassuring. Kirsty and her uncle crept round to a side entrance. How different from the wee school at Aberannoch. Inside a long, severely polished corridor stretched before them, and yet another staircase climbed up to a second floor. It was as dark and silent as a church.

'Mr Buchanan has gone round the corner to his dinner,' said a voice from the gloom. 'I am Miss McNeil, the senior pupil teacher.'

Miss McNeil had come quietly from a room further along the brown-painted corridor. She wore a brown dress and a heavy hand-knitted brown cardigan, and the little amount of stocking that could be glimpsed beneath the hem was also brown.

Kirsty took the hand that was held out to her. It was cold and thin. She smiled at Miss McNeil, but there was no answering smile in the cold eyes. Were they brown too?

'She's a sparrow,' thought Kirsty, 'a little grey-brown sparrow – but without the charm.'

'This is my dinner break too,' said Miss McNeil resentfully, 'and there's so little free time. Mr Buchanan is expecting you. His house is just around the corner. Go out that way,' she said, gesturing down the gloomy corridor. 'It's the boys' door but it doesn't matter if you're a teacher. The house is the big one just to the right of the gates. It's a beautiful house,' she added and Kirsty smiled. So Miss McNeil was human.

'Thank you,' she said, and with the silent Uncle Chay in tow she set off along the corridor.

This will soon be so familiar to me, Kirsty thought. I will know these doors and who is behind them and it will be as if I have known them all my life.

Chay did not speak until they were outside in the playground and then he expelled his breath in a long, deep sigh. 'No' a very friendly lassie, Kirsty. She'd fright the bairns.'

'She's dignified, Uncle, not like me. Maybe I'll have to be dignified too and not sit on the floor with the wee ones while I read them a story.'

They walked quickly to the gates, dodging the games of racing or football that all stopped with horrified murmurs of apology when the players saw the strangers.

'A grand enough house, lassie,' said Uncle Chay.

'And look at the gardens,' exclaimed Kirsty, her heart rising. Who could fail to be happy in such beautiful surroundings?

She pulled the bell rope and somewhere in the bowels of the house they heard a dull sound, and then there was silence until the door opened tentatively. A small, thin woman in grey silk smiled rather shyly at them.

'You'll be the new pupil teacher. Come in, lassie. Mr Buchanan's at his dinner. He's expecting you. I'm Mrs Buchanan,' she added almost as an afterthought.

Kirsty introduced herself and her uncle and they followed the headmaster's wife into a cheerless hall. The furniture was much grander than in the little Schoolhouse at Aberannoch. 'Strange,' thought Kirsty, 'it's such good stuff, but it doesn't feel like a home. The furniture doesn't look . . . loved.'

Mrs Buchanan opened a door. 'Angus, dear. Here is Miss Robertson and her uncle.'

Kirsty had time to notice that the table was set for only one person before her hand was crushed and pumped up and down by the exuberance of the Dominie's greeting. 'My dear Miss Robertson, let me say how delighted we are to have you with us' – his voice dropped mournfully – 'even though we are painfully aware of the sad circumstances, the very sad circumstances that have brought about our acquaintance.'

Tears pricked at the backs of Kirsty's eyes and she forced them away. 'How do you do, sir,' she said. 'May I introduce my uncle, Mr Robertson.'

Chay's hand received the same treatment, but his was stronger.

'Mr Robertson. Delighted, sir, delighted. I had thought our Miss Robertson was quite alone in the world' – again the voice dropped – 'apart from her poor grieving parent.'

Uncle Chay murmured something inaudible and twisted his bonnet around in his work-worn hands.

'My uncle lives in Ayrshire, Mr Buchanan,' explained Kirsty, 'and will be returning there with my mother.'

'Admirable, sir, admirable.' Mr Buchanan turned to his wife, a smile on his face which did not quite reach his eyes. 'Tea for our guests, Mrs Buchanan. Where are your manners?'

Mrs Buchanan turned quickly to the polished sideboard. 'I have it ready, Angus', she said, 'and a nice cake to go with it.'

'Yon cake was like the back end o' a carpet ... and as foosty,' said Uncle Chay later as they walked back home.

Kirsty giggled. 'Poor Mrs Buchanan – but the Dominie ate two slices, Uncle, so maybe he thought it was good.'

'And whit did ye think on him, lass?' Uncle Chay's voice was worried.

'He's not Father ... and I suppose I resented it a little when he said I probably hadn't learned much out in the country ... but he seemed very kind ... maybe a little too ...'

'Full of hissel?' suggested Chay.

Kirsty giggled again. 'I think I was going to say ... loud, Uncle. He's not like Father, and I mustn't hold that against him, and she's a nice wee soul, even though he bullies her. I hope he doesn't bully the children.' Kirsty sighed. 'Come on, let's get home. I still have two whole days before I have to move in. I'm sure everything will be fine, and the house is very pretty if . . . well, a bit gloomy. Maybe I can encourage Mrs Buchanan to put big bowls of flowers everywhere.' She turned to her uncle. 'It'll all work out, Uncle. Don't worry.' But she could not help worrying herself.

To her great joy Meg was at the Schoolhouse when they returned. She jumped to her feet when she saw Kirsty, rushed to meet her and started talking at once.

'Oh, Kirsty, why did you not tell me you were staying in Arbroath? You'd be better off staying with my mam; you can share a room with me, I've talked to Mrs Robertson about it.' She turned back to Kirsty's mother who was smiling at them both as she fussed over the tea-table. 'You'll be happier if she's with us, won't you, Mrs Robertson?'

'Oh, I couldn't impose like that. The Buchanans have a huge house and there's lots of room.' Kirsty was delighted to see how much good Meg's visit had done her mother, but she was surprised to see her friend during school hours. 'What's wrong, Meg? Why aren't you at school?'

'My headmaster has taken the class. What a nice man he is. I hope your Mr Buchanan will be as thoughtful. Mr Grieve asked how you were, and when I told him you were leaving this week he gave me the afternoon off to come to visit.'

Everyone agreed that Mr Grieve was the soul of kindness, and they laughed at Uncle Chay's description of the cake.

'Our Kirsty will hardly get fat in that house, Jessie, but it's a clean house and Mrs Buchanan's a nice enough woman.'

'And the Dominie, Chay?'

'Ach, I don't know. He's no' our John: he's a loudish man and talks a lot. I didnae take tae him.'

'Oh, he was all right, Mother,' said Kirsty. It would hardly do for her mother to be worried more than she need be. 'He's, well, maybe a bit full of his own importance, but kind enough, anxious that I like the house and the school. He very kindly said he thought I should do quite well.'

'Oh, the cheek, as if my John hadn't taught you well.'

Kirsty laughed, delighted to see her mother so stimulated. 'You want everybody to be like Father. Besides, I am just a pupil teacher. There is a lot for me to learn, isn't there, Meg?'

Meg stirred her tea slowly before answering. 'I'm still learning. But oh, I wish you had spoken to me at the funeral. My mam said to talk to you then, but we were sure you would go with your mother.'

'No, no. I want Kirsty to continue with her teaching. It's what her father wished.' Jessie turned to her daughter. 'I have to say I'd be happier if you were living with the

Stewarts, Kirsty, instead of complete strangers . . . who can't even make a decent cake!'

'Mother, there are many good reasons for living with the Buchanans. It's right next door to the school. No walking in the rain and snow like Meg, and I've never lived in a town. There's a library and . . . shops, and I can see Meg at weekends – and then I'll come to see you and Uncle Chay for my holidays. I think we have nearly a week at the end of the year.'

'And if the weather is too bad she can come to us, Mrs Robertson, and every weekend too.'

And that is how it happened. The first few months after her father's death flew past so quickly that Kirsty sometimes felt she was spinning like a child's top. Perhaps that was as well; there was no time to feel lonely, no time to mourn her father or to miss her mother. She had soon settled into the routine of Burnside School. Almost every one of the eight classes was bigger than the whole of Aberannoch School. Most classes had two teachers, or a fully qualified teacher helped by one or even two pupil teachers. Kirsty and the other new pupil teacher, Mr Cargill, replaced Mr Brown, who had already officially replaced Kirsty's father. Mr Cargill too was beginning his third year, and unlike Kirsty he was planning to go to the teachers' training college in Edinburgh when he had completed his four years. Like Meg, his father was a fisherman, and he and Kirsty soon became firm friends. It was not so with Miss McNeil, who had deliberately spurned all Kirsty's offers of friendship.

'You must not think that because we live in the same house and work in the same establishment we are equals, Miss Robertson,' she had said coldly on Kirsty's very first night at her new home. 'I am the senior pupil teacher and I have a position to uphold before all the other pupil teachers. Naturally,' and here she smiled a little, 'in the house, you may call me Sarah and I shall address you as Kirsty, but you must understand that Mr Buchanan has forecast a great future for me, and I will do nothing to impede my progress.'

'Well, I should certainly hate friendliness or a welcoming manner to a new colleague to get in the way of your progress, *Miss McNeil*,' said Kirsty hotly. 'I will look for my friends elsewhere,' she finished and walked off grandly, cheering herself up by remembering that the weekend would bring a visit to Meg's warm, loving home.

Mr Cargill also asked her to visit his home at Auchmithie. They were standing talking in the teachers' room because there were not enough chairs to accommodate all the staff.

'I think old Buchanan does it deliberately, Kirsty,' laughed Bob Cargill. 'He wants one of us to sit down and then be embarrassed when a *real* teacher comes in and demands a seat.'

Kirsty said nothing, for she was rapidly coming to the conclusion that Bob was right. Mr Buchanan seemed constantly to be trying to cause discomfort. Should a pupil teacher be sitting when a permanent member of staff came into the room it gave him, on his rare visits, a grand opportunity for a lecture on good manners.

Night classes continued twice a week and there were occasional classes on Saturday mornings. There were also classes for the pupil teachers, including Miss McNeil, two mornings a week from eight to nine. Kirsty loved these, and her academic ability brought her to the top of every class, much to Miss McNeil's annoyance. The lessons were to broaden their possibly narrow education, but under her father's careful tutelage Kirsty had become well versed in several areas. Most of the literature, history and science presented to the pupil teachers was merely revision for Kirsty.

'You're in grave danger of being loathed by every man in Arbroath, and not a few of the women,' Bob teased her as she helped him with his homework essay. 'Our reverend "Senior Pupil Teacher" – funny how we think of Miss Sarah McNeil in capital letters – tells everyone that there's more to teaching than book knowledge.'

Bob was laughing, but Kirsty decided to try not to be quite so overpowering at the classes. She hadn't meant to show off: it was just that she was so well taught. Now she would try to be demure and feminine. 'Dash, dash,' she swore at her mirror. 'Father never told me that being maidenly meant pretending I don't have a brain in my head. Men are such tender creatures, and yet we're supposed to be the weak ones. I know I couldn't possibly grasp, "Oh, Mr Buchanan, how exciting and frightening modern science is". ' That was what Miss McNeil had said when Mr Buchanan had explained a recent eclipse of the sun.

Living arrangements were adequate. Usually all four members of the household met in the morning; the girls took a sandwich for lunch and all four had tea together after school. Unlike her baking, Mrs Buchanan's basic cooking was adequate and there were still gifts of fresh fish which were gratefully accepted and shared with the small household.

The school was to close on the 30th of December – and if Mr Buchanan was in a festive spirit, the staff were sure he would close at noon, just after giving his customary gift of an orange to every child in the school. It was not to reopen until January 6th, 1911 – a whole week's holiday!

The weather worsened towards the end of the year, but no one expected fair weather in November and December. One evening late in December, Kirsty and some fellow pupil teachers remained for over an hour in the school where they had been attending a class, sheltering from a storm.

'It's not letting up at all, Bob,' said Kirsty as she peered out at the rain that seemed to fall in solid sheets. 'I'm going to make a run for it. I don't have far to go.'

'You'll never get to Auchmithie the night either,' said Tom Christie, one of the senior students. 'You can share my bed if you like, Bob. You'll be blown off the cliff gin you try for home the night.'

The boys helped Kirsty struggle against the wind as far as Burnside Schoolhouse and she stood for a moment in the door, watching their unsteady progress. Suddenly there was a movement behind her; the door opened and there stood Mr Buchanan, a frightening figure in nightshirt and dressing gown.

'Jezebel!' He seemed to almost hiss the word as he grabbed Kirsty by the hair and pulled her into the house. She was too startled to scream.

'What were you doing with those lads?' he went on, still in that frightening, hissing voice. He had pushed Kirsty up against the wall and his bulk pressed against her. Never in her life had she been so close to a man. 'Answer me, you strumpet, answer me!'

Kirsty began to struggle, but he still had a hold on her hair and his face loomed so near to hers, the eyes staring wildly.

'Please,' she managed to gasp, 'please.'

He shook her the way a dog shakes a rat it has caught. His eyes stared wildly into hers, and that smell, that awful smell that made her want to gag . . .

'Mr Buchanan.' The voice was clear and firm. 'Let Miss Robertson go. She has merely been sheltering from the storm.'

His grip slackened but he did not release her. 'Miss McNeil,' he said. 'Arm in arm with two lads she came, and lingered in the door watching her lovers leave.'

'A courteous gesture, no more,' said Miss McNeil. She dropped her voice. 'Let her go, Angus dear. She is only a child.'

'And needs discipline,' he answered, but the painful grip on her hair was gone and Kirsty almost fell against the wall as her knees seemed to refuse to bear her weight a moment longer. Behind the headmaster she could see the wraithlike figure of Miss McNeil and, on the stairs above, wrapped in a dark plaid dressing gown, stood Mrs Buchanan. When she saw Kirsty looking at her, the head-master's wife turned and scuttled back up the stairs.

'Go upstairs, Miss Robertson. You are very late and we have all been concerned for you.'

For a second Kirsty stood looking at Miss McNeil while her mind tried to understand what was going on. Then her legs found some strength and she fled past them up the stairs. As she reached the door of her room she vaguely saw Miss McNeil lead the headmaster, still muttering 'Jezebel' under his breath, to the staircase.

'It should be his wife,' her mind told her as she thrust her door shut against a world gone mad and turned the key in the lock.

5

SHE HAD TO GET OUT, to get away.

Kirsty had thought that she would not sleep, but when she had hung up her clothes, washed her face, brushed her hair, done all the other things that she always did in the routine before going to bed, and had then slipped between the cold clean sheets, she had very quickly fallen into a deep sleep. However, she had wakened a few hours later and had lain for the rest of the night waiting for the wag-at-the-wall clock in the hall to tell her the hours as it marked them off.

What would he say or do in the morning? What had been wrong with him? His eyes, so wild and unbalanced; his breath, that horrid breath; his face so close to her own that she had wanted to be sick; and his heavy body pressed against hers. Silent tears streamed down her face and she turned her head into the pillow for fear that she would make a noise and someone might come. She could bear none of them near her: not him, not that little shadow on the stairs who was his wife, not the frighteningly calm Miss McNeil. Miss McNeil had called him Angus, Angus dear, him the Dominie, the headmaster, and she was not a relation but merely a pupil teacher, and his wife had allowed it and had not intervened. Surely Mrs Buchanan should have been the one to help him?

Kirsty tried desperately to see if there had been any fault in what she herself had done. She had been late returning from her night class, but that had been because of the rain. Anyone could understand that she should take shelter. Father would have understood: he would have . . .

She could not bear it. Great racking sobs tore at her. He would have been there to shelter her from the rain, to walk home beside her, to protect her from suddenly frightening men like Mr Buchanan who pulled her hair and called her Jezebel. Why Jezebel? Was she not the shameless woman in the Bible, the Queen of Israel, Ahab's wife? How was she like Kirsty Robertson?

Like hurt children everywhere, Kirsty cried for her mother and the safety of her arms. But Mother was in Ayrshire, regaining her strength, almost ready to face life without her husband, and it would do her no good at all to be told that her daughter was lonely and frightened.

'I can't tell her,' decided Kirsty, suddenly grown up, 'but I have to get away from here.'

But where could she go?

The morning brought no answers, only a dull-eyed pupil teacher with a raging headache, but as the clock calmly announced that it was half-past five on a damp November morning, it also brought Miss McNeil to Kirsty's room. She carried a tray with tea and hot buttered toast, a real luxury.

'Mrs Buchanan has slept a little later this morning, Kirsty, and so I am doing breakfast.'

Kirsty said nothing and the other girl put the tray down on the small table at the window: a little window looking over the garden with the cherry tree that would be a riot of pink blossom in the spring.

'I hope you appreciate how concerned Mr Buchanan was for you last night, Kirsty. He takes such a fatherly interest in any young girl living in his house, and when you were so very late ... and then to come home arm in arm with two gentlemen who were not related ...'

Kirsty was stung by this interpretation of a very innocent event. 'I was not arm in arm as you put it, Miss McNeil, with anybody, and even if I had been ... that man had no right to ... to ... pull my hair and ... breathe on me.'

'A fatherly overreaction, Miss Robertson. Mr Buchanan is responsible to the Board for not only the welfare but the morals of those pupil teachers in his charge, and we both saw you walking home in the dark arm in arm with two men who are not related to you in any way. If it should get to the Board ...'

'Oh, that's nonsense and you know it. I shall apply for another position and leave . . .'

'Three of us saw you, Miss Robertson.' Miss McNeil paused as she saw the full significance of what she was saying sink into Kirsty's understanding. 'Certainly it was acceptable that you were out after eight o'clock in the evening because you were upon school business, but the Code states that a teacher may not be in the company of a man to whom she is not related – and there were two of them, Miss Robertson. Now Mr Buchanan is prepared to be lenient, on condition of course that your behaviour from now on is totally responsible. Hurry up and eat your toast. You've let it go cold, and it's your turn to go and stoke the stoves.'

She turned and was gone. Kirsty stared at the door behind her for some time. It was true, it was all so appallingly true. Who would believe her if she were to tell her innocent little story when the full force of the Dominie, his wife and the senior pupil teacher was ranged against her? She gulped down the still warm tea while great sobs again shook her and then, hurriedly, she washed in the cold water in the ewer on the dressing table and dressed as quickly as she could. It would be a pleasure to hurry to the school to help with the fires that seemed to do no more than take the chill off the rooms. Anything would be better than to be here in this house.

Outside, November echoed her depression. The night's rain was over, but clouds seem to hang like wet laundry from the trees and she walked out into the road to avoid the drips from the branches. Her mind was still busy with her problem, so she did not see the car until it was almost upon her. There was a scream of brakes, and the next moment she was being shouted at by a very angry driver.

'You damned stupid woman! Are you trying to get yourself killed, walking in the middle of the road like a partridge?'

'I'm sorry,' began Kirsty, and then stopped, for blue eyes that had once merrily looked into hers were now staring down at her in a fury. She began to cry.

'Look here, it's all right, don't cry, but you were in the middle of the road. Perhaps I was driving too fast: I'm horribly late.' And then he peered down at her again through the November murk. 'Good heavens, it can't be but it is, it's Miss Robertson, isn't it? Look, get in and I'll drive you home. What on earth are you doing so far from Aberannoch?' He stopped his tirade and looked at her for a moment. 'Can't you talk?'

'You haven't given me a chance,' sniffed Kirsty and tried to smile up at Hugh Granville-Baker through her tears.

'That's better. Now hop in off the road and I'll take you home.'

How wonderful to climb into the beautiful car and to be whisked somewhere, anywhere. 'I am home, Mister . . . or should I say Colonel or something?'

'Good lord, no! A humble lieutenant at your service, Miss Robertson. What do you mean – home?'

And so she told him, but left out her misery and her fear and her loneliness.

'A working woman! Well, I suppose I can understand that. Independence: it's a great life, isn't it?' But Kirsty thought she detected a little bitterness in his young voice, the voice that still had that ability to churn her stomach with feelings she didn't understand.

'It was so good to see you,' she said impulsively, and then blushed furiously for fear he would think her shameless. 'I mean, someone from home. I . . . miss the village, and the children. Now, I must hurry to school.'

'Burnside? Hop in. I pass it on my way. Ugly old place, isn't it?'

'Yes, and cold. I'm on fire duty this morning. But I can't get into the car with you – school regulations for unmarried women.'

'Good lord! How medieval and, of course, my car would be recognized. I don't think there are five cars in the area. Well, I shall swear we're related: we're seventh cousins twice removed. Hop in.'

Kirsty looked at him. Oh, how she wanted to be in that magnificent machine, protected by him for even the few moments it would take to turn the corner. Then she heard the screaming in her head, 'Jezebel, Jezebel!'

'I can't really, it's only round the corner.' She had to keep him, had to hear his voice just once more, just once. 'The janitor would have to report me,' she finished regretfully.

'If you insist. You are sure you're all right? I almost ran you down.'

'I'm fine.' Inside I'm crying, Hugh. Can't you hear me crying? She smiled.

'Delightful to see you again,' he said politely, and then the devil of mischief danced in his eyes again, 'cousin.'

Kirsty stood and watched as the dark blue car disappeared into the fog, then she walked through the gates and into the reality of school and the stoves that needed stoking before the senior teachers arrived to go over lessons with the pupil teachers.

The school was open, for the janitor had been there for an hour already and the great pot-bellied stoves in all the rooms were lit.

'Morning, Miss Robertson,' he said. 'I've put a bucket of coal in every room, but there's something bluidy wrong wi' the stove in the Dominie's class. It's a stubborn bugger, a wee bit like himself. Come on back here where it's warm when you're done an' I'll make you a cup of tea wi' a nice buttered bap.'

'Thanks, Mr McGillivray,' smiled Kirsty. The janitor was always the same. His complaints were constant: the stoves, the children, the Dominie, all, in his opinion, 'thrawn buggers' whose sole purpose in life was to ruin his clean school. Kirsty laughed and went off to work, cheered by his normality and looking forward to the tea which he always said 'will pit hairs on yer chest, Miss, if you'll pardon the familiarity'.

She was sitting toasting herself at the open fire in the janitor's room when Bob Cargill arrived, and with him the memories of the night before came flooding back from the recesses of her mind where she had tried to bury them.

'Morning, Kirsty. What a night! Did you see the rain, Mr McGillivray? What my grannie calls the stotting kind. "It comes down and goes back up." That tea looks good. Any chance of a cup?'

'I've mair tae dae than stand here feeding every useless pupil teacher that comes in,' complained the janitor, but he was already filling a mug with the hot, sweet brew.

'I hope your parents won't be too worried, Bob,' said Kirsty.

'Fisherfolk are used to their men staying out all night, but I'll be glad to get home. Was everything all right with you?'

Kirsty looked at his fresh, open face and longed to confide in him, to tell him that her world had gone mad, but she bit the words back, and then she heard the voice that she had been subconsciously waiting for, and to her horror she began to tremble.

'Quick, lassie, pick up that spare bucket and pretend you were in here for coal.'

'Morning, McGillivray, Miss Robertson, Cargill. Good to see you on time, Cargill. Give Miss Robertson a hand with that coal, laddie. Where are your manners?' He was gone in a swirl of black gown, down the corridor to his room. Kirsty stared after him. How normally he had behaved. Had he forgotten? Surely he could not have forgotten.

'Finish yer tea, lassie,' said the janitor. 'It'll pit heart into you. Don't show the Dominie you're feard of him – he bullies the bairns who're scared, and the teachers an' all. Pit that extra bucket in Mr Wallace's room, Mr Cargill. His bluidy stove eats coal.'

'Come on, Kirsty, it's Mr Wallace who's teaching us this morning. Let's get the best seats.'

Mr Wallace was already in his room and soon the other pupil teachers, including Miss McNeil, arrived. Kirsty could not concentrate, although as a rule she liked Mr Wallace's history lessons. Had Mr Buchanan forgotten that terrible few seconds by the front door, or was he merely ignoring the event?

'My dear Miss Robertson,' Mr Wallace's quiet voice interrupted her thoughts. 'You are to take an examination in this subject on Saturday morning. Please try to at least pretend an interest.'

The tears started behind her eyes again. Oh God, was she going to cry every time anyone spoke to her for the rest of her life? Bob looked at her sympathetically, Nell Carson, a third-year pupil teacher, giggled and Miss McNeil frowned. When the hour was over and they were on their way out to the playground to collect the classes, she fell into step beside Kirsty.

'Pull yourself together, Miss Robertson,' she said. 'The Buchanans have decided to ignore your questionable behaviour. Stay away from Mr Cargill in future, and pay attention to your studies if you want to be commended to the Board.'

A hot wave of fury swept over Kirsty. So that was to be their attitude. She was the one in the wrong because she had innocently walked home after dark with two young men. Nothing was to be said about the violence with which the headmaster had accosted her. Who would believe her if she were to complain? Hugh. A vision of his smiling face flashed into her mind; his warm, deep, cultured voice filled her head. 'Seventh cousin, twice removed.' What a ridiculous relationship. Could such a one even exist? She smiled and hugged the happiness to herself. Hugh would believe her and he would know what to do, how to help. And then the glow faded, for Hugh was gone and who could say if she would ever see him again? He was the knight and, since he was so obviously twentieth-century, his white charger was a dark blue motor. Would he ride into her life again? 'Don't be silly, Kirsty,' she chided herself in an effort to cheer up. 'You know where he lives. A letter would be forwarded to him, wouldn't it?'

It was a dreadful day. Kirsty was in the infants' classroom all morning and so never saw the headmaster. She dreaded the dinner hour: surely he would seek her out. But he never did. As usual she saw him stride purposefully through the school, and when he was out of the gates she went slowly to the female teachers' cloakroom and washed her face in cold water. Then she sat down in the single armchair and closed her eyes to ease her blinding headache.

'Time of the month, lass? You delicate ones never can endure it.' It was Miss Purdy, the infants' mistress. 'I thought you weren't yourself this morning.'

'No, I'm all right, Miss Purdy, it's just a headache. I didn't sleep well.'

'If you slept at all. You're all right with the Buchanans, aren't you, lass? She's a wee mouse but nice enough, I think.'

Kirsty looked up into the honest, scrubbed face. 'Yes, thank you. Everything's fine.'

A chance missed. Should she say something? No, not yet. This was, after all, her first real conversation with Miss Purdy. She could hardly blurt out that she was suddenly afraid of the Dominie.

'Here. I've a powder in my bag.'

The world swam before Kirsty's eyes, and before she could fall her head was pushed firmly down between her knees.

'I hope you haven't been stupid, lassie. There's only two reasons I've ever known for a lassie fainting. One is when it's her time of the month, and the other is when she wishes it was.'

Released, Kirsty looked up at her. What was she saying? Why would anyone want to have . . . She blushed.

'No, no. It's just that I'm hungry. I couldn't eat breakfast and I forgot my piece.' Better not mention Mr McGillivray and his roll and tea.

Miss Purdy stared down at her for some minutes without speaking. 'I've enough for two, lass. Go back to my classroom and I'll fetch us both a cup of tea. Sit by the fire and warm up.'

Kirsty returned to the classroom, which was warm and quiet without the seventy-eight children who usually covered every inch of floor space. Miss Purdy had swept the floor and stoked the fire and it blazed invitingly. Kirsty flushed guiltily. Should she have cleaned up after the class instead of the senior teacher? She turned hesitantly when the infants' mistress bustled in.

'You've swept the floor, Miss Purdy.'

'I can't abide a mess, and the wee ones certainly make enough to please anyone, don't they? Don't fret, Miss Robertson. It's not in your contract to sweep my floor before dinner, you know. Here, have a sandwich. My favourite moment of the day, lass – the only time I'm ever on my own.'

Kirsty ate the sandwich and drank the hot sweet tea, and then Miss Purdy insisted that she take the headache powder. When the bell rang for the afternoon classes, she not only felt better but knew that she had made a friend. She had told Miss Purdy all about her parents and the school at Aberannoch, and she had learned a great deal about Miss Purdy, who had spent her early womanhood looking after a disabled father and then, after his death, had cheerfully taken over the running of her brother's home when his wife had died giving birth to their eighth child. There was no note of complaint in her voice, but Kirsty could appreciate why the infants' mistress enjoyed a quiet break in her classroom.

'You have my address, Kirsty,' said Miss Purdy as they walked to the wobbly lines of small children. 'Michael will certainly squeeze you in somewhere should you ever feel the need.'

Kirsty could say nothing. Those dratted tears once again hovering on the roots of her eyelashes, she smiled and hurried out to her afternoon class.

It was tea-time before she actually saw Mr Buchanan alone. It was Miss McNeil's turn to help in the kitchen and so Kirsty found herself sitting in the cold dining room with the headmaster, her host, her employer.

'Miss McNeil tells me you weren't quite yourself this morning, Miss Robertson. Perhaps now you'll agree with me about the value of eight hours' sound sleep. No running around the town after class like one of the fisher lassies. I shall be writing to the Board at Christmas about your first full term with us and, of course, I want that report to be as positive as possible.' He looked at Kirsty in a kindly and almost jovial manner.

'He's mad,' thought Kirsty. She could not answer him. A sick feeling was growing in the pit of her stomach.

'And your dear mother,' he went on. He lowered his voice in that way Kirsty had supposed denoted pity and sympathy. 'She will want to know that her child is progressing well in her chosen career: a credit to her mother's upbringing and to the memory of her own dear husband.'

To Kirsty's relief – for she had been sure that in another second she would have been violently ill – the door swung open and Mrs Buchanan bustled in with a tureen of soup. Miss McNeil followed with plates and hot bread.

'Nothing like soup on a November evening, is there, lassies?' she asked. 'Will we have the blessing, Mr Buchanan, afore the soup grows cold?'

'Before, Mrs Buchanan, before the soup grows cold,' said the Dominie, almost gently, and Kirsty saw his wife wince slightly.

'He's a horrible little man, and I never noticed until last night,' she thought as she bent her head for the blessing. 'What a hypocrite he is, and Miss McNeil too, and me if I stay in this house a minute longer.'

She sat at the table and ate her meal, and she supposed she joined in the conversation, for sometimes she seemed to hear her own voice as if from a long way off, but her mind was busy, busy, busy. Hugh, with his merry eyes and his lovely voice – she could have told Hugh. 'But you have no right to tell a complete stranger all your worries,' she argued with herself. 'He's not a complete stranger, we're friends.' And they were. Somehow she knew that there was a bond between her and the young soldier that she did not understand but was ready to accept. They had met only twice, but it did not matter. The bond had been forged that first day as they stood together in the playground worrying about poor wee Tam and his wet trousers. She must have smiled at the memory, for Miss McNeil's voice jerked her back to the tea-table.

'A smile at last, Miss Robertson. Thank goodness. Do you know, Mrs Buchanan, I even heard the head of the French department – and we all know what a misery he is – complain that our pretty little Miss Robertson was looking unhappy today.'

Kirsty said nothing.

'I do hope you are not unhappy, Miss Robertson?' said Mrs Buchanan anxiously.

'Good gracious, Mrs Buchanan. Why ever should the girl be unhappy? She has an excellent appointment, a fine home with good food, every chance for advancement like Miss McNeil here. Is that not so, Miss Robertson?'

'If you say so, Mr Buchanan,' said Kirsty. 'Now, if you will all excuse me, I find I'm not very hungry this evening.' She rose from the table, dissuading Mrs Buchanan – who was developing a remarkable resemblance to a clucking hen – from following her, and went upstairs to her room. What was going on in this house? Mr Buchanan had been so strange, so frightening, so brutal less than twenty-four hours before ... and now it was all being passed off as if it had never happened. Something was wrong: with him, with Miss McNeil, who seemed to have a somewhat unusual relationship with him, and with the overanxious Mrs Buchanan, who had stood hidden on the stairs last night while her husband had berated a girl in his care. And the remarks of the infants' mistress and the janitor ... their protectiveness ... had there always been undercurrents at Burnside School, and had she merely been too preoccupied or too grief-stricken to notice them? How she longed for the peace and beauty of Aberannoch. She would suggest that she and Meg go out there on Saturday afternoon, on their old second-hand bicycles, and have a picnic in the castle valley. They might even meet some old friend.

They did. They met Jamie.

6

Saturday was dry and cold, not at all like November, which was normally *dreich* and miserable. As usual the girls met at the little bridge over the Brothock, the place Meg called The Fit o' the Toon.

'A picnic, in November?' she said, a shiver in her voice. 'You're daft, Kirsty. We'll cycle out if you like, visit your father's grave and then cycle back. My mam's expecting us for our tea.'

They cycled slowly up through the town, talking all the way, while Kirsty gathered confidence on the ancient machine. Once out on the country road, they stopped to look back at the red sandstone bulk of the ruined abbey rising almost protectively above it.

'It must have been beautiful before it was destroyed,' said Kirsty. 'I'd love to have seen it back then.'

'But if you had been alive in those days, Kirsty, you'd probably have been a serving wench and you'd never have been a teacher.'

'I'd never have learned to read. That must have been awful, don't you think, Meg, never to have been able to read?'

'Imagine, no Co-op,' said Meg ruefully as she surveyed her very smart new boots which were perhaps designed more for the classroom than for country roads.

They turned away from the abbey and set off towards Aberannoch. Kirsty grew quieter as they approached the village, and Meg understood and was quiet in sympathy. The blacksmith was busy in his forge and he waved his hand as he saw them. The air was heavy with the smell of bread and cakes from the open bakery where two or three children were playing, drawn by the enticing smells. It was all as it had always been. Nothing had changed because John Robertson was dead and Kirsty Robertson no longer lived there.

'I wish I had some flowers,' said Kirsty as they dismounted at the little churchyard and went in.

Someone else had been at the grave very recently, for some long, slim branches with their dead leaves still attached lay on the mound under which John Robertson rested.

'Beech,' whispered Kirsty as she reached down to touch them. 'They must have been lovely. I wonder who . . .?'

She stayed for several minutes until she became conscious of the damp forcing its way up through her boots. 'Oh, Meg. I miss him so.'

'Take your time,' said Meg sympathetically, but Kirsty had turned and together they walked back along the neat little path to the beautifully wrought iron gates.

They mounted their bikes in silence and pedalled slowly up the hill away from the graveyard, towards the Schoolhouse and the castle entrance. The gates were closed against the world, the great eagles looking down broodingly, their thoughts their own.

'It was an Englishman who bought the castle, wasn't it?' said Meg as they dismounted in order to push their bicycles up the hill towards Kirsty's old home.

'Yes, a soldier. He was always very nice but the family isn't there much, I don't think,' said Kirsty. 'They have a son called Hugh,' she added, aware that she spoke aloud just to hear his name on her lips. 'I met him in the town the other morning.' She blushed furiously and turned her bicycle away from the gates, but Meg was kind enough to say nothing.

They laboured up the steep hill, but as always in nature were rewarded by the gratifying freewheel down the hill at the other side. Kirsty was in the lead and so exhilarated was she by the speed of her descent that she lifted her feet from the pedals and stuck her legs out at either side as she had done, always, as a little girl. Meg followed more sedately, just in time to see Kirsty and a huge Clydesdale swerve to avoid colliding with one another.

'Of a' the daftlike irresponsible . . .' the man leading the horse began to shout, and then the anger on his young face changed to an expression of joy. 'Kirsty,' he said, his voice dropping to an almost loverlike tone. 'Oh, Kirsty, you daft wee besom! Man, but it's good to see you.'

'Jamie.' It was all she could say as she looked at him. Jamie: the friend of her childhood, her father's favourite among all his pupils. Meg and the Clydesdale stood quietly while they greeted one another. Kirsty forgot Meg for a moment, so happy was she to see this sharer of childhood's secrets, but at last she became aware of the patience of the girl and the giant beast and stopped, embarrassed.

'Meg. This is Jamie. We went to school together, here in Aberannoch.' Kirsty turned to Jamie again. 'It's so good to see you.'

'Aye, it's good to see you, and you too, Meg. You'll have been to the grave?'

And then Kirsty knew. It was Jamie who had left the beech branches. 'Oh, Jamie, thank you. You visit him, don't you?'

Jamie looked behind him up the quiet winding road to the school. He ignored her question. 'I'll have to take Sergeant here intae the smiddy. Johnstone is waiting on him and, forbye, we'd best get aff the road. The laddie from the castle is hame and he drives yon motor car of his like a loon.'

She didn't want him to leave, but how could she keep him? 'You've grown, Jamie. Are you reading? Your father . . .?'

'All's well, Kirsty: am I not earning a man's wage? I'll tell Cissie I saw you.'

He was leading the horse away. She was aware that she might never see him again and she knew she didn't want that to happen. He was a tie, a special link with her father and her childhood. He was Jamie.

'Cissie's doing well?' she called after him.

'Aye,' he said, but already his face was turned towards the village. 'She likes the new Dominie.'

Childishly that hurt. No one should like the new teacher: they should be in perpetual mourning for her father.

'Good-looking laddie,' said Meg eventually.

'Oh, Meg, I'm sorry. It's just that we were such friends, and my father thought he had a good mind . . .'

'Is his father the farmer?'

'No, they both work on Balcundrum Farm.'

Meg said nothing, but her disapproving silence spoke loudly enough while they continued the long push up the next hill. Eventually there was the school and the Schoolhouse and the few cottages near it. Before they came abreast of the school, Kirsty turned and began to cycle back into the village, but more sedately this time as befitted a young lady schoolteacher. They stopped at the bottom again and pushed their bicycles for a while.

'I couldn't bear to see the house after all, Meg.'

'I understand.'

They cycled through the village and could see Sergeant's large haunches as he stood in the smiddy, and at his head the slender figure of Jamie. Kirsty deliberately kept her face turned towards the road, and so she did not see him come out to the street and watch her until she had pedalled out of sight.

'I won't go back again, Meg,' she said, 'not until the spring, and just to the graveyard.'

'Your mother will be glad to hear it's being tended. Won't it be lovely to see her at the New Year?'

Dear Meg. They were able to steer the conversation away from the dangerous topic of teachers and farm boys and walking out. Not that there had been a question of walking out with Jamie. He was an old friend, but the rules of her employment stated that she should never be seen in public with a man who was not her father or brother; or did it merely say that she could not be in a vehicle with a man? She had had no interest in that area of the teachers' code, not until that awful night of the storm. Male teachers of good character were awarded one or two evenings a week for courting purposes. How female teachers ever married was a mystery. There were no married teachers at Burnside, and all the women teaching there were ancient, like Miss Purdy: married teachers, such as Kirsty's mother, were allowed to help as sewing or cooking instructors. It must be that most dedicated teachers never married but remained in their posts, pillars of the community, until maidenly and virtuous retirement. It was a very depressing thought.

Kirsty's spirits lifted when they reached the harbour and Meg's cottage. At the back of her mind, nibbling away, had been the memory of Mr Buchanan's behaviour. The visit to Aberannoch had not eased it, but perhaps she could talk to Mrs Stewart – or was she making too much of it? Sometimes it loomed large in her mind, and at other times she felt that she might have exaggerated the incident as Miss McNeil had suggested. She propped her bicycle against the door and made a decision. She would wait to see if such a thing ever happened again, and if it did she would talk to Miss Purdy. Had not Miss Purdy promised her refuge with her brother and his large, motherless family, and why should she do such a thing if there was no cause for concern? All was not well in the Buchanan household and at least some members of staff suspected it.

Her mind at last at rest and a course of sensible action decided upon, Kirsty gave herself up to enjoying the Stewarts and especially Mrs Stewart's cooking.

'Sam and me'll walk you back with our Meg, Kirsty lass,' said Mrs Stewart as Kirsty at last rose to go. It was so warm and friendly at the Stewarts. There were no undercurrents in the house, that was filled with noise and laughter and light. That was what was wrong at the Buchanan's: no lights streamed from laughter-filled rooms.

*

The term went on and Kirsty continued to attend night classes at Keptie School. She became more and more friendly with Bob Cargill and with Miss Purdy, the senior teacher with whom she spent most of her teaching time. In the evenings after tea she would go straight to her room: there was studying to do, there were lessons to prepare and, in the exciting run down to the end of the year, presents to make. She avoided the Buchanans and Miss McNeil as much as possible.

In the middle of December, Bob was caught in a storm on his way to school and, having spent the entire day in wet clothes, developed a terrible cold.

Miss Purdy took the pupil teachers for their lessons in the morning. 'Since Mr Cargill is to be off for the rest of the week at the very least, you'll need to take his place with the senior class, Kirsty,' she said. 'It will be excellent experience. You can't spend all your practice time with the babies.'

'No, Miss Purdy,' answered Kirsty, but her heart sank into her fur-lined little boots. She would have dreaded the senior classes at any time, but the teacher was the Dominie, and the longer she had stayed with Miss Purdy and her infants, the more she had hoped to avoid Mr Buchanan.

When the bell rang she went outside to bring the class in. They were lined up like soldiers in the playground, and not for the first time was she struck by the difference between the Burnside School and Aberannoch, where the children had milled around like calves in a field until the appearance of the headmaster. Mr Buchanan was waiting for them in the classroom.

'Ah, Miss Robertson. Well, we must be very good today, boys and girls, and not frighten away our pupil teacher.' He smiled at the children and they shuffled nervously and a few sniggered. 'Perhaps you'd like to correct the homework exercises, Miss Robertson, while I mark the register and hear the reading.'

Thankfully, Kirsty walked around the class collecting the exercises. She could sit quietly for a while absorbing the feelings of the class. The homework exercise was a bill, and since the Dominie didn't give her the figures or the answer she was absorbed for a while going through the papers to find six with the same figures so that she could work out the correct answers. The work was of a relatively high standard. Her father would have approved of the neatness of presentation and the accuracy. Most of the twenty-eight exercises were correct; one, however, had not even been attempted, and two had errors in multiplication. '193 apples at 3 ½d each'. Expensive apples, but it was obvious that two of the children had no idea of the wonders of the three times table or how to deal with halfpennies.

'Have you found Mary McDougall's bill yet, Miss Robertson?' The Dominie interrupted her corrections. 'Ah, that tear-soaked mess in your hand looks the very one. Bring it here if you would be so kind.'

Kirsty looked at Mary McDougall, whose halting attempts at reading had disturbed her concentration. There was a terrible inevitability on Mary's bovine face, and fear together with patient acceptance.

Mr Buchanan held the bill by one end as if not to contaminate his fingers. '193 apples at 3½d each. £107, says Miss McDougall.' Some children giggled but most were quiet. 'Miss McDougall plans to marry a rich man to throw his money away on apples for her children. 18 eggs at ¾d each; ⅛d, says Miss McDougall. Well, that was closer than the apples, was it not, boys and girls?' Mr Buchanan turned to Kirsty. 'You would not believe the time I have spent trying to teach this young lady her tables, Miss Robertson.' His voice was quiet and sad. 'She refuses to learn, don't you, Mary McDougall,' and his voice rose almost to a scream. Kirsty jumped. It had been so unexpected. 'What would you do with a obstinate lassie who refuses to do as she is told, Miss Robertson?'

Kirsty was as white as Mary McDougall. What could she say or do? She had no idea whether Mary would not learn or whether, as was more likely, she *could* not learn. She said nothing, but looked down at the corrected exercises in her hand. Mary had moved from her bench to the Dominie's desk – this was obviously a morning ritual. Why did she even bother to come to school if this was her reception? Mr Buchanan had taken the ugly leather tawse from his desk. Nothing was said. Some children watched avidly but most turned away. Mary held out her hand, her lips trembling and her rather vacant eyes filling with unshed tears. She made no sound as the leather strap crashed down on her hand with all the force of a large man behind it.

'As stupid as a cow,' said Mr Buchanan.

'Then why hit her for it?' thought Kirsty.

The awful morning went on, the only sounds the scraping of nibs and smothered sobs from poor Mary. No one was more relieved than the pupil teacher when the bell for the morning interval sounded. She had gone about her work as the Dominie had bid her, desperately trying to prevent the vomit from rising in her throat. She stayed outside in the damp air until the cold forced her into the teachers' room for a hot cup of tea.

Miss Purdy met her. 'A good morning, Kirsty?'

'Different.'

'Aye, we all have our methods, lass. He gets good results – they're well taught.'

'They're scared.'

'Careful, Kirsty.' Miss Purdy looked round as if to see who was within hearing. 'Have some tea, you look chilled. It's a big room for such a wee stove.'

'There were only twenty-eight children in this morning.'

'They tend to drift away as they get older, Kirsty, and forbye, the weather's been so awful, half of them will have chilblains or colds.'

Mary McDougall was not at school the next morning, and Kirsty never saw her in school again. She was near to leaving age and her parents applied for, and were given, permission for her to leave because she was needed at home. Mrs McDougall already had four children under school age and another was on the way. Kirsty felt sure that poor Mary had eagerly welcomed the news of the impending arrival, even if her mother had not. Bob stayed off for the rest of the week and Kirsty remained with the senior class and observed the headmaster. He did teach well, she was forced to admit, on the days when he taught at all and did not leave it to her. Mr Buchanan was subject to migraine headaches and often stayed in his darkened office all day. Once or twice, since the beginning of term, he had been forced to remain in bed at home. On those days it had seemed to Kirsty that even the very walls of the old school seemed to breathe more easily and, in his classroom, she could see a tremendous difference in the attitudes of the children. Luckily Mr Cost, the assistant head teacher, took his class on those days, for Kirsty knew she could not have handled the children. With Bob back, Kirsty was delighted to return to the infants, who were busily making the unbelievable mess that they called 'a present for Mam'.

And then it was the last day of term. The weather was kind in that there was no snow, and Kirsty set off on the long journey to her uncle's farm. To her surprise she had a gaily wrapped parcel from Miss Purdy as well as the gift she had been expecting from Meg, and the two bright boxes sat on top of her overflowing bag and cheered her up as she waited at cold stations or rattled at an amazing speed across the Ayrshire countryside.

7

UNCLE CHAY MET HER AT the station. He had borrowed the farmer's trap, and Jessie had covered a hot brick with a blanket and put them on the floor to warm her daughter with. As she wrapped the warmed blanket around her shoulders, Kirsty felt her mother's warmth and love enfold her and she relaxed, determined to enjoy the few days of holiday.

'Your mam's fine, Kirsty,' said Chay. 'She gets on fine wi' the lassie, teaches her cooking and sewing and such. Bett's walking out. She'll make some man a fine wife, thanks tae Jessie.'

And Kirsty was delighted to see for herself that her mother was much better in body and had almost come to terms with her loss.

'Your Uncle Chay's a fine man, Kirsty, but I miss you so much. If we could only get a wee cottage or a house in Arbroath, I could come back and look after you.'

'That would be so wonderful, Mother.' Should she tell her mother her worries over the headmaster's erratic behaviour?

No, better to keep it to herself and look forward to the day she qualified. Not long now.

'I've had time to think,' Jessie went on, 'and I believe we should have approached the Colonel about a cottage on the estate. There might have been one we could have had.'

'You are happy with Uncle Chay, aren't you, Mother? I couldn't bear it if you were miserable.' Both of us, thought Kirsty sadly, both of us miserable and unable to help one another.

'As happy as I can be without you and my dear John, but I have high hopes for Uncle Chay and young Bett.'

Kirsty looked at her mother, shock and disbelief written large on her face, and Jessie laughed.

'Kirsty Robertson,' she said, 'why so shocked? He's a good man, and not fifty yet.'

'But he's old enough to be Bett's father, and besides, she's walking out.'

'Just because the man she wants hasn't asked her yet doesn't mean she should sit at home and knit with me,' said Jessie complacently.

'Oh, Mother,' laughed Kirsty happily. She was still shocked by her mother's – and Bett's – attitude to love and marriage, but it was wonderful to see Jessie beginning to emerge from the cocoon of grief which she had wrapped around herself.

'What plans are you two hatching for the holiday?' asked Chay as he came in from feeding the cattle. 'Here's Bett with a meal ready for a queen . . .'

'Or a king, Uncle Chay,' said Kirsty, and giggled at the mystified look on his face.

Later as she snuggled down beside her mother in the best feather bed, she gave herself up to imagining the unbelievable joy it would be to live with her mother and to set off for school in the morning knowing that Jessie would be waiting in their own little home for her return.

'When I qualify, Mother,' she vowed as she fell asleep. 'There's just a little over a year left.'

Just a little over a year. It sounded no time at all, but it was to be the longest year of Kirsty's life.

8

Two days after the beginning of the new term, Bob Cargill had a row with Mr Buchanan. The Dominie had caught the pupil teacher with his coat on before the bell rang for the afternoon dismissal. Possibly if Bob had apologized the matter would have gone no further, but Bob had refused to do so.

'He's being unreasonable,' he told the other pupil teachers angrily. 'I put my coat on to get a head start for the journey home. The bairns are tidying up when I do it – it's not that I'm taking time away from my duties.'

A letter about insubordination was sent to the Board and Bob was summoned to a meeting to explain himself.

'They were nice enough,' he told the staff in the teachers' room. 'Said they could understand in the winter how I'd want to get on the road, even said they'd see about a school placement nearer home, but I'm still to wait till I hear the bell. I've got to grovel to old Buchanan.'

That should have been the end of the matter, but from that day Bob could do nothing right for the Dominie. His class was never lined up properly in the playground. They made too much noise filing up the stairs. His lessons were not adequately prepared. His marking was sloppy and insufficient. Twice he had had the audacity to be late: no matter that a gale had been blowing and it was a wonder to the rest of the staff that he ever arrived at all.

Every evening, it seemed to Kirsty, Mr Buchanan went over and over all the faults he found with poor Bob.

'He doesn't realize how lucky he is, as we all are, to have you as his headmaster,' said Miss McNeil soothingly.

Kirsty said nothing, and when pressed by Miss McNeil said quietly that since she was never in the same classroom with Mr Cargill she was not in a position to comment.

'You'll have to do better than that, Miss Robertson,' said Miss McNeil. 'You have the advantage of actually living under the same roof with Mr Buchanan, and Mrs Buchanan too,' she added, looking to the foot of the table where the quiet little woman sat taking no part in the discussion.

'You're forgetting, Miss McNeil, that our little Miss Robertson is an intimate friend of Mr Cargill,' said the Dominie, and a chill went through Kirsty at the undisguised venom in his voice.

The next morning Mr Buchanan had a migraine. It had come on after supper, explained Mrs Buchanan quietly, when he had been struggling to correct some essays from the Supplementary Class. He had hardly been able to get upstairs to bed.

'I think he may have accidentally fallen against your door, Miss Robertson,' Mrs Buchanan said. 'I hope you weren't frightened.'

Kirsty looked at her and at Miss McNeil. They were both watching her very closely. She had heard Mr Buchanan stumbling up the stairs in the dark; she often did. Light seemed to make his migraines worse and he usually came upstairs without a lamp, brushing against tables, chairs and doors as he did so.

'It's all right, Mrs Buchanan,' she said. 'I think I heard him bump into the chair in the hall outside my room. I'm really sorry he gets such terrible headaches.'

Was she imagining things or did the Dominie's wife look rather too relieved?

It was Kirsty's week for the fires, and so she arrived at school before any of the other teachers.

'Mr Buchanan won't be in this morning,' she told the janitor. 'Have you lit the fire in his office?'

'First one that's lit, lass. What's wrong wi' his nibs this morning, or do I need to ask?'

'He gets terrible migraines,' said the very healthy Kirsty sympathetically.

The janitor looked at her as if he was going to say something and then he changed his mind. 'Aye, I get them

maself, lassie. Every Friday night when I'm finished wi'
this place.'

Kirsty was stoking the fire in Miss Purdy's room when
the realization hit her. It was well known that Mr McGillivray spent every Friday evening in the Mariners' Rest,
a public house at the Fit o' the Toon. She sat back on her
heels, heedless of the dust. Was the janitor saying that
Mr Buchanan *drank*? The smell, that awful smell on his
breath the night of the storm – was that alcohol? She cast
her mind back to her father's funeral. The men had been
drinking whisky. Was that the same smell, or had it been
more sickly?

'Morning, Kirsty. Saying your prayers?'

Miss Purdy with her common sense, her kindness, her
no-nonsense approach to life.

'Does Mr Buchanan drink?' There, it was out.

Miss Purdy rapidly closed the door behind her. 'Well,
good morning to you too, Kirsty.' She took off her heavy
tweed coat, shook the moisture from it and hung it up
near the fire to steam.

'You should have known him when he was young,
Kirsty.' She avoided a direct answer. 'Those of us who grew
up with him . . . make allowances, I suppose, and perhaps
we shouldn't. He wanted children . . .' She laughed suddenly, not a bitter laugh but the laugh of someone who
sees a joke. 'But then, so did I. Women never expect men

to be able to manage – it's one of our failings. Yes, he drinks, gin, I think, and when he's drinking we say he has a migraine headache. We can see it coming: he's harder on the bairns, he picks on a teacher or a pupil teacher. We worried about you, but it's poor Bob Cargill that gets the bullying. We don't know what goes on in that mausoleum he calls a home, but McNeil seems all right, and you ... you'll tell me if anything's wrong, won't you?'

She doesn't really want to know, thought Kirsty. No direct questions. But then nothing was wrong, was it? Just that one night when Miss McNeil had stopped him from ... from what, shaking her? Now that she knew, and she blushed a little at her naivety in not realizing the problem, Kirsty determined to be more watchful and to work towards her goal as conscientiously as possible. Whatever happened, she would become a qualified teacher; she would rent a little cottage from Colonel Granville-Baker and she would live there with her mother.

9

WOULD SPRING EVER COME? THE children were miserable: colds and coughs, measles, even the dreaded diphtheria raged over the first months of the year. Kirsty moved to the middle classes and although she missed the little ones, she found that the mental development of nine- and ten-year-olds really interested her. They were too old to wet themselves in the classroom, had achieved a certain standard in basic reading, writing and arithmetic, and were not so old that they could not be handled by an unsure pupil teacher – usually. It had been quite a blow to her self-conceit to find that she was not so perfect in the classroom as her father's uncritical love had led her to believe. The classes she attended gave her knowledge in academic subjects, but only experience could teach her how to deal with sometimes belligerent, aggressive or even violent pupils.

Bob seemed to have no trouble when he was left alone in the classroom, although sometimes a little too much laughter was heard echoing down the dark corridor and there were a few tut-tuts from some of the established teachers. Kirsty, however, sometimes dreaded the time she spent alone with her class: the children sensed her nervousness, and misbehaved just to see how she would handle them. To these children she was not the Dominie's lassie but just another pupil teacher, which was a lowering reflection. The class teacher asked her for the names of those who did not behave when he was out of the room, but 'Miss Robertson' was determined to handle discipline for herself.

'Don't you have trouble making the children behave when your class teacher is out of the room?' Kirsty asked Bob when she recuperated with a cup of tea in the staff room after an hour alone with eighty-three eight-year-olds.

'Well, I have an advantage because I'm a man,' said seventeen-year-old Bob complacently, 'but I think you've got to make the little beggars believe you're not afraid of them.'

'I thought I had done that till Billy McGuire started rolling around the floor with the waste basket on his head.'

'I hope you gave him the strap.'

'No, I took it off his head and threatened to fill it with water and then let him put his head back in again.'

Bob laughed. 'Aren't we progressive? Next time you'll have to belt him because you certainly won't be allowed to drown him.'

Bob was right because the very next time Kirsty was left alone to manage the class, there on the floor was Billy McGuire with a tin waste bucket on his head, banging into desks and the legs of other children who crowded around him yelling their heads off. Into the tumult walked the Dominie.

Kirsty was aware only of a sudden frightened silence as she struggled with the eight-year-old, and then young Billy became aware that he was no longer the centre of attention and stopped rolling.

'A small problem with discipline, Miss Robertson?' Mr Buchanan did not wait for an answer but grabbed the now whimpering little boy by the arm and hauled him out of the classroom. 'Report to me in my office at four o'clock, Miss Robertson,' he said quietly from the door. 'Is there anyone else in the class who does not mind the pupil teacher when she is alone in the room?' he asked the children, now quiet at their desks. No one spoke. 'Send each and every malefactor to me, Miss Robertson,' he finished as he slammed the door behind him.

Kirsty and the children looked at one another. 'I feel sick,' thought Kirsty. 'I mustn't be sick.'

'We will discuss verbs,' she said. 'Everyone is to think of a verb, present, simple past, or future tense, and I will write them on the board. What a list of verbs we will have to use in our sentences.'

The afternoon dragged on. The class teacher returned and, if he was surprised by the level of industry, he said nothing. At four o'clock the children seemed more relieved than ever at hearing the bell. Not Kirsty.

'I'm to see Mr Buchanan,' she said hesitantly.

'I'll dismiss the children. Don't worry, Kirsty. His bark's worse than his bite, as they say.'

Kirsty hurried along to the headmaster's office.

'Come,' said his voice in answer to her knock.

Kirsty swallowed nervously and tried to steady the butterflies that insisted on dancing in the pit of her stomach. 'I don't want to go in there,' she thought. 'I don't want to be alone with that man for any reason whatsoever.' She opened the door.

'Come in, lassie, come in. Wee Billy is not here, if that's what's worrying you. He's away home with six of the best and will probably get another six when his father gets home. All your fault, Miss Robertson. It happened before, didn't it, and you did nothing? Psychology you were trying, was it?'

He waited.

'I thought the child was seeking attention and therefore probably needed attention.'

'Oh, he did, Miss, and he got it, more than he bargained for. It seems I'll need to take the pupil teachers for some classes in discipline. You have them rolling all over the floor with buckets on their heads, and Mr Cargill has them laughing like loons all day and learning nothing, as far as I can see.'

'I have to stand up for Bob: he'd do it for me, wouldn't he?' she thought, and nervously cleared her throat.

'I . . . I . . . don't think that's very fair, Mr Buchanan. They say Mr Cargill does some really interesting lessons.'

He got up from his desk and came round to stand beside her. She took a small step away from him and then decided to stand her ground.

'Does he indeed, Miss Robertson? You would know, of course. I had forgotten what . . . intimate . . . friends you two young people are.'

'We discuss our methods and our lessons with Miss Purdy and Mr Watson.'

'Naturally.' Had he moved closer? His nearness was oppressive; he seemed to dominate her. 'Mrs Buchanan and I might enjoy discussing your work with you, Miss Robertson, but you are always off to your room to study, or off to classes with our young friend, Cargill, and then there are the Saturday meetings with Miss Stewart. She has several handsome young brothers too, I believe. What a popular young lady you are.'

Kirsty refused to be drawn. Her friendship with Meg was none of his business, and she would say nothing about Meg's brothers. Let him think what he liked.

'How is your mother?' he asked suddenly.

'She's well, thank you.'

'I would not want her distressed.' He was closer and she could smell wood smoke and chalk on his gown. She glanced up at him and saw he was looking at her in the strangest way. She could not read the message in his eyes. Mother. Their hopes for a cottage together could only come to fruition if she gained her teaching certificates, and Mr Buchanan could ensure that she either did or did not. His hand was on her shoulder. She could feel the heat and the weight through the thin wool of her dress.

'Ye cannae go in wi'oot I tell him.' It was the janitor's voice.

'Aye, I can, and I'll gang in an' brak his bluidy neck for him.'

Mr Buchanan had moved quickly back to the other side of his desk. 'Open the door to our visitor, Miss Robertson.'

But before Kirsty could reach it the door was hurled open and a small plump woman came in, followed by the janitor. 'Ye auld bastard, Buchanan,' she yelled. 'Whit did my Billy dae tae get his hands blistered like that? I'll get ma man tae tell the Board on ye.'

'Sit down, Mrs McGuire. It is Mrs McGuire, isn't it? Miss Robertson and I have just been discussing young Billy's constant disruption of the class. Thank you, Miss Robertson. I am sorry you had such a distressing afternoon.'

'He'll hae her eatin oot o' his haun' afore ye reach yer classroom, Miss Robertson,' said the janitor. 'Dinna fret, lassie', he continued as Kirsty said nothing, 'ye'll hae tae learn tae deal wi' parents and dominies as weel as bairns gin ye bide in the teaching profession. Best get ye a guid man an' hae yer ain bairns, a braw wee thing like you.'

He couldn't have said anything more likely to strengthen Kirsty's resolve to stay in teaching. 'Thank you, Mr McGillivray,' she said. 'I'm sure you mean well, but I have no intention of getting myself a man, well, at least not yet,' added Kirsty honestly and awarded him a smile. 'I have a class tonight, so I'd best sweep the classroom and then I'll go home for my tea.'

'Aye, and I'll hae nae sooner got this tip cleaned up and aboot fifty of you will be fleeing through here for yer lessons dripping water aff yer wet raincoats all over the place. I'd better redd up the fires in Miss Purdy's room.'

'In my room, I think, janitor,' came the headmaster's voice behind them. 'Good night, Mrs McGuire, don't let your man be too hard on wee Billy. Laddies like a bit of attention from bonny pupil teachers.' He waited until Mrs McGuire, not completely calm, had left the school and then turned back to Kirsty and the janitor. 'I've decided to teach the pupil teachers tonight. Do the fires, McGillivray, and then cycle over to Mr Purdy's and tell Miss Purdy I will take her class. We'll put something besides ancient civilizations into these young heads, eh, Miss Robertson? Can't have bairns acting like idiots in the classroom, even if that's all they are.'

They watched him stride down the corridor, his gown billowing around him.

'Ye'd best away hame fer yer tea, Miss Robertson. I'll sweep the classroom for you. You're nae use at corners – but dinnae tell the others.'

'There's time, Mr McGillivray, thanks,' said Kirsty and hurried off. She did not want to go home, home to the Buchanans. She wanted to go home to her mother. How wonderful it would be to hurry home knowing that her mother was there. A little cottage, no more than a but 'n' ben, a room and a kitchen, that's all they would need. As soon as she had her teaching certificate she would write to Hugh. He would help. Was he not her seventh cousin, twice removed? Perhaps she should write now. If plans were actually being made, would she not be happier, better able to deal with ... with what ... with any difficulties that might arise? She swept the dust happily from one end of the classroom to the other. Mr McGillivray was right; she was no good at corners.

'I'm sorry for you, Kirsty,' said Bob in the staff room the next morning, 'but last night it was nice to have someone else at the end of old Buchanan's tongue for a change.'

'Glad to be of help,' smiled Kirsty, who had been the embarrassed recipient of all the Dominie's ridicule the evening before. 'I've been practising severe looks all morning in the classroom. I think the children must believe I have a pain. Three of them have been quite concerned and asked me if I was all right.'

'Discipline is not a laughing matter, Mr Cargill,' broke in another voice. 'I know how frivolous Miss Robertson is, but since you, as a man, must want a career in teaching, I should hope you would take everything Mr Buchanan says to heart.'

'Kirsty is not frivolous, Miss McNeil.' Bob rushed in to Kirsty's defence, then stopped for a moment and looked at the senior pupil teacher very deliberately. 'Would a dried-up stick like you recognize frivolity if it hit you in the eye?'

For the first time in the six months she had known her, Kirsty saw Miss McNeil lose her composure. Her sallow face went bright red and even her disciplined hair seemed to burst from its restricting pins. 'How dare you speak to me like that, you . . . you . . . I am not a dried-up . . .'

'Yes, you are,' interrupted Bob. 'You, Miss McNeil, senior pupil teacher, are about a hundred years older than Miss Purdy and have as much . . . frivolity in you as that chair.'

'You've done it now, lad.' Mr Watson's calm voice broke the silence as the astonished staff watched Miss McNeil run from the staff room. 'Even if our Kirsty doesn't know, our senior pupil teacher certainly knows what synonym you had in mind for frivolity.'

'Is sex a synonym for frivolity, Mr Watson?' asked Miss Purdy calmly. 'Come, children, let's get the lines in.' At the door she turned to Bob. 'And thanks for the compliment, laddie.'

'Into the valley of death,' quoted Bob, and followed her into the playground.

10

MR BUCHANAN HAD A MIGRAINE. Kirsty lay in her bed and listened to him stumbling around the house, bumping into furniture, crashing against doors. She heard Mrs Buchanan's quiet voice soothing, restraining, and then a loud slap, a muffled cry. A few minutes later, the sobbing woman ran past Kirsty's door and into her own room at the end of the corridor.

'He hit her, the old devil,' said an angry Kirsty into the darkness, and wondered for a second whether to get up and say something to the headmaster.

Kirsty was angry with herself. She couldn't believe how naive she had been. She knew the cause of his *migraines* – oh, yes, she knew now, as everyone in the entire school seemed to have always known. Had he not left the school very shortly after the appalling row he had had with Bob Cargill had echoed around the walls of the old school? Had he not stayed in his study here in the house, *correcting papers*, according to the quieter than usual Dominie's wife?

Kirsty had sat down to tea almost alone with Miss McNeil; one could hardly count the withered figure who had desperately tried to play serene hostess at the head of her own dining room table.

'Poor Mr Buchanan,' soothed Miss McNeil, and Kirsty surprised a look of dislike on Mrs Buchanan's face that would have stopped a more sensitive woman. 'Mr Cargill will have to go. He has fought with Mr Buchanan every step of the way, ignored his teachings, which were all for his own good, and he was a bad influence on Miss Robertson here.'

'I'll get the mince,' said Mrs Buchanan as Kirsty rushed to Bob's defence.

'Bob has not defied Mr Buchanan and you know it, but he's not going to be bullied, and if he's dismissed for telling you a few home truths I'll write to the Board.'

'I wouldn't do that if I were you. They won't believe you against Mr Buchanan. He has a long-established reputation as a conscientious and hard-working Dominie who gets results, from his pupils and from his pupil teachers,' said Miss McNeil, calmly buttering bread. 'Two of his pupil teachers won scholarships to the University of Glasgow last year, and I myself hope and expect to attend the Methodist College in Edinburgh this October. And I would look out for yourself, Miss, with your lace collars and swirling petticoats. Having Bob Cargill's faults to correct kept the Dominie's attention from you.'

Kirsty stared at her as she calmly helped herself to a minute serving of mince. 'I'll write to the Board, Miss McNeil. I have friends on it.' Please God, let the Colonel be at home if I have to write. He would know, wouldn't he, that she would tell only the truth. Hugh, she would write to Hugh.

'Mince, Kirsty?' asked Mrs Buchanan and pushed the casserole into the silence between the two young women.

In her room after the awful, interminable meal, she started letter after letter to Colonel Granville-Baker.

Dear Colonel,
    We met once when my father was Dominie of Aberannoch School.

Dear Colonel,
    I write to inform you of a grave miscarriage of justice.

Dear Colonel,

She tore them up. How could she write a letter in defence of Bob before she knew whether or not he was being wrongfully dismissed?

Dear Hugh,
    How nice it was to meet you again before Christmas.
    I had been so homesick for Aberannoch . . .

Dear Hugh, Dear Hugh Dear, dear Hugh.

She could not finish the letters. The words refused to marshal themselves on the paper. But there had been a threat in Miss McNeil's voice, and she would have to deal with that threat.

Now she lay in bed and listened to the Dominie's progress around his house. Another sixteen months before she could leave this house, before she could hope to be transferred to another school.

She saw Bob next morning. He had obviously had even less sleep and was white and drawn, with dark shadows under his eyes and on his chin. For the first time in six months he looked more man than boy.

'He's written to the Board about what he calls my insubordination. Can you believe it? Because I yelled at his little pet.'

'What will you do, Bob?'

'Wait and see. They'll summon me to a meeting, but the Dominie'll win, Kirsty, they always do. I'll lose my job, and then it's me for the fishing like every other man in my family since the beginning of time. You know, I had begun to think about applying for one of those university scholarships.'

'I know two men on the Board, Bob. Colonel Granville-Baker and the minister from my old home. I'll write to them.'

'I don't want you involved, Kirsty. If they're prepared to listen to me, maybe they'll transfer me . . . only I transferred already from Authmithie because I needed a different experience.'

The Dominie did not come to school that day or the next. At home the house was quiet and, when asked, Mrs Buchanan would only say that the migraine was a bad one and that her husband was now resting in a darkened room.

'He can't bear light when he's bad, Kirsty,' she explained, and Kirsty looked at her and wondered at her bravery as she deluded herself. Or was pretending her husband had a headache her only way of coping with an insurmountable problem? Would it be easier for her if I were to say, 'Mrs Buchanan, I know your husband drinks. You don't have to pretend with me'? Maybe not. Mrs Buchanan needed her pride, her dignity. 'I can be nicer to her,' Kirsty resolved.

'What a shame the Dominie isn't well enough to enjoy this delicious fish pie,' she said.

Mrs Buchanan gave her a small smile. 'Do you really like it? I know I'm not a good cook. Cakes never turn out well, but I do quite well with plain cooking.'

'This is really tasty.'

'Thank you, dear. You never say, and Miss McNeil hardly eats enough to get the taste of her food, and my husband . . . well, some men just shovel it in, don't they?'

Poor Mrs Buchanan. Surely her husband's failure to appreciate her cooking was only one of her problems. No wonder she drifted around her own house like a shadow.

The next morning the Dominie appeared at breakfast. In two days he seemed to have shrunk. 'And what have Mr Cargill and Miss Robertson here been up to in my absence?'

Kirsty stared at him woodenly.

'I explained your forbearance to Miss Robertson, Mr Buchanan,' said Miss McNeil.

'There are limits to even my forbearance, Miss McNeil, as you will find, Miss Robertson. I have informed the Board of your encouragement of young Cargill – your interest in him, should I say?'

This was so unjust. How could he twist the truth so badly? Unsteadily, Kirsty got to her feet. She couldn't say anything sitting in her chair; she felt too small and helpless. 'You are a bad man,' she finally managed as the bile rose in her throat.

At once the Dominie was up and around the table. 'A bad man, am I? How dare you speak to me like that? Sit down!'

'Sit down,' he said again as Kirsty refused to move and then she felt his hand on her shoulder as he pushed her into her chair. 'I have tolerated enough from you, Miss.' He pushed his face against hers, and this time she could smell vomit and that other smell – alcohol, gin, was it? Hysteria and fear threatened to overcome her. She must not cry, must not scream, must not lose control. 'Do you want to be thrown out in the street without a reference? You have defied me at every turn, you and young Cargill. The teaching profession, our bairns, they deserve more than the likes of you.'

'Or you either,' began Kirsty hotly before she could stop herself, and she stared at him aghast as his face went white and then purple with rage. He drew back his hand and slapped her hard across the face.

'Angus.' It was Mrs Buchanan. 'Stop it! I won't put up with it, I won't. I'll leave the house this day and never return.'

'Go? You? What a good day that would be for this house. The woman of the house?' He laughed, a horrible leering sound. 'What kind of woman is it who does not welcome her own lawful husband to her bed, and then when he does manage to get himself between her legs, can't get herself with child!'

Mrs Buchanan stared at them all for a moment, the colour ebbing and flowing in her thin cheeks, and then she turned and fled from the room. Kirsty made to follow her.

'Get to school,' said Miss McNeil, and she held Kirsty's wrist so brutally that a mark could be seen for days. 'Get to school, and not a word of this. I'll handle everything here. Go.'

Kirsty continued to stare as the Dominie slumped back in his seat, his head hidden by his hands. 'My head, oh dear God, my head.'

Miss McNeil bent over him solicitously. 'There, Angus my dear, it's all right. Let me take you to your room. You can rest there.' She helped him to his feet, his face still hidden by his hands, then she turned again to Kirsty. 'Get out, you stupid girl, if you want to salvage anything of your career.'

School: the children and their openness, their innocence and natural charm. Without a bite of breakfast Kirsty hurried to be with them. Their worries would wipe away the memory of that scene for a time.

'Who's chasing you, lassie?' It was the janitor. 'You're no' on fires this morning. It's Mr Watson.'

Kirsty slowed down and tried to calm her breathing. 'I . . . I had a few things to do before the lessons this morning.'

'Fine, they'll wait till ye warm yersel. I've baps still warm frae the bakery. I must hae kent I was going to have company this morning.' He looked at her steadily. 'There's little in life cannae be mended efter a decent cup of tea.'

'I'm not hungry, Mr McGillivray,' said Kirsty, but the warmth of the fire drew her. She sat down and the janitor handed her a mug of hot sweet tea. She sipped it and looked up at him.

'Aye, I ken you never take sugar, but it'll dae you good.'

He said nothing, asked nothing, but handed her a hot buttered roll and, when she had eaten that, a second one, and he watched the colour return to her cheeks and the fear ebb from her eyes.

'Miss Purdy's an awful sensible old woman,' he said, and left the room to attend to his morning duties.

Yes. Miss Purdy. Obviously she had expected something, or why should she have talked about finding room for Kirsty in her brother's overflowing house? Kirsty made up her mind to tell the whole story to the infant mistress as soon as she could see her on her own. The first opportunity seemed to be playtime when the children were all outside. Cheered by the janitor's sympathy and shared breakfast, Kirsty looked forward to the moment when she could unburden herself of her worries. Bob arrived for the pupil teachers' lessons, and although he was pale and drawn with a faint dark line along his jaw, he smiled at her gamely. There was no chance to speak for Mr Watson began straight away with his talks on the history of education in Scotland. As a rule he would have infuriated Kirsty by sounding as if education for women was a real privilege awarded them by men, instead of a right, but her own worries were too overpowering today. What was happening in that dark house around the corner? Where was Miss McNeil?

Miss McNeil walked in at half-past eight and, ignoring her fellow students completely, went straight to the master's desk to talk quietly to him for a minute or two. Then, still managing to avoid looking at Kirsty, she sat down at one of the desks and appeared to give her complete attention to the lecture.

She grabbed Kirsty as they were walking out to the playground to bring in the classes of children who had lined up when Mr McGillivray rang the bell.

'I've had to send for a doctor,' she whispered. 'Nothing happened at breakfast this morning, nothing, do you understand? Mr Buchanan won't remember and Mrs Buchanan will say nothing. I've seen it before. No one will back you up. Be a sensible girl and get through the next fifteen months.'

She went off, leaving Kirsty staring after her open-mouthed.

'You do intend to bring the lines in, Miss Robertson?' It was Mr Watson.

Kirsty looked at him for a moment and then hurried out into the playground.

11

Dear Hugh,

How very good it was to see you just before Christmas. You will remember that I told you that after my father's death, Mother moved to Ayrshire to live with my uncle, my father's brother, and, since I am a pupil teacher at Burnside Primary, I am living in the house of the headmaster . . .

Kirsty chewed the end of her pen while she deliberated and then added:

. . . a Mr Buchanan. I spent a few days at the end of the year with my mother and we discussed the possibility of living together again. Mother has recovered from the trauma of my father's death and I think she will be happier if she can have a home of her own again and, of course, I cannot tell you the joy living with my mother would be to me.

I wonder if there is a cottage somewhere on the estate – that Colonel Granville-Baker does not need for a farmworker – which we might rent for a nominal sum. I believe ⅓d to ⅑d is the going rate for a farm cottage.

The end of the pen received further rough treatment. Was that the price to the farmworker who was also employed on the farm? Well, Hugh could only laugh at her stupidity and tell her the proper rental.

I hope you and your parents are well and that your career . . .

What did you say to a soldier about his career? She rubbed the offending words with breadcrumbs until they were almost invisible and finished the letter with the words:

I hope you and your parents are well and that you excuse my impertinence in writing to you.

Yours sincerely,
Kirsty Robertson

She put the letter into an envelope without rereading it and slipped it into her bag to post the next time she was in the town.

*

Hugh received the letter almost a month later. He was lying in a wicker chair on the verandah of the Officers' Club in Calcutta sipping a long, cool Pimm's.

'Looks like a lady's hand, Hugh,' laughed Captain Mansfield who had picked up the letters. 'The rest are tailors' bills, by the looks of things, plus the usual half-dozen from your devoted mama.'

'If you ever wrote a letter, Oliver, you might receive some,' answered Hugh mildly, trying to hide his irritation at the pile of letters from his mother, letters that would tell her 'darling boy' that society was nothing without him, that his father was the world's most selfish and thoughtless husband, and that she had had to close the castle for the season because 'Scotland is too positively wet'.

He closed his eyes for a moment, the better to conjure up an image of Aberannoch, but the brutal Indian sun would not be ignored and forced its way through his eyelids. He opened them and read the letter.

'Kirsty Robertson. Who on earth is . . .?' And then he remembered the little school and the afternoon he had gone there with his father in an attempt to relieve the boredom of another leave spent listening to his mother's complaints about the thirteenth-century castle her husband had bought her. 'And was it Jock or Tam who had wet his pants, and young Kirsty . . .' His mind conjured up a picture of nut-brown curls and a determined little chin as she had set the child standing in the playground to dry in the fresh air. 'Poor wee laddie,' laughed Hugh to himself. 'And Miss Kirsty wants to return to Aberannoch. Me too, Kirsty,' he said across the miles. He rose, stretched and went indoors to the writing room.

Dear Kirsty,

How nice to hear from you; it was no impertinence, believe me. Are we not sixth — or is it seventh — cousins, twice removed? You see, I have remembered.

I am glad your mother is well, and I will send your letter to my father by the next post. If there is an empty cottage on the estate, I am sure he will be happy to rent it to you for a nominal rate. Had Father been at home when your father died, I am sure he would have discussed the future with you and your mother, and offered help.

No need to say that Lady Sybill should have been there to take a real interest in the people of the estaste, that this was how his father saw his role.

As you see, I am stationed for a time in India, but my father is in Surrey and so the letter may take some time to reach him, but I am sure he will contact his agent to see about the availability of a cottage.

Are you still enjoying teaching all those small children? You are very brave. The thought of being in a room alone with forty-odd scruffy little people makes me quake in my shoes.

Yours,
Hugh

P.S. By the way, since February 14th we have had an aerial post in India and so you should receive this reply quite quickly. I hope so.

Hugh sealed the letter, then he sent Kirsty's letter back to Britain with a covering note:

I have no idea what the rents are, Father, but I think from the way Miss Robertson has phrased her letter, she must be financially strapped. The Dominie couldn't have left much, if anything, and I shouldn't think a pupil teacher makes a great deal of money.

Why it should be, I do not know, but her letter has left me feeling slightly uneasy. Did I ever hear you say anything about this headmaster, Buchanan, after one of those School Board meetings? I should also tell you that I met Miss Robertson one morning before Christmas in Arbroath when I was returning from a party. I'd had rather too much to drink, and it was only later that I thought she had seemed somewhat distraught.

There, aren't you pleased that I am taking an interest in the estate, even if, I suppose, technically Mrs Robertson was never really a tenant of ours since the Schoolhouse belongs to the education wallahs.

Life here is as you remember it. Too little to do and too much to drink. Their Majesties are to come to Delhi in December. That, at least, should give us something to do.

Love,
Hugh

His duty, as he saw it, done, Hugh sealed his letter and returned to the verandah.

Kirsty waited for a reply to her letter. Every morning for a week she ran to the front hall when she heard the postman's step on the path, but when no letter came from Hugh she very sensibly decided that either he was abroad or he was ignoring her, in which case there was nothing constructive for her to do.

The Board met and Bob was transferred to another school.

'In my best interests – that's all they said, Kirsty. Not a word about Buchanan's complaints. I'm to start tomorrow. Can you believe it, just like that? I'm off to the Abbey.'

'But Bob, that's a lovely school with a really good Dominie. You'll be very happy.' Kirsty was trying hard to be delighted for Bob. No need to say what was really in her mind, that she wished she were the one to be leaving. 'Are we to have another pupil teacher? Did they tell you?'

'No, but Mr Watson did.'

Mr Watson had been acting headmaster while Mr Buchanan had been ill.

'He says it's another final year student, a Mr Hunt. That'll upset the Queen, don't you think?'

Kirsty thought before answering. How could she tell Bob of the unusual relationship that seemed to exist between Miss McNeil and the Dominie? It was doubtful that anyone, male or female, could usurp the senior pupil teacher's position.

'Because he's a man, you mean,' she said finally. 'I doubt that will worry Miss McNeil, Bob, especially since Mr Buchanan comes back on Monday and he thinks the sun rises and sets on her head.'

'You're looking a wee bit drawn these days, Kirsty. Is it difficult living in that house? Mrs Buchanan strikes me as a definite non-person – not much personality there.'

'She's nice.' She could say nothing of the rows that raged in the house, of Mrs Buchanan's threats to leave, of the Dominie's horrible taunts about her childlessness. 'I'd leave,' thought Kirsty fiercely. 'I'd never tolerate that nonsense from any man. Even if I had nowhere to go and no money, I'd leave. Perhaps it's different when you're old . . .

and scared, and she's obviously more afraid of the world outside than of her horrid little world inside.'

To her dismay, Mr Buchanan met her as she walked up the path to the house that same evening after school.

'Spring is here, Miss Robertson,' he said. 'Fresh new growth everywhere. A joyous season, is it not?'

Kirsty looked at him warily but answered steadily enough. 'Yes, I always enjoy the daffodils, Mr Buchanan.'

'I came out into the garden specifically to have a word with you, Miss Robertson. You'll take a turn around with me?' He gave her no chance to protest but took her arm in an almost fierce grip. 'Almost April, and you have been with us nearly a year. Miss McNeil has been with us for four years. She's been like a daughter to me. You'll have noticed, Miss Robertson? Well, naturally Mrs Buchanan and I hope that she will be able to stay with us, but that will depend on where she is given a post. I had thought Miss Purdy might retire, but no, she insists that she will stay. Finance, of course. Her brother is a minister, did you know? No money, no wife, and too many children.' He stopped talking but continued to stroll quietly along the paths, up and down, up and down, with Kirsty unwillingly towed along. How had she ever thought she would find solace and joy in this garden?

'And Mr Cargill is to go. You will be disappointed. I know how ... fond of him you were, but he defied me at every turn.' Kirsty tensed, waiting for his voice to change to that almost-scream that constantly startled her, but his voice remained calm . . . dangerously calm? 'I feel, however, that I have worried so much about Mr Cargill's intransigence that I have quite neglected you – and then, I looked out of my window this morning and watched you as you walked to school, and do you know what I thought, Miss Robertson? I thought, "Good heavens, Angus, a wee lassie walked in your door last September and it's a woman who's walked out of it this morning."' He stopped and pulled her round to face him and she stared at him in growing fear, though fear of what she hardly knew. 'A very lovely young woman,' he breathed, 'a woman who could do such things for a man, oh, such things.'

'Stop it,' cried Kirsty, and with an effort she pulled herself free and ran from him along the path bordered by pure white snowdrops. She brushed past Mrs Buchanan, hurried up the stairs to her room and after locking the door, threw herself against it as if she and the lock together would better keep out any danger. She stood for a few moments catching her breath, then hurried to the bed and pulled her suitcase out from under it and began frantically to throw clothes into it – dresses, blouses, petticoats, stockings. And then she stopped, and slowly and carefully put the clothes back on their pegs or on the shelves in the large oak wardrobe. Suddenly she understood Mrs Buchanan. Where could she go? To Ayrshire, to tell her mother that their dreams of Miss Robertson, qualified teacher, and of a home together were gone? To gallant Miss Purdy, with her overfull house and overfull heart? It was only in the early hours of the morning – when she had carefully thought out exactly how she could keep well out of the Dominie's way – that she remembered Meg. She could have gone to Meg. And she should have, of course, but things never look so bad in the morning as they do in the night when only the house seems to be alive. In the morning all four members of the ill-assorted household met at the breakfast table.

'Is your headache better, Kirsty?' asked Mrs Buchanan, who had dropped the formal 'Miss Robertson' after that distressing breakfast. 'I've scrambled you some eggs. The carrier brought them this morning from Carmyllie; they're nice and fresh.'

Kirsty managed a faint smile. 'I'm much better, thank you, and hungry. I'll enjoy the eggs.'

Miss McNeil sat, as usual, with her thin toast and a cup of tea, and the Dominie emerged from time to time from behind his newspaper to shovel in more food.

'It's as I thought,' said Kirsty to herself. 'He can't possibly taste anything.'

At school she met the new pupil teacher, Willie Hunt, a scholarly-looking young man.

'He could never cycle all the way from Auchmithie,' thought Kirsty, and then heard him tell Miss Purdy that,

'Yes, Ma'am. My father is Dominie at Fern, and sends his very best wishes to you and the Reverend.'

'What a long way to come every day,' exclaimed Kirsty, revising her opinion of the young man's muscles.

'By the new session I shall have found somewhere in Arbroath – if, of course, I'm not accepted at the university.'

'Mr Hunt could join our happy home, could he not?' Kirsty had not seen Mr Buchanan and Miss McNeil join them. 'My wife has always wanted a son, and we could find an attic for him, could we not, girls?'

No reply was needed, for he was already leading the new pupil teacher off to the office and, without a word, Miss McNeil followed them.

'Willie's father and I taught together in the early days, Kirsty. What a fine man. Willie looks just like him.' She paused reflectively. 'I never could resist red hair on a man – very attractive, don't you think?'

Kirsty was too stunned to answer. Miss Purdy and a man?

Miss Purdy laughed. 'I did not spring from the head of Zeus fully formed, you know.'

Kirsty, reared on classical mythology, understood the slight rebuke. Of course Miss Purdy had once been young, had formed a young girl's fancies, had . . . loved?

Love. Her thoughts went to Hugh and her letter. Had it reached him? Had he ignored it? Had he and some bright young socialite laughed at her hesitant phrases? She should have written in a businesslike fashion to the Colonel and Lady Sybill. She could hardly do that now. If Hugh had tossed away, in disdain, her first letter to a man, she had cut off her only avenue of escape. Another year before qualifying, if she qualified. The headmaster had seemed perfectly normal this morning. Could she avoid him, in his own house, for over a year?

This morning there was not even the comfort of a cup of tea with the janitor.

'It's sleep I need, not food,' she decided and went off to answer the persistent clanging of the bell.

At last, at last, it was four o'clock and Kirsty finished her classroom chores as quickly as possible. She had some last-minute studying to do for her Saturday class, but first she would just lie down on her bed and rest until Mrs Buchanan called her for tea.

The house was quiet. Perhaps there was no one at home. Kirsty threw her cape over its peg in the front hall, and did not notice the thin blue airmail letter on the oak table as she slipped silently upstairs. She would rest, just rest, for half an hour or so. Sound asleep in no time, she did not hear her door open.

She woke to unbelievable terror. The depressing of the bedsprings as he sat down stirred her into consciousness and she opened her mouth to scream as she looked into his face so close, so horribly close to hers. His hand covered her open mouth and the scream died in her throat as she struggled wildly like a hare caught in a thresher.

'Don't scream, Kirsty, my wee Kirsty,' he crooned and he pressed his face to hers, his wet lips on her open eyes, his breath rank. Her stomach heaved and she kicked again. His other hand was on her shoulder and he lowered his body onto hers and pinned her to the bed. The weight of a man – how could women welcome it night after night? She would stifle. Every rib would break.

What was he doing? If this is what men and women did together it was not what she had expected.

He lifted his head. 'Oh, wee Kirsty, you'll make it happen for Angus, won't you, my love, my lassie with the light brown hair?' He went on muttering and grinding his body against hers in that obscene way, but his hand against her mouth relaxed and from somewhere she summoned the strength to bite him, and when he snatched his hand away from her mouth she screamed, a scream that reflected all the terrors of hell.

He hit her then. 'Bitch,' he screamed, 'Bitch! You made it happen for Cargill, didn't you, and the fisher laddies, no doubt.'

His hand was inside the neck of her dress, a new dress, her hand-stitched gift from her mother at Christmas, and

Kirsty began to struggle again as she felt it rip to her waist, and then his body fell across her and she heard another voice.

'I'll kill him! I'll kill him!' Mrs Buchanan stood there, the frying pan in which she had been cooking sausages for tea still in her hand. She raised the pan to strike her unconscious husband again.

'No,' screamed Kirsty and jumped from the bed.

'I'm sorry, lassie. Oh, dear God in Heaven above, I am so sorry.'

Kirsty looked at her standing there, the frying pan dripping fat still clenched in her hand. Automatically she held out her shaking arms and found herself comforting the older woman.

'It's not your fault. He didn't hurt me but I have to get away, you understand that, don't you? I can't stay here. I'll go to my friend Meg, or to Miss Purdy.'

That threat calmed Mrs Buchanan. 'No, not Miss Purdy. Her brother will tell the Board.'

'The Board.' Kirsty hadn't thought of the Board, hadn't thought of revenge, only of getting away from the sight and sound of him. She began to shake uncontrollably, but there was nowhere to fall; he was still on the bed where she had pushed him. He was so still . . . A frightening thought . . . so still . . . so still.

'Is he . . . all right?'

Mrs Buchanan approached the still form of her husband, the frying pan held warily as if, at any minute, she might need to strike again.

'He's not dead,' she said flatly, turning to Kirsty who stood with the two sides of the top of her dress hanging limp like sails when there's no wind. 'I wouldn't have cared,' she said. 'Thou shalt not kill – that's what the Good Book says – but I wouldn't have cared. Get another dress, lass. We need to decide what to say, what to do before he comes round.' She touched her husband almost gently. 'Well, his migraine will be real enough the morn, won't it?' and she began to laugh.

12

SHE COULDN'T SAY SHE WAS glad it had happened, never glad, but it had brought everything, the seething mass of suppurating undercurrents out into the open.

'Into the open,' said Kirsty to herself as she tugged furiously at the weeds threatening to strangle her aquilegia, 'is not exactly the right word. It never quite smelled the pure, fresh air.' She looked up from her digging, saw the open windows of her little kitchen and smiled at the knowledge that somewhere inside those four strong walls, her mother was preparing dinner.

'And Hugh might come,' she told the weed and, with a mighty tug, wrestled it free from the flowers and threw it into her pail.

In two years they had done wonderful things to the cottage. It was amazing what a difference hard work and talent made for there was, at least for that first year, very little money. When Kirsty had qualified, her first salary of £65 per annum had seemed a fortune, and now when they had an extra $2.10s. and the prospect of an annual increment of another £2.10s. more per year to look forward to, they felt secure and more than content. They had even opened a bank account in their joint names. One day, they would have a holiday. For now it was enough to have their own home, to go to bed at night content to be together.

'Grand farmer you'd make.' Kirsty hadn't seen him arrive, but she looked up and smiled in pleasure. She smiled because she was always pleased to see Jamie, her first friend, but also because he was very good to look at. The skinny laddie had grown into a powerfully built young man, but the blond hair that still hung thick over his weather-beaten face no longer looked like a haystack but more as if art rather than nature had made it fall like that.

'D'ye need a hand?'

'Haven't you done enough?' For it was Jamie who had ploughed the overgrown garden. 'Anyway, I enjoy struggling with weeds as a change from verbs and multiplication tables.'

He smiled. 'I was on the train this afternoon. Was I not in Arbroath before I sat down in my seat?'

'It's wonderful, isn't it, although I still like my bicycle on good days like this, but what a boon the new railway will be in the winter.'

'Aye, 1914 has brought us amazing progress. Well, if you don't want a hand, I'll get home. The wee ones will be in, needing help with their homework.'

'And Cissie?'

His face darkened and he straightened up from the wall. 'She's supposed to be in the Supplementary Class. The Dominie wants her to go to the secondary school, but it's the dairy at Pitmirmir or the kitchens at the castle for the likes of Cissie.' His face, his whole demeanour had changed. 'My regards to your mother, and thank her for the shirt. Don't I feel like a toff in a handmade shirt.'

Jessie had made Jamie a new shirt as a thank-you for all the labouring he had done in the garden. She had thought to pay him, but he had seemed ready to be insulted when she made the tentative suggestion.

Had he made the silly remark about feeling like a toff because he had picked up the sound of a car on the road from the castle? He touched his hair, almost mockingly, and walked away, not quickly but yet he seemed to cover the ground. Kirsty watched him lightly vault over the dry-stane dyke at the corner and then she turned to welcome Captain Hugh Granville-Baker.

Hugh's letter to his father had been attended to at once by the Colonel, who was disciplined about everything. Colonel Granville-Baker had written to his factor about the Dingle cottage, which was almost dilapidated but sturdy. Oh, the joy of receiving that long-looked-for letter from the factor offering them the cottage as soon as repairs were made. The Colonel's man had had trouble finding Kirsty, for by the time he had received his orders from his employer she had moved in with Meg.

She no longer had nightmares about that dreadful day, but she could never forget it. It was Miss McNeil who had taken charge, showing a practical side Kirsty had never imagined.

'Poor old man,' she had said as she walked into the bedroom, 'hasn't he got enough to deal with? He'll need a doctor, Mrs Buchanan. Better send her before she falls down.'

And Kirsty had gone for the doctor and by the time he had arrived, Mr Buchanan was out of Kirsty's bedroom and into his own.

'I'm reporting him to the Board,' Kirsty had told Miss McNeil as they waited outside.

'Oh, it'll make a lovely story for the *Arbroath Herald*. The nationals will pick it up too, and they'll all wonder how far he got with you.' She had allowed that to sink in. 'Probably be a picture. You'll see it on new stands at every station as you go to visit your mother.'

Kirsty had jumped to her feet. 'I won't pretend it never happened. He's a wicked man . . .'

'A sick man, Kirsty.' For a moment a look of such remembered horrors passed across Miss McNeil's face that Kirsty was jerked out of her self-absorption. 'You don't know what evil is yet, lassie.'

'I won't stay here . . .'

In the end, Kirsty went to live with Meg and her family because it was announced to the community that the Dominie's ill health made it difficult for Mrs Buchanan to manage. The Board met in closed session and Mr Buchanan was retired early on medical grounds.

'It's up to you, Kirsty,' the doctor had said after he had examined Mr Buchanan. 'If you want to press charges, I will have no option but to inform the police of what really went on here tonight. Had you been physically harmed, lassie, I would be the first at the police station' – he gave no thought then or at any other time to the emotional shock Kirsty might have suffered – 'but I want you to think of Mrs Buchanan, who has surely suffered enough. I can ensure that Buchanan is retired and that he accepts medical treatment, but there's no need for the world to know his shame. A good night's sleep and you'll be fine, lassie, and it'll be the spring holidays in a day or two. You can get away to Ayrshire and breathe nice clean air. In the meantime you have friends among the fisherfolk you can go to, have you not?'

Kirsty had agreed for Mrs Buchanan's sake and had been welcomed warmly into Meg's close, loving family. She had been happy there, but after two months of sharing a bed with Meg, and the washing facilities with all members of the large family who were at home, she had been overjoyed to find the letter marked 'Aberannoch Estates' on the table.

'A cottage just outside the castle gates, Meg, and it'll be ready in June.'

The cottage had welcomed her from the start. Even in its semi-dilapidated condition she had admired it. It was honey-coloured in the warm spring sun when Kirsty and Meg first went to see it, and honeysuckle and wild roses bound up with brambles rioted over everything.

'There's room for flowers and vegetables and a dry-ing green. Look, Meg,' Kirsty had cried in her joy as she struggled to pull her skirts from the briars. 'There was a well-laid-out garden here, and it will be again.'

And two years later it was a joy, a garden that provided enough flowers to satisfy Kirsty and more than enough vegetables to supply a small family. Kirsty had no thought of the picture she made as she stood in the evening sun, but young Hugh certainly appreciated it as he drew up in his latest car, a gift from his mother for his last birthday.

'Miss Robertson,' he said, touching his hat but without the mockery Jamie had used. 'Your beauty is an antidote to too much Indian sun.'

His voice was serious; so too was his face. He laughed lightly as he saw Kirsty blush. How different she was from the girls he saw in London.

'Father and I have been fishing, Kirsty, and have an embar-rassment of sea trout. Can Mrs Robertson help us out of our predicament?' He was reaching into the car as he spoke and reappeared with three large fish. 'We could drive into Arbroath and give two of them to your friend Meg to smoke.'

'You're very kind,' said Kirsty, dimpling with pleasure. 'Come in and give them to Mother and we'll see what she suggests. I'd need to change if we're to go to the town. I couldn't be seen in this old dress.'

'At least in this enlightened age you can be seen. No more pretending to be related – and I find I'm very glad we're not: related, I mean.'

He saw her blush again in confusion and, carrying the trout, he followed her into the little cottage, effectively cutting out all light to the interior as he filled the doorway. He couldn't understand the attraction Kirsty held for him. She was so young, so innocent, so inexperienced. Perhaps it was her very freshness which appealed. He tried to picture her in her cotton frock at a dinner in the Officers' Mess among all the regimental silver and smiled at the bizarre picture. 'But with the correct dress,' his mind suggested, and he pushed the suggestion away. No, he didn't want a Kirsty in silk and satin with crimped hair and rouged lips.

'Captain Granville-Baker, how very kind, but we can't possibly use three huge fish.' Mrs Robertson smiled at him. 'Put them on the table and do sit down.' She didn't add, 'Your height is overpowering in such a small room.'

'Hugh thought we might take them to Mr Stewart to smoke, Mother. I'll change my dress if you say it's all right.'

Kirsty looked anxiously at her mother, for it was already after eight.

'We wouldn't be more than an hour, Mrs Robertson. Actually, I haven't told Kirsty yet, but I've been recalled to my regiment. Rather nasty goings-on in Europe at the moment. Nothing to worry about, of course, but Father thinks we may have had our last day of fishing for a while. I'm glad we've had such a glorious holiday. Mother's in Europe, and Father and I have done nothing but walk and ride . . .'

'And fish,' Kirsty finished for him, and he laughed and looked doubtfully at the trout.

'We did overdo it a bit, but they just kept jumping to the fly today. Pity to let them go to waste.'

'Go and change your dress, Kirsty. I don't want you driving through the town in your gardening frock,' said her mother.

'I think she looks perfectly lovely,' said Hugh as he stood up when Kirsty hurried from the room. He looked at Kirsty's mother and saw the dilemma in his eyes reflected in hers. 'Perfectly lovely,' he said again, as if he had learned something that he had been struggling to learn for some time.

Dear Kirsty,

I had hoped it was all going to be a bit of a damp squib. Can you believe we'd all been worried about Mexico, where there have been some real fisticuffs for some time. There's a chap called Villa who is rebelling with the people against their new President, Carranza, who was in fact Villa's chum until this coup. All to do with agrarian reforms, and as a farmer; I find myself in sympathy with Pancho . . . sounds like a comedy act, doesn't it . . . Pancho Villa? Anyway, we're leaving the Mexicans to sort themselves out because of this trouble in Sarajevo . . .

Kirsty knew all about Sarajevo. Hadn't she been pointing it out on the map of Europe to her class since June 28th, when the news of the assassination of the Archduke Francis Ferdinand, heir to the Emperor of Austria, had stunned the world? So stupid, too: the man was a liberal even when it had been against his own interests. Thank goodness for the summer holidays. On June 11th a bomb had exploded in Westminster Abbey – more work of the suffragettes? She could not belong to a group that did such stupid things, no matter how splendid the cause. Now Mr Chamberlain had died . . . a Minister had been murdered in Paris. The world was going insane. No doubt by the time school reconvened in September everyone would have cooled down. Kirsty put the last box of books neatly on the shelf and left her classroom. Everything would be fine after the holidays.

But on August 4th, a particularly glorious day, Britain declared herself at war.

13

Germanophobia had been rife in Britain for some time, but the Cabinet had been divided. Prime Minister Asquith abhorred the thought of war, but he hated even more the idea that Britain should break her word. Britain had pledged to safeguard Belgium and therefore had no choice. The Lord Chancellor, Lord Haldane, who had lived many years in Germany and was a distinguished philosopher of the German school, felt the same. The Chancellor of the Exchequer, Lloyd George, wavered until the last moment, but John Burns, President of the Board of Trade, resigned his office rather than be in a Cabinet of whose position he disapproved. The War Party centred on Winston Churchill, the young man whom the people felt had the vision and imagination to conduct a war.

'Over by Christmas,' said the visionaries and enthusiasts.

'At least three years,' pronounced the realists like Lord Kitchener and Lord Roberts, and they began to prepare for a long conflict. Lord Haldane's Territorials were recalled from their summer camps and London stations were full of them. Keir Hardie harangued the crowds in Trafalgar Square from the plinth of Nelson's Column, hardly the best place for a speech advocating retraction. The crowds outside Buckingham Palace went mad with delight when the proclamation of war was declared. Did they not realize that like crowds were shouting themselves hoarse in Berlin?

In the first months of the war, little changed in Aberannoch. Farmers were not conscripted and so the harvest went on as it had always done. Kirsty and her mother read about the bank rate jumping to 10 per cent and back down to 5 per cent, but that hardly affected their little nest-egg. They saw pictures of London's bus drivers enlisting en masse and heading off to Avonmouth, and 'H' Company, the Post Office Recruits Column, learning to march in Regent's Park.

'Who on earth will deliver letters if the entire Post Office joins the army?' asked Jessie.

'Women, I suppose,' muttered Kirsty as she struggled with the Merit Class essays, and Jessie chuckled, for surely the world could not go quite so mad as that.

Kirsty took the train to Arbroath every morning that autumn and winter of 1914. Cycling in the rain was no fun, and it seemed as if it would never stop raining. She was supposed to have had an infants' class, but had come back after the summer holidays to find herself in charge of the

Merit Class, which was composed of most of the oldest and brightest children. Every young male teacher had rushed off to enlist almost before war had been declared.

'What do you think of my promotion chances when I return as a decorated veteran?' young Mr Tobias had asked the staff.

'Director of Education, lad, straight away.' Mr Watson, who had tried to enlist but who had been turned down because of his age, slapped the young man on the shoulder. 'Give 'em hell for me, lad. Your job will be here for you, never fret.'

Miss Purdy had agreed to delay her retirement until the cessation of hostilities. 'If I live that long,' she had said sadly in the staff room. She remembered the Boer War, and agreed with Lord Kitchener that this would be a long struggle.

The infants were probably unaware of the war, but the older children followed every event and their teacher had to read the papers closely every day to keep herself informed. She took out a subscription to the *Glasgow Herald* and had it delivered to the school, and part of each day was set aside for what the teacher called 'Current Affairs' and her pupils called 'The War'.

Every evening, Kirsty corrected papers and read the newspapers while Jessie sewed. To their great surprise, Lady Sybill Granville-Baker had returned to Aberannoch as soon as war was declared and had turned the castle into a hive of industry. A sewing circle was started, and to Kirsty's delight her mother's name had been among the first suggested to Lady Sybill.

'Don't you think being a teacher is enough duty for me, Mother?' Kirsty had asked rather wickedly. She still loathed needlework of any kind, but the entire county seemed to be sewing: bandages, pyjamas for wounded soldiers, baby clothes for destitute wives. 'I'll be much better off growing vegetables and saving my pennies for the "Cigarettes for Soldiers" campaign.'

'Save for cigarettes, by all means, Kirsty – after all, the men do deserve their little luxuries – but you should join Lady Sybill's group. All the nice people have joined. It's lovely.'

All the nice people. Kirsty could hear the joy in her mother's voice, and she was happy for her. Jessie Robertson's married life had been very narrow, and the past four years even more restricted. Jessie had devoted herself exclusively to her daughter but now, thanks to the war, she was meeting *all the nice people.* For herself, she didn't want to meet the right people, especially if one of them was called Hugh.

Since they had moved into the little cottage, Hugh had visited at least once during each of his leaves, and each of these visits left Kirsty feeling unsatisfied, vaguely unhappy. Why, she did not know. His car or his horse would appear at the gate where it would be either parked or tethered, and he would stroll in to chat, perfectly and naturally at home in the tiny cottage. Once Kirsty had even found him sitting on the hearth balancing a mug of tea and a scone while Jessie cut out curtains at the table.

'Little snob,' he'd teased when Kirsty had made to change his mug for the Sunday china.

'We do know how to behave,' she'd snapped.

'Your mother does,' he'd laughed back at her.

Apart from the drive into Arbroath to deliver the trout to Meg's parents, Kirsty had never really been alone with him.

'He treats me like a . . . I don't know what he treats me like, another boy? A chum, a sister? And I can't get him out of my mind. I think about him all day, every day and I even dream about him at night, and why?'

On his last leave Hugh had even driven past the cottage with not one but two beautiful, sophisticated young women in his car, and had tooted and waved enthusiastically to Kirsty. She had stopped weeding to watch him disappear in a swirl of dust, the laughter of the carefree young people blowing back on the wind to where she stood. Conscious of her old dress, her hair, her labourer's smock, she had looked down at her hands clutching the heavy fork and seen the dirt under her nails and ingrained in the skin.

'He sees me as some wee lassie who must be humoured by the knight in shining armour,' she said to her reflection in the mirror as, her weeding abandoned, she viciously scrubbed her dirty hands. From that day she wore gloves in the garden and rigorously obeyed a suggestion in her mother's herbal that, twice a week, she steep her hands first in warm oil and then in a horsetail decoction for ten minutes. She also resolved to apply chamomile lotion to her hands every day. Luckily Jessie believed strongly in the medicinal benefits of chamomile and always had plenty of dried flowers in her store cupboard for winter use.

Hugh knew exactly what he thought of Kirsty. She was a young girl living on his father's estate who needed protection. The reason given for Mr Buchanan's early retirement was ill health, a euphemism – thought the town of Arbroath – for alcoholism. Colonel Granville-Baker was one of the few who knew the whole truth.

'That poor child,' he had said to his son, 'barely sixteen years old and entrusted to his care . . .'

Hugh had looked at his father incredulously. 'You don't mean . . . he didn't . . . she hasn't been . . .'

'The bastard's impotent. I suppose one ought to have a feeling of pity for him,' said the Colonel, 'but to try to reawaken his manhood by abusing a young girl? Fella ought to be horsewhipped, but there's his wife, poor woman, and

Miss Robertson, of course. The truth came out, there would bound to be some idiot who preferred to believe she'd been raped, although being handled by that madman must have been frightening enough for such a cloistered child. Keep an eye on them when I'm away, Hugh. We ought, perhaps, to have been more alert when the Dominie died.'

And so Hugh had taken to dropping in on the Robertsons, no hardship since Kirsty really was a pretty little thing and Mrs Robertson gave a fellow such a good tea. He had stayed well away from Kirsty physically for several months, feeling, wrongly, that she might well be afraid of all men. Now, as he prepared to leave for France, it was her face that came between him and the nightmare of war he was trying not to think about. Like most young men of his class, Hugh had several young ladies who shared his leisure hours and, occasionally, his bed. He smiled ruefully when he thought of his last few days in London. A chap could have a really good time in town, could forget a place called Mons where several of his class at Sandhurst had bought it. Alex Carlyle was dead – Alex, who'd been to prep school with him and Oxford and Sandhurst, who'd shared his London flat and his London girls, and who'd wanted to retire, a general at forty, to an island anywhere. Death was so bloody permanent: he'd never see Alex again, or Buff, or stupid old George whom he'd never really liked but who certainly hadn't deserved to have half his body blown into the next county or whatever the hell they called counties in *la belle France*. Not so bloody *belle* now. Did it hurt to die? Falling off a horse hurt; bashing against the other side in rugby hurt. God, he was scared. Scared of dying, scared of not being able to bear the pain, scared of letting everyone else see that he was scared. Kirsty. Think of Kirsty and keep sane.

'Come on, chaps. Let's get this over with. There's a girl at home I have to get back to. Come on, look lively. Seasick? That the only thing that worries you till you get home again, McNaught, you'll be a very lucky man.'

14

Jamie Cameron asked Kirsty to dance at the Aberannoch Castle Sewing Society's social evening on New Year's Eve 1914. She accepted even though she was aware that Jamie, like too many of the other young farmers, had been fortifying his courage from a communal whisky bottle. The measures of the 'Gay Gordons', which Jamie danced with more exuberance than skill, meant that Kirsty did not spend the whole run of the dance in his arms. She began to regret the eight bars of waltzing into which he whirled her at the end of each run-through of the dance.

'Jamie,' she protested finally. 'You're holding me far too closely, and frankly, I don't like the way your breath smells.'

His face reddened and he stumbled over his feet but he did loosen his grip.

'I apologize, Miss Robertson,' he said. 'No doubt French champagne is more what you're used to smelling.'

'Don't be silly. And stop calling me Miss Robertson. You called me Kirsty when you asked me to dance.'

'I forget myself. I thought you looked like a wee lassie that was at the school wi' me.'

They had stopped dancing now and were standing glaring at one another while the dance rushed to its exhilarating close around them. Kirsty was embarrassed; she could see her mother and several other 'sewing ladies' looking at them. Jamie, for the moment, was beyond embarrassment.

'Nae dout you have champagne by the bucketful when you dance here with Captain Granville-Baker, except they probably dance in the ballroom and no' here in the hall. Grand enough oot here for the proletariat.'

Kirsty considered walking away from him but thought he might just shout after her and that she could not bear, not so much for herself but for her mother, so happy in the 'Dowagers' Corner' with *the right people*.

'I've never had champagne in my entire life, Jamie, and if it's any of your business, I've never been to the castle before, so I don't know where the Granville-Bakers entertain their guests,' she said quietly, just as the music ended.

'I'm sorry, Kirsty. It is none of my business.' His broad Scots vocabulary had drifted away with his bad temper.

The awkward moment was broken by a deep Scots voice. 'Are you twa planning on geein' us a demonstration?' laughed an old farmer. 'For if you're no', get aff the flair and leave it tae the dancing.'

'Dance with me again, Kirsty. I'll behave myself this time. Come on, it's an Eightsome. I can't be belligerent in the middle of that.'

'I can't,' said Kirsty and saw him stiffen. 'Jamie,' she added pleadingly, 'I promised to dance the Eightsome with the minister.'

'Oh, aye. You'd dump him soon enough if Granville-Baker turned up.'

Kirsty looked at him sadly. 'Colonel Granville-Baker is somewhere in Belgium, the very heart of the conflict, and his son is probably at this very moment leaving South-ampton. Excuse me.' She turned, left a discomfited Jamie standing in the middle of the floor and went to find the elderly minister who had come to take services at Aberan-noch, the incumbent minister having been one of the first to answer Kitchener's pleading cry, 'Your country needs YOU'. She went through the dance like a clockwork doll. What had happened to Jamie? Was that what growing up did to a man? The poetic farm boy with the corn-coloured shock of hair – was he gone for ever, or was he merely hidden beneath a veneer of hair brilliantine? She looked around as she and her partner laughingly skipped round in their circle, and saw Jamie standing morosely against the wall.

'Why hasn't he danced with someone else?' she asked herself in exasperation. 'It's New Year's Eve. He should be rejoicing that 1914 is over. The New Year will surely bring an end to this war.' Kirsty tucked her arm into her partner's and found herself hurled with surprising agility round and round. She could see the holly and the paper streamers that decorated the rafters blending dizzily into a solid mass of colour, like an infant's first painting. She laughed happily and when the room and her head had stopped spinning, Jamie was gone.

'Well, let him be childish,' she determined, and allowed the elderly man to lead her off to the outer room where the sewing circle ladies were serving lemonade.

'Have you seen my mother?' she asked Mrs Lamont of Pitmirmir farm.

'Aye, Kirsty, she's away over tae the castle kitchens for a pot of stovies. The men'll be starving wi' all that hopping around.'

'I'll go and help her with it.'

'Straight across the courtyard. There's a wee door even you'll hiv tae bend doon tae get through.'

Kirsty looked across the hall to the door. The music had stopped and everyone in the large panelled room was searching for the person with whom they wanted to bring in the New Year, the year that would surely bring lasting peace.

'I'll run and find her. I don't want her to miss the stroke of twelve.'

'Aye, lass, and ask her if she got someone to first-fit us.'

The first foot. The man, preferably with dark hair, who would cross the threshold of the castle on the stroke of midnight to wish everyone 'A Guid New Year'. He would carry coal to bring warmth to the hearth, wheat to ensure that everyone had enough to eat for the year, and perhaps a little silver to guarantee that all bills would be paid. An ancient custom, and one that the superstitious Jessie would not wish to miss.

The courtyard was lit only by a hesitant moon and already one or two happy couples were plighting their troth against ancient walls that for centuries had witnessed both truth and lies. Kirsty smiled and hurried across to the kitchen as quietly as possible.

A figure loomed up out of the shadows and caught her arm. For a moment it seemed to Kirsty that her heart stopped beating as she looked up into an intense young face.

'Jamie, what a fright you gave me. What are you doing?'

'Mrs Robertson asked me to be first foot,' he said, showing her his large lump of coal. 'It's sae big since I'm sae fair. Kirsty, Kirsty, wait.'

She pulled away from him. 'Please let me go, Jamie. I need to help my mother with the stovies.'

'Aw, Kirsty lass. I'm daein' this all wrong, but it's Hogmanay and sometimes a lassie'll listen at Hogmanay.' He took a deep breath. 'I love you, lass. I always have, and I ken you're a teacher and far above me, but I'll no' always be a farm laddie . . .'

'Please, Jamie, stop.' Kirsty had no idea what to say or do. A declaration of love was the last thing she had expected, and she said the first thing that came into her mind: 'You're only nineteen years old.'

With a sound, half groan, half moan, he turned from her. He pulled apart a courting couple and thrust the coal into the boy's hands. 'Here, Sandy, be first fit. Yer darker nor me,' and then he ran across the courtyard and disappeared through the great wooden doors that led to the driveway.

Kirsty watched him go. 'The taste of ashes,' she said to herself sadly, and it was true. So many clichés were true. Her mouth was full of the taste of ashes and her heart was curiously heavy. 'Oh, Jamie lad,' she whispered. 'I never meant to hurt you. I didn't know what to say.'

'Oh, good, Kirsty. Take one end of this, dear. We'll never get to the hall before midnight.' It was Jessie, struggling out of the old kitchens with a huge tub of stoved potatoes. The smell enticed Kirsty's taste buds but could not quite dispel the ashes.

The New Year was brought in on January 1st, 1915 by two dark-haired women carrying not coal nor wheat but hot potatoes. For a moment there was a stunned silence, and then an old farmer came forward to take the heavy pot.

'Aye, it's a new order o' things, and maybe you lassies wi' yer tatties'll bring us mair joy than last year's first fit. Useless bugger you turned oot tae be, Pitmirmir. It was you brought the New Year intae the church hall.'

Then there was laughter and hugs and kisses and slapping of backs and tears, too many tears, for had not everyone a cousin or friend on his way to the Belgian front? The war had not yet really touched the farming community; they fought by trying to provide food. No one even dared to whisper, 'Over by Christmas, please God,' for Christmas was a year away.

Work, the antidote to pain. After an unhappy, restless night during which Kirsty went over and over all the sensible things she should have said to Jamie – and would have, if he hadn't taken her so much by surprise – she woke to find that, for once, Jessie was not up before her.

'Do me good,' she said to herself as, shivering in the intense cold, she cleaned out the grate and laid a new fire. She had taken a lit fire in the morning for granted all her life, first at the Schoolhouse and then at the Buchanans.

'Mother must rise in the cold every morning to put on the fire for me, and Mrs Buchanan must have done it too. What a lot I have always taken for granted.' She revelled in the discomfort, feeling that somehow she was exonerating herself a little. She would make a New Year's resolution:

every morning she would light the fire for Jessie, and today at least she would make her breakfast in bed. At last the fire was lit and two fresh farm eggs were boiling gently on the hob. The events of the night before came flooding back, and now anger took the place of unhappiness. Jamie had had no right to be so silly. He had been drinking and said things he didn't mean.

'Oh, heavens,' said Kirsty, sitting back on her heels as she watched the eggs. 'What if he did mean them? How could he love me? We've only talked to each other in passing for years. Men. They spoil everything.'

'Spoil what, dear?' It was Jessie.

'Go back to bed,' ordered Kirsty, smiling brightly at her mother and deliberately ignoring the question. 'I'm bringing you a treat, breakfast in bed.'

'Sounds lovely, but I'd rather have it with you here before the fire. Oh, how welcoming it is to come in to a nice warm room.'

'You really spoiled Father and me, Mother.'

'Nonsense, Kirsty,' said Jessie as she began to set the plain oak table. 'It's a woman's job to look after her family. You'll be just the same when you marry.'

'Oh, no, I won't. I'm much too lazy, and it's all your fault.'

'My, we are gloomy this fine New Year's morning.' Jessie paused and ruthlessly chopped the top off her egg. 'There. What do men spoil, dear?'

Kirsty decapitated her own egg before she spoke, gazing at the round brown shell as if it were a head, the head of some young man? 'Jamie, he behaved so stupidly.' There was a long pause while Jessie calmly ate her boiled egg and toast and Kirsty looked strangely at her egg, growing colder in its little cup that bore the legend, 'A Present from Ayr'. 'I was really embarrassed, Mother. He held me so tightly when we were waltzing and then he said he loved me.'

'What a nice gift to bring the New Year in, dear, a young man's love.'

Kirsty pushed her chair out almost violently and stood up. 'Mother, he's a farm boy. He's nineteen years old, nine months younger than I am. We were good friends, *friends* – and now he's spoiled everything.'

'Sit down, dear, and finish your lovely egg.' When Kirsty had complied Jessie went on, 'Jamie Cameron has always loved you, Kirsty. Maybe it's changed from a laddie's admiration to a man's love, I don't know. Time will tell. But a lassie could do worse than have the love of a lad like Jamie Cameron.'

'I like Jamie, Mother, I always have. We played together, not just because we were the two eldest in the school but because we were like one another. We liked the same things, we liked books and learning and listening to Father talk, even when he was on his hobby horse and going on about parsing analysis ... but I don't love Jamie and he shouldn't love me. He's got no right to love me and he doesn't,' she finished with a return of her initial fire. 'He's too young to love anybody.'

'What about Captain Granville-Baker?'

'He's a man,' whispered Kirsty and blushed to the roots of her hair. She had not yet worked out her own feelings for Hugh. All she knew was that she thought of him constantly, that even when she knew he was with his regiment she still found herself looking for him as she hurried for the train or walked through the streets of Arbroath to the station. When she did see him or, more wonderfully, when she talked to him, she was in a daze of happiness. She wanted the moment to go on for ever, and when he rushed off – and he invariably seemed to be hurrying somewhere – she felt curiously bereft. When he sat in the little cottage kitchen and laughed and joked with her mother, always teasing – or was it true, that he came only for Jessie's baking? – she felt that life could offer nothing better. She loved just to listen to his deep, well-modulated voice, to watch his face and the play of emotions across the fine features. It was enough: for now it was enough, but something deep down inside her told her that one day she would want much, much more from Hugh Granville-Baker.

'Kirsty,' said Jessie, and there was such sadness in her voice that Kirsty put down her bone egg-spoon to listen attentively, 'you're between these two men. Jamie is a nice laddie, and if he'd been able to stay at the school he might have made something of himself, but he's a farmworker. I know your Uncle Chay is a farmworker, but he'd be the first to say that he wants better for you.' Jessie looked at her daughter, who seemed to be fascinated by the pattern of congealing egg yolk on the back of her spoon. 'Hugh is a gentleman, Kirsty, by birth and by nature. Don't misunderstand his natural good manners. It wouldn't work, an army officer, public school . . . Kirsty, his mother is a titled lady. Your mother is the daughter of a shop assistant. He lives in a castle. Look around you . . .'

'Mother, please. I'm not ready for any of this. I haven't thought of Jamie . . . or Hugh . . . as, well, as men.' Kirsty stopped talking. Was she being truthful? In the dark of the night, had she not dreamed of a future with Hugh? No, no, or if she had, had she not been aware that it was only a dream, a dream like the dreams that one day she might wake up as a princess with golden hair, or that she might suddenly grow wings and fly, or even just burst into glorious song at the morning service at school? 'Let's forget all this. Jamie went off with hurt feelings and Hugh is . . . God knows where, some battlefield in Belgium. When the war is over he'll be older and he probably won't think of us any more. There will be too much on his mind.' A picture of the two lovely girls laughing, their hair blowing in the wind, came into her mind and she ruthlessly thrust it away. Mother was right. Hugh was the son of the laird and she was a tenant of a very small cottage. She must stop thinking of him.

And she did until his letter arrived.

Dear Kirsty,

I don't know when this letter will arrive but I wish you and Mrs Robertson a Happy New Year. Tell her the food in Belgium is absolutely appalling and I shall need serious feeding up when I get home.

Home. I miss Aberannoch very much and I thought I would miss London. Would you write to me and tell me how everything is? It will be nice to know that there is somewhere not touched by this senseless waste. Why did I join the army, Kirsty? I suppose it never occurred to me not to, but if I'd thought I might have said, 'I think a soldier's job is to keep the peace.' We're civilized men and we're doing utterly unbelievable things to one another. It just doesn't make sense. Anyway, I'm sure it will all be over soon. Right will prevail, or so the politicians keep telling us.

Tell me about your class. What are you teaching them?

Hugh

Kirsty decided to write back and to do exactly as Hugh had asked. She told him about Aberannoch and she told him about the class. There were one or two boys and even a girl or two who tried to undermine her authority:

I wish I was taller and then I could tower over Alec Wattie and frighten him into being good. One day I may have to use the tawse, but I'm more scared of it than Alec is. I know he makes faces behind my back and he's just civil and no more . . .

Several weeks later the reply came back.

As to young Master Wattie, in the army we have a charge called 'Dumb Insolence'. Perhaps you should haul him up before the Dominie on the educational equivalent. This pupil has been guilty of dumb insolence, Saaar. Permission to wallop. Saaar?'

Kirsty had had to report the ringleader of her unruly pupils to the headmaster long before Hugh's tongue-in-cheek advice had been received, and Mr Watson had punished him. So far, he had not returned to school.

'Don't let it worry you, Kirsty,' said Mr Watson. 'There will be an Alec Wattie in every class you will ever teach, and you will have to bring yourself to stand up to them.

Just one good whack with the belt two months ago might have done it.'

'I can't bring myself to use it. My father never did, or very rarely, and . . .'

'Buchanan used it too often.'

'Not too often, too hard and on the wrong children.'

'Face it, Kirsty. If you stay in teaching you will inevitably get older, but without some miracle of medical science you are not going to get any taller. When the war ends we can get a man back in your classroom, although academically you do well, and you can get back to the infants where you belong. Until then, discipline your class as soon as problems arise or you'll have no authority. Now, off to class like a good girl.'

Kirsty stood up and looked at the acting Dominie. A nice man, Mr Watson, a little too old for the job now, but capable . . . and so unbearably patronizing that she felt if she didn't leave the room now, she would smack the smug self-satisfaction off his face.

'He very grandly said I was doing quite well academically, Miss Purdy,' she moaned in the staff room. 'He, a man whose knowledge stops at Napoleon's conquest of Russia, tells me condescendingly that I'm doing quite well and then, have you any idea what he had the nerve to say next?'

'Sit down and drink your tea, lass, before you explode. He told you kindly not to worry too much because as soon as the war is over a nice big strong man will come along either to sweep you off your feet to domestic bliss and seven bairns of your own, or to take your class and let you scuttle back to the baby classes where you belong.'

Kirsty almost finished her cooling tea in one gulp. 'It's happened to you then?'

'It's the order of things, lassie, and it will never change.'

'Why can't it change? The suffragettes say women should be able to vote. If we can vote, we can vote, for equal pay for women, equal career opportunities . . . I could even be a Dominie one day. You can handle the big laddies better than anybody.'

'It's old age that gives me authority, lass, but you won't spend your life in a school, Kirsty. Any boy that survives this war is going to come back looking for peace, and peace means a wife and a home and bairns.'

'Why can't we have it all?'

Miss Purdy could not have looked more shocked if Kirsty had blasphemed. 'Lassie, lassie! Thank heavens for the bell. Away to your class and calm down. Have it all, indeed!'

Kirsty said nothing but as she walked to the play-ground, newly coated with metal chips to make it more comfortable in wet weather – unless you happened to fall down on it – her mind was saying, 'Why not, why can't women have it all? Why ever not? Men do it all the time.'

15

OFFICERS AND GENTLEMEN WERE GIVEN leave when they had been under fire for a period. It was all very civilized. Hugh spent most of his leave in London. His mother too had fled to Town to recoup from the rigours of a winter spent in Scotland and, to his delight, Hugh was able to see his father who was also on home leave. As they had dinner together in a hotel, Hugh looked around incredulously. There was a war on, wasn't there? Men, women, and children were dying horribly all over Europe, weren't they, or was that part of that dreadful nightmare from which he hoped one day to wake up? There were no shortages here. Wine flowed more freely than the waters through the Flanders trenches, and the food – oh, God, the guilt as he ate as he hadn't eaten for months.

Despite the good food and the champagne with which the family toasted the safe return of its men, it was soon obvious that the incredible politeness which had held together the marriage bonds of his parents was wearing perilously thin. Lady Sybill had recovered from the delight experienced when she realized that she was not going to be a war widow, at least not yet, and that her only child was being returned, and not before time, to her maternal bosom. Her usual disaffection with the state of her life had therefore returned.

'I have spent months in that draughty place, Hugo, and with absolutely no society. How can you expect me to go back yet? Besides, I have nothing to wear.'

Since Lady Sybill was wearing a new, rather fetching and obviously expensive dinner gown as she spoke, her husband and son looked at one another deprecatingly.

'I detest it when you look down your superior nose and smile as if to say, "Silly little thing", when I utter no more than the truth, Hugo – and you are just as bad as your father, Hugh. I will not return to Scotland. I can't even pronounce the name of that godforsaken place where you found that castle. Castle? A pile of stones: wasn't even a decent battle fought over it. The English didn't want it, being men of taste.'

Hugh saw the muscles in his father's jaw tighten but he knew the Colonel would say nothing. He never did. To fight with a woman offended his code of honour. Lady Sybill, who would have loved a good squabble, thought her husband spineless. 'Mummy,' Hugh laughed, 'you're being a teeny-weeny bit naughty. Father's more English than you are. Grandpapa's family is all Norman, or so he says.'

Lady Sybill leapt eagerly on the bait offered by her son and, as Hugh had foreseen, the conversation avoided the ugly lane for which it had been headed.

'I'll go up to Aberannoch after you've left, Pa. Young Kirsty Robertson at Dingle Cottage has been writing to me and keeping me *au courant* with all the goings-on. I know all about the sewing ladies and the pennies for cigarettes, and that the primroses were out early in the valley this year. Wish I'd seen them.'

'Next year, Hugh. We'll have a picnic, do a bit of fishing.'

'Who is Kirsty Robertson?' demanded Lady Sybill. 'Surely, Hugh, you are not corresponding with the daughter of a sewing teacher?'

'Miss Robertson is a teacher like her late father, m'dear, and she's writing to Hugh. Hugh didn't say he was writing to her.'

His parents had forgotten their own animosity and were staring at him. He felt about twelve years old. In a second his father would say, 'Go to your room.'

'Actually, I started writing to her after she wrote and asked about the cottage. You remember, sir? I sent the letter on to you?'

'The insolence!' Lady Sybill was righteously angry. 'This young person actually wrote to you and asked for a cottage? Really, the effrontery of the working classes.'

'Are you wise, Hugh?' asked the Colonel. 'Think carefully, boy. Women, and especially young ones, are frightfully impressionable. Wouldn't want her to get the wrong idea.'

'Good heavens, Pa. What are you thinking about? Actually I tend to drop in on Kirsty, and Mrs Robertson of course, frightfully nice woman – Mummy, you must know her. She's the leading light of your sewing ladies.'

'Exactly, Hugh, my sewing ladies. I shall leave you two to your port. Hugo, I expect you to talk to your son.'

The men stood up as Lady Sybill swept from the table in a fury of satin and lace.

'You're a little big to be spanked, Hugh,' said the Colonel when they were seated again, 'but your mother has a point.'

'Mummy's a frightful snob. Oh, don't glare at me and do your "women are to be cherished" routine, Pa. Kirsty writes funny little letters about her school, and they take me out of hell for a moment or two.'

They sat silently for a few minutes watching the candles burning down in their holders.

'Well,' said the Colonel, 'if that's all it is.'

Hugh was able to leave his mother to her London social round, his conscience clear. His father had gone back to the Front and wanted news of his estate. Blandly Hugh ignored the fact that the factor wrote to the Colonel every Monday morning; he always had done so, and would no doubt continue until he retired. Again, as he drove through the beautiful Angus fields, Hugh had that feeling of displacement. Was there a war on? The barley was high and golden; the briar roses and bramble blossoms fought with one another on the hedgerows, which were a mass of purple rosebay willowherb. He stopped for a while on the approach to the castle and looked over the calm waters of the firth.

'This is the picture I want to keep in my mind,' he decided. 'If I can remember every field, every hill, every little cottage . . . if I can remember the way the barley nods when the wind runs through it and the way it seems to change colour as it moves. God, how I'd have laughed at Eton if any chap had said I'd be silly over flowers – and wild ones at that. I'd have blacked his eye for him.'

He started the car and drove quickly to the castle.

Kirsty was in the little front room of the cottage when he drove by. She had been filling up a record of work for her own information.

ARITHMETIC

The rules learned in previous classes.
Compound Practice
Compound Proportion

Percentages
Discount
Averages
Simple Interest
Arithmetical problems worked MENTALLY

'Not bad for a mere woman,' she said to herself, and then wrote the next heading in her fine flowing script:

NATURE STUDY

March

Sun and Pole Star
Compass
Map of school grounds
Quarries, etc., pebbles, sand
Frog spawn, tadpoles, frogs
Migratory birds
'Bledding' of trees
Daffodils
Flowers on leafless trees

April

Migratory birds
Mustard seedlings

Was that a car? It couldn't be a car. Only Hugh or the Colonel . . . No, she would not get up from the table and rush to the window like a yokel to see the grand car drive by. It would be Lady Sybill with her condescending smile for the local riff-raff.

Daisy, etc.
Wallflower

The car had stopped at the gate. She heard the gate swing open and someone stride purposefully up the path. Kirsty reached the door and opened it just as her visitor raised his hand to knock.

'Hugh.' For a moment she stood looking up at him while her heart did strange things and her stomach seemed suddenly to have become a home for thousands of butterflies.

'I'm sorry. Is this a bad time? Do you have guests? I'll come back . . .'

Kirsty blushed in confusion. 'I'm sorry. I thought you were in Flanders. Come in, please. Mother's in the garden, I'll get her. She's embroidering a tea-cloth, and she doesn't want anyone to see her so she can't sit in the front. She should be working on baby clothes, but she's not allowed to embroider them any more . . .'

She stopped the talking, which had given her heart time to settle itself down and the butterflies to alight.

183

'Because Lady Sybill says plain smocking is good enough for the poor in time of war,' he finished for her. 'Actually, Mother's wrong about that. More need for lovely embroidery in time of war.'

She laughed in relief. He wasn't angry and, of course, that was exactly what her unruly tongue had wanted to say.

She went through to the kitchen to call her mother and turned in surprise to find that he had followed her.

'How right she looks,' he said, and following his gaze Kirsty saw her mother in her long black skirt and high-necked blouse sitting under an apple tree, setting exquisite stitches into a linen cloth.

'It'll be briar roses,' she said because she was embarrassed by his closeness to her, 'or bluebells. Scottish harebells, you know.'

'I don't, and I'd like to. Would you take me for a walk, Kirsty, and show me the bluebells so that I can remember them when I go back?'

She looked up at him and for a breathless moment they gazed wonderingly into each other's eyes. Then Jessie looked up from her sewing and saw them standing at the kitchen window. She waved her tea-cloth and, after gathering up her threads, hurried in to join them.

'Captain Granville-Baker, what a very pleasant surprise. I thought there was no one in residence.'

'There isn't, but Father is anxious about the state of the harvest. My grandfather in Surrey is watching his crops rot in the fields for want of workers.'

Jessie had shepherded them back to the front room and they were seated before the fireplace where a huge pot of geraniums blazed in the otherwise empty grate.

'But what's happened to the farm workers?' asked Kirsty. 'We lost our minister although he wasn't allowed to be a combatant, but only a very few of our local men have joined up. The country needs fishermen and farmers.'

Hugh sipped from his teacup and smiled gratefully at Jessie as he silently accepted a second scone.

'We've had a tremendous recruitment campaign in England. Baroness Orczy – you must have read her romantic novels – published an appeal in the *Daily Mail* to all women and girls in England, saying that since we've all laughed and cried over the fictional exploits of the Scarlet Pimpernel and his league, women should form another league to encourage all their menfolk to join up.' He stood up, put his hand on his heart and then squeaked in a falsetto tone, 'I won't ever, ever be seen in public with any fit and free man who isn't in uniform.' In his normal voice he continued, 'Have you got the white feathers up here? It's pretty awful in the south. Friend of mine went up to town in civvies the other day and was accosted by a whole group of "holier than thou" young women. He took the feather they handed him and then threw open his overcoat to show his VC. "Thanks for the present, ladies," he said. 'His Majesty gave me this other gift this morning.'

'How dreadful for him,' said Jessie.

'Actually he regretted saying it: a cheap shot, he called it. They were only doing what they thought was right.'

Kirsty stood up because the feelings of anger inside her were so strong that she felt they would burst out if she stayed seated. 'How dare they!' she said finally. 'How dare any woman encourage a man to enlist? War is madness, insanity ... and death must hurt, mustn't it? I couldn't fight, I'm a coward. I should have a white feather. I ... I think you're wonderful, Hugh, and all the other soldiers, of course, of all ranks ...' She stopped talking. She had said he was wonderful, and she was so embarrassed she wanted to crawl into a little hole.

He rescued her. 'We *are* wonderful,' he laughed, 'and I'm especially wonderful. I know because my mama keeps telling me. Am I wonderful enough to be taken for a walk on this lovely afternoon?'

'Mother?' Kirsty looked at her mother, her eyes shining, and Jessie gave her permission. Her eyes were sad, but Kirsty was too happy to notice.

They drove up to the castle. 'I'll have to let them know I'm here so that they can rustle up some food. Come in . . .'

Kirsty held back. 'Your parents? I . . . I . . .'

'They're not here. I'll tell the staff.'

He was ringing the doorbell as he spoke and soon Kirsty heard footsteps and then the door was pulled open and the butler, hastily buttoning his frock coat, beamed at his employer's son in delight.

'Master Hugh, we weren't expecting you.'

'I should have sent a telegram – sorry. My bag's in the car. I'll take Miss Robertson up to the library while I change. Come on, Kirsty.'

Meekly Kirsty allowed herself to be propelled up the stone stairs. She had been aware of a look of surprise from the butler at her presence, and lifted her head firmly. 'Let him be surprised,' she thought. 'Why shouldn't I be with Hugh?'

'Are these unbelievably ugly women your ancestors, Hugh?' she asked as she passed under the unseeing gaze of a line of portraits.

'They are awful, aren't they? A fifteenth-century job lot, Pa calls them, but don't let Mama hear you say anything. Blue-blooded, every one.'

'That's why they're so grey,' said Kirsty quietly and thrilled to hear him laugh.

'Wait in here for me,' he said, opening a door. 'I won't be a sec.' Kirsty was alone in a beautifully proportioned room and she almost gasped at its beauty. The walls were lined with bookcases that drew the eyes upwards to an

ornately carved ceiling. On one wall a carved oak fireplace, big enough to roast a cow, supported a magnificent
mirror, and she turned in awe to examine the portrait that
was mirrored there. It was of a girl of the Regency period;
she was caught, for ever poised, ready to dance, one small
foot in its delicate little shoe pointed forward. It was as if
at any moment she might slip from the canvas and dance
across the room. Her gown was white muslin and below
the rounded young bosom was a ribbon of rosebuds. She
was astonishingly lovely, but it was the eyes that held
Kirsty; they were deep blue, fringed with black lashes.

'Grannie,' said Hugh behind her. 'Quite a Regency belle,
wasn't she? She died when I was two.'

'Not related to any of these visions,' teased Kirsty as they
walked down the stairs again. 'I think they disapprove of me.'

'They disapprove of everyone. They were a wedding gift
from my maternal grandfather. That'd put a blight on any
marriage, wouldn't it? They're supposed to be incredibly
valuable.'

'No excuse,' said Kirsty firmly and was amazed at her
sophistication.

Hugh took her hand as they walked across the courtyard
and down the path to the Dell.

'Come on, teacher. Tell me all the names of the flowers.'

'I haven't seen a bluebell yet,' said Kirsty, suddenly shy
because his face was so close to hers. 'That's willowherb,

and down here by the burn there are celandines, and water forget-me-nots. They're sisters to these lovely blue forget-me-nots over here, and—

'This is willowherb,' he interrupted.

'No, that's purple loosestrife. It's quite similar. Oh, look, Hugh, these are bluebells – they're lovely, aren't they?'

'Not so lovely as you,' he said quietly. 'Willowherb,' he murmured and kissed her forehead, 'and bluebells,' and he kissed her eyebrows, 'and purple loosestrife,' and he kissed her cheek, 'but my favourite is forget-me-not,' and he claimed her mouth.

It was right, so right. His mouth was soft and warm, the kiss almost as delicate as a butterfly's wing. He held her gently against his chest and it seemed exactly the right place to be. They stood for a few moments in the quiet flower-filled glade and then walked on, stopping every now and again to look at yet another flower and to kiss, kisses that grew firmer and that began to do such delicious things to Kirsty's heart that it seemed to be free of whatever held it in its rightful place. Kirsty threw her arms around his neck and returned the kisses with innocent abandon.

'I'd best get you home, Kirsty,' he said, and his voice was strangely breathless. 'Summer evenings are deceptive – it's later than I said.'

Kirsty wanted the moment and the kisses to go on for ever. She wanted to be caught in time, to stand there with

Hugh in the enchanted meadow, and never ever go back to reality.

He took her hand and they wandered back towards the driveway.

'What's that pretty orange one in the meadow?' asked Hugh as if he needed to find normality.

'Poppies,' said Kirsty, her own voice rather breathless. 'They're awfully pretty, aren't they?'

16

GRAMMAR

Parsing and Analysis of Simple, Complex and Compound Sentences.

What else, what else was there to English grammar? Kirsty's mind refused to work. Hugh was returning to the Front and this evening they were going to visit the Aberannoch Dell for a last time. His staff were to provide a picnic. She stopped trying to conjure up English grammar out of her head, which seemed to be full of images of Hugh Granville-Baker: his eyes, his lips, his hands with their long, slim, but strong fingers, the way his hair curled darkly at the nape of his neck but shone almost like gold at his wrists.

COMPOSITION

The Garden

A Visit to the Harbour
Libraries

The '45
Our Bodies and Alcohol
The Life Story of a Bird
A Walk in the Woods

'A Walk in the Woods'. Perhaps she should rub out that title. Even writing it made her fingertips tingle. The Merit Class essays would surely not talk of the delicious delights of soft kisses, sweeter than the wild strawberries that grew in the wood. They would not mention the heady perfume of the honeysuckle that made her forget everything until a breathless Hugh pulled her up to stand beside him for one last kiss. Somewhere, not so very far away, men were dying. How could that be when the Aberannoch Dell was so peaceful, a bower formed by briar roses and bramble blossom? The School Year. What else had she done last year? How would she improve this year?

She took a new page.

GEOGRAPHY

What matter? The class and their teacher would be interested only in the geography of Europe.

HISTORY

Who cared about the landing of the Romans or the Saxons? In Europe history was being made; geography was being unmade; and in Scotland in August 1915 Kirsty Robertson fell in love with Hugh Granville-Baker in the Aberannoch Dell. There was history and geography for you.

Jessie watched her daughter chew the end of her pen. Her attention was wandering from the job she had set herself and Jessie knew what – or rather who – was on the girl's mind, and her own heart was troubled. It wouldn't do; it just wouldn't do. But how to tell a girl who had wandered around for three days as if her feet didn't even feel the hard ground beneath them? Thank God he was leaving tomorrow, and when he came back on his next leave surely he would have come to his senses and realized the extent of the gulf between the king in his castle and the maid in the cottage at the end of his mile-long driveway.

'Perhaps we should ask Hugh for a meal this evening, Kirsty?' she said. Keep it casual. A lonely boy needing company. They could have a nice supper and then play 'Freddie the Fox' on the card table – a silly child's game, but just the thing to distract from the knowledge the morning would bring.

'Look at these peas. I pick them every day, and every day more appear. Hugh can help us eat them.'

'We're having a picnic, Mother.' Kirsty turned to her mother, her eyes shining. 'The staff are preparing it. Doesn't that sound elegant? It won't be cheese sandwiches . . .'

'What's wrong with cheese sandwiches?'

'Nothing, when *you* make them,' laughed Kirsty. 'Oh, Mother, I'm so happy. He's so wonderful, isn't he?'

Jessie wanted to plead, 'Don't fall in love, Kirsty', but she could see that Kirsty already had, and girls in love saw and heard only what they wanted to see and hear.

'He's a nice laddie, Kirsty. He must have lots of friends. It's unusual for him to come back on his own, isn't it?'

A little of the light went out of Kirsty's eyes but Jessie hardened her heart. 'If his parents were here, if there wasn't a war on, the castle would be full of young people, Hugh's friends, the ones he grew up with, the ones he sees in London.'

'He didn't want to stay in London with his society friends, Mother,' said Kirsty quietly. 'He wanted . . .'

'What, dear? To see for himself how the estate was handling the harvest, and it's nice that you're here to keep him company. That draughty old place must be miserable if you're on your own. He must rattle around like one of these little peas.'

'Don't spoil it, Mother, please.' Kirsty stood up and turned her back on her mother. 'I know I'm in a dream,' she said in a voice so low that Jessie could hardly hear, 'and I'll wake up. When I'm sane I know that, and then sometimes I say, it doesn't matter that he lives in a castle and that I live in a cottage. When we're together we laugh, and talk and talk . . .'

'And kiss,' Jessie thought. 'Please, God, nothing else. Innocent kisses among the wild flowers. A romantic dream for a boy escaping from the hell of war . . . but my wee girl? She has seen no hell to hide from. Her memories are not his memories.'

Jessie sighed and said aloud, 'Have a lovely picnic, my dear, but tomorrow, Kirsty, tomorrow Cinderella has to come back from the palace. I don't want you hurt, my wee lass. There are no glass slippers in real life.' There, she'd said it, as much as she could say. 'I'll take these peas down to the Camerons. Jamie brought me a hare this afternoon and I know he doesn't have time to grow vegetables.'

She doubted that Kirsty even heard her go.

Jamie Cameron saw Kirsty drive off in Hugh's car. He'd managed to avoid her since New Year's Eve. Several times he'd started a note of apology, or a poem, a poem that would explain, but he couldn't get further than 'I've loved a lass for near ten year', and he didn't think that was very good poetry. He saw the way Kirsty looked at Hugh, just the way he would like her to look at *him*. He couldn't tell whether there was love in the Captain's eyes. What twinkled there – amusement, friendship, affection? Maybe all three. 'I'll kill him, gin he hurts her,' thought Jamie fiercely, and his mind shied away from all the ways that she could be hurt. 'She looks right in a big fancy car. Maybe he's no' just killing time. Why shouldn't he love her like I love her?'

But no one could ever love Kirsty like that. Sometimes the power of the passion inside him frightened Jamie, and to rid himself of it he would walk for miles, or sit at the slit that passed for a window in the byre where he lived since he had stopped sharing with all his brothers, and he would write and write and write. He wrote about the country-side, and he wrote about the sea, which he could see from the hill above the cottage, and he wrote about his mother and his brothers and sisters and he tried, so hard, to write about his love for Kirsty.

The briar blooms sae fresh and fair,
But fairer far is Kirsty . . .

Damn, he was stealing from Burns and she wasn't fair, anyway, she was dark, except that fair meant beautiful to look at. That's what the Dominie's dictionary told him, and Kirsty, oh aye, she was fair.

'Where was he taking her in his big car, and her with her best blue frock on?' He'd seen them wandering around the castle grounds – the 'Policies' as Lady Sybill cried them. Jamie's feelings were in a turmoil too. He didn't want Kirsty to go out with Hugh Granville-Baker, but if they were going out together why couldn't it be to the fancy restaurants where the nobs took their lassies, and not just for a walk in the woods like farm laddies? Kirsty was good enough for the swanky places and if Hugh Granville-Baker did not agree then he, Jamie Cameron, would personally draw his cork for him. Coming to that decision made him feel a great deal better and he went off to inspect the traps he'd put in the woods. The gamie didn't like it, but finding nourishing food for seven bairns and his mother – his father seemed to manage on whisky and great doorsteps of bread and cheese when he was sober – was not easy on one lad's wages. His mother had offered herself for the harvest; his mother, pregnant again and her near forty, cutting hay with a scythe while her man slept it off under a tree.

'One day I'll hit him.' Jamie made another decision that raised his spirits. 'Soon I'll be strong enough tae handle him. Honour they father and they mother,' the words sprang unbidden into his head. 'I've tried, Lord, ye cannae say I haven't tried.' He jumped the dry-stane dyke and skirted round the field. 'What a bonny sight is a field of barley.'

'If I ever thought of having champagne,' said Kirsty, 'I would never have thought my first sip would be at a picnic.'

'Why not?' asked Hugh as he refilled her crystal glass and then his own. 'Champagne, cold chicken breasts, asparagus and luscious strawberries. Here, pop a strawberry into your glass. Now, how does that taste?' He held the dripping fruit to her lips and, her eyes on his, she bit it.

'No,' she whispered, strangely breathless. 'Champagne is for drinking and strawberries are for eating on their own.'

'Not even with cream, Miss Purist?'

She shook her head. She was drinking champagne; she was sophisticated, witty. 'A strawberry, my poor disadvantaged boy,' she said, 'is at its best picked warm from the sun.'

'Next year, Kirsty. Next year the war will be over and we'll pick strawberries and eat them straight from the field.' He was so close, so very close. It was so right, so inevitable, so perfect. He leaned over her and his lips met hers, warm, soft, sweet from the taste of strawberries and very slightly sour from the champagne. She looked up over his shoulder and saw the wild pink roses and the white blossoms of the bramble, and she could smell so strongly the scent of honeysuckle, and then everything was blotted out by Hugh, the strength of him, the feel of him. The blood raced in her veins, faster and faster and she could hear his breathing and hers, mingled, and words ... what was she saying, what was he saying? It didn't matter, nothing mattered but this feeling. She would die; she could not bear this pleasure.

'Hugh, Hugh,' she heard a voice shriek, and it was hers, and he fell against her and she could feel the tears running down her cheeks.

'Oh, God, Kirsty, I didn't mean . . .'

She put her hand over his mouth. 'Don't talk, don't talk,' she begged.

She had to hold him, to hold the moment, for even as she smelled the blossom which waved above her, something, something deep, deep inside, told her that nothing would ever be so perfect again.

Jamie had seen them kiss as he slipped through the Dell with his rabbits. They did not see him and he was no voyeur: he would not watch, he could not watch. 'Oh, Kirsty lass,' his heart cried. 'What I'd give tae have you look at me like that.'

He was unaware of the tears that streamed down his cheeks as he handed his mother the rabbits. 'I'll kill him gin he hurts her,' he vowed as he climbed the ladder to his loft.

I've loved a lass for near ten year.
I'll love her till I die . . .

'I can't write poetry. It stinks. Oh, Kirsty lass, could I find the words . . .'

In the Dell, the honeysuckle, the briar roses and the bramble blossoms slept. Hugh and Kirsty tidied up their picnic, a slow job, for they stopped too often to kiss.

'Oh, Kirsty, Kirsty, my dearest girl . . .' Hugh began, but she stopped the words with her lips or her hand.

'Don't speak, oh, Hugh, my heart, don't spoil the moment.'

17

THE ARMIES OF BOTH SIDES spent the summer of 1915 resting, reorganizing and reinforcing. It was all so civilized.

Civilization tried to find normality. In France, Chagall and Dufy were painting and Debussy was composing piano music. In Britain, Rupert Brooke was writing poetry, Somerset Maugham completed *Of Human Bondage*, a Scotsman called John Buchan published a book entitled *The Thirty-Nine Steps,* and people began to talk about a writer called Virginia Woolf. There was even time, while armies slept, for science to march forward, and the first automatic telephone exchange was set up. Impending disaster was smouldering in Russia where a monk called Rasputin was effectively ruler. In America a divinely handsome film star with twinkling eyes began to make women all over the world forget their worries for a few celluloid moments: his name was Douglas Fairbanks.

In Scotland, Kirsty Robertson's class collected £1.0.9d. for the Red Cross Appeal and each child was presented with a Red Cross stamp as a memento of such sacrifice. At home Kirsty spent a great deal of time staring into space when she wasn't wandering around humming the popular new Novello song 'Keep the Home Fires Burning'.

On the first Saturday after school started, Meg Stewart cycled out to Aberannoch. The girls had long since given up their Saturday-morning meetings, tending instead to meet for a cup of tea after school during the week. Meg had been walking out for over a year with a neighbouring fisherman, a friend of her brother Alex.

Kirsty and her mother were delighted to see her and they spent the first few minutes catching up on the news of their families. Then Meg got down to the real purpose of her visit.

'Kirsty, I want you to stand up for me next Saturday. Will and I want to get married – he's joining the Army.'

Getting married! Jealousy flowed into Kirsty's mouth like a wave of bitter gall. She swallowed both the jealousy and her own pain. This was Meg, her friend, and impulsively she hugged her. 'What wonderful news: the wedding bit, not the joining up. Fisher lads don't have to join up, Meg.'

'I know, but he wants to do his bit. We planned to wed next summer, but Will says if we don't get in and finish those Germans quickly it'll go on for ever.'

Kirsty poured more tea. 'And your job?' She remembered how much Meg had wanted a job where she wouldn't have to smell like fish. She remembered how she had cried over homework assignments, and how Meg had sat in the schoolroom at Aberannoch every Saturday afternoon while John Robertson had coached her. All to be tossed away.

'I'm going to stay at home and help Will's mother,' said Meg easily.

'I'd do it too,' thought Kirsty, 'but it wouldn't be painless.'

'We want to get married on Saturday,' Meg went on. 'I told the headmaster yesterday and he was very nice and understanding. He says maybe soon they'll allow married women to teach – they'll need them, the way the men are joining up.' She turned to Jessie. 'Will you come too, Mrs Robertson? It'll be a small wedding, my family and Will's, the ones at home, and you and Kirsty. We're going to Dundee for the weekend and then Will will enlist there on Monday. I'm very, very proud of him,' she finished bravely.

'Of course I'll come,' said Jessie. 'Have you decided what to wear, Meg? I'll run up something for Kirsty that complements you.' She looked at her daughter who, after the first enthusiastic reception of the news, had quietened down and was sitting almost unaware of the excited chattering that was going on around her. 'Kirsty, Meg will look lovely in blue, won't she?'

'Yes, and I'm so happy for you, dearest Meg,' said Kirsty and burst into tears.

Jessie and Meg stared at her aghast. 'Kirsty, what's wrong?' exclaimed Meg.

'I'm sorry, I'm so sorry. It's just that I'm so happy for you, Meg. It's so romantic. You and Will in love and being married. It's just perfect, well, almost, isn't it?'

'It would be if he wasn't going to war, but then we've been walking out for a year and he never even said he loved me until last Sunday. Maybe he would have taken years . . .'

'All men are slow, then?' said Kirsty, and she seemed to brighten up. 'Tell me again about your dress, Meg. No, it was a suit, wasn't it?'

Later Kirsty cycled a little of the way towards Arbroath with Meg.

'You heard Bob Cargill enlisted during the holidays, didn't you, Kirsty? He's in the new Flying Corps. Can you imagine a fisher laddie in an aeroplane?'

'I haven't seen Bob for ages. We lost touch when he went to the university.' She recalled old memories. 'He was such a nice lad.'

'You should write to him,' suggested Meg, 'or are you keeping company yourself – your farmer, perhaps?'

'No, I'm not keeping company exactly, I don't think so anyway. I write to someone on active service and I see him when he's on leave.'

'That's keeping company, Kirsty,' said Meg positively. 'Have you made plans?'

'No, it's all very casual, just friends, you know,' and Kirsty felt that annoying blush that always let her down sweeping across her face and neck as those last moments in the Dell came rushing into her mind. Casual, casual – there had been nothing casual about that!

'And what about your rustic swain?'

'Don't be silly, Meg.' What a change a tiny diamond chip on the fourth finger of her left hand was making to Meg. Her complacency after Saturday's ceremony would make her unbearable. Then Kirsty remembered all the early years and Meg's unswerving help and friendship after her father's death, and the old affection swept away the annoyance.

'I'll see you on Saturday, Meg, and I'm so pleased you want me to be your bridesmaid.'

'Couldn't be anyone else, now, could it? I'll get Bob's address for you. He wasn't walking out with anyone: too busy with all those extra courses. He'll be a head teacher one day soon if this awful war ends quickly.'

'With your Will and Bob Cargill on our side, how could it not?'

Meg laughed happily, the laugh of a girl who loved and was loved and was being married in a few days. Kirsty envied her. She didn't turn back towards the cottage as Meg cycled away but cycled on. Almost before she realized it, she was at the castle gates but she turned away. Without Hugh there would be no beauty in the Dell. She dismounted and stood for a moment looking up at the eagles, then turned slowly and began to cycle home.

'May I walk with you, Kirsty?' Where had Jamie appeared from?

Kirsty looked at him for a long moment. She had not seen him for nearly a year, not since the social on New Year's Eve, and he had changed. If anything he was even thinner, but he was taller and somehow he looked stronger. The eyes that looked down at her were clear and bright, but the skin around them was wrinkled from years of working out in all weathers. He exuded health. She could afford to forgive him for embarrassing her; she could even understand, for was she not now the one who had sworn undying love and who had seen it . . . not rejected, no, but hardly accepted, and certainly not reciprocated. Not once, not once in those beautiful moments in the Dell when Kirsty Robertson had given her love with her whole heart and soul, had the object of that love and desire said, 'I love you too, Kirsty.'

She smiled now at Jamie. 'I'll be glad of your company, Jamie. My friend Meg was just asking if I saw much of you.'

'I saw her go past.'

'She's getting married on Saturday. Her fiancé wants to enlist.'

'Seems a daftlike thing to do. Marry and then enlist.'

'Will feels that the more men who join up, the quicker the war will be over.'

'There's only one thing sure, Kirsty. The more men that join up, the more'll get killt. War is not something for civilized men to be doing with. If I take a gun and shoot a man in Aberannoch, I'm a murderer and I hang. If I take a gun and shoot a German in France, I'm a conquering hero. What bluidy arrogance!'

'It's not the same thing at all.' They were ten years old again, talking and arguing as they had always done, but Jamie was no longer awed by the power and position of the Dominie's lassie. He was a man who had suffered, who had read and listened and, more importantly, learned.

'The Germans were the aggressors,' said Kirsty hotly.

'Aye, but since when do two wrongs make a right? If these educated men are that clever, can they no' sit down and talk sensibly and get this all ironed out? My God, Kirsty lass, it's madness. It won't end with Right conquering Wrong. There does'nae seem much in the way of tactics being thought out here. It's just, if one battalion gets wiped out, find two more to fill up the hole. It'll be the army with most men that wins, most money, for I'll tell you something, Kirsty Robertson. Somebody's making a lot of money out of this war.'

What he said seemed to make sense, but he had to be wrong. Hugh was out there, and Bob Cargill, and soon Meg's Will. There had to be more to it than self-seeking, self-aggrandizement.

'The old minister at Aberannoch has three sons in the Army, Jamie. His youngest's only sixteen and he wants to go, to fight for Right, and his father is a man of God. He wouldn't have three boys in uniform if it wasn't right. The aggressor has to be beaten and punished, to make sure he doesn't do it again. It's like teaching. I can hardly bear to punish children, but I've been a teacher long enough to have learned that if you don't act really firmly with naughty children they soon become bad children.'

'Europe's hardly a classroom full of bad bairns.'

'Sometimes to me that's exactly what it seems like.'

They had reached the cottage and were so involved in their argument that they almost passed, but Jessie hailed them.

'How nice to see you, Jamie. Watching you two took me back nearly ten years.'

'Aye, we were always arguing, but not about the rights and wrongs of war.'

'How is your mother?'

'Better off in the fields than in one of those munitions factories. Our Cissie's gone off to London, did you hear? They're offering wages of 12/6d. a week and 2d. an hour overtime, but since she's not eighteen she can't work nights, otherwise I don't think the lass would sleep at all. Mind you, the man that had the job before her got near £3 for the same work. Is that not the war we should be fighting? Inequality.'

'You sound like Meg's brother. He even wants women to vote,' said Kirsty incredulously.

Jamie looked at her almost scornfully. 'Kirsty Robertson, did your father not show you you had a brain in your head better than most boys in the school?' He laughed like the young Jamie. 'In fact, I sometimes thought it was near as good as mine. Why should *I* vote for my government, and not you? Think, lass.'

'Heavens, Jamie, don't turn my daughter into a suffragist.'

All three laughed and, happier than she had been for some time, Kirsty said good night and went indoors. It was good not to be at outs with Jamie. If only a letter would come from Hugh! He had to write; it had to have meant something to him. She should have let him speak, and then perhaps he might have said the words she wanted to hear. But she had been so terrified that he would say he hadn't meant it to happen, that it didn't mean anything to him. He had tried to apologize, to say he was sorry, and she couldn't have that. She wasn't sorry, would never be sorry, ever, ever, even if . . . even if . . . No, to say that would make it true and it couldn't be true, mustn't be, not yet, not yet till he'd written and said he wasn't sorry – that he had wanted it as much as she had.

Not for the first time since the night in the Dell, Kirsty Robertson cried herself to sleep.

18

In 1915 in Britain, in stately mansions in the south of England, in farm cottages in Angus, in tiny crofts in the Western Isles, two names became known by everyone. One was Edith Cavell, a British nurse who had been working in Brussels since 1906. In August, while Kirsty waited for a letter from Hugh and Meg prepared for her wedding to her Will, Miss Cavell was arrested by the Germans for helping Allied servicemen to escape to Holland.

The other name was that of Flight Sub-Lieutenant R.A.J. Warneford, and it was the exploits of this young airman and his fellows that caused many young men, including Bob Cargill, to rush to join this new band of heroes. There had been a number of air raids that summer and all Britain looked forward to a fight between a German Zeppelin and a British aeroplane. It happened on June 7th between Ghent and Brussels. Warneford, in a very light monoplane, found himself above one of the huge ungainly monsters at a height of some 6,000 feet. He swooped down on top of the Zeppelin and dropped six bombs on it, one of which burst open the envelope, and in the tremendous explosion the little plane was turned upside down. Warneford had barely graduated from the Central Flying School. This new force in the air was, in fact, scarcely a year old, but the fledgling pilot managed to right his machine and to land safely – in enemy territory. Before he could be captured he restarted the plane and flew back to Britain and immortality.

Hugh Granville-Baker heard neither of Warneford, nor of Nurse Cavell, whose execution in October filled the nation with righteous anger and made the British people more determined than ever to win the war. Hugh was in the midst of a nightmare not of his own making at a place called Loos. Hugh did think of Kirsty. He did not try to hide his thoughts; he welcomed them. He could stand exhausted, held up by the mud that almost held his trench together, his boots rotting on his feet, and his soul would be in Scotland lying in a bower of roses and honeysuckle, and in his arms would be a girl who smelled cleaner and sweeter than either. He had tried to tell her he was sorry – their lovemaking had got out of hand.

'I should have been stronger: I'm experienced. Dear God, I'm a man.' He went over it again and again. 'I should have guarded her, protected her. She didn't know what was going on. Please God, let her be all right until I get back.'

The thought of what life would be like for Kirsty if she was not all right brought him out in a cold sweat. He looked for a letter. Kirsty wrote every day: she told of the harvest, of her new class, of the bramble blossoms turning to berries on the bushes. None of the letters had, so far, reached him.

Loos is in that area that became known as the Western Front. The German armies had begun their huge offensive in the East in May, and so it had seemed only sensible to hit them as hard as possible in the West. There were no Gettysburgs in the First World War, no Waterloos: no battles that lasted a day or a little more and decisively changed the course of war and of history itself. The great battles of this First World War dragged on for days, for weeks, for months. Now Hugh stood hardly aware of the continuous bombardment, the likes of which men had never heard before. It was like thunder that rolled above his head hour after sleepless hour. The thunder rose every now and again to a crescendo and there would come the cry from somebody, 'Here it comes, lads, man the parapets,' and ... nothing, nothing but the boom, whine, boom. General Joffre had encouraged the quietening down of activity. He needed time to reinforce, to repair the roads that would bring in supplies: tents, huts, food, drink, ammunition and men – in the British case, since they had lost most of their trained soldiers in 1914, raw, confused recruits.

One night, towards the end of September, Hugh stood in a blessed break from the shelling, the lull before the storm, and reached inside his vest for the little box sent by Princess Mary as a Christmas gift for the soldiers. He'd meant to give it to Kirsty; she would have loved the little silver pencil he had been given because he was one of the few men who did not smoke. Paper? Surely to God, somewhere he had a piece of paper. His paybook. He'd write on the back page and square that breach of regulations with the CO later. Christ, he was the CO! Forsyth was dead, and Hendry, and Smythe, and, and, and . . . Dear God, would it ever end?

Dear Kirsty,

You wouldn't let me speak. I would have said, what would I have said? That those moments with you in the Dell would stay in my heart for ever. I pray you are well. As soon as this is over I'll come back to you, I promise. Meet me in . . .

'Captain, Captain,' the hoarse voice interrupted him, and hurriedly he pushed the paybook and the little pencil into his pocket. 'We're to expect another attack, sir. All hell's . . .'

It was as bright as noon on Midsummer's Day. And the noise! After that moment of quiet he felt his head would burst. He ignored it. Now that it had started again the hideous fear that sat constantly in his belly, so that sweat broke out on his cold body, disappeared. He straightened his shoulders. He was not a man with loves and fears, he was an expensively trained machine. His voice, strong where a moment ago it had barely croaked, shouted the right orders.

'We'll do our bit with what we have, Sergeant.' They had more men, and the British had instigated the attack and so they had surprise, but there was too little ammunition.

'Keep your heads down.' As yet there were no steel helmets; military caps afforded no protection, even if they stayed on the head.

'What's going on?'

'Oh, sweet Christ, the wind's changed. Put your masks on,' he shouted above the bombardment, but the sergeant didn't hear and Hugh hurried over to him. 'Your mask – not that it's much use, but better than nothing.'

'Come on, Frazer, lad.' The private was about seventeen, his eyes wide and staring, his mouth open in a silent scream for his mother, for sanity. 'It's all right, lad. We'll beat the buggers. Here, get your mask on.' Mask, what mask: an impregnated flannel bag with a celluloid window. The Germans were uncivilized, there had been an outcry when they had first used gas. Now, he, Hugh Granville-Baker, was ordering his troops to throw gas at the Germans. Science dehumanizes.

The boy clung to him. Hugh smelled the smell of urine and for a moment his mind went back through the years to wee Tam and the school at Aberannoch.

'Pull yourself together, lad. That's it, that's it. Got a girl, have you? Wait till she sees your medals.'

'It's our own gas blowing back on us,' Hugh mouthed to his sergeant.

'It's the bluidy shells the Germans are throwing that I could dae withoot.'

Hugh managed a smile.

The madness went on. Noise, silence, darkness, brilliant light, screaming, blood, mud, stumps of trees – or were those bodies slumped over fence posts? Pain, pain, and always, always trying to make sense, trying to do the right thing. Was he thinking, rationalizing, making conscious decisions, or was some inner force outside looking down objectively and forcing his exhausted mind and body through the motions? He saw Frazer, or what was left of Frazer, still with his mouth open. Where were the boy's legs? He scrabbled in the bloody mud. He had to find the legs. What was that bloody lump of meat over there? 'I've got your legs, lad. Don't fret. I've got your legs.' Fingers. Legs didn't have fingers. Whose arm? Whose arm? Where was everyone? He crawled back to Frazer and tried to close the mouth but the jaw wouldn't move. *Rigor mortis* – How could that have set in? Didn't it take time? Surely he'd only chivvied the lad a few minutes ago.

He wiped the rivers of sweat from his brow. How warm it was – it wasn't sweat, it was blood. He looked at it dispassionately and the smell, warm and sickly, rose to him. It changed . . . it was honeysuckle. Honeysuckle in September – or was it October now? Honeysuckle and wild roses and in the field there, on the left of the Dell, barley red-gold like the tips of the waves in Kirsty's hair when the sun caressed it. He would wait here in the Dell for Kirsty to come. He was so tired. He could sleep now with the scent of honeysuckle. He pulled a rose from the briar and sat down on the fallen log.

'I'll wait for you in the Dell, Kirsty.'

He smiled.

Meg's wedding was as perfect as any hastily arranged wedding can be. The bride was radiant, and the groom proud, nervous and very shy.

'Don't ask,' said Meg's grandfather as he happily poured real and very expensive French champagne into newly bought crystal glasses. 'There's never been champagne in this hoos and certainly nae fancy glesses, but for wir wee lass, the best of a'thing we kin get. No much o' a waddin',

Kirsty. Landsakes, there should be dancin' fer days – and her in a blue suit! She should hae her mammy's veil.'

'It's a lovely wedding, Mr Stewart,' Kirsty consoled him honestly and then very abruptly, so abruptly that she almost broke its delicate stem, she set the glass down on a table. Her head reeled and her stomach heaved.

'Losh, lassie, ye've only hid ae sip. Kin ye no haud yer drink?'

Kirsty waved him away and ran for the door of the cottage. 'So hot, so hot,' she explained to those she rushed past.

Outside she managed to reach the nettles and willow-herb that grew among the rubble at the back of the cottage before she was violently sick.

'Kirsty, how could you, how could you?' It was her mother. 'You're pregnant, aren't you? You gave yourself to him, didn't you? How could you? How could you?' she asked the unanswerable question again and again and again. Maybe if she asked enough times she would get the answer she needed. 'Thank God, oh, thank God, I never thought I would ever say it, but I'm glad your father is dead. University, he wanted for you. "Why, John?" I asked. "She's a girl. Some lad will come and wed her, and what price a university education then?" And do you know what he said? He said, "Education is never wasted, and I want it for our lass. She'll be a better mother." A better mother? Oh, Kirsty. In a million years, would the likes of Hugh Granville-hyphen-Baker wed a lass like you?'

Kirsty, white and shaken, looked up at her mother, at the face of someone she had never before seen. She was not afraid. She was not angry. Suddenly she was a hundred years old and she understood the pain that was making Jessie scream abuse at her.

'I'm so sorry, Mother, sorry that I've hurt you.'

She wiped her mouth with the handkerchief that Jessie had embroidered for her.

'Oh, Kirsty, my bairn,' Jessie whispered and held out her arms to her daughter.

'What am I going to do?' Kirsty sobbed in her mother's arms. 'Help me. Mother, I'm so frightened.'

'We'll get home quietly and then we'll talk. Can you pull yourself together? We'll need to say our goodbyes.'

'The heat ...' 'The excitement ...' They made their excuses and left before the bride and groom. Knowing looks followed them and people nodded at one another. They said nothing as they walked to the station; nothing as they sat and waited for a train. Jessie held her daughter's hand as if it was a lifeline that she dare not let go. At last, at last the cottage welcomed them.

'I'll make a cup of tea and bring it in to you, lass. Take your shoes off and lie down on your bed.'

'I'm fine now, Mother. I'll sit in the front room.'

She noticed the best china. Why? What was Jessie saying? 'He's been gone a month' – he was no longer Hugh, but he, he the seducer, the ruiner of young girls – 'and he was only here a few days.'

Kirsty wanted to laugh. It didn't matter how long Hugh's leave had been; *it* had only taken a few minutes. She answered Jessie's unasked question.

'The last day.'

'Not that that makes much difference. Have you told him?'

'No. I didn't know myself, tried to hide from the truth, I suppose. I've been late before. When Mr Buchanan . . . when I lived there . . .'

'He must be told. He will admit responsibility, won't he? He always seemed like a nice boy. You can write tonight. He has to marry you . . .' Jessie turned away to dry her tears.

'Mother, there's a war on. It might be months before Hugh comes back.'

'He's an officer. They have power, and his father is high up, isn't he? And Lady Sybill? Her father's a lord. They can pull strings.'

Then Kirsty admitted to the nightmare, to the fear that had been growing with her knowledge of what had happened. 'He hasn't written since he left. Perhaps he doesn't care for me . . . perhaps he thinks I'm a bad girl.'

Jessie stood up. 'You've never even walked out with anyone else. I'll tell him that. You write. I'll walk into Arbroath and post it. It must go out as quickly as possible.'

Dear Hugh . . . Kirsty bit the end of the pen. What could she write? How do you tell someone something that, in the right circumstances, is so wonderful that it should only be spoken face to face, so that the joy in each soul could be seen reflected in the eyes. There was no joy here, only acute fear. Hugh hadn't written. He had lost all respect for her. She was easy. Men didn't marry girls who were easy. Oh, dear God, what was she going to do? The tears blotted the paper and she sniffed loudly, blew her nose, and started again.

> *Dear Hugh,*
> *I haven't heard from you and I hope you are well. The news from the Front is not good and I hate to think of you out there.*
> *Hugh, I need to hear from you because I'm going to have a baby.*

There, she had said it, coldly, badly. She wouldn't beg, wouldn't plead, wouldn't assure him of her virtue. Hugh would know all that. He would not deny the baby was his, and if he didn't want to marry her . . . Never once, never once had he said, 'I love you, Kirsty.' She could handle it. She would manage, somehow.

Please tell me what you want me to do. I'm all right for a few months.
Please write to me.

Kirsty

She wouldn't say that she loved him. She had said that often enough in the Dell, in every way.

'I'll post it myself, Mother. I'm perfectly well, really.'

She walked back towards the town and looked out over the sea. How incredibly beautiful and peaceful it was. Not for the first time she thought how difficult it was to believe that there was a war on. The haystacks stood golden in the fields; a few early brambles were almost ripe. 'A few days and we'll be making jelly,' thought Kirsty, 'and while I'm making jam, soldiers not so far away will be killing each other.' For the first time she thought not of her own soldier but of the French and Flemish, and even the German women who should by rights also be looking forward to making jam. Were their fields lying golden in the sun? Were the brambles in France, and the grapes, ripe and luscious and ready to pick? If the papers were correct and the drawings of the official war artists, Nash and Nevinson, true to life – or death – the fertile fields of France were blown to smithereens or churned up by the countless feet of marching men.

She continued her walk and did not know that she was followed by Jamie, who wondered what letter was so important that Kirsty could not wait for tomorrow for the train.

19

Kirsty watched and waited for a letter, but none came. She tried to hide her growing despair from Jessie and from her class. From them too, she had to hide her pregnancy. If only it wasn't accompanied by this awful morning sickness ... but at least by the time she had reached school her stomach was behaving itself again.

The papers talked of a great battle at Loos and of a piper in one of the Scottish regiments who held onto his battle honours and, despite his wounds, refused to let them droop in the mud. Later they reported the death of one Captain Hugh Granville-Baker.

But before that day Kirsty saw the flag and understood. The caretaker, Wilson, with tears streaming down his old cheeks, had found a flag and flown it from the ramparts of the castle to honour a boy he scarcely knew.

Kirsty's first feelings were not of grief, or fear. They would come later. She felt peaceful. He was dead; he hadn't ignored her, denied her. She turned in at the gates that old

Wilson had not yet thought to close and made her way to the Dell. For a moment she thought she saw a figure sitting on the fallen tree where they had picnicked, but October was too cold for picnics. A strong wind was blowing the leaves from the trees and they were dancing on the ground. There was someone there. It couldn't be. It was: it was a soldier. Hugh. She could see him clearly and she began to run. The figure turned, saw her and stood up. He smiled and held out his hands. She heard his voice, his dear, dear voice.

'I waited as I promised. Goodbye, my dearest little love.'

She stopped. The Dell was empty. 'Oh, Hugh.' And then the tears came, at first for him, for the young life cut off before its prime, and then for herself, and at last for the child who would never know its father, but who should know only shame.

'I'll never be ashamed, Hugh, never, and neither will he. He'll be loved, I promise, loved and cherished.' She lay on the tree trunk and cried for all the unfulfilled promise.

'Kirsty, Kirsty, get up. You're freezing.'

She looked up at Jamie and realized that there was no need to tell him anything. He knew.

'I've been sent to close the gates – the estate's in mourning. I'll have to put you out, lass, or you'll spend a cold night in the wood.'

She walked quietly beside him to the gates and stood waiting as he locked them and pocketed the key.

'I'll walk you home.'

She drew herself up, dignified, proud. 'I'm fine, Jamie, and I'd rather be alone, if you don't mind. But can you tell me when it happened?'

'Her ladyship didn't tell us the exact date. I don't think she knows. Some awful battle that's been going on for weeks: Loos, they called it.'

'I should have known. Goodbye, Jamie.'

He watched her go and then ran after her. 'I'll not intrude on your grief, lass, but I'm here, Kirsty, if I can do anything.'

'Thank you, Jamie, but there's nothing anyone can do.'

Jessie allowed her daughter a few hours only to mourn. She walked around her bedroom frantically. Kirsty hadn't thought of the shame, the humiliation. For one awful moment Jessie even considered abortion and then, so horrified was she by her own thoughts, she fell down on her knees beside the bed and begged God's forgiveness. Maybe grief would do it. That would be the best solution. Sometimes that happened. She watched Kirsty carefully. Nothing.

'What are we going to do, Kirsty? We have to think. You'll let the Colonel know, and Lady Sybill?'

Kirsty, thinner and paler than ever, looked at her mother sadly. 'No, I can't. I'll stay on at school until the end of the year. I'm so thin, maybe I'll be able to stay until the end of January.'

'Five months pregnant! You'll be stoned in the street. You'll have to go away. I'll write to Uncle Chay.'

'No. Oh, Mother, please, there's no room – him with a young wife and a babe now of his own. I'll work as long as I can, and we'll save, and then I'll have the baby here.'

Jessie looked at her daughter incredulously. 'You're insane. You can't know what you're saying. You're a schoolteacher, Kirsty. Your morals are supposed to be . . .'

'They are, Mother. My morals are admirable. I'm not ashamed of loving Hugh. He loved me . . .'

'He never even wrote . . .'

'Mother.'

Jessie looked at her daughter and saw the belief shining out of her dark eyes.

'He loved me. I know, and no one can ever take that knowledge away from me or my baby. I don't want to stay here and be pointed out as a loose woman every time I go out of that door any more than you do, but we have nowhere else to go. Besides, perhaps attitudes will be different because of the war.'

'Maybe for some farm lassie, or some fisher lassie, but you're the teacher, the Dominie's lassie. Everybody expects you to be perfect. Will you tell the name of the father?'

'No, and you mustn't either, Mother, please. Try to understand. I never met Hugh's parents. We never spoke about them, just about us. They probably don't know I exist and now, when they're mourning their only son . . . for me to turn up and say that I'm carrying his child. No, Mother.'

'But they should help. They would want to know, Kirsty. They have a right to their grandchild.'

'I can't explain, Mother, but I can't tell them, not yet, maybe not ever.'

Kirsty had considered writing to Hugh's parents. She had imagined them, grief-stricken, heartbroken, pictured them receiving the news, the wonderful news that she was to have their son's child. Then the doubts had rushed in. Would they want the child? Would they even believe her? As far as she knew, Hugh had never mentioned her to his parents. How often had she seen him, been with him? This last leave had been three days and they had spent only a few hours together. She thought of her child. Hugh's parents were wealthy. The baby had a right to the same type of upbringing as his father had had.

Night after night Kirsty lay awake. She tried to sleep. She needed to be healthy and strong for the coming child, and for her job – even more stressful now that she tried to hide her condition and her worries from both the children and the staff. But sleep would not come. She had nursed one faint and slender hope, a hope that Hugh would have been able to write to her. She no longer doubted his love for her. She knew that he had died thinking of her, and that his spirit had waited for her in the Dell to assure her of his feelings. If he had written she could have gone to his parents, for no matter how brave she was for Jessie during the day, in the cold watches of the night her heart failed her. She was unmarried and she was going to have a child; she would be mocked at, jeered at, sworn at in the street. And the shame and embarrassment to Jessie – it didn't bear thinking about. She could not stay in her job much longer. Already Miss Purdy had asked her if she was well. How would they eat, how would they pay the rent, when she had to leave school? Kirsty tossed and turned, and in the room next door, Jessie tossed in equal agony.

Jessie wanted Kirsty to go to Hugh's parents. They had a right to know, and they might help even if they would not officially acknowledge an illegitimate grandchild. Jessie no longer worried about right and wrong. Even more than Kirsty, she feared the scorn of the people of the village. Some would stand by them; some would whisper behind their curtains. Jessie sighed for her tenuous position among *the right people*. They would not be quite so friendly when they found out. Bravely she put her personal feelings aside. She would support her daughter and the child as much as she could. Now she turned her thoughts to ways of earning money.

The next morning the headmaster asked the staff to meet him for a few minutes before school started. This was very unusual and there was a buzz of excitement in the staff room.

'You're not interested in Messages from on High, Kirsty?' Miss Purdy had sat down beside Kirsty without her even noticing.

Kirsty blushed. 'Of course. It's just that new chips for the playground, or making sure that we comply with National Registration, don't really seem too relevant.'

'Maybe it's the date for opening the soup kitchen.'

It was not.

The Dominie came in in a flurry of black gown.

'I think it's something bigger, lass,' whispered Miss Purdy and received a frown from the Dominie for speaking.

'Ladies, gentlemen, pupil teachers, last night I received a communication from the Board that affects us all. We are to be used for billeting by the Military Authorities and therefore the school will close at the New Year holiday.'

The reception of the news was all that he could have anticipated. There was an immediate storm of protest from the men – 'Worried about their jobs,' thought Kirsty scornfully and unkindly – and an excited buzzing from most of the women.

The words Military Authorities rang in Kirsty's ears. 'Hugh, oh, Hugh,' she thought, and Miss Purdy noticed the sadness on the girl's pale face. 'You are the only military I can think about,' and just then she felt a tiny flip inside her, like a small goldfish turning over in a jar. She put her hands wonderingly on her stomach and again Miss Purdy noticed.

'The children, Dominie?' protested Allan Inglis, the drill instructor. 'What on earth is to happen to the children?'

'A good question, Inglis, and one that the Board in its wisdom has seen fit to answer.'

'How patronizing even the nicest men get when they have a bit of power,' whispered Miss Purdy and was glad to see Kirsty smile.

'We are to go to Parkhouse School, where we will alternate with their staff and students. We will be half-timers, as I believe was the habit in Dundee, though the children will not have to work in the mills but will be free to study.'

Everyone laughed at that sally.

'I'm quite sure one or even two may well spend some time at their books. We will not as yet tell the pupils, although I am sure rumours will go the rounds as they always do. I will be meeting with my colleague from Parkhouse and with the Board, and will try to obtain the best terms. You will be pleased to hear that your salaries will not be affected but, naturally, you will be expected to earn them. I rather think that we shall teach straight through, with a break only for your babies, Miss Purdy, and there will be alternate dinner hours. That is, the school that works the morning shift will work through what was the dinner hour, and the others will start after it. Thank you for your time. I will keep you all informed. The soup kitchen, for those of you who had questions, will open in December and dinner will be from

1 to 1.30, so we will close at 3.35 p.m. I hope that won't affect train timetables too much.'

The staff had no time to discuss the news because the bell rang for the first class. Kirsty went through her lessons mechanically. 'I can't go to another school. I'll have to leave at the holiday. One month less salary. One month less salary. One month less salary.'

'Miss, are you all right, Miss?'

Kirsty waved the child away. 'Of course, Sadie. I was thinking, that's all.'

'You don't look well, Miss. Will I get the jannie?'

Kirsty looked at the girl. Did she know? Had she guessed? 'The janitor isn't needed, Sadie. Thank you.'

She collected her thoughts. 'Take out the Palmerston Reader.' There was the expected groan from the less able readers. 'Fergie,' she turned to her brightest pupil, 'if you would like to read *Dombey and Son* until playtime you can sit out in the corridor. I would like you to finish Dickens by Christmas and go on to Thackeray's *Vanity Fair*. I have a bound copy of my own you may borrow, and who is able to read Dickens after Fergie? You, Sadie, or is it to be you, Willie? Let's see who is the best reader today. Charlie, begin at page forty-seven.'

She kept her attention firmly focused on teaching them reading. It was not enough that the children could pronounce the words; reading was for enjoyment, not only for the reader but for the listener. Some were pleased and some disappointed when the bell rang.

In the staff room there was more consternation. Robert Bell, the senior pupil teacher, had walked out of school and enlisted.

'By God, I'll go with you, lad.' It was Allan Inglis. 'They'll be conscripting us soon, and who knows what kind of situation this half-time school is going to be? We'll away and win the war for you, ladies. Who'll give me a favour to hang on my rifle?'

Bile rose in Kirsty's throat and she stumbled from the room. Miss Purdy followed her into the lavatory.

'War's not a joke, is it, lassie?'

'No, it's a horrible mess.'

'Do you want to talk to me about it? Can I help you in any way?'

Dumbly Kirsty shook her head.

'I offered to help you once before, lass. The offer still stands, and you've more need of help now, I think.'

'I'll be fine, really. It's nothing, just him making a joke of war and death and destruction.'

'My mother had nine pregnancies, my poor, dead sister-in-law had seven. I'm not blind, lass.'

'No . . . no,' Kirsty whispered.

'It doesn't show yet, lass, just in the eyes, but a woman would know. Your mother?'

Kirsty nodded.

'Thank God for that. Will she help you?'

'Yes.'

'The father, Kirsty. Marriage?'

Slowly Kirsty shook her head. Her voice was so low that Miss Purdy could scarcely hear. 'He's dead.'

The older woman sat down abruptly on the lavatory seat. 'Oh, God, you poor wee lass.'

Perhaps the sympathy was what Kirsty needed. She straightened up. 'I'll be fine, Miss Purdy. Really. Don't worry. Quick, there's the bell.'

That night she told Jessie about the takeover of the school. 'I'll have to leave a month early, Mother. I just can't bear another group of people knowing and talking, and I think Miss McNeil is still at Parkhouse and I don't want her to know.'

'We'll manage. Kirsty, Jamie Cameron was here this afternoon. He brought a hare.'

'That was kind.'

'He asked how you were. He knows, Kirsty.'

Kirsty looked at her mother incredulously. 'How could he know?'

'He loves you, Kirsty. I suppose that gives him a sixth sense. He didn't exactly say that he knew you were in trouble . . .'

Kirsty interrupted her mother fiercely. 'I'm not in trouble. I'm not, I'm *not*.'

'Oh, Kirsty, love. That's what the village will say.'

'I don't care what they say. I loved Hugh and he loved me and I'm glad, glad to be having his baby.' She broke down sobbing and her mother held her in her arms.

'Can you bear to have everyone talking about you, laughing at you? The schoolteacher, the Dominie's lassie, with an illegitimate baby. How will we be able to hold up our heads, lass? Your father's memory . . .'

'I think about him, in the night, when I think about Hugh. Everyone will say I've disgraced him. Is that what you think?'

'Oh, lassie. I scarce know what to think.' And then Kirsty looked at her mother and saw, for the first time, the changes in her. She too was thinner and paler. The eyes were tired, loving still, but oh, so tired.

'You lie awake too. Oh, Mother, I'm sorry. I've only thought of myself. I had it worked out. I can't go back to teaching, can't ever be what Father wanted, but next summer I'll go to the harvest. There'll be no men, except the farmworkers like Jamie. I'll get a job. You could look after the baby. That's what I'd planned, but you're ashamed. Your sewing ladies . . .'

'I'd prefer that you had waited till Hugh put a ring on your finger, lass, but I can understand. It was easy for Father and me – there was no worry, no strain, everything so nice and tidy. War's not tidy. I'll stand beside you with my head up, Kirsty, but could we not go to Uncle Chay? We could say you were a widow. God knows there are enough of them.'

'Mother, you haven't thought of Uncle Chay's feelings. I could pretend to the neighbours that I was a widow, but I couldn't lie to him. He deserves better from me than that.'

'Let him decide, Kirsty, please.'

'No. I won't put him in the position of having to decide. Oh, Mother, please. It will be terrible at first, but people will get over it. I'll get over it. People will forget.'

She was not surprised to find Jamie outside waiting for her next morning.

'Have you no work to go to, Jamie?'

'I'm taking the train in to order feedstuffs for the winter. I thought I'd chum you to the station. Carry your books, Miss?'

'I'm perfectly capable of carrying my own books, thank you.'

'I really came to tell you the Colonel's closing the castle for the duration.'

'What's that to me?' she asked sharply.

'They won't be back, Kirsty. The factor says no decisions will be made . . . no' while they're still shocked. But I think they'll sell up. Her ladyship never liked it – wasn't what she'd had in mind when she asked for a castle. Balmoral was more what she wanted, if you ask me, but the residents weren't keen to sell.'

Still she said nothing.

'I can always find the London address . . . should anybody want it?'

'I can't think of anyone remotely interested.'

They walked in silence for a while. Frost was everywhere, covering the ground with crisp, clean whiteness. Their breath formed clouds before them and Kirsty remembered how, years before, a little boy and girl had stood in the playground at Aberannoch, blowing clouds into the frosty air.

'If the estate's sold, will you be out of a job, Jamie?'

'Wouldn't think so. Good cattlemen are hard to find.'

'I'm glad you'll be all right.'

He put out his hand and held her arm. 'And you, Kirsty? Are you going to be all right?' He looked fiercely into her eyes and she blushed and dropped her lashes, almost with shame.

'Christ,' he said viciously. 'I hoped . . . but you never get what you hope for in this world, it seems. We'll need to hurry if we're tae catch the train. For God's sake, gie me your books. I'd dae it for any lassie.'

For the rest of the journey to Arbroath he said nothing. He touched his workman's cap in salute at the station and left her looking after him.

'Well, he's found out what he really wanted to know,' thought Kirsty, 'and he's the first to abandon me. Square your shoulders, Miss Robertson. You are on your own.'

20

KIRSTY ROBERTSON AND JAMIE CAMERON were married on New Year's Eve, 1915. There were no guests, no reception and no honeymoon. The bride was attended by her mother and by the groom's sister, Cissie, who had taken two days' holiday from her lucrative employment in the south of England. Jessie had made an effort to provide a special dinner but none of the wedding party seemed very hungry: even seventeen-year-old Cissie could not be tempted.

'I just seem that tired these days, Mrs Robertson,' she explained.

'You don't look well, lass, and your hair's a funny colour. I thought it was fashion at first, but it's not, is it?'

Cissie explained that there was a dust that hung in the air in the factory all the time, day and night, although, she hastened to assure her brother, she was not allowed to work at night. She was underage and her employers in the munitions factory were honourable men.

'I'll walk Ciss home,' said Jamie to his new bride after the dishes had been washed and put away. 'I doubt anyone wants to see the New Year in.'

'Good night, Mrs Robertson, Miss Robertson.' Cissie stopped talking and laughed. 'Here's me still crying you Miss Robertson: it's Mrs Cameron now. I'd never have believed when I was at the school that my brother would wed the Dominie's lassie, though mind, he aye thought the sun rose and set on your head, didn't you, Jamie?'

'Aye, lass, but Kirsty's your sister now. It'll be Kirsty and Cissie atween you.'

'Good night, Cissie,' said Kirsty and impulsively hugged the younger girl.

'Good night . . . Kirsty, and a very Happy New Year to you, to us all. I'll no' see you the morn, we'll all leave the newlyweds in peace, and I'm away south on the first train I can catch.'

'Leave the newlyweds in peace,' said Jessie bitterly when Kirsty had closed the door behind her husband and new sister-in-law. 'Whatever for? I'll go off to bed . . .'

'Oh, don't, Mother, we can't go to bed and leave Jamie alone on his first night in the house.' She looked at her mother. 'We'll get used to it, really we will.'

'It's not right, Kirsty. What bride sleeps with her mother on her wedding night?'

'That's the way it has to be. It's the way Jamie wants it . . . and me too,' she finished softly.

They sat down in the big armchairs before the fire and Jessie took up her sewing, new sewing, a baby's dress.

'Oh, Mother.'

'No one has seen it. I'm knitting, too. Some preparations have to be made.'

Kirsty lay back in the chair and as she rested she felt the baby move and her hands went protectively to her stomach, still almost flat. Four mouths. There was no way to disguise the fact that the Cameron baby would arrive suspiciously soon after his parents' wedding. The village would know, and most of the town of Arbroath, that the Dominie's lassie was nae better nor other lassies and had anticipated matrimony. And she'd mairrit a fermer laddie, her with all her education, her that her faither had aye said he'd intended for the university. He'd be turnin' in his grave, John Robertson.

'But you'd be pleased with Jamie, Father,' said Kirsty to the silent ghost.

For Jamie had not abandoned Kirsty when his fears about her condition were realized. Never once had it occurred to him to reject her.

Two days after he had left her at the station he had come to the cottage.

'Will you take a walk with me, Kirsty?'

Kirsty had looked at him standing there on the doorstep, his cap twisted in his hand, his Sunday tie around his neck.

'Jamie, you know . . .'

'Aye, I know, and we have to talk. Will you come, or will I say what I have to say here on the doorstep?'

They had walked away from the village, away from the Dell, up towards the pine woods. It was a cold, crisp, clear night and they had no difficulty in finding a good path.

'The Jerry aeroplanes will have no problem finding targets tonight, will they, lass?'

'Are we to talk about the war, Jamie? I have corrections to do.'

He turned to face her. 'I want you to marry me. I'll not have you shamed in the village, or your mother, or the Dominie's memory.'

Had she expected it? If so, not so baldly.

She looked into his face, but could not read the expression. His face was blank, only the eyes shone with the intensity of his feelings, but she could not interpret those emotions . . . love? Lust? Anger?

'I can't marry you, Jamie,' she said sadly and turned away from him to walk back to the cottage.

She had not gone far when he caught up with her, but he must have stood watching her and thinking: thinking of what? The shame to the Dominie's memory. Why should he care that she and her mother were shamed? He did not say they, she, meant anything to him.

'You've forgot Ella Grieve, the tinkler lass?'

'No, I remember her.'

'You remember she had a bairn and her with no man. They hounded her family from the area and she was but a tinkler lassie that nobody really expected tae ken better. You're the Dominie's lassie, Kirsty, next below the meenister on the steps to the Deity.'

'Oh, don't be silly. I know people will talk and wonder, but it will be over eventually.'

'And the bairn? Hugh Granville-Baker's bairn. Is he to be laughed at and cried the bairn of a whore?'

The word tore at her entrails like her mother's knife through the carcass of Jamie's hare. No, her mother was gentler, far. She stared at him for a moment, wide-eyed with horror, and then turned and ran, gasping for breath, towards the road.

A whore. Was that what people would say? Could she bear it? Could she tolerate being shunned and perhaps even spat at in the street? And her mother? Would Jessie be able to continue as a senior member of the castle sewing ladies, now meeting in the Manse? How would her precarious state of health, her fiercely won new serenity stand up to the knowledge of her daughter's shame?

'I should keep running,' thought Kirsty desperately. 'I should run and run into the sea, and that would solve the problem.' She stopped, bent over to ease the stitch in her side, and looked back to where Jamie still stood like a sentinel on the path. 'How can I marry him? How can he even ask me?'

She was crying as she let herself into the cottage. Jessie rose expectantly.

'Did you know?' Kirsty's voice was harsh.

Jessie looked troubled. 'Know what, lass? I hoped . . . well, that you two could . . . one day.'

'Jamie asked me to marry him, to save my name, for Father's sake, I think, or maybe even for the baby or for Hugh, though why he should care what folk say of an illegitimate child . . . What kind of marriage could we have? I loved Hugh, Mother. I could never, ever marry anyone else.'

She picked up her notebooks and carried them along to her room. Corrections had to be done. She was still the teacher, still the Dominie's lassie.

Jamie Cameron let himself into the byre where he slept above the beasts and cursed himself for a fool.

'You think yourself a poet, man, and you can't find the words to tell a lass what you feel. I should have said, "Kirsty, lass, I love you, I've always loved you, and I want to marry you even though you love someone else." He's dead. The Captain's dead, and I want to protect her: I have to protect her, for who else will? I can't see Lady Sybill welcoming a cottage lassie into her family, even though the lass is a teacher. Would he have married her if he'd come back? Did he know about the child?'

Jamie relived and relived his moments with Kirsty. Should he have held her in his arms as his whole body cried out for him to do? No, she would have hated that. She loved

EILEEN RAMSAY

another. 'I should have told her I'd ask nothing from her, just the right to care for her, to have her share my name, not my bed.' A vision of Kirsty in Hugh's arms came into his mind and he thrust it away. 'With my body I thee worship. With my heart and soul, too, Kirsty. Oh, yon was a cheap shot calling her a whore. I hurt you, my lass, and I could cut out my tongue. I wanted to shock you, to let you know what it will be like for you, to frighten you into letting me take care of you and the bairn. It should have a castle by right, and it's to be born in a cottage. Should I tell the Colonel? He's a decent man. Maybe he knows already, or is Kirsty Robertson too proud to tell him, to ask him for help?'

Neither Jamie nor Kirsty slept much that night, nor for a few nights after that. Jamie continued to berate himself for his lack of finesse and Kirsty saw the word 'whore' swim in the air above her everywhere. 'I can stand it for a few months. People will tire of laughing at me, there will be some new scandal. I'll get a job – there are plenty available with all the men at the war. Maybe I could give lessons to slow bairns here in the cottage. Who has money to pay? Should we move away? Where? Where would we go? If I marry Jamie we could stay. People will still talk but they'll think the baby is Jamie's. And when he's in school he won't be shamed.'

She remembered the illegitimate lass at Burnside who had always got the strap harder than anyone else, who had been picked on constantly. 'That never happened at Aberannoch school when Father was the Dominie. It won't happen now. This is a nice place to bring up a bairn.' If she married Jamie he would expect other children, wouldn't he? How could she be with Jamie as she had been with Hugh? 'I like Jamie well enough: it wouldn't be too bad, would it?'

Round and round went the questions but no answers came. Every morning she walked to the station and every night when she came back, Jamie was waiting at the station to walk her to the cottage.

'Please, Jamie. Why are you doing this?'

'There's riff-raff around since the war. I've no work in the dark and can spare the time to walk you home.'

They walked in silence for a while.

'I was upset the other night, Jamie. I should have thanked you for the proposal. It's not every man who would take on another's bairn.'

'Bairn?' Jamie sounded surprised. 'I wasn't thinking of the bairn, lass. It's you I love. Of course I'd love the bairn. They're easier than lassies. You love a bairn, it loves you back.'

Kirsty held the words, 'It's you I love', in her mind to savour later. 'I'd forgotten you knew a lot about children,' she said.

'Aye, maybe even more than you, Miss Teacher,' he laughed.

'People will talk if you walk me home every night.'

'Marry me to save my name, lass.'

'This is too serious for humour, Jamie.'

'Laughing's aye better than greeting, lass. I did enough of that, and maybe so have you. I don't ask to take his place. Think on it, Kirsty.'

'It wouldn't be fair to you. I can't stop loving Hugh because he's dead. I'll always love him, and I'm carrying his child. The baby will always be there to remind you.'

'I'll hold no grudge against a helpless bairn, Kirsty, and I'm the best judge of what's good for me. Think on it, lass.'

And Kirsty thought and decided to accept Jamie's offer. It had been an incident in school which triggered her decision. Sadie, the same lass who had seen her unwell, seemed always to be watching her closely, slyly.

'I'm imagining things,' Kirsty told herself, 'but she seems rather insolent. Not so bad that I could punish her or report her to the Dominie – and what would I say? "I think Sadie has found out that I'm pregnant." But if she does suspect . . .'

The suspicions came to a head when Kirsty overheard several of her class talking and giggling in the corridor.

'Fur coats and nae underwear: that's these stuck-up teachers that think they're better nor abody else.'

'Miss Robertson's no stuck-up, she's aye been really nice.'

'Aye weel, she's been affie nice tae somebody, I'm thinking.'

Kirsty turned with flaming face and returned to her classroom, where Miss Purdy sought her out.

'I brought you a cup of tea, Kirsty. Are you all right, lass?'

'The children, the girls . . .'

'You can't hide much from such big lassies, Kirsty. They've more experience of life than you have, for all the mess you've got yourself into. My mother used to say it was the good girls that got caught – the bad ones knew how to take care of themselves.'

'I must stay until Christmas. Another month's salary will make so much difference. The staff don't suspect, do they?'

'No one has . . . said anything.'

The inference was obvious and really, thought Kirsty, if the children suspected, then the staff – both ladies of inde-terminate years, and married men – must be considering the possibility too.

That evening Kirsty told Jamie she would marry him.

'I want to be totally honest with you, Jamie,' she began. All day she had been rehearsing her speech and she knew that Jamie might reject her when she had finished. 'I'm marrying you because I'm a coward. The girls in my class were laughing at me today, and I realized I couldn't bear the shame. It'll be bad enough that the baby arrives so soon after the wedding, if you still want to marry me, that is.'

'I love you, Kirsty. I always have,' he said so simply that there was no doubting his sincerity.

EILEEN RAMSAY

'I like you. I don't love you, but I'll try to . . . one day. Do you still want to marry me knowing that?'

'Your father was the only good thing in my life growing up, Kirsty. Your friendship. The things we shared, the wee triumphs, the tragedies. Do you remember when you fell down and tore the frill of your new apron? What a vain wee thing you were, but you were that clean, and smelled so sweet, like the meadow after the rain, and you sat beside me when nobody else would . . .'

'I sat beside you because we were the top of the class, Jamie, and I admired your intelligence.'

'We were friends.'

'Friends, good friends. Is that enough for a marriage?'

'It'll dae. I'll not ask more and one day, when your grief is no' sae new, maybe there'll be room for more.'

'I'll try.'

Jessie was delighted, of course, and wanted the wedding to take place as soon as possible, but Kirsty held out for the holidays. She could resign properly; there was no need for anyone to know anything other than that she was to be married.

'I'll move my things out of the big room and leave it for you and Jamie. He will want to live here, won't he? You can't possibly go down to the Camerons' cottage.'

'Mother, sit down, please, and listen.' Kirsty had wondered how to tell her mother the truth about her marriage, and this was the opportunity. 'Jamie and I will have a marriage in name only. Maybe later, after the baby is born . . . He wants me to have some time to . . . well . . . he hopes I'll get over Hugh.'

'You mean you're not in love with Jamie? Oh, Kirsty lass, marriage is hard enough where there's love.'

'We'll make do with liking and respect, Mother, for now anyway.'

'But Jamie's a man. He'll want . . . and you, Kirsty. You'll want . . . children.' Jessie was becoming more and more confused.

'Mother, I'll move my things out of the wee room. Jamie's delighted. He's been sleeping on the straw of a byre since he was twelve. Give us time, please, and we'll work it all out.'

And so they had arranged the strange wedding. Kirsty had decided not to invite even Meg or Miss Purdy, thinking that others would be hurt if left out and so it was better, in a time of war, to have a small wedding.

'It's so small it hardly exists at all, Kirsty. What would your father say?'

'He'd thank Jamie and he'd thank God for Jamie.'

Kirsty, Mrs Cameron, sat with her mother on the evening of her wedding day, because she was too shy to face her groom alone.

'We'll start as we mean to go on, Mother. When Jamie comes back I'll make cocoa, or maybe I'll offer him a dram since it's Hogmanay.'

'Best stay away from the alcohol,' warned Jessie quickly as she heard Jamie knock at the door.

'Don't chap, Jamie,' Kirsty greeted her husband.

'You're the tenant here now,' said Jessie. 'I gave your name to the grieve, and he said he'd inform the factor.'

'Thank you, Mrs Robertson. That was a kind gesture.'

'Only right, Jamie. Now if you'll excuse me, I'll away to my bed. We can have a long lie-in tomorrow since it's New Year's Day.'

'Cattle don't care about holidays. I'll be up at five, but don't worry about me. I'm used to doing for myself. Good night to you both.'

Kirsty watched her husband walk across the tiny kitchen and enter the small bedroom that for two years had been her own.

'Good night, Jamie, and thank you.' Strange words to say to your husband on your wedding night. She looked down at the slim gold band on her finger and felt the baby turn in her womb. Into her mind leapt an image of Hugh, so strong that she could almost feel his presence. It would not be banished, but stayed with her while she readied herself for bed and while she tossed and turned in the bed beside her mother.

'I'm married to one man, and my heart and mind and my very body are filled with the sound and smell and the child of another. Oh, Hugh, you must leave me in peace. Your child will grow up as Jamie Cameron's child. Leave us in peace.'

But the spectre or dream only smiled and, in her sleep, Kirsty smelled the scent of honeysuckle.

21

On the Sunday after her wedding Kirsty Cameron walked to the church where she had been married with her new husband and her mother. Apart from the minister and two elders, Jamie was the only man there. Balcundrum and his wife congratulated them.

'You're no' joining up, Jamie, lad?' asked the farmer. 'I hear the estate might change hands, and should ye find yourself out of a job there's aye one at Balcundrum, and a bigger hoos to go with it.'

'Thanks, Mr Lovett, but as yet I've no plans to leave the Colonel.'

'We'd never have thought you and Jamie, lass,' said Mrs Lovett, 'Not that you've not got yourself a good man – there's little of his father in Jamie Cameron, besides a strong back.'

She looked measuringly at Kirsty's figure, but as yet there was nothing to see.

'You were a naughty girl' – was there a slight hesitation? – 'not to tell anyone. Do we no' all need an excuse for a celebration? Hogmanay passing, and not one community party. I don't remember a Ne'erday like that in all my life. You won't have heard the auld meenister lost two of his boys at the close of the year? Aye, and the laddie wants to join up and him only sixteen years old.'

'Poor, poor man,' said Jessie.

The community had grown to like old Mr Close since he had come out of retirement to replace their own young minister, who was one of the first clergymen to join the army as a hospital chaplain. Now, almost two years later, everyone knew that Mr Close had married late to a wife almost too old for childbearing who had surprised herself and her husband by presenting him with three sons, one after the other in quick succession. She had died ten years before when her fourth totally unexpected son had been six years old. His father called the boy his 'ewe lamb', which was poetic if not biologically accurate. And now the poor man had lost two of his older sons, one a soldier and one a sailor.

'Oh, dear God,' thought Kirsty as she sat beside her brand-new husband in the pew and watched the old man, suddenly grown even more frail and bowed, climb into the pulpit, 'I'm almost glad there's something more excit-ing to talk about in the village than my marriage. What a horrid person I am.'

The minister's sermon was not, as she might have expected, on the futility of war, but on the theme, 'Love thine enemies'.

'He's too good for this world,' was the general assessment of the village. 'Did you notice the laddie wasnae in the Kirk? Him that's sat there every Sunday looking up at his faither as if at the Lord himself. It's a sad hoos this day: twa laddies dead, and a third that angry he willnae enter the Kirk.'

'Perhaps he's overcome by grief,' suggested Kirsty.

'Aye, he is, lass,' said the woman who had spoken. 'But he's angry with God for letting it happen and angry wi' his faither fer no' letting him at the Germans. And whit's this aboot a surprise wedding on Hogmanay? There'll be another wee surprise afore very long, I'm thinkin'.'

Kirsty blushed furiously and saw the knowing looks on the faces around her. She turned away to where Jessie already stood with her new son-in-law.

'I'd never have expected it o' the Dominie's lassie,' she heard the voice say. 'Juist shows we're a' the same under wir skirts.'

'Haud yer tongue.' It was Balcundrum's voice. 'You're in the Lord's hoos.'

There were tears in Kirsty's eyes; she could hardly see. This was what it was going to be like. Already there had been talk all over the village and the surrounding farms, and in such a closed community there was room for two stories at the same time.

'I can't bear it, I can't bear it. I thought I was strong enough, but I'm not. I'll never come to church again. They can talk about me but I won't have to look at them.'

'A good New Year to you, Mrs Cameron.' It was the minister, not bowed with grief but standing smiling at the door of his church, greeting his parishioners, getting on with his job.

'I'm so sorry,' Kirsty stumbled over the words.

'I have three angels in Heaven now, lass. A little more work and I'll be free to join them.'

He shook her hand and turned to his next parishioner.

Kirsty walked to her husband and her mother. She took the hand that Jamie held out to her and felt his strength. How could she survive if he was not there by her side?

'I should maybe think of a job at Balcundrum, Kirsty,' he said as if he was unaware of all the undercurrents. 'I never wanted to work with my father, but . . . What do you think, Mrs Robertson?'

'You must do what you think is right, Jamie,' said Jessie, who in the few days since the wedding had begun to treat Jamie with the same deference with which she had treated her husband.

'You'd come with us if we moved, wouldn't you?'

Kirsty looked anxiously at her mother. Moving? She and Jamie in one cottage, with the baby, of course. Jessie in another? How would they pay the rents? How could she live alone with her husband?

'We'll go on as we are while I'm useful, Jamie. But you won't always want a mother-in-law with you.'

'Mother, what are you saying? We agreed that Jamie should come and live with us.'

'Things will change, Kirsty. You will need more room eventually.'

'Not for a long time,' said Kirsty desperately. 'Will we, Jamie? We'll manage.'

Jamie squeezed her hand. 'I had no' thought of changing anything, lass. Balcundrum took me by surprise, and I could see myself grieve there one day. Who knows, though? There might be a bigger house, a better job at the castle. We'll wait to see how things go.' It was Jamie's turn to blush. 'I mean as far as jobs are concerned. The way folk are joining up, I'll be able to work anywhere.'

February 21st, 1916. Verdun. The Germans had decided to wear out the French army. They had to be ready to break, said the German generals at the end of 1915. France can stand no more; then we'll wear out England.

'There's too much fuckin' artillery in this bloody war.'

Only a Tommie could make a sardonic comment like that in a moment of extreme terror. But the terror wasn't over in a moment. It became as much a part of a soldier as the nails on his fingers or the hairs on his head. Had he ever known a life without this fear?

Shells screamed, 105s, 150s, 210s, and men screamed as they began to recognize just what shell was coming to blow their heads off, even the heads in the new steel helmets.

The minister's third and eldest surviving son, a boy who had wanted to be a concert violinist, died in the mud, his right arm blow to smithereens.

'You'll let me go now, Father,' cried the boy, George. 'They've killed Hamish. Hamish that couldn't squash a bluebottle but had to catch it and let it out the door.'

'Vengeance is mine,' said the old man while the tears for lost dreams, lost promise, ran down his paper-thin cheeks. 'The Lord will avenge him, lad.'

'Let me go. I'm ashamed not to be in uniform. Every man who is able, who is not a coward, has joined up.'

'No, lad. The good God has spared my ewe lamb to me.'

Old Jack Lovett, farmer at Balcundrum, found the boy's body hanging in the barn at the church glebe.

'He must have been unsound,' wept Kirsty. 'To kill himself because he wasn't allowed to join the Army?'

'His friends at the secondary school had all joined up,' said Jessie sadly. 'They called him a coward.'

'A coward? Three brothers dead in the mud. His father nearly seventy years old. Oh, the poor man. What will become of him?'

There were even fewer men at the Kirk the following Sunday. The Reverend Mr Close looked older and frailer than ever but his voice was strong. He preached on the text, 'The work Thou gavest me to do . . .'

After the service, after he had greeted the few parishioners who had turned up, he went back to the manse and sat down in his chair in his study while Balcundrum's wife prepared his lunch. It was his special chair, the chair where his boys knew they could always find a hug or a cuddle, where they could curl up with their father and tell the tale of woe and know that their side would be listened to, believed.

'There's time for a game of cricket before dinner, Father.'

Hamish. His pride and joy; his arms held out in welcome – both his arms.

Mr Close smiled.

'Two's hardly enough for a decent game, lad. I'll bowl for you.'

'We're all here, sir. You bowl, I'll bat and the bairns will field. Come on, young John. Help Father. He's not so young as he used to be.'

'John, my dear lad.'

'There's music, Father. You should hear our Hamish play.'

'My ewe lamb?'

'I'm here, Father. He understands and He forgives. Come on.'

And then the sweetest voice of all: 'I've missed you, dearest Andrew. Come on. It's time, it's time. We're all here, all waiting for you.'

'I've never seen anything like it.' Balcundrum's wife told the story over and over again. 'Died and gone to Heaven. How often have I said that? Looked as if he'd died and gone to Heaven. He looked thirty years old, not a day more. And the smile? Oh, please God, I'll be let die with a smile like that for the welcome I receive.'

'His text?' Jessie was almost in tears.

'The work Thou gavest me to do . . .' whispered Kirsty.

'A grand way to die, right enough, with a smile on your face,' said Jamie bitterly. 'He's another death that won't be counted. He died of grief, of a broken heart. Three men . . . three laddies blown to bits in action, and a fourth wee bairn by his own hand. He could thole no more, and dressing it up with Mrs Lovett's stories of last texts and last smiles doesn't change that. War kills mair than the soldiers in the field. Where will it say, "Killed in action, the Reverend Andrew Close. Killed in Action, wee George Close, aged just sixteen?"'

Kirsty looked at her husband. He sounded so bitter, but it was not his usual anger against the war: it seemed more directed against himself.

'Jamie, you don't want to go, do you?'

'Only madmen want to go to war.'

Jamie could not speak of the battles that raged not in Europe, but within himself. Living in the same house with Kirsty, seeing her body blooming with the fruit of another man, filled him with such longings.

'It should be mine.' He would clench his teeth together in the stillness of the night to save himself from crying out his plea. In the first few weeks of their marriage she had been up before him every morning to make his breakfast, determined to be the best wife she could be in their unusual circumstances.

'If you didnae fill me full of food at five in the morning I could get back to my bed, Kirsty lass, and have another hour's sleep. There's little I can do in the dark.'

'But I thought you always got up at five, Jamie, and you need to be fed.'

'Like the cattle,' he said bitterly. 'Sometimes I'm up at three, lass, but I pull my clothes on, run to the byre, feed the animals and I'm back afore the bed gets cold. Stay in your bed, lass, till the sun comes up. It's the sun directs a farmer's day, not a clock.'

'I only wanted to be a good wife,' Kirsty had almost sobbed, and the urge to hold her in his arms and console her and tell her that she was the best, most beautiful wife in the world, made him rush out into the darkness with no words said at all.

Jamie had decided that he would make no claims of any kind on his wife. He had seen marriage only as a way to lessen the shame the village would heap on the girl he loved: an extension of the life he had lived above the cattle in the byre. He had slept there, visiting his parents' cottage twice a day to eat. That is what he had thought marriage to Kirsty would be like, except that he would live in the house. He slept in the bed where Kirsty had slept, and the feelings and desires that swept over him as he tried to find some smell or trace of her on the sheets made him blush with shame. Several nights he ended up trying to sleep on the drugget rug that covered the wooden floor, so humiliated was he by the thoughts that came to him in the narrow bed.

Sometimes he would allow himself to dream of what life could be after the birth of the baby when Hugh Granville-Baker would be at least out of her body if not out of her mind. One day, one day, he prayed, Kirsty would turn to him. He did not expect her to love him the way she had loved the father of her child. Second-best would be enough.

'She always liked me fine at the school. Surely friends can love as well as like? I'll not rush her, frighten her, and she likes me a bit or she wouldn't have married me. She's afraid to be alone with me when her mother's at the sewing. Does she think I'll try to claim my rights?'

'Kirsty, can't you sit by the fire and read your book? You're that restless.'

She sat down holding the book almost defensively.

'It's easier to read if it's the right way up, lass. Would you be happier if I spent the evening in my room?'

She looked at him sadly. 'You said you loved me, Jamie, but you never want to . . . well, to kiss me or anything.'

He looked at her. What answer did she want? Was her vanity hurt that he made no attempt to touch her? Was she saying she would welcome more intimacy than the holding of hands in the village to present a combined show to their neighbours? Would he ever understand her?

'I love you, lass, but we made a bargain and I'll stick to it . . . if that's what you want.' He allowed no hope into his voice.

'Yes,' she answered with her head bowed so that the curls fell down around her cheeks.

'She's a bairn herself for all she's twenty-two,' he thought.

'Should you feel different after the bairn's born . . . well, I'd like to . . . we could start with courting, as if we weren't married at all.'

'All right, Jamie.' She raised her head and looked fully at him. 'I still love Hugh, you see. I can't get him out of my mind.'

'Or heart,' thought her husband sadly. 'That's fine, lass,' he said. 'You can't turn love on and off like a spicket for the water. Now, relax and read your book. We'll sit here like old married folk and be easy with one another.'

But keeping his feelings inside was not easy, and he found more and more to do around the farm, avoiding the Dell when he could for sometimes he thought he smelled honeysuckle there, or saw a shadowy figure. More than anyone he welcomed the longer days, days he could fill with work, so that he returned to the cottage too tired to do anything but eat and sleep.

And as the spring came, Kirsty answered the questions about the expected date of her delivery with as much equanimity as she could, and felt more and more gratitude to her husband, for at least she received no slurs for not having a ring on her finger.

There was talk of conscription, and a thing called British Summer Time which would change the very hours of the day and night.

'More time for us to be in the fields,' said Jamie. He had come to a decision, but he would wait for the birth in early May before he told his wife.

On the Western Front there was a continuing crisis at Verdun and General Joffre planned a joint offensive. A rebellion in Ireland at Easter caught the attention of the press for a while. James Joyce was preparing to publish *A Portrait of the Artist as a Young Man*, and John Buchan was writing his great war novel, *Greenmantle*. The composer Edward Elgar was writing 'The Spirit of England' and, jogged by the thousands of needless deaths on the battle-fields of Europe, scientists were experimenting with the refrigeration of blood for transfusions. Out of the darkness always comes the light.

Kirsty waited for the surge of energy that would tell her her baby was willing to be born, but it never came. She stayed quiet, almost lethargic, as fertile as the garden in which she sat dreamily watching the daffodils.

'There will be roses soon in the Dell,' she thought, and the pain struck her.

'Mother!' she cried in primeval fear, and Jessie was there beside her.

There was no time to send for Jamie from the fields, and no need. Kirsty's son came into the world as if determined to prove that he had caused enough trouble and would cause no more.

Wrapped in an exquisite hand-knitted shawl, he lay in his mother's arms and waited until his foster-father entered the room. Jamie tiptoed over to the bed.

'We're fine, Jamie,' said Kirsty. 'Don't tiptoe. He's had a good feed and now he's asleep.'

She was different, older. She had been somewhere he could never go, achieved something he could never achieve. He felt humble, in the presence of something sacred, miraculous.

'Oh, clever wee Kirsty,' he smiled. 'Isn't it you that's definitely top of the class!'

Had he heard the deep voice in his sleep? The baby stirred, yawned a delicate pink yawn and opened his eyes. Hugh Granville-Baker's eyes looked directly at Jamie and smiled.

'Goodness,' cooed Jessie. 'I know they say babies can't smile, but he smiled at Jamie.'

'Wind,' said Jamie, who had had time to control himself. He had never expected it, thought the baby would look something like his mother's last baby. All babies look the same . . . but not this one. Had Kirsty noticed?

'He's a grand lad, Kirsty. Have you a name for him yet?

'John,' said Kirsty definitely, 'after my father.' She smiled, a smile of such beauty, at her husband, 'and James, after you. If you'd like me to, that is?'

'I'd be honoured, lass. Welcome to the world, John Jamie Cameron.'

'Jamie-John,' said Kirsty. 'It sounds better.'

22

It was June. June flowed into July. Wild roses bloomed along the dykes and hedgerows at Aberannoch. Brambles grew strong among them and the delicate white blossom gave promise of the berries to come. The barley turned to beaten gold in the fields and the sun recast the still waters of the Firth into fields of silver to march beside the gold.

Kirsty sat in the garden, Hugh Granville-Baker's child at her breast, and Jamie watched. Oh, the look in her eyes, as if she was looking upon the face of God himself.

'All new mothers are like that,' he told himself. 'She's besotted with her bairn, not his father . . . or his foster-father either, I'm thinking.' He worked longer hours, and managed to put some money into the small savings account at the bank.

'Could I get a tenancy one day? There's no son at Pitmirmir.'

There was no change at the estate either. The Colonel and Lady Sybill Granville-Baker had no stomach for dealing with Aberannoch.

'Sell it,' Lady Sybill had said one day in the darkest hours of grief when she finally accepted that her bright boy was gone.

'The lad was happy there,' said his father, and the estate was no longer discussed.

Jamie-John was a good baby but when he cried, no one could quiet him like Jamie. He would lift the crying bundle in his strong arms and almost at once the furious yelling would die down to a sob and then the child would lie peacefully looking up at Jamie out of his beautiful blue eyes, eyes that had not changed in his two months of life.

'That's a good laddie,' Jamie crooned. 'Be a good laddie for Jamie.'

Kirsty smiled at the picture they presented. 'No, Jamie,' she said. 'He's not to call you by your first name. Haven't you earned the right to be called "Father"? If you'd like to, that is?'

'Like?' said Jamie. 'Like? Am I to be your daddy, my wee man?' And he danced the baby around the garden.

'He'll lose his dinner,' Kirsty warned, but it was too late.

'I'll clean him up,' said a chastened Jamie.

'And yourself as well.'

Jamie put the baby on the table in the front room and washed and changed him, and all the time he talked to him and Jamie-John followed the sound of his voice with his big blue eyes.

'We'll go fishing, Jamie-John, and I'll teach you to guddle salmon. It won't really be stealing because they belong to your grandfather. I'll show you the best places to watch the daft wee birds. Will you like that, wee mannie?'

Jamie-John burped and smiled at his surrogate father. Jamie looked into the eyes smiling into his own and his heart turned over in his breast.

'I'll not show you the best place. Your mammy will show you the Dell.' Again he saw Kirsty smiling, not at her baby but at the man she had loved. 'Ach, wee lamb, who could hold anything against you? One day, maybe your mammy will love me a little and what a happy family we'll be. I'll work all the hours God gives, laddie, for my two treasures.'

Life was almost perfect, but the war would not stay out of the little heaven Jamie had tried to create in the cottage at Aberannoch. There were rumours of great battles, battles won by feats of engineering. Whole German towns or trenches encircled by miners working like silent moles – and then the mines blown like volcanic eruptions. A new weapon, a bullet-proof machine that could crawl across any terrain like a caterpillar, was whispered about and then developed. They would be over thirty feet long and weigh nearly thirty tons, and they would end the war. They didn't . . .

And Jamie looked at Jamie-John at Kirsty's breast and almost died of pleasure when she smiled at him over the baby's downy head. Yes, his decision had been right. He kissed the baby, and very daringly and gently kissed the mother's cheek, and then walked to Arbroath, took a train to Dundee and enlisted.

'You'll be all right while I'm away, lass. My wages will be sent to you. It's for Jamie-John and you. I love you, Kirsty, with all my heart and I always will, but working the land isn't enough any longer. I don't believe in fighting and killing but if I can help, if my going shortens this war in any way so that this wee laddie can grow up free . . . And not just Jamie-John. Sometimes in my mind I see countless wee bairns: German ones, and Belgian, and Italian, and Russians and others forbye. War's an evil thing, Kirsty lass. Man's arrogance, that he thinks he's better nor another just because of the colour of his skin or his eyes or the way he eats or worships his God, makes me weep with shame. The war will end, no' by who is right and who is wrong but by who is stronger and richer, and that's the Western powers.'

He stopped talking, the longest speech he had ever made in his life, and blushed furiously, and Kirsty looked at him and wondered. What depths were there to this farm laddie who had had so little schooling but who was so wise and so kind?

'You're a good man, Jamie Cameron,' she said. 'I don't think I've ever realized just how good.'

269

He came closer. 'Ach, Kirsty, I'm not good. If you know the thoughts that sometimes come to me: thoughts about you . . . about you and me thegither.'

She looked down at the baby sleeping soundly at her breast, his little mouth still firmly attached. Asleep, he looked just like any baby. It was when he looked at her with his father's eyes, the eyes that everyone avoided talking about, that Hugh was closest to her.

'We could try, Jamie, to make a life, I mean,' and this time it was her turn to blush.

He knelt down beside her chair and put his arms around her and the baby together and laid his head on Kirsty's breast.

'This moment I'll cherish, lass. It's this I'll think on, and when I come back, I'll do my courting. I want you, dear God in Heaven, I ache for the warmth of you, but I'll not take you till all the ghosts rest in peace.' He stood up and looked down at her bowed head.

'I'll away to my bed. I'm up tae catch a train for Edinburgh the morn. Me in Edinburgh! I'll send you a picture postcard, and one for you to read to the bairn.'

Kirsty looked after him and, unchecked, the tears rolled down her cheeks. She admitted to herself that she had wanted nothing more than to lie in Jamie's arms as she had once lain in Hugh's.

'Am I fickle? I loved Hugh desperately. I thought I could never ever love anyone else.' But her body tingled with unfulfilled desire and she admitted to herself that she had wanted Jamie to kiss and to love her the way Hugh had loved her. She knew that had Jamie made one move she would have willingly gone into the little room with him. She sat down again by the fireside and imagined herself putting the baby in his crib and walking to Jamie's door. Jamie had done so much for her and here he was going off to war. He could be killed, hideously wounded.

'I'll go to him.' But still she sat while the room grew colder around her, and in his narrow little bed Jamie tossed and turned, and pondered that nobility could sometimes be a highly overrated virtue.

23

JAMIE WAS GONE, AND TRUE to his promise a card arrived from Edinburgh. It was for Jamie-John and read:

What a bonny place. I'll take you one day.
Love from Daddy. x for Mammy.

Kirsty could almost feel the pride – and the great daring – with which her husband had written the card. She pressed her lips to the X, to the kiss for Mammy. Had Jamie kissed the card too before he put it in the post box? Not for the first time did she wish she had overcome her inhibitions and gone to Jamie in his room.

'I loved Hugh and I always will love him, but I have to make a life with Jamie. I owe him that much.'

She did not believe that she could ever recapture the melting tenderness or consuming passion that she had experienced with Jamie-John's father, but she liked Jamie, had always liked him, and surely a deeper affection could grow? She remembered teaching the Merit Class about the system of arranged marriages in Japan. She had not thought much about the feelings of the young people involved in such marriages, but a child in the class had worried.

'Is all the fowk in Japan miserable then, Miss?'

And Kirsty had decided that no doubt many of them managed to get along together quite happily.

'Love grows,' she had added quite grandly without having any real knowledge of this fact.

'And it must,' she added to herself softly now, 'because I wanted to be with Jamie and I couldn't be like that with just anyone. Feelings grow: mine have changed for Jamie.'

There was not the breathless tingling that had been conjured up by even the very thought of Hugh, but still her feelings were not those of the young child, the Dominie's lassie, who had made a friend of the farmworker's laddie.

Jamie had joined the Royal Artillery and was now Bombardier Cameron.

'*I had the chance of the Black Watch,*' he had told Kirsty in his first letter, '*but I've never been keen on the kilt.*'

Jamie was a Scot who found no thrill at the skirl of the pipes or the whirl of the kilt. He thought the pipes shrill, preferring the fiddle. And as for the kilt? He could not, of course, tell Kirsty, but felt strongly that if he was to fall in the mud, he would much prefer that his limbs be decently covered.

Can you believe that I am across the Firth in Fife at a grand place, Mugdrum House, me, Jamie Cameron, that slept in a barn till an angel married him. I'm learning to ride a motor cycle, and what a brave man I am roaring up the driveways like the laird himself. I have to admit to enjoying the power of machines, but have a feeling I'll spend most of my time on somebody's old bike. Seemingly they telephone messages from one part of the battlefield to another and, the telephone being a distinctly unreliable instrument, they have to depend on pedal power.

Will they give me a medal to make my bonny laddie proud? Will I make his mammy proud? Is that not what I want more than anything? Oh, Kirsty lass, do I not know that it will be hard for you? I thought it out carefully. There should be enough for you to pay the rent and feed the three of you, if you're careful, and was I not the cleverest man in Angus to choose Jessie Robertson for my mother-in-law?

I have to face the fact, and so do you, my love, my heart, my soul — oh, Kirsty, could I speak to you the way I can write — but I may be killed, and God knows I would prefer to die than to be left hideously *deformed, but should I die, Kirsty, will you please write to the Colonel? He has the right to know about the bairn and he was aye a good man.*

Kirsty read the letter a hundred times and could not doubt that her husband loved her as a woman wants to be loved by a man. She was a churchgoer because her parents had taken her to the Kirk regularly, but now she went to church and prayed for Jamie and for the repose of the soul of Hugh Granville-Baker, who had died without knowing that he had fathered a son. She would not think of the possibility of Jamie dying, and therefore she did not consider informing the Colonel of the facts of Jamie-John's parentage.

Jamie's next letter came from the Front and said little other than that he missed her. He did not tell her what life was like on the 133rd day of the battle of the Somme, when the British called off their action. On the first day of that 133 days, Britain alone had lost 57,470 men. Jamie, who had never seen a hundred people together in his entire life, could hardly conceive of such numbers. He did not tell her of the horror of living, no, of existing, covered in slime, amid the stench of rotting corpses, desperately firing shells – one-third of which failed even to explode – at an enemy as exhausted and demoralized as himself. As Kirsty prepared happily for her child's first Christmas, Jamie did not tell her of huddling in a trench during one of the worst recorded winters ever experienced in Europe.

Kirsty bought a paper streamer and draped it around the front room to welcome 1917. Jamie woke from a doze to the sound of guns, the guns that were never silent. The thunder of one battle died down and the roar of another began. He could not conjure up the sound of bird calls in Aberannoch. He tried to hear Kirsty's voice, little Jamie-John's cry, but they refused to come. Only the boom of guns and the screams of dying men came. He tried to make part of his mind work with the lovely words the Dominie had taught him. Other men were writing poetry – could he? The words, like the birds' songs, eluded him.

When Jamie-John was a year old Kirsty decided to try to get a job. The baby was already walking and needed shoes so that he could play safely in the garden.

'Imagine having to think about the price of a pair of shoes,' said Jessie. 'We'll take it out of the bank.'

'The bank's for emergencies, Mother. I'll manage out of housekeeping. I wish I could teach. It's so stupid. Here's me, a qualified teacher, and the village school making do with an old man well past retirement.'

'He's a man, Kirsty.'

Kirsty looked at her mother in astonishment. Obviously Jessie still believed that a woman's place was in the home.

Had the war changed nothing for her? Was her mind still firmly anchored in the last great days of Victoria?

'Mother, can you possibly still believe that it's right to throw away education, talent, just because a woman gets married – and oh, please don't tell me that motherhood is a woman's crowning achievement.'

Jamie-John, who was playing with building blocks on the rug at their feet, looked up at the sound of the almost angry voices and smiled his devastating smile. Kirsty caught him up in her arms and covered his plump little face with kisses.

'It is, it is,' she said, setting him down again, 'but why can't we have both – motherhood and jobs – especially when we need the money? I'll sign on at the estate as a land girl.'

It was the very opening Jessie had wanted. For months she had been thinking about the every-day-more-obvious fact of the baby's parentage, and now she could quite naturally speak of it. 'The estate your son's grandfather owns, Kirsty. I've never ever said a word about it, but shouldn't you consider showing the baby to Lady Sybill?'

'The baby is Jamie's.'

'Kirsty . . .'

'Mother, please. Had Hugh lived it would have been different, but he's dead. I want nothing from his parents. That's not why I loved Hugh. I loved *him*, not the son of a great estate. Can't you understand that?'

'Very noble,' said Jessie drily. 'Oh, Kirsty, the bairn has the right to grow up the way his father grew up.'

'Morally, yes. Legally, no. I'll give Jamie-John what I can, Mother.'

'So you'll go and work all hours of daylight as a land girl and come home to him at night too exhausted to play.'

'Jamie will be a tenant one day. He'll work for Jamie-John and we'll give him a good home and love. That's all he needs.'

'Perhaps.' Jessie was still heavily involved in the village war effort: sewing circles, sphagnum moss collections for wounds, fresh eggs for wounded soldiers in the nearby hospitals, and so she saw and heard a great deal of what went on in the area. Now she said casually, 'I did tell you the castle is open again? The Colonel is here for a day or two. The poor man was wounded in the spring and has come back to recuperate for a wee while. There's a big house at Craiglockhart in Edinburgh being used as a hospital for wounded officers, gas cases and suchlike. He was there and took the opportunity to come north to decide about the estate.'

Jessie could see no change in Kirsty's expression.

'That's a splendid hospital,' she said. 'I did read that the poet, Siegfried Sassoon, was there. Wouldn't it be wonderful if he is well enough to write some poetry?'

Jessie rose angrily and put her constant sewing – this time a blouse for Jamie-John – on the table. 'Kirsty, consider your child. If the Colonel sells up, he'll never return and Jamie-John will have lost his grandfather. Here are we worrying about the price of a pair of shoes, and a few miles away sits a rich man ... Och, lassie, I know there was no thought of worldly gain in you when you ... fell in love with Hugh, but he could do so much for the bairn – schools, clothes, the university even.'

Neither of them considered the baby's legal grand-father – Jamie's father – who lived less than a mile away but whom they seldom saw.

'Had Jamie not married me, I might, just might have gone to the Colonel. I thought it all out, Mother. Perhaps he would have believed me – he'd have to believe me now ...' added Kirsty, looking down at the child with his blue-black hair and Hugh Granville-Baker's eyes. 'But what if he'd said he would support the baby if I gave him up? Could you give him up, Mother?' Kirsty did not wait for an answer. 'I couldn't.'

Jessie looked at the firm line of her daughter's jaw and saw that there was no more to be said.

In the panelled library of Aberannoch Castle, Hugo Gran-ville-Baker looked into the fire which he needed even in the summer and saw his son's face. The boy seemed more alive to him in Scotland than anywhere else. Sometimes it seemed to him that his son was more alive than his own marriage, which had deteriorated even further since Hugh's death. It was now strictly pretence: neither wanted the shame of a divorce, and neither admitted to having found someone else to love.

'Sybill can enjoy her discreet flings without sullying her family name, and me . . .?'

The Colonel thought of his constant companions for the last few years: fear, pain, cold, hunger, worry and, the hardest of all to bear, grief. A spark shot out of the fire and went black on the hearth. So bright and short had been his son's life. He looked at the portrait hanging above the carved fireplace. Hugh's merry blue eyes smiled back at him and he could not bear the pain. He rang the bell furiously and soon heard the limping steps of his batman.

'Pack us up, Frazer. I'll find out about trains.'

Kirsty Cameron had made up her mind: she would become a land girl for the rest of the war. When Jamie returned, everything would be different. He might even get a tenancy – if not at first, then in a year or two. Meantime she had a duty to do her bit. It was a lovely day and she would take Jamie-John with her, especially since she would soon be leaving him for hours at a time.

'Walk, Jamie-John. We'll go for a long walk today. All the way into the village, and then Mother has to see a nice man and you'll be a good boy and read your book.'

At fourteen months, Jamie-John was walking quite well, and he tried to help his mother get him ready for his outing. He submitted to having his face washed and his curls combed. He was not so happy about having to wait while his clothes were changed, but at last he sat in the second-hand baby carriage that Kirsty had found in Arbroath and rode like a king towards the village. In each fat little hand he held a chop-bone, for he was teething and Jessie firmly believed that the bone of a lamb chop was much better for him than any of the patent devices on the market.

'As well as easing his poor wee gums, he gets some nourishment from them,' she had said and Jamie-John, when he was given a bone, carried it everywhere with him.

It was a lovely day for a walk and it was almost two years since Kirsty had walked that way with Hugh, and his image came to her stronger and more strongly still as they approached the village. Tears, unbidden, flooded her brown eyes.

'Oh, Hugh, will I ever be free of you?' her mind whispered. 'This morning I wrote words of love to one man, and here is my whole body trembling at the thought of another?' But it was not a trembling with passion but the pain of loss.

'Oh, blast.'

Kirsty had not kept to the road but had wandered onto the grass verge and a wheel had come off the old baby carriage. Jamie-John was tipped sideways and expressed his displeasure in no uncertain terms.

EILEEN RAMSAY

'Hush, lambie. You're not hurt. Mother will lift you out and then I'll try to fix this stupid wheel.'

'Weel,' said Jamie-John, and was rewarded with a hug for being such a very clever boy.

Colonel Granville-Baker saw the girl in some difficulty as his car swept down the driveway.

'Stop, Frazer, and I'll give her a hand. No, not you, you old goat. My legs are better than yours.'

'Car,' said Jamie-John, and Kirsty looked up to see her nightmare realized. Her baby's grandfather was about to see him. She picked up the baby and pressed him close against her shoulder.

'It's all right, sir, I'll manage,' she said breathlessly.

'Glad to be of assistance,' said the Colonel and lifted the carriage out of the verge.

Jamie-John heard the deep voice. He pulled his head away from his mother's shoulder and turned to the sound.

'Bome,' he said, and with a devastating smile offered Colonel Hugo Granville-Baker a damp and well-chewed lamb bone.

24

MEN WERE SO SCARCE THAT Kirsty did get a job on the estate. Conscription had come in and most able-bodied men had gone to the Front. The work was hard and the hours were long but, to her surprise, she found that she was healthier than she had ever been before. She missed Jamie-John terribly but when she was working in nearby fields, Jessie would wheel him down to watch his mother at work and they could eat their midday meal together. Kirsty wrote to Jamie every week: the letters of a woman who had been married for years and years, not those of a breathless young bride. She painted a picture of the changing seasons and of the progress of their small son. Jamie wrote as often as he could. Sometimes weeks would pass without a letter and then several would arrive at once:

This is not the land in the Dominie's geography books . . . I would like fine to see France when its fertile fields are not swimming in blood or its blue sky not hidden by choking clouds.

Mostly, however, he wrote about his hopes for their marriage and its future:

> *Oh, Kirsty lass, what a man you have married, for I should tell you that I never slept a wink that last night. I kept thinking of you and wondering, dare I be brave enough to go to her . . . to ask her. I wanted so much to hold you, Kirsty, but was so feared that you would turn from me in horror. No, I made a promise and I'll keep it, but oh, I love you, lass. Does not the smell of you that comes to me in dreams keep me sane in this insanity. I wish I could really believe in why I'm here, or at least understand. Sanity is you and Jamie-John and the land.*

Kirsty wept over that letter. 'I should have gone to him. Why didn't I? I wanted him, and in the Dell I wanted Hugh.' Hugh?

The Colonel obviously had seen nothing in the baby's face. When they came face to face outside the castle, Kirsty's heart had certainly played a tattoo, but he had said only, 'Grand wee laddie,' as he returned to his car. It was several days, however, before Kirsty quite relaxed, and by that time she had been well into working with the harvest.

'Oh, I'll never take a simple slice of bread so much for granted again, Mother,' she said as she stretched out in front of the fire, tea over, the baby in bed.

'You're looking well on it.'

'I'll have bigger muscles than Jamie when he returns.'

Jessie laughed. 'The old Scots saying, "Hard work never killed anybody", must be true, Kirsty, for you've never looked better.'

'I enjoy being out in the fresh air, but there'll be no work in the winter unless I can get something with cattle, and I'm afraid of the big brutes.'

'Surely we've saved enough to help us through?'

'We'll manage, I suppose, but we must have depended quite a bit on Jamie's poaching, and there's been no fish from Meg for a while.'

'She's got over not being asked to the wedding?'

'She's forgiven me, I think, but she hasn't really forgotten. Then there's the baby.'

Meg had hoped to conceive a child during her brief honeymoon, but had not.

'Oh, sometimes it takes a while,' said Jessie. 'When this war is over . . .'

Everything was 'When this war is over'. Would it ever be over? Had there been a time when it never was? The days at Burnside with the Buchanans and Miss McNeil seemed like a life that must have belonged to another girl. The innocent lass, interested mainly in the swing of her petticoats or her shining brown curls, who had been so shocked and disgusted by Mr Buchanan's abhorrent behaviour, seemed to have nothing to do with this strong, supple young woman who looked back from Kirsty's mirror. 'You did take your teaching seriously,' Kirstly consoled her mirror image, 'and you were good, or' – and here maturity helped her out – 'at least you were well on your way to being good, and it's a senseless waste.'

'I shall join the suffrage movement, Mother, when this war is over, and petition for women's rights.'

'I don't think there is a suffrage movement any more,' said Jessie in a tone that said quite plainly, 'Thank goodness.'

The suffragettes had been quiet over the period of hostilities, directing their not inconsiderable efforts to fighting the common foe instead of injustice.

'Mother, I'm surprised at you. We're fighting a war such as man has never before experienced or even contemplated. More men are dying in a day than fell in whole wars, and you think we'll go back to what we were before. Never! Maybe no actual battles have been fought on British soil, but things like attitudes and prejudices are being wiped out and life will never be the same.'

'The papers say it has to be over soon. There will be a final push and it'll all be over.'

A few weeks later Kirsty took Jamie-John into Arbroath on the train to visit his Auntie Meg. There had been a letter from Meg telling how lonely she was with her husband and brothers away, and how bored she was since there was little fish being caught.

Mrs Stewart was in the town at the little family shop and Kirsty and Meg looked at each other a little warily after many months of avoiding one another.

'I'm sorry we haven't kept up, Meg,' said Kirsty after the first few strained minutes, when they had exhausted the questions about their husbands and families. 'I've been so involved with the baby and then working. I'm a land girl, you know.'

'I wondered why you were so brown, but it suits you, Kirsty.'

'So Mother says.'

They drank tea and nibbled biscuits in an awkward silence and finally Kirsty bent down to fuss over Jamie-John, who was perfectly content on the floor with some spoons.

'To be honest with you, I was hurt you never invited me to your wedding,' Meg burst out at last. 'And then when the baby came so early I understood and I was angry again . . .' She stopped in mid-sentence as Kirsty stood up. 'Och, Kirsty, I wasn't making a moral judgement. I was hurt you didn't trust me to understand, to be there with you.'

Kirsty looked at her. How could she explain that she had never once thought of Meg or her appraisal, that all she had been able to think of for months was Hugh Granville-Baker dead on a battlefield? Obviously, since Meg knew neither Hugh nor Jamie, she had not realized the truth of the baby's parentage. There was surely no need for her to know. Very few people in the Aberannoch community had even met Hugh, and she was doing her best to keep the baby as sheltered as possible. Soon, surely, Hugh's parents would sell the castle and then she and her secret would be safe.

'I didn't doubt your friendship, Meg,' she was able to say honestly. 'It just wasn't an easy time for me.'

'Oh, morning sickness, you poor thing.' Meg was obviously very happy to wallow in a lovely woman-to-woman talk about marriage and pregnancy. 'You know, for a few weeks after Will went, I was sure I was . . . in the family way. I even bought some things, nappies and a wee rattle. Silly, isn't it?'

'I'm sorry, Meg, but you'll have children when Will comes back. Sometimes it takes time.'

'Time? You got married and didn't even tell me about it, and the next thing I hear is that there's a baby on the way sooner than it should – and, oh Kirsty, I was so jealous, I almost hated you.'

What could she say?

'I'm sorry, Meg.'

'He is beautiful and so good. Will he come to me, do you think?'

Jamie-John Cameron had made another conquest.

Mrs Stewart came back from the shop and was delighted to renew her old friendship.

'You shouldnae hae held away, lassie. Is it no' the guid lassies that get caught? You're aye welcome in this house, and this braw wee mannie forbye. And noo tell me all aboot yer mither and yer man. Are no' a' my laddies away and we miss them sair, do we no', Meggie?'

It had been a successful visit and on the train back to Aberannoch Kirsty was deeply content. She had missed her friendship with Meg, and could now look forward to renewed visiting. And in the basket by her side, under a covering of damp seaweed, lay a fine healthy haddock.

Winter came and with it an end to Kirsty's employment, but her allowance from Jamie came regularly and there was little hardship at the Dingle Cottage. She ached for the war to end and for Jamie to return. The baby was growing so quickly and she was sad that Jamie missed all the firsts: the first tooth, the first words. By the end of 1917 Jamie-John was already talking quite coherently and his mother and grandmother wondered at his intelligence. Had there ever been such an advanced child?

'If only the war would end . . . if only Jamie would come home . . .' Kirsty echoed the thoughts of women all over Europe.

Kirsty sat alone beside the fire and waited for 1918 to come in. It had somehow seemed important that, this Hogmanay, she stay awake and welcome the New Year.

Surely, surely this year of 1918 would bring an end to the war and a beginning to a new and fulfilling life with Jamie, the Jamie she had come to know and to love through his letters. Kirsty sat, her book forgotten on her lap, and admitted what she had never before fully accepted: she loved Jamie Cameron and she wanted him in every way. He was not Hugh. Hugh: she saw him, heard his voice, every time she looked at his child. She would never forget him, she did not want to forget. But her mourning was over and she wanted Jamie, Jamie who had given her a name to save her from disgrace and who had given her baby a father. She rose from her chair, and as 1918 came in she wrote to Jamie and poured out her love and longing.

In May 1918, five weak British divisions were sent to the quiet sector of the Chemin des Dames to recuperate. Jamie's section went with them. He did not know of the indecision among the Chiefs of Staff as to how, or even if, to defend the area. He did not particularly care. Only Kirsty's letters pressed against his heart reminded him that he was a human being. She loved him: she loved him and he longed for the war to be over. He did not know that French Intelligence was lulled into a sense of security and that a heavy German build-up was not even suspected.

At 1 a.m. on the 27th May, Jamie-John Cameron's second birthday, the third battle of the Aisne began. The zone of fire was over ten miles behind the front line and every position, every village, farm, chicken coop, every road, bridge, railway line and bus stop was systematically shelled. Gas came with the shells, so that the British were blinded, and to make matters worse there was a morning fog.

'They're in league with the devil,' cried the corporal next to Jamie. 'They can make the fog come whenever they want it.'

Jamie did not reply.

The Corporal turned. He was alone. Where Jamie Cameron had been was a pool of mud and blood and some bits of clothing.

'Pair bugger,' said the Corporal. 'And on his bairn's birthday.'

Kirsty had to tell Jamie's parents of his death. They had never responded to any invitation she had issued, and she had never been asked to visit their small cottage.

'You're still the Dominie's lassie to them,' Jamie had explained, 'and you know I never got on with my father. It's best to keep away. Cissie will visit you if you ask her.'

The telegram arrived on a Wednesday morning when Kirsty was alone with her son. She opened it dully, knowing full well what it would say, and then she sat for a long time staring at nothing, at years and years of nothing, until the baby demanded her attention and she rose, like an old woman, to attend to him.

'Why, Jamie-John?' she asked as she unbuttoned him. 'Why? He was such a good laddie all his life.'

She helped the toddler sit on his pot and sat down beside him on the carpet. 'Your daddy's not coming back, Jamie-John.'

That was when she realized that Jamie's parents would have to be told. She should, perhaps, have waited for Jessie.

'I can't write a note,' she told the little boy. 'I wrote a note when you were born, but they never said anything. I can't write them a note today, I'll have to see them. Come on. Let's go for a walk.'

She wrapped the child up warmly and set off across the fields to Pitmirmir farm. The outside of the Cameron cottage was neat and tidy, but there were no rows of cabbages or potatoes or Brussels sprouts growing to keep the family through the winter. Jamie had always planted vegetables for his mother and her large family, and no one had taken on this task when he had gone to the war. Kirsty knocked at the door and eventually it was opened and thick smoke and a blond little boy tumbled out together.

'Mammy, it's a wuman wi' a bairn,' the boy yelled back into the house.

A moment later Kirsty was face to face with her mother-in-law. She held out her hand to Jamie's mother.

'Hello, Mrs Cameron. I'm Kirsty, Jamie's wife.'

The woman looked at her coldly. In the worn face Kirsty could see the remains of what had once been freshness like Jamie's. 'I ken fine who ye are. Whit dae ye want here?'

'I have bad news, Mrs Cameron. May I come in?' The truth of the news she was carrying had only just hit Kirsty, and she knew that if she did not sit down she would fall. 'My Jamie, my Jamie came from this?' her heart was crying.

Mrs Cameron staggered back into the smoke-filled front room. 'My laddie,' she said. 'It's my laddie.'

'Yes,' began Kirsty . . .

'Don't you come in here, bitch, whore! Don't you come in here! You took my laddie, the only good thing in my life, and you sent him away tae get killt. He wouldnae hurt nothing, my Jamie, a gentle laddie that liked books and flooers and playing wi' his wee brithers. He'd nivir hae gone tae the war if he'd been happy. He found oot that bastard wisnae his, didn't he, ye jade? Look at him, look at him. His faither's face is plainted on him. Ye werenae guid enough fer him, were ye? Jist guid enough tae lie wi'. Get away afore I hit ye, ye slut!'

The door slammed shut with a violence Kirsty had only once before experienced. 'Slut, whore!' She had been called that before. Was it more accurate now?

She grabbed Jamie-John's hand and ran and stumbled across the stubble fields, the child protesting and crying all the way. Jessie met them on her way back from the castle and without asking anything picked up the child and soothed him.

'There, there, Grandma's wee darling. It's all right. Hush now, hush,' she murmured as she hurried beside her daughter to the security of their cottage.

'I'm sorry, I'm sorry. Oh, Jamie-John, did Mother frighten you?' Kirsty took her child and held him closely. Over his head she looked up at her mother. 'Jamie's dead,' she said, 'and I thought I should tell his parents. Oh, Mother, I'll never forgive myself, never.'

'Tea,' said Jessie. 'Sit down, Kirsty. I'll see to the child and then we'll talk.'

And so Kirsty was allowed to mourn for Jamie and, in mourning for her husband, she was able to mourn for Hugh. The tears that she had kept hidden two years before flowed now and mixed with the genuine outpouring of grief for Jamie: Jamie, her husband who had never been her husband; Jamie, the poet who had been unable to write poetry. After the grief came anger, anger at the futile waste of young men, of old people, of unborn babies, of the very buildings ravaged by war. She cuddled Jamie-John to her until he protested vehemently and restored her equilibrium.

'His own mother didn't know just how good a man he was. She thought I'd tricked him into believing Jamie-John was his child. But he didn't go because he was unhappy, Mother, did he? He said it was time.'

'He'd have been called up anyway, dear. You mustn't feel guilty. He knew you loved him.'

'I was never a wife to him. I gave him nothing and I don't even know whether he got the last letters I wrote to him.'

That was the nightmare that Kirsty took to bed with her night after night. If only Jamie had known of her growing love for him. If only he had known that she had wanted to be his wife in every way. Every night, unable to sleep, she sat and stared into the fire.

'I'm twenty-four years old. I have loved two men and they are both dead. I have a two-year-old son and an ageing mother. How am I going to keep them alive? I am a teacher who is not allowed to teach. I must find a job.'

The future for Kirsty Robertson Cameron looked very bleak.

25

KIRSTY CLOSED THE DOOR OF the flower shop and, with a thankful sigh, locked it and slipped the key into her pocket. It had been a hard day and tomorrow would be even harder. Everyone who could afford it wanted flowers or wreaths for the holidays. Her fingers were red and almost raw from forcing holly around the wire circles which formed the foundation of the wreaths. She shuddered with distaste; she could not understand this liking for putting holly wreaths on graves. For her, holly was a happy flower, no matter its connections with Christ's death. Mind you, she had no grave on which to put mourning flowers. Jamie and Hugh were in unmarked graves in France; only their names remained – carved on the new memorial in the village church.

She and Jessie made no special effort to visit John Robertson's grave at the festive season. If the weather was good on the Sunday nearest to Christmas, they slipped into the churchyard for a few minutes.

'I think about him every day,' Jessie said, 'and he would not have liked a wreath of holly. He liked a sprig of it behind the old photograph of his mother at the New Year.'

'If there's any holly left tomorrow, I'll buy her some,' Kirsty thought as she hurried in the sleet towards the station.

There was no one on the train she knew well enough to chat with, so she was able to relax completely on the short journey to Aberannoch. She surveyed her shopping bag with satisfaction. She had stockings for Jessie, and Kirsty smiled to herself as she thought of her mother's face when she opened the small parcel. All her life Jessie had knitted her own stockings, and would certainly find the new stockings quite decadent.

'She'll probably save them for taking Jamie-John to school for the first time,' Kirsty thought fondly.

Jamie-John. At four and a half he resembled his father more and more every day. Next year, 1921, he would be going to the village school where his grandfather had been Dominie so many years before. Jessie threatened to look for some paid employment when her grandson was at school all day, for she was determined that Jamie-John should go to the university as his father had done and as his mother should have done had she been able.

Kirsty smiled again at the thought of her small, sturdy son at university, and looked down at her bag where a little box of toy soldiers and a bright red ball were hidden away for wrapping for Christmas morning.

The train pulled into Aberannoch station and Kirsty gathered her shopping together for the part of the journey she hated. She still had to walk to Dingle Cottage. It was a pleasant enough walk on a summer evening, but in the winter, when it was pitch-dark and the rain and sleet soaked her despite her umbrella, she could imagine a bogey-man, or worse, around every corner.

'Keep to the middle of the road,' she told herself, 'or you'll end up in the ditch and be really wet.'

She refused to acknowledge her feeling that, should anyone be skulking in the hedge to leap out on her, she would possibly hear if not see them from the middle of the road.

As she turned the corner from the churchyard Kirsty was surprised to see lights from the trees that hid the bulk of the old castle. Her heartbeat quickened. There were so many lights it could only mean that some member of the family was in residence. Who? Why? As far as she knew the family had never spent Christmas at Aberannoch Castle. They came for the shooting around the start of the New Year, but no one had been since the end of the war. Only the caretaker and his wife lived there now.

'Whit a cushy job,' was the verdict of some of the villagers. 'Naethin' tae dae but dust a few bits furniture and watch the money roll in.'

'They couldnae pay me enough tae stay there,' said others. 'That many rooms tae clean, and the place must be hoochin' wi' ghosts, and bluidy draughty forbye.'

'Someone's taking an inventory for a sale,' decided Kirsty, and her musings on the effect of a change of ownership kept her mind busy until she was home.

'Och, you're wet,' said Jamie-John after his first rapturous greeting of his mother.

'Doesn't he sound like an old woman,' laughed Jessie, but Kirsty didn't join in the laughter. Jamie-John spent most of his time with his grandmother, and did indeed have the vocabulary and sentence structure of someone much older than four.

'Sooner I get you into school with other bairns the better,' she thought, but she said nothing. Jessie looked after the little boy six days a week. She doted on him and cared for him devotedly. No child in the area, Jessie had decreed, was good enough to play with her grandson; she did not want his accent adulterated by the sounds of Angus.

'He'll pick it up at school,' thought Kirsty, 'and I can easily see that he becomes bilingual. No reason why he shouldn't manage English and Scots.'

But she kept these thoughts to herself and went off to change her wet clothes.

'I wish we kept Christmas Day as a holiday,' she said as she came back into the warm front room.

'Irish stew,' said Jessie, gesturing with a ladle. 'What about the New Year? It's tradition to have a holiday at the New Year.'

'We could have both.'

'Both,' echoed Jamie-John and the doting women laughed.

Later, when he was in bed and Jessie was working on the sewing that Kirsty pretended not to see and never to recognize on Christmas morning, Kirsty mentioned the lights in the castle.

'I'd choose a warmer time of year to sell,' said Jessie practically. 'We sat through some chilly sewing afternoons during the war. And that was despite a fire roaring up the chimney.'

'Lady Sybill hasn't been back since 1914. It will hardly be her.'

'There was a picture of her once in a fancy magazine,' said Jessie. 'I meant to show you. "Lady Sybill Granville-Baker and Lord Somebody or other enjoying a day at the races". You know the kind of thing. It certainly wasn't the Colonel in the photograph. What a handsome man he was when Father and I first met him – Hugh would have looked just . . .' Jessie bit off her thread in her confusion.

'It's all right, Mother. I'm aware of Hugh every time I see his son, and so Hugh's father is bound to see a resemblance too, this time. Thank goodness he's come in the winter. No need for long walks with Jamie-John.'

'I'll make some cocoa and we'll get off to bed. You work harder in that shop than you ever did on the land, Kirsty.'

'No, it's just that I don't like the work so much, and Netta does enjoy playing the boss. We really created our own wee monster there when we suggested a career in flower arranging!'

Kirsty's employer was Netta Humphreys, once Netta Spink. She had managed to accumulate enough money – she said – from working in a munitions factory in the south of England during the war, to start her own little business. She had been delighted to hire 'the Dominie's lassie' as a shop girl.

'I saw flower shops in London, Kirsty,' she had explained. 'There was always someone in the front to speak nice to the customers, somebody a bit superior. It's great you needing a job but, of course, till I really get started you'll need to help out in the back shop a bit too.'

A year later Kirsty was still doing two jobs, running from the freezing-cold back premises, where she sorted flowers and made bouquets, to the front shop every time she heard the bell as the door opened. Too often, unfortunately, it was Netta's husband, ostensibly the delivery man.

Sam Humphreys was the kind of man who thought of himself as all things to all women. He had offered, after three months of wandering hands and suggestive talk, to 'help the little widow out'.

Kirsty had looked at him, at first in amusement and then in growing dismay. He really meant it.

'You know,' he said, 'you must be really needing it now and I've got plenty to go around.'

'I'll pretend you didn't say that, Mr Humphreys.'

'Sam, darling, Sam. Come on, a pretty bit like you. Netta's told me all about you. You must be gasping by now, unless there's another farmer waits for you in the hedges.'

Kirsty pushed his hands away from her waist. 'How dare you!'

'Oh, lah-di-dah, aren't we? Don't try to play the grand lady with me. You need it, I've got it, and I'm willing to share.'

'One more word and I'll speak to Mrs Humphreys.'

'She won't believe you, sweetheart,' said Sam, but he did move away from her. 'Thinks the sun rises and sets on my head, she does. Besides, Netta's used to all the women chasing me. If you knew what she had to do to catch me. Whew!'

He went out laughing and Kirsty sat down in a chair until the trembling in her legs stopped.

What an arrogant and unpleasant man. She should leave right now: leave and never come back. But she had to stay, at least until she could find another job. She would look for advertisements as she did her shopping. She could even clean houses, although it was a job she hated and had never had to do. Jessie had always done everything.

'Oh, Mother, how you spoiled me. I can't ever let you know about this. I've given you enough grief already.'

Now, at her own fireside, Kirsty smiled at her mother and took the proffered cocoa.

'I should have made that, Mother. You work all day long.'

'In my own wee house with my own wee boy. It's you that has the hard job, Kirsty. I wish you weren't always so tired.'

'It's the winter. I'll feel better in the spring.'

'Kirsty, I've been thinking. Well, you know dear, you haven't really had much luck with men . . .'

It was Sam Humphreys' face that swam before Kirsty's eyes but she did not speak of him. 'Of course I have, Mother. Hugh was wonderful. Sometimes, it all feels like a beautiful dream, and then I see his son and I think, "Hugh loved me." And Jamie? One day I'll tell Jamie-John all about Jamie, everything.'

'Yes, dear, but they're dead. I don't want to be brutal but you have to start again.'

'I have started again.'

'You want to spend the rest of your life working yourself to death for Netta Spink?'

'I'm working for my son,' Kirsty interrupted.

'Who needs a father.'

Having delivered her bombshell, Jessie lay back in her chair and watched her daughter.

'He's had two.' Kirsty's laugh was rather thin. Until the moment her mother had spoken she had truly never thought of trying to find another husband, and she certainly wanted no 'arrangement' with Sam Humphreys.

'I had sixteen happy years with your father. I have things to remember. You're so young, Kirsty. I married your father when I was your age, and here you are widowed and with a wee boy and you've never really been married.'

'I've never thought of marrying again,' said Kirsty thoughtfully, and until that moment she never had. She looked into the fire. Eventually she and Jamie-John would be alone, and then the boy would grow up and go his own way and she would be left in the little cottage. Years stretched ahead of her, filled with employers like Sam Humphreys and boring jobs that she was unqualified to do.

'I've been in love twice, Mother, and I'm glad I had that much. I'll never love again, and besides, there are no men left to love.'

It was New Year's Eve and the shop was busy. Even Netta had come in; she was making a superb arrangement.

'You'll never guess where this is going, Kirsty,' she said with a smirk.

Kirsty tried to think of who among their customers could afford such an expensive arrangement.

'It's for the castle,' said Netta. 'I wrote to them when I started in business. You've got to be aggressive, you know, or you won't get anywhere . . . told the Colonel he'd really started me off and how grateful I was . . . and then three days ago there's this letter on fancy paper saying "Good Luck" and, although his own man usually does the flowers, would I do something special for the New Year. A shooting party, I shouldn't wonder, with lords and dukes, but, of course, you'd know all about that, wouldn't you?'

Kirsty looked at her in distaste and saw, hidden away under the folds of flesh, a little fresh-faced girl with a bunch of field flowers in a jam jar. 'I know nothing of the Colonel or his movements, Netta. If you'll excuse me, I'll finish this holly wreath.'

Netta said no more, but Kirsty was left with a feeling in the pit of her stomach as cold as her red hands. What had Netta meant? Why should she assume that Kirsty knew anything about the Colonel? Surely all the gossip about little Jamie-John had died down, replaced by a newer and juicier piece of gossip? Besides, no one could connect her with Hugh, could they?

'I'm away tae find Sam tae deliver these flowers.' Netta poked her head round the door. 'You'd think he'd be here waiting, knowing I had this important order, but he'll be at a pub telling everybody how he won the war. I'll go look for him, but tell him where tae go if he gets back afore me.'

'Wouldn't I just love to tell him,' thought Kirsty, but she called, 'Fine, Netta,' and went back to her arrangements.

She heard the bell on the door and a few seconds later it rang again. She pulled off her apron and tidied her hair for the front shop, then went in with a smile that froze as soon as she saw her 'customer'.

'Your wife's looking for you. You just missed her,' she said, and turned to go into the back shop. 'That big arrangement's to go to the castle.'

'I know,' he said, and to her horror he had followed her into the workshop.

'You'd best take it before she gets back.'

'She'll be ages. I saw her go. There's plenty of time for what I came for.'

He pulled her up from the stool where she was sitting and made as if to take her in his arms. She could smell the alcohol on his breath and terror rose like bile in her throat. It was Mr Buchanan all over again, but this man was not impotent – far from it. She could feel him strong against her as he pulled her to her feet.

She screamed, 'Let go of me, let go!'

He seemed to enjoy her struggles. 'That's it, darling,' he mouthed against her hair. 'Did you struggle for all the others afore you gave it to them? Is it better that way?'

His mouth was on hers blotting out the memory of Hugh and his gentle kisses, and she retched. Then his hand was inside her blouse and he was pushing her up against the wall.

Oh, God in Heaven, this could not be happening.

His hand left her breast and began to push her skirt up around her waist. Desperately she struggled and then, salvation, over his head she saw the furious face of Netta Spink.

'You wee slut!' yelled Netta. 'I knew you couldn't leave them alone.'

Kirsty almost fell as Sam released her. 'Slut!' That word again. She stared at Netta. Surely she couldn't believe Kirsty had led Sam on? She couldn't have seen what she saw as she entered the shop and believe her husband innocent?

'I'm sorry, Netta hen,' said a cowed Sam. 'You know my wee weakness, and she's been at me since she started. I came in for the deliveries and next minute she's got me ben the back shop tae wish me a Happy New Year, and I'm no' strong, Netta. I wish I was.'

Netta looked at her husband with distaste. 'Aye, I ken your weaknesses fine, Sam Humphreys.' She turned to the still trembling Kirsty.

'I've wantit tae say this to you since the minute you came crawling in here looking for a job. Get oot, you slut, afore I throw you oot. The Dominie's lassie, wi' her bouncing curls and bonny ribbons, wi' her starched petticoats. And the habits o' a rabbit. Get oot before I take an ad in the *Herald* tae tell the world you had a go at my man.'

Kirsty could not speak; she could scarcely breathe. Netta could not believe she had propositioned Sam unless, of course, she wanted to believe it. Blindly she felt behind her for her coat and her bag and rushed wildly from the shop.

'Run tae yer fancy man. Tell him I'm bringing the flowers.' Netta's words followed her along the street.

Kirsty stopped running. People were hurrying, but mad flight like this would cause comment. She started to walk towards the station, and then went right past and began the long walk to Aberannoch. She needed time to compose herself. It was New Year's Eve; she had no job and had forgotten to ask for her week's wages, and no force on earth could make her go back for it.

'Happy New Year, Kirsty,' she whispered softly.

26

THE FIRST FEW MONTHS OF 1921 were sheer hell for Kirsty. She had told Jessie that she had walked out of the flower shop on New Year's Eve because of Netta's demands, and if Jessie ever felt that it was silly to throw one job away when there was no others available, she made no complaints. Every day, when the weather allowed, Kirsty walked into Arbroath and looked for a job, any job, but the ones that were available were always given to returned soldiers. Every Friday she went to the bank and withdrew the minimum amount of money needed to supplement her income so that they could live reasonably for the next week, and panic rose in her throat as she saw the balance dropping, always dropping. She would have to leave Aberannoch, and Jamie-John. There was nothing else for it. Only in an industrial city could work be found. She began to frequent the library, too, on Fridays. She was no longer interested in whether or not John Buchan was writing, or Picasso was painting or Elgar composing. The city newspapers listed jobs available and surely, surely soon there would be a factory somewhere advertising for unqualified help.

Once a month, with Jamie-John, she visited Meg and Will in the fishermen's cottages, and that weekend she withdrew a shilling less for Will always gave her fish to take home. Meg's husband was a quiet, shy man and he would not make the journey out to Aberannoch when it was Meg's turn to visit, but he loved to sit quietly in a corner of his front room and play with Jamie-John, who always gravitated towards Will when the women had stopped fussing over him. Meg no longer spoke about babies. After three years she had decided that there were to be no children and she made the most of the nephews and nieces, who arrived with amazing regularity every year, and of Jamie-John.

Meg's two oldest brothers, Alex and Tam, had survived the war and were more political than ever. Often when Kirsty visited, the entire clan would assemble and the adults would drink quantities of strong tea and talk and talk while the children played with Grampa or quiet Will, neither of whom took much part in political arguing.

'The war tae end all wars,' Alex would quote every time he had the chance of an audience. 'A country fit for heroes. Well, if grinding poverty and ill health is whit this country thinks its heroes deserve, then I want nane o' this country. We'll change things, Kirsty. Come and join us. Whit has Britain done for you? A widow woman wi' a wee laddie, and they're tellin ye they dinnae gie a damn that yer man's deid, that a woman wi' your education is washed up like one o' faither's auld boats. And oor Meg that loves bairns wi' a passion and wis that guid wi' them? Do they say, "Take yer love o' bairns and yer talent for teachin' them intae the schools?" No, they gie the jobs tae men because they're men, no' because they're better teachers – and some o' the pare bit walkin' wounded that's teaching these days. It breaks yer heart tae see them, jumping in the playground when a laddie that needs his backside skelped slips up behind them and claps his hands.'

'Men have families to keep, Alex.'

'And you don't? Come on, lassie. We want equal rights for all, men and women baith, and a clever lass like you should join the movement.'

For a moment she longed to tell him that she would if she were staying in Angus, but she could not speak, not yet, not until she had found a job, any job that would keep a roof, albeit a rather leaky one, above their heads.

Alex's talk of job opportunities and civil rights reminded Meg that Kirsty still had found no work. She interrupted her brother.

'Kirsty, Tam's wife is in the family way.'

'Oh, how nice.'

'She works in the shop on the High Street, and she'll need to leave. It's mainly selling. The fish is usually cleaned down here.'

'Ach, Kirsty's too fine for gutting fish.'

Tam seemed not to resent his grandfather's supposition that what was good enough for the wife of his grandson was not good enough for his granddaughter's friend.

'There's nae workin' wi' the fish, Grandfather, juist sellin' them. Kirsty could dae that, and it's nae caulder than Netta Spink's flower shop, Kirsty.'

'It's very good of you, Tam. To be honest I'd actually thought of moving away – getting a job, maybe even in England.'

'England?' Meg made it sound as uncultivated and as far away as Outer Mongolia. 'Why on earth would you want to go to England? And what about your mother and wee Jamie-John?'

'I'd leave them until I could find another house.'

'My case entirely, Kirsty,' said Alex triumphantly. 'You'll maybe land a job, lassie, that pays you half whit it pays the man beside you, but a hoos? Gin there was one available who'd gie it tae a young lassie when there's veterans wi' families lining up like shoals of mackerel ready tae dive intae the net? Join the real world, Kirsty, and fight for the rights of women here in Angus.'

Kirsty's head was buzzing when Meg and Will had finally seen her onto the train and it started its ponderous run to Aberannoch. Selling fish, the Dominie's lassie selling fish? Why not? 'Oh, Father,' she thought, 'you wanted so much more for me and I've let you down badly. I'll take the job and do it as well as I can, but a life of fish? We used to laugh together at dear Meg because she always smelled of fish. Your grandson smells of it now, but his little tummy is full of it lovingly caught and cooked for him by fine, fine people who are giving me a chance. I won't have to uproot Mother. And I'll join the Women's Suffrage Movement, and maybe Alex's people too.'

Jessie was at the station to meet them.

'Mother!' cried Kirsty, her heart beginning to beat rapidly. 'What's wrong?'

'Nothing, dear,' Jessie said as she wrinkled her nose in distaste at the smell of her small grandson wriggling delightedly in her arms. 'I thought you might be tired and I came to help.'

'Will took him on the boat – no, no, not out to sea, but he was allowed to "help", weren't you, my lamb?'

'I'm a fisher laddie, Gramma,' said Jamie-John.

'Not if I have anything to do with it,' smiled his grandmother grimly. 'Hot baths for you two, and then lovely macaroni and cheese.'

'Yum, yum,' said Jamie-John. 'We had roast beef, Gramma, and we've brought all my fishes with us for tomorrow.'

'There's a letter from the estate, Kirsty, probably about the leak. I hope they won't put the rent up.'

'I'll get him off to bed first. Don't worry, Mother. The Stewarts are giving me a job and so, even if we have to contribute to repairs, we'll manage.'

Kirsty could tell from the expression on her mother's face that Jessie did not relish the idea of her daughter working in a fish shop. A mulish expression came over her own face: it was honest work and she was lucky to get it.

'We'll talk about it after I get him off to bed, Mother, and then I'll see what the factor has to say.'

Deliberately they changed the subject: no talk of any business until Jamie-John was in bed and everything tidy again for the morning – Sunday, a day of rest. There had been too many for Kirsty Cameron lately, and she could almost look forward to going back to work. Next time she went to the bank, it might even be to put money in. She smiled as she walked along beside her skipping son who was recounting, with a bit of embellishment, his adventures.

She was so tired that she almost decided to leave the letter until the next day. If she ignored it and went to bed, she knew that she would worry about its contents; if she read it and learned that the rent was going up, she would worry just as much.

'I'd best see what the factor has to say about my complaints,' she said as Jessie was about to retire to Kirsty's old room.

Kirsty neatly and carefully slit open the letter with her father's old brass opener and read it. Then she sat down abruptly on the chair beside the table and let the letter flutter from her fingers.

'He wants to see me,' she said, her face as chalk white as the expensive paper. 'The Colonel. Tomorrow. Oh, Mother, he must know about Jamie-John. What if they want to take him from me?'

Colonel Hugo Granville-Baker had not immediately recognized his son's face in that of the small child whose perambulator he had righted. He had thought the child handsome and had said so to the mother, the Dominie's lassie, if he recalled right. He'd heard she'd married some farm laddie. A bit of a comedown after all that education, but rumours of the state of the morals of the new Mrs Cameron had infiltrated the castle walls more easily than English spears had ever been able to do, and he had sighed, said, 'Ah well, who am I to judge?' and dismissed them from his mind. Or tried to, because that small face with the big blue eyes and the engaging gap between the front teeth kept coming between his eyes and the papers he was reading.

'Dear God in Heaven above,' he had exclaimed loudly in his club one night when he had tried vainly several times to locate the price of his shares, and his disturbing of the peace and earned him several loud 'Tut-tuts' from aged members. The child was Hugh's. There could be no doubt!

He pored over baby pictures, pencil sketches, portraits. The eyes, the teeth, the set of the little ears, the curling black hair. The child was his child, born again. But how? Mind you, the boy had always loved Aberannoch and had been there on leave several times, and by himself. And then one day the Colonel had opened the little parcel of Hugh's effects and the bloodstained letter had slipped from the back of the paybook where it had rested for five years: a letter of love that had never been posted because the writer had died before he finished it. The Colonel had cried over that letter as he had not wept when the news of his son's death was brought to him. He was a man, for God's sake, a Colonel in His Majesty's Forces. His crying would be done inside where only God could see it.

But another man had acknowledged Hugh's child. Had he thought it his own? Was the girl promiscuous? His grandson the child of a slut? He would tear him from her! No, no, slowly, slowly. Watch and listen as you have done all your life, Hugo, and come to an educated man's conclusion. Now the girl was widowed, it would be easier to take the child. Nannies, prep school, Eton, Sandhurst. Hugh again, all to himself, without Sybill and her wretched blue-blooded interference.

'Shall I come with you?' asked a trembling Jessie next afternoon.

'No. I'm sure it's nothing. I was overwrought yesterday, I overreacted. He didn't mention Jamie-John. He can't know, and even if he guessed, I can deny it. Jamie saved us. He's Jamie's child in the eyes of the law.'

'The Colonel is so wealthy, and Lady Sybill – she's related to lords.'

'Then she won't want to acknowledge a bastard grandson,' said Kirsty brutally, and was furious with herself when she saw Jessie wince. She kissed her mother softly. 'Don't worry, Mother. I won't let anyone take Jamie-John away from us. If we have to, we'll go to England and get a job there. I'll change my name, anything. No one will take my child.'

Bravely said, but after a few minutes in the Colonel's magnificent panelled library, a room she had seen only once before, Kirsty laughed at her foolishness. The Colonel never even mentioned Jamie-John.

He had poured coffee into cups of a porcelain so fine that Kirsty had marvelled that it could even tolerate the weight of the liquid.

'Milk or cream, Mrs Cameron? Sugar?'

Would he get to the point?

'Mrs Cameron, I have a proposition to put to you.' He saw her stiffen and regretted his choice of words. How often had he gone over this conversation in his head, and still he hadn't got it right? 'Not just me. The Board.'

She looked at him strangely. Of course, for her the Board had always meant the school board, and he laughed. It was almost the same thing.

'Several friends and colleagues of mine met here over the New Year period, Mrs Cameron. We are all men with one particular thing in common: we lost at least one child in the war.' His face clouded for a second, and he paused and did not say, 'For some it was an only child.' 'We don't want marble memorials to our children. No cold winged ladies on great columns bearing their names. We want a living memorial. They were young. We thought of the young who survived, who should have a chance to do with their lives what our boys ... and girls had no chance to do. In short, a school, Mrs Cameron. A school here ... for orphans. What do you say?' He looked at her excitedly.

'I don't know what you want me to say, Colonel. It's a lovely and generous idea, I think.'

'I want to turn the castle into a school. A great deal of work has been done already, and the first group of boys will be here in August. Later there will be girls, and perhaps even children from Belgium and France. We can't mend all of Europe's wounds, but maybe some. And we want you, in a way a casualty of the war, to be our first teacher.'

There, he had said it. Should he have started with that? Her face had lit up. An enchanting little thing. With her eyes shining like that, he could understand what Hugh had seen in her. The war had not been kind. He looked at her hands, rough and red, on the Crown Derby. The thin gold wedding ring. Would Hugh have put one there, had he survived? She was looking at him very straightly and directly.

'Why me, Colonel? You important men must know many men who would want a job like this?'

'I liked your father, Mrs Cameron. I know he taught you well, and your references from former colleagues are exceptionally good. And then, you are the mother of a war orphan and will surely have an affinity with these children.' He could not say what his heart wanted him to say: 'And because my son loved you and you are the mother of his child.'

'Could I explain a little more of what we have in mind – our long-term plan, as it were. We have ten boys from Glasgow, London, Liverpool. I think that's the first lot. Their ages range from five to ten, and you are used to teaching a wide age range in one classroom. Next year, we'll add a class and another teacher, a man to help with physical education, although I hope to find an old soldier in the area who'll come in once or twice a week. Each year we'll add a class, and perhaps we'll have girls too. The top floors will be turned into dormitories, and we'll need a matron. I thought of Mrs Robertson. Some rooms on this floor will be converted into a flat for you, or whoever takes the job. You would need to be on the premises, you see. This room we would keep the way it is: ideal for interviews, don't you think, and a lovely view of the gardens?'

He rose and invited her to join him at one of the windows. Below them lay the walled gardens.

'Pretty bleak now, Mrs Cameron, but see the snowdrops, and in a week or two there will be thousands of daffodils, and in the summer, roses. Do you like roses?'

She did not answer, her eyes full of unshed tears. He left her and returned to the fireplace while she composed herself.

'It'll be hard work: practically twenty-four hours a day for a while, but worthwhile, I think.'

'My son?' she asked softly.

'Oh, there'll be room for him,' he said lightly. 'Ten boys or eleven? There are a couple of nippers. They'll be company for one another.'

'I'll take the job, Colonel.'

He reached out his hand and she put hers into it, and as they shook hands she looked up into his eyes – Hugh's eyes.

He offered to send her home in his chauffeur-driven car, but she needed to walk, to think, to pinch herself to make herself believe it was true. A job doing the only thing she was good at, a generous salary and a rent-free home! And Jamie-John would be growing up in his father's old home. Hugh had never played in the walled garden where Jamie-John would play, but he had been there, had loved it.

Hugh's father watched her walk away and his hand fingered the wallet, inside which was Hugh's letter. By rights it belonged to the girl, and he had meant to give it to her. She should know that her lover had been thinking of her just before he died. But the time wasn't right for her to know that he was aware of the boy's parentage. For her sake she had to believe the job was hers because of her ability.

'You wouldn't have thought of a woman for the first teacher if she wasn't your grandson's mother, Hugo,' his conscience told him and he replied to it firmly. 'We wouldn't ever have thought of a school as a memorial if it wasn't for the boy.'

'What does he want from you, from Jamie-John?' asked Jessie when the news was broken to her.

'From me he wants a devoted and caring teacher, Mother – and Jamie-John? I don't know. He said he could come too, quite lightly. Perhaps he doesn't know. He's only seen him once.'

'How often will he be there? If he's there constantly he'll see the child . . .'

'Don't worry, he won't be there, not often. There's a Board, a Trust, of eight men. The Colonel has given the castle and the gardens, but not the farms, and each of the others has put in money to keep it running. They have lawyers and accountants and bankers to make the money . . . well, make money, I suppose. The children's families can't contribute. I start, with a salary, from today, and you too. We need to supervise the conversion of the castle and ordering of supplies: books, crayons, slates, chalk, toilet paper, food, everything . . . sheets. The lawyer is coming tomorrow to see both of us. Oh, Mother, you will come with me and be Matron, won't you?'

'I don't know, Kirsty. The idea is exciting but terrifying, and what will everyone in the village think?'

'About what? There will be other jobs, Mother. We'll need cleaning staff and a cook and a janitor. The Board or Trust will pay the gardeners, if they want to stay on with eleven little boys running all over the place. I'm terrified, but oh, so thrilled. It's the chance of a lifetime. Teaching, Mother! The only thing I ever wanted to do . . .'

'In Hugh's home, Kirsty, with memories of him everywhere.'

'My memories make me happy, and just think, you didn't want Jamie-John to have an Angus accent.'

'No,' Jessie brightened.

'Glasgow's much worse,' Kirsty laughed and went off to put her son to bed.

The next day all three of them set off for the castle. The Colonel watched for them from the drawing room windows, and as he saw his grandson skip between his mother and his grandmother a groan of agonizing pain forced itself between his lips. Could he bear to see the child, the unacknowledged child, to hear his laughter echoing in the empty rooms?

'The ladies are here, Matthew. No need for me to interview them. I'll see you at lunch.'

The Colonel's manservant, who acted as butler when the Colonel was at the castle, opened the door to the little family.

'Good morning, ladies, young gentleman,' he said. 'Mr Matthews will see you in the library.'

They followed him up the stairs slowly as Jamie-John's sturdy little legs struggled with the height and depth of each stone step.

A man rose from the chair by the Colonel's desk and came towards them and, to her surprise, Kirsty saw that he was quite young. She had thought all lawyers were elderly, balding, stooping figures, but this man was no more than thirty and certainly seemed to have all his hair. She realized that she was staring and blushed, pulling her hand away, conscious for the first time in months of how rough and red her skin was.

'I'm Matthew Matthews, Mrs Cameron, Mrs Robertson, lawyer for the Aberannoch Trust.'

They could never be ready in time. Kirsty would stand in a dust-filled room and look at bare walls and floors and try to see the rooms filled with beds or desks, and could not. For weeks the workmen seemed to do more harm than good as they pulled down one wall here, erected two there, discovered dry rot in a floor and pulled everything out again to replace the bad with good. Then came an army of women with buckets of hot soapy water who scrubbed and cleaned and rinsed and, under Jessie's eagle eyes, left not one speck of dirt. The painters came and soon there was a 'Blue Dorm' and a 'Yellow Dorm'. The smaller boys would be in 'Blue', the older ones in 'Yellow'.

Matthew Matthews came in often from his office in Arbroath, and never seemed to flinch when Kirsty discovered that they had completely forgotten yet another item without which the school could not possibly function.

'I had a telegram from the Trust yesterday,' he told Kirsty one morning in late July. 'Sir John's found five more boys in Edinburgh.'

Kirsty looked at him in mock despair.

'Seems only right to have two Scottish cities represented,' he said.

'Sixteen boys?'

'The Trust thinks you should hire another teacher.'

They were sitting on boxes in what was supposed to be the classroom and Kirsty looked around. 'Another teacher? Where? We're supposed to open in two weeks.'

'You must know someone – a married woman, perhaps.'

'A married woman – not necessarily a widow?'

'A good teacher, Mrs Robertson. Someone who can relate to boys, some of whom are quite disturbed by trauma.'

'There's room for five more desks in here, if we can get five more desks, and I just might know someone. She lives in Arbroath.'

'I live in Arbroath and I'm going back there now. May I drive you? There isn't much time.'

'Well, that's very kind of you.' Kirsty looked at the watch pinned to her blouse.

'It's lunchtime,' said Matthew. 'We could have a bite somewhere.'

'A bite,' Kirsty echoed in confusion.

'Yes.' Matthew laughed and it was, Kirsty decided, a very nice sound. 'Food, Mrs Cameron. You seem to manage very well on air, but I starve following you around this great barn with my notebook. If we drive in, on business, to Arbroath, to see this teacher, well, why not stop at the inn and have a little lunch? You do eat, don't you?'

'Of course I do.'

'Good, then may I take you to lunch?'

Kirsty hesitated. Lunch? She had never been out to lunch, to any meal with a man. A picnic, oh, a picnic, once, oh so long ago, she had gone on a picnic.

'Mrs Cameron?'

She blushed. 'I'm sorry, Mr Matthews. No, I mean, yes, I would like to have a bite.'

'Good, we could discuss converting another room. Bigger boys in here, little ones . . .?'

'Somewhere with a view of the gardens,' said Kirsty, picking up her hat. 'Oh, my mother. I forgot. My mother and son are in the flat. I should tell her.'

'I'll wait outside.'

A few minutes later Kirsty joined him and turned to wave to a small figure with face pressed against a window. How Jamie-John would have loved a ride in a motor car!

'I'll drive him around the courtyard when we get back, Mrs Cameron,' said Matthew, and Kirsty smiled gratefully at his discernment.

'You have children, Mr Matthews?'

'No. I'm unmarried.'

'This is a business meeting,' thought Kirsty, 'but I'm glad he's not married. It wouldn't seem right having lunch, even a business lunch, with a married man.'

They couldn't talk in the car for the wind, and the noise of the motor took the sound away. Kirsty lay back against the leather upholstery and submitted to the enjoyment of speed.

They lingered over lunch. There were so many things to discuss. A simple little thing, lunch in a public restaurant with an attentive and, yes, an attractive man. Matthew was a different man from Mr Matthews the lawyer with his codes and figures and strictures, and Kirsty Cameron felt light years away from Mrs Cameron, head teacher of the soon – God and the plumbers willing – to be opened

Aberannoch Castle Preparatory School for the sons of servicemen. The most important decision in the world was whether or not to have syllabub or apple tart for pudding, or even whether to have a dessert at all. Kirsty relaxed and visibly softened. It was with real regret that she finally stood and announced that they must see Mrs Barber soon, or they would arrive just as she was preparing an evening meal for her husband.

Matthew's hand lingered on hers a little longer than strictly necessary as he handed her into the car. They were each aware that a new stage in their relationship had been reached. They were Matthew and Kirsty, and already took it for granted that there would be another lunch soon.

'Or a concert, Kirsty, or a play. I'll find out what's on in Dundee. You need a break from constant concern about the school.'

A play – she had been to a play once when she had been at Burnside Primary. The breathless hush when the curtains opened, when the lights went up . . . she could never forget it and now she would go again.

But for now, Cinderella had better go back to her fireplace and her cinders.

'Lovely, Matthew, I would enjoy that very much, but now we must see Mrs Barber and then I must get home to Jamie-John.'

27

THE ABERANNOCH CASTLE PREPARATORY SCHOOL opened not with a blaze, but more with a small glow of publicity. The Trust did not think newspaper reports too helpful to the work it was trying to do, and none of the members relished reading the names of their own lost children again in the press – once had been more than enough.

There were 'Letters to the Editor'. Some wondered how a bunch of women could handle sixteen sturdy boys. Others applauded the Trust for hiring qualified women whose only fault in the eyes of the law was that they had chosen to marry as well as to teach. There were men on the staff, of course: a janitor, three gardeners, one of whom had committed himself to giving a gardening lesson every Thursday afternoon – weather permitting – and Sergeant Sydney Kinloch, late Black Watch. Sergeant Kinloch was to take the boys for drill: big boys Monday, Wednesday and Friday; small boys Tuesday and Thursday. For the next ten years he was to bemoan to Kirsty that if he could only get a few bigger laddies he would have a better football team, and that what so-and-so needed was a good hiding. Sometimes Kirsty felt he was right on both counts.

A football team had not been discussed when the school opened. Jamie-John was the smallest, but there were six others under eight, and only nine boys between the ages of eight and eleven. By Christmas the boys had been divided into two teams, eight-a-side, and Kirsty, Meg and Jessie would watch them from the windows as they ran shrieking up and down the lawn. Meg had relished the idea of going back to work, but Will had been adamant that he wanted his wife at home.

'I'll usually be here when you get back, Will,' had been Meg's argument.

'It's no' right, a married woman working.'

'But I help out in the shop sometimes.'

'That's different,' was Will's male logic.

'How is it different?'

Will had cast around in his mind for an answer. 'Women's always worked wi' fish.' He heard his answer and thought for a moment as Meg waited. 'So why no wi' bairns, Meggie? Is that it?'

'Aye, Will, that's it, love.'

It had been agreed that Meg would start with the first term but if she found the work too demanding, she could resign at the end of term with proper notice to the Trust.

Meg was to take the smaller boys, who included Jamie-John. Kirsty was to take the older ones, and that was how she got a third qualified member of staff.

A few days before the proposed opening of the school, she went into Arbroath to visit the now retired Miss Purdy, to ask for her advice.

'Keep them interested,' had been her advice over a cup of tea, 'and keep them busy.'

Kirsty had looked around the tiny room. 'You must miss your family,' she said.

Miss Purdy's brother had died during the war, and his eldest son had established his wife and family in an already overcrowded house. Miss Purdy had been lucky to find a tiny house on a pleasant side street quite near her old home.

'They didn't ask me to go, you understand, Kirsty dear, but we were always too many generations in one house and my room was needed. I have most of my dear mama's best pieces here,' she stopped and looked rather sadly around the crowded room, 'and I would like my eldest niece, Sarah, to have them one day. Her husband was wounded in the war, poor man, and there's little money. I do miss the hustle and bustle of a house full of children. Although at my age, peace and quiet are nice too, but not all day, every day. Still, enough of my moans. Tell me all about this wonderful new school.'

And Kirsty had told her, and as she had talked an idea had been slowly forming in her head. Some boys had suffered incalculable trauma during the war: there would be remedial work to be done, and who was to do it? Her own programme was already as tight as possible, and Meg was to leave every evening to catch the four o'clock train. At four the boys were to have tea, and then time to play before six o'clock when they were to do homework. After homework it would be baths and bed. During the home-work period Kirsty hoped to do tutorial work. What if they all need extra help? she thought now as she listened and talked to Miss Purdy and, even worse, what if some were so clever that they needed extra stretching?

'I'll pop in to see you again when I'm in the town,' she said as she rose to go and Miss Purdy, who had always seemed to know exactly what was in Kirsty's mind, said, 'And if I can ever help with a little coaching, or even just listening to or being with a laddie – sometimes some-body to be with is all a bad laddie needs – I'd be more than glad to help out. I wouldn't need wages: I've enough to manage on.'

Kirsty had gone straight from the little house to Mat-thew's office. He rose from his desk when his secretary announced her with a smile of pleasure on his face. The door closed behind Miss Smith and, still holding her hand, he leaned down to brush Kirsty's lips with his. It was the second time he had kissed her; it was pleasant, no more.

'Matt, this is business.'

'I honestly didn't think my charm had brought you. Something to do with the school?'

She told him all about Miss Purdy and her years of experience with boys, both in and out of school. She did not hide how old the former teacher was.

'It's the evenings that worry me, Matt: just Mother and me and fifteen boys, and I have to find special time for Jamie-John.'

'And for me, I hope, Kirsty.' He looked at her anxiously.

Kirsty smiled at him. For two weeks Matthew had been almost as underfoot as her little boy, and almost as much of a nuisance, but it was nice to have a motor car to whip her into Arbroath or even to Dundee if something was quickly needed. They had had coffee at Lamb's Coffee House and last night had gone to the theatre. It was when they had returned from that excursion that Matthew had kissed her. A fast worker, Matthew, she had thought, much faster even than Hugh. She had been surprised and had drawn quickly away from his arms.

'I'm sorry,' he had said at once, 'but I had hoped you were no longer in mourning for your husband.'

She had looked at him steadily. Wasn't this what Jessie wanted for her? And what did she want for herself?

'I'm not mourning anyone, Matt,' she had said, and they had smiled at one another as if a bargain had been sealed.

Now he smiled at her again. 'I'll need to inform the Trust, but if you say she doesn't need a full salary . . .?'

'I didn't discuss it with her, Matt, but I think we might ask her to live in – it would be another adult – and she could sell her house or let it to her niece whom she obviously worries about. But she would be wonderful as a remedial teacher.'

Miss Purdy moved in. At first she had no official duties but, by their first Christmas, Kirsty wondered how she would ever have been able to manage without her. Meg too was devoted to her work but, come what may, she had to leave after classes so as to be with her husband. In the winter months the fishermen did line fishing near the coasts and went out in smaller boats that returned to harbour and, in Will's case, to a loving wife, a hot bath and a meal.

'In the summer, when he's deep-sea fishing, I could even stay overnight occasionally, Kirsty.'

Kirsty smiled gratefully. No more talk of leaving at Christmas!

The entire Trust visited them the first term, not all together but two or three at a time, and Kirsty was able to hand over her logbooks without a qualm.

Colonel Granville-Baker looked at her appreciatively. She had blossomed, and the hand that rested in his for a moment was white and soft. Something stirred in his heart and he found himself wanting to press it. Her clothes had always been neat, but now there was a new sophistication that suited Mrs Cameron, head teacher.

'Brave little thing,' he thought, and watched with approval as she showed his colleagues around the converted castle.

'It's just possible Her Majesty might pop in when she's in Arbroath next week, Mrs Cameron.'

'Her Majesty the Queen?' Kirsty almost stuttered and he smiled to see the sophistication fly away.

'The Queen. Luckily, there isn't time for word to get to m'wife, or you'd have Lady Sybill to entertain too and she's much more difficult. Take it that Her Majesty will be here around five for a cup of tea and a tour. Let her see the school working. A runner will come out from Arbroath if there's a change.' He shook hands with her again and left her at the door to walk with his colleagues to their car.

'Mrs Cameron's doing a fine job, Matthew,' he told the lawyer and almost laughed as he saw Matthew's face light up with pride. 'Something brewing here,' he thought. 'Well, why not, as long as it doesn't affect the running of the school.'

'Help her out on the 21st, that's a Wednesday. Shouldn't be a problem: private visit. Wyngate's father will be with her.'

The Colonel might take a royal visitor in his stride but, for Jessie especially, the honour involved a great deal of work.

'And all for less than an hour,' she moaned to Kirsty on Wednesday evening as, with the boys lined up like a football team, they waved their royal visitor off down the driveway.

'But what an hour, Jessie dear,' said Miss Purdy, her flag waving as enthusiastically as any of those brandished by the children. 'Well worth coming out of retirement for. Oh dear, a preposition at the end of a sentence. I hope none of the boys heard me!'

Kirsty laughed. Two of the boys, each almost twelve years old, had still not learned to read. Prepositions out of place would hardly worry them.

The school closed for a holiday over Christmas and New Year. The boys went to their homes; Miss Purdy returned to the room that had been lovingly kept for her in her own little house; Meg went to Will; and Kirsty, Jamie-John and Jessie were left alone without even the domestic staff. They sat in the drawing room on New Year's Eve and savoured the peace and quiet.

'You should have gone out to dinner with Matt, Kirsty,' said Jessie.

'I wanted to be here with you and Jamie-John. Remember last New Year's Eve? We were sitting in a damp cottage – the leak's been fixed, by the way – and I was wondering how on earth to tell you that I'd lost my job. This year we're sitting in a castle. It's like a fairy tale.'

'Is there a Prince Charming?'

EILEEN RAMSAY

'Don't rush me, Mother. I like Matt and he's very good with Jamie-John.'

'Jamie-John thinks he's wonderful,' interrupted Jessie.

'Jamie-John thinks his car is wonderful,' said Kirsty drily.

'Oh, there's more to it than that, dear.'

'Mother, Matt's moving too fast. I'm only just getting into the routine of running a school, and I love it. I love every frantic minute. The Trust talked about more children, more teachers. I haven't time for anything else just now. I like Matt: I enjoy being with him, I enjoy going out to dinner, to the theatre, but right now the school has to come first.'

'The school won't keep you warm on cold winter nights . . . and what of Jamie-John?'

'It's enough that he's living in his father's old home,' answered Kirsty before she realized that her son, crawling around the carpet at her feet arranging his toy soldiers, could hear every word. She looked down at him to see that he had stopped recreating Waterloo and was looking at her very measuringly. He was only five; he couldn't possibly understand what he had heard.

'Come on, young man,' she said with a smile. 'Time to say "Goodbye" to 1921. When you wake up it will be a different year.'

'And Matt's coming to tea.'

'Yes, dear.'

'Will there be sausages?'

'Something a little more special,' said Kirsty as she helped him put Wellington and Napoleon into their cardboard beds.

'Sausages is special.'

'*Are* special.'

'Oh, good, you like them too, Mummy?'

He laughed and she laughed with him and led him off, after he had kissed his grandmother, to his room. Had it been Hugh's room? The Colonel had left a great deal of the furniture with the house, and Jamie-John's room had a carved oak single bed and a matching wardrobe, just right for the son of the house. It could, of course, have been merely a guest room for a single male guest. Surely Lady Sybill would have wanted her son's furniture with her?

'I'm removing cherished family antiques, Mrs Cameron,' the Colonel had explained, 'but we have two other homes and extra furniture is of no use to us. The Trust feels the head teacher's quarters should reflect her importance to the school and so, if you don't mind, I'll leave the public rooms and some of the private ones just as they are – apart from the removal of the pieces I've already mentioned.'

Jessie had been overwhelmed when she saw the flat where she was to live.

'I've never been close to furniture like this, Kirsty, and to live with it! Mind you,' and she had cast a critical home economist's eye over it, 'the last housekeeper fairly ruined that fine wood with cheap polish. It'll take me a while to get that build-up off, but when I'm finished, the Colonel won't recognize it.'

'And he won't,' thought Kirsty now as she closed the door softly on her already sleeping son. 'I only hope he doesn't change his mind and take some of the pieces away.'

The year 1922 came in, and brought snow and Matt together. To Kirsty's relief, he behaved as no more than a family friend. He brought New Year gifts for the three of them, took Jamie-John for a furious drive around the castle policies, and then sat down to the special tea without trying to get Kirsty to himself.

'That was excellent, Mrs Robertson,' he said as he finished his second large piece of game pie. 'I should have suggested that you keep it in the larder in case the Colonel calls.'

Kirsty's heart skipped a beat.

'The Colonel? Is he in Scotland? Why should he call? Usually the secretary of the Trust writes to me.'

'The Colonel is shooting in Perthshire. I thought he might take the opportunity to drop in. He'll send a telegram, I should imagine.'

But he didn't. Two days after the New Year Kirsty looked out of the library window that faced towards the driveway and saw a long black car slowly edging its way down towards the inner keep. A small figure in a red jumper was standing on the dashboard talking animatedly to the driver, and at the same time waving his right arm forward just as the senior officer in the Charge of the Light Brigade must have done.

'It's done then,' she thought, and felt her heart sigh with relief. The Colonel had visited the school several times since the day in the spring when he had hired her, but she had managed to keep Jamie-John firmly out of sight. At least now there would be no more worry. The Colonel would either challenge her about the child's parentage or he would not. She went slowly down the stairs to meet him . . . she waited for the bell to ring, and waited, and finally opened the door. The car was just outside, the bonnet was open and Jamie-John was examining the wonders of its insides, firmly prevented from falling in by his grandfather's tight grasp on his shorts.

The Colonel turned and smiled at her. 'They're all the same, aren't they, Mrs Cameron? Anything that moves!'

'Anything that's dirty and noisy, Colonel,' she answered as he set Jamie-John down and came towards her, hand outstretched.

'Happy New Year,' he said. 'Do forgive me for barging in.'

'You're welcome, Colonel. I have already sent the end-of-term reports to the Trust secretary, but I'll be happy to show you around and discuss them with you.'

'No, I've seen the reports. Excellent. I came for something else: something that's been on my mind for years. Ah, Mrs Robertson. Happy New Year to you! I hoped you might give me tea.'

'We're delighted to see you, Colonel,' said Jessie, who had been standing at the top of the stairs beside an ancient suit of armour.

'That not been knocked down the stairs yet?' asked the Colonel with a laugh. 'I'd forgotten I meant to move it: not because it means anything, but because it might be dangerous.'

'We like him, the boys and me,' said Jamie-John. 'He tells us when bad people are coming.'

'Then he must stay,' said the Colonel and followed Jessie into the library.

There seemed to be somebody outside Kirsty's body watching the pleasant little tea party. She could see herself, laughing and joking with Hugh's father as he tucked into Jessie's excellent baking and agreed to join in a hilarious card game, 'Freddie the Fox'. He always seemed to finish up with the Fox and smiled as Jamie-John, who always won, roared with laughter.

'He has to know,' the voice told her. 'But just enjoy being a family, relaxed and happy, for a few hours. Then we'll see what he has to say. Does he want to take him away or, beneath that charm, is he furious that this child is here?'

'I'll see you to your car, Colonel,' she said firmly when at last he rose to go. 'Help Grandma tidy up, Jamie-John.'

The little boy looked mutinous but he did as he was told, and Kirsty walked down the stairs with her son's grandfather and waited for whatever blow was to fall.

'I have something for you, Mrs Cameron. I should have given it to you years ago, but I honestly didn't know I had it. Couldn't bear to examine the boy's things, y'know.' He felt inside his breast pocket and then handed her a leather wallet. 'Hugh's paybook is in there. He was using it to write to you just before . . . just before he was killed.'

His hand was still over hers and the wallet and she stood as if turned to stone. He bent and kissed her lightly on the cheek.

'I'll come again, if I may. He's a fine chappie.'

Kirsty could say nothing; her eyes full of tears, she lifted her hand that held the wallet and put it on her cheek where he had kissed her. She stood in the gathering dark and the cold until the lights of the car had completely vanished, and then she turned and slowly walked back up the stairs towards the library. At the suit of armour she turned and went to her bedroom, where she sat for what seemed like hours on the bed and felt the tears course down her cheeks, and then at last she brushed them away and opened the wallet. The brown-stained scrap of paper was still inside the back cover.

'Hugh's blood,' she thought and tenderly held it to her breast, and then at last she read the letter that had waited over five years.

'Oh, Hugh, my darling. You did wait for me in the Dell.'

Later she rose and returned the letter to its bloody bed, then put the wallet in the drawer of her bedside table. She would not need to look at it again but, one day, Jamie-John would want to see it.

'Kirsty, you were an age,' Jessie exclaimed when she returned to the library. She looked warningly at the child's bent head. 'Is there a problem?'

Kirsty held out her arms and hugged her mother. 'No problems at all. He knows, and it's all going to be all right.'

28

MATT ASKED KIRSTY TO marry him in May 1922.

'I won't give up asking,' he said when he had received her negative answer, 'until you tell me that there is someone else. There isn't anyone else, is there?'

'Matt? Who would you suggest? One of the gardeners? Sergeant Kinloch?'

'The Colonel,' he said almost defiantly.

She was shocked and stared at him in disbelief. The Colonel was old; he was Hugh's father, Jamie-John's grandfather. Matt couldn't know that, of course. 'The Colonel is already married, or didn't you know?'

'It's a shaky marriage, from what I hear. And he has been spending a great deal of time here since he retired.'

'This was his home, Matt. It was an extremely generous gift and, naturally, he wants to keep an eye on things.'

'That's why the Trust hired me,' he said pettishly and then, 'Forgive me, Kirsty, I'm being silly. It's just that my mother thinks I'm wonderful and she can't understand why I haven't been snapped up.'

Kirsty knew that Matt's fiancée had been unable to bear his long absence during the war and had married someone else. Matt, too, was a casualty of the war. She looked at him measuringly.

'You would be, or will be, if you stop wasting your time with me.'

'I'm not sure that I'm wasting my time.'

She could not explain about the letter, the letter that had confirmed that Hugh had loved her, that she had seen him and heard him speak to her in the Dell days after his death. That was love, and she had been preparing to settle for second best. No, she couldn't do that, to herself or to Matt. She liked him, admired him, respected him, but he did not make her heart race the way Hugh had been able to do. He did not fill her being with gentleness and promise the way Jamie had begun to do.

'Give both of us a chance, Matt. Come as often as you need to, on business . . .'

'But, otherwise, stay away.'

She nodded sadly. 'Yes.'

When she found that he had taken her at her word, she missed him. 'You miss having an escort to the theatre. You miss being taken out to dinner. And that's all you miss, Kirsty. You don't really miss Matt at all,' she told herself.

She set herself to composing an advertisement for *The Times* and the *Scotsman*. There would be another class in September and she would need another teacher, a man perhaps. A married man could have the flat over the converted coach house. One day they would have a school shooting brake; they would need to take the boys on outings, or to the football matches Sergeant Kinloch talked about.

She heard the sound of scurrying feet. If that was Alice, the maid, and not one of the boys, she would be quite cross. Alice really must learn to walk sedately, no matter who her visitor was. There was the expected knock at the door.

'I know my way, girl. This is my house,' said a voice that Kirsty recognized immediately, although she had never before heard it. She rose, trembling, to her feet and forced back the terror the voice had evoked. Why should a visit from Lady Sybill worry her?

'Thank you, Alice. Please ask Mrs Robertson for some tea.'

The girl curtseyed and withdrew and Kirsty was left confronting, for the first time, Hugh's mother.

Lady Sybill smiled. 'Forgive me, Mrs Cameron, I should have said "was my house", I suppose, but bumbling servants do distress one so. I hope you had someone a little more *au fait* when the dear Queen visited.'

'Her Majesty didn't appear . . . distressed by Alice, nor Alice by Her Majesty.'

Reluctant admiration appeared for a moment in Lady Sybill's eyes.

'I am Sybill Granville-Baker.'

'What can I do for you, Lady Sybill? I should be more than happy to conduct you round the school. We are very conscious of your generosity in gifting us the building.'

'Not my generosity, girl. Not a penny of my money ever went into the place and Hugo removed all my furniture, every last little piece. He always was so honourable, my wonderful husband. No, I wanted to meet you.' She sat down in the chair Kirsty indicated, disposing of her coat and bag in an effortlessly elegant gesture. 'You're much younger than I imagined. Actually, I'm surprised at Hugo. Well, we haven't had much of a marriage since the war, nothing since the boy . . . died, but I would have thought someone a bit older, his own class. It's the novelty, I suppose. They do say men get . . . peculiar as they get older, but Hugo? I could have sworn he was the type to tear out any unworthy thoughts – you know, like a medieval knight, lying on his belly on a cold altar to defeat the urges of the flesh.'

Kirsty rose to her feet. Whatever she had expected from Lady Sybill's visit, it was not this.

'I must ask you to leave, Lady Sybill. I will not sit here and listen to such vilification of one of the noblest . . .' She got no further, for the door opened and the tea and Jamie-John arrived together.

'Mummy, there's a super car . . .' He stopped on seeing Lady Sybill and then turned his blue eyes on his mother's visitor and awarded her a beautiful smile. He well knew how to earn himself a drive in that marvellous machine – but his charm did not work this time. Lady Sybill was looking at him, not in shocked realization but in anger.

'You slut,' she said in a low voice to Kirsty. 'I never dreamed . . . and Hugo . . . Hugo, the pure, the undefiled.' She swept up her belongings which she had draped so negligently on her chair and pushed past the gaping Alice. 'You'll hear from my lawyers, Mrs Cameron.'

'What's a slut, Mummy?' asked Jamie-John.

'Matt's a lawyer. Perhaps you should talk to him?' Jessie was furious. 'Oh, if I'd been there . . .'

In spite of her deep fear and worry, Kirsty smiled. She could not imagine her gentle mother who had so loved 'the right people', Lady Sybill's people, squaring up to anyone.

'I keep hoping it will go away, like a bad cold or a headache. That's been a weakness of mine all my life, Mother, trying to pretend that the awful thing that is happening isn't really happening at all. At least I faced the fact that Hugh was dead.' Her voice dropped so low that Jessie could barely hear it. 'And now Hugh's mother is calling me a slut. She's the third person to call me that, and it's not true. First, old Buchanan because I let Bob Cargill walk me home, then Jamie's mother and now Lady Sybill. I looked it up in a dictionary. It says a slut is an immoral woman. Am I immoral? I suppose some people would say I am. You've never said so, or Jamie, or the Colonel.'

'Of course you're not immoral, Kirsty.'

'I wasn't married to Hugh.' Kirsty paced across the beautiful room, the room which had so recently echoed to Lady Sybill's cruel words, and looked out of the windows. Boys were playing on the lawns. One, Alfie Briggs, was sitting with his back against the old sun-warmed wall, and he was reading. He was reading the new comic, the *Hotspur*, that the big Dundee company, Thomson Leng, had commissioned in order to give jobs to men coming back from the war. Alfie was unaware of the football that narrowly missed his head, and for a few minutes he had forgotten the misery that was his home life.

'She'll spoil it for Alfie and the others, Mother. She'll make it all dirty and horrible, and the school will close because of the scandal. Why should she want to hurt the Colonel this way?'

'I don't know, Kirsty.' Jessie had no experience of unhappy marriage. She said again, 'Please tell Matt.'

Later Kirsty sat by her son and watched him as he slept. The blue eyes were closed but he still looked like Hugh, like the Colonel. It was the hair, the shape of the head, the ears. 'I thought she might be broken-hearted when she saw you, my lamb,' the words went round and round in her head, 'but it was anger on her face, not unhappiness. She can't really believe the Colonel is your father. On the train south she is bound to have worked it all out, but Matt's coming tomorrow and we'll tell him everything.' She winced as if with pain, for Matt would have to be told about Hugh. She looked carefully at the sleeping child. 'Perhaps he knows already.'

Matt bounded up the stairs to greet her, but one look at her face told him that he was not here to receive good news.

'Kirsty, what is it?' he asked. 'You look as if you haven't slept.'

'I haven't, Matt, and I'm sorry to drag you into this mess, but I wasn't able to contact the Colonel last night . . .'

'I had a telegram from his office this morning. He's on his way. What on earth is this about?'

'Lady Sybill came . . .' Kirsty stood up abruptly and walked to the window, to the solace of the gardens. No, she had to face Matt; she had to see his face, the anger, the scorn, the derision. She turned again. 'She thinks Jamie-John is the Colonel's child. I don't know what she means to do, but she's planning something.'

'Divorce,' said Matt quietly.

'Divorce,' Kirsty echoed.

'Yes. It's common knowledge that the marriage has been a sham for some time. Now Lady Sybill has seen a way to become the injured party. She wants a divorce with her name unsullied.' He stood up, avoiding looking at Kirsty. 'Perhaps it would be better if we wait for the Colonel? Obviously she or her lawyers have already been in touch. He might prefer that you both consult a lawyer more versed in this kind of litigation.'

'Both. Oh, Matt, you don't believe it, do you?'

'I honestly never thought about it before. We did think it odd that the Trust should choose such a young woman, but you were a war widow and you were qualified, and everything in the school has gone so well. You seemed to justify the Colonel's faith in you. You worked so damned hard those first few months, and since, of course. But a scandal involving the head teacher and the Chairman of the Trust . . .'

'Colonel Granville-Baker is the noblest, kindest man I have ever met, Matt. And you know me. You must know that nothing has ever happened between us.'

'Jamie-John?'

'Is his grandson.' There, she had said it out loud for the first time.

He was looking at her so oddly. What was he thinking?

'I think the best thing would be to wait for the Colonel, Mrs Cameron,' he said stiffly.

'Mrs Cameron?' And then she understood. He was like Jamie's mother, making the same calculations, the same judgements, probably wondering too if Jamie knew about the child's parentage or if he had been able to believe that he himself was the father. She drew herself up scornfully.

'You're right, Mr Matthews. It would be better if you left.'

'Try to understand, Kirsty. I wanted to marry you.'

'I was married, Mr Matthews, to a truly good and noble man. I'm ashamed that I ever considered settling for anything less.'

He winced as if he had been physically struck and she rejoiced as she turned back to the window and let him leave by himself. There were other lawyers who would not make moral judgements. She would wait for the Colonel, and for the first time they would have to really discuss Jamie-John's parentage. For the sake of the school she might have to leave, but surely Lady Sybill would not proceed with her action when she learned the truth.

There was another scratching at the door. Alice really would have to learn if she was to stay on. Oh, God, would there be a school for her to stay on *in*?

She summoned a smile. No one, children or frightened little servants, learned when they were afraid.

'Yes, Alice?'

'There's a gentleman, ma'am, come about a job.'

But the advertisement had not even been received at the newspaper offices yet.

'Show him in, Alice.' Perhaps it was yet another former soldier looking for something, anything. Could she hire anyone? Proceed as normal, Kirsty.

There was something familiar about the tall, too-thin man who limped into her office and held out his left hand. He had no right arm. The eyes that looked into hers were still shadowed by pain and fear.

'Good morning, Mrs Cameron. I am a fully qualified teacher. I have been abroad for some years and now can also offer you French and Italian. Three teachers for the price of one!'

A ghost of an old grin, that she struggled to recognize, played across those tormented eyes.

'Bob,' she whispered incredulously as she put out both her hands to take the one offered her. 'Bob Cargill?'

He came closer to stare into her face. The eyes lit up for a moment with pure joy.

'Kirsty?' he breathed. 'You're no' telling me it's wee Kirsty Robertson!'

29

Lady Sybill had stayed awake on the train all the way to London. She was still wide awake when the porter helped her into a cab that took her to the beautiful house on Lowndes Street which her parents had bought for her as a wedding gift almost forty years before. She ordered coffee, a hot bath, her lawyer and her lover in that order, and in that order she dealt with them. The evening's dalliance with darling Arthur was the most satisfying part of the day's negotiations. Really, neither of them was cut out for a life of sin and deception. She did love him so and he was – face it, Sybill – becoming tired of trying to pretend at house parties that they were no more than close friends.

'At last, at last,' he had breathed as they reached the most satisfying climax in years. 'To be able to call you mine, Sybill.'

Really, he was beginning to sound the teeniest, weeniest bit like dull, honourable old Hugo.

'One is supposed to enjoy it more when one's not really allowed, Arthur,' she had said pettishly.

'You can't mean that, Sybill. You know I've loathed these years of sneaking in at back doors. It will be wonderful for you to be divorced honourably, the injured party, with all the sympathy of Society. When shall we plan to marry?'

Sybill eased herself up against the pillows, so much more feminine since Hugo had stopped sleeping there. He had said that yards of lace on his pillows terrified him.

'We still have to be a little circumspect, my darling, but by Christmas, I think, we should be able to announce our engagement, at least to family and close friends. Hugo won't fight. Perhaps he wants to marry his little friend.'

Arthur lit cigarettes and handed one to Lady Sybill. 'You know,' he said reflectively as he blew smoke against the pink ceiling, 'I just can't see Hugo and a girl half his age.'

'If you'd seen the boy . . .' Lady Sybill gritted her teeth as she remembered the shock, the pain, the unbelievable anger. 'I was livid. The image of my dearest child.' The tears, genuine enough, swelled in her faded blue eyes and spilled over. 'Hugo must have gone to his hussy for comfort as soon as we heard the news. He certainly didn't come to me.' Comfortably she forgot that the news of Captain Granville-Baker's death in action had followed her around the country as she and a few other wealthy socialites had sought release from the horrors of war in a never-ending social round. 'And to install her as head teacher in the very school set up as a memorial to Hugh and the other poor, dead boys. I'll drag him and his harlot through every sordid paper in England!'

'The proverbial storm in the proverbial teacup, my dear,' the Colonel said, accepting a second cup of coffee from Kirsty. 'I deeply regret that you had to suffer such verbal abuse.'

'But how can we prove . . .?'

'Sybill will realize herself upon reflection, Kirsty. I may call you Kirsty after all this?'

Kirsty nodded, her eyes full of tears.

'We have to sit down one day soon and talk about Hugh and little Jamie-John and Jamie Cameron, Kirsty. I only need to know a few details. It was obvious to me when I saw the letter that my son loved you. Had he lived you would have been my daughter-in-law, and that is how I think of you. This case won't come to court, simply because I was in France for most of 1915. It's quite clearly documented. I'll go back to London and see Sybill. End of story.'

'People must be talking. Lady Sybill was told something.'

'She won't want Hugh's name muddied any more than I do, m'dear. Our marriage finished a long time ago, but our love for our boy . . . In a way, I'm almost glad that she has forced the issue. Jamie-John is my grandson and I'm delighted to be able to admit it.'

'But Colonel, for his sake . . . and mine?'

'I know, Kirsty. People will think and people will talk, but only we two will really know. Let me take care of the boy financially, school, and so on. I want him to go to Hugh's old school. My friends who see him will realize he's Hugh's child, and by the time he's old enough to go to school it will be accepted without very much thought. The war has ensured that too many children won't bear their father's name: if there are any decent men left alive to marry all those poor little widows, that is. Now, tell me about this fellow you hired.'

Kirsty did not realize how her face lit up as she described her reunion with her former colleague.

'He was always so funny, Colonel. The Dominie at our first school had no sense of humour' – that was all she would ever say about Mr Buchanan – 'and he was furious as laughter rang down those dark old corridors. Bob has lost an arm, but little else, though he was badly injured and lost his memory for a time. He was in a hospital in France and was thought to be French: when a nurse spoke to him in the language he automatically replied in French. He had studied French for a year at a college in Edinburgh, but the war put an end to his formal studies.'

'As it did for so many young men,' interrupted the Colonel. 'He had no thought of returning to university?'

'No, when his memory returned and they realized that he was British, they sent him back to a hospital in

England and then up here to Edinburgh. He's been living in Auchmithie for a year. His family were fishermen. He read in the *Courier* about the school starting but waited a year to see if there was an opening, in the hope that he would be really well and able to handle the work.'

'He'll live in, I suppose? It would be excellent security to have an old soldier actually in the building at night. We could do something for him in the block above the old stables.'

The fear engendered by Lady Sybill's harsh words receded. How wonderful it was to sit there with Hugh's father and feel that, at last, everything was out in the open unashamedly. He knew about Jamie-John. The child's future was secure – his grandfather would make sure that Jamie-John Cameron received a good education after he left this preparatory school. Her son would fulfil the promise of both his father and his foster-father and, incidentally, of his mother who had been unable to attend a university. Quite a burden for one little boy, and she would have to see that there was never too much pressure. He must be allowed to be himself.

The evening and the visit came to a close.

'I'll return to town tomorrow, Kirsty, and you should hear no more from Lady Sybill. There are probably communications already in the post from her solicitors, but send them to me directly and I'll deal with them. As for Jamie-John, I'll come as often as I can to watch him grow, but we'll keep our secret until he's old enough to handle it.'

She smiled at him in relief. 'You're welcome here at any time, Colonel. All the boys like to see you.'

'Yes, it's the extra pudding the cooks make when there is a visitor!'

She laughed. They both knew there was more to it than pudding. 'Goodbye, Colonel, and thank you.'

When the car lights had disappeared down the drive-way Kirsty turned and went back upstairs, where Jessie was waiting with her never-failing remedy for grief and worry – hot cocoa.

'Everything is going to be fine, Mother,' said Kirsty, 'and we're to go ahead with the plans for expansion. I'll be happier when Lady Sybill drops her action, if she has started it, but for the moment I'm going to arrange for a flat to be prepared for Bob above the old stables. You'll like him, Mother, and so will the boys. A real hero in the house. And dear Miss Purdy will be absolutely delighted.'

*

Colonel Granville-Baker had himself announced at his old home upon his return to London. He had spent over thirty years as joint owner of the house, yet he no longer felt a part of it. Lady Sybill was seated at her desk when he entered the library and she turned to look at him.

'Come to beg, Hugo darling?' she asked mockingly.

'It won't wash, Sybill, and if you think, you will realize it.'

'You look exhausted: all this running up and down to Scotland. I'll ring for coffee.' She rose gracefully.

He reflected as he watched her cross the room that she always had been the most extraordinarily graceful woman. Hugh had inherited it, and the little chap, though she might not like to be told that. A blot on the family escutcheon, little Jamie-John.

'So much better to have it all out in the open like this,' she said.

'The boy is Hugh's child, Sybill, and I think you've already realized that.'

She turned swiftly to face him and he saw disbelief, shock and pain in her eyes. The thought had never occurred to her.

'I don't believe it,' she said, her hand at her throat as if to hold back the worlds. 'I won't believe it. My son and some working-class little schoolteacher? Never!'

He saw the tears swimming in the once-lovely eyes. Was she crying for her shattered hopes of a socially acceptable divorce, or for her dreams of her son?

'You'd like Kirsty if you tried, Sybill, and the boy is . . .'

'A bastard.' She spat out the word with venom. 'Whoever his father is.'

'Yes,' he said simply, 'there are too many like him around now: all casualties of the war. I'm seeing my solicitors this morning and changing my will. You won't need anything, will you, my dear? You have this house and your father's money, and I'll arrange to give you cause for divorce if you want old Arthur so badly, but not at the expense of Mrs Cameron or the child.'

'Hugh was in love with one of the Ponsonby girls. Clara is still in mourning for him.'

'I'm sorry for her then. But I know he loved Kirsty . . . Mrs Cameron. There was the most heartbreaking note in his paybook. He was writing to Kirsty a few minutes before he was killed.'

She stood up again. 'Don't,' she said and put out her hands as if to push away the thought of her child, dead.

'He's gone, Sybill, but knowing his son has brought me incredible peace. I wish . . .'

'Just go, Hugo, please.'

He rose at once. 'Very well, my dear. I'll see about arranging everything nicely for you and Arthur.'

She did not watch him leave but sat with head bowed while tears for her son and her dead marriage rained down her face. What a mess it was, what a bloody mess. Where had all the promise gone, all the early happiness? To come to this . . .

Hugo ran lightly down the steps to the road and decided not to hail a cab but to walk across town to his solicitors' offices. Poor old Sybill. If marrying Arthur would compensate a little for the loss of her child . . .? Could anything? Not for him it couldn't, although knowing the boy was such a joy. He wondered what he would have to do to give Sybill cause to divorce him. Have a photograph taken in some seedy hotel with some poor woman? To my grandson, Jamie-John Cameron, I leave everything of which I die possessed. What a pleasure that would be, to have that done. Should have done it years ago.

He did not see the omnibus that hit him. His eyes were full of pictures of little boys with bright blue eyes.

30

And we are, therefore, delighted to be able to add Lady Sybill's illustrious name to the list of Trustees. We feel sure it is what the Colonel would have wished.

Kirsty read the letter from Sir John Banniman, London solicitor to the Trust, several times. Lady Sybill to replace the Colonel! She shook her head as if to brush away the pain that thinking of either of them always brought.

'Bad news, Kirsty?'

She looked up and smiled at her old friend, now her colleague, Bob Cargill. 'No, not really. Lady Sybill Granville-Baker has been persuaded to lend her name and title, I suppose, to the School Trust. I really don't want to see her here, at any time. Her one and only visit was not a success.'

She looked at him again, taking time to register how much his appearance had improved in the last two years. He was heavier and his face was no longer so lined with pain. His eyes were clearer and either he had bought a suit to fit his filled-out frame, or good food and rest had allowed him to fit into clothes that for too long had merely draped his bent body.

'I don't know how I could have borne the last few years without you, Bob,' she said suddenly. 'You have been such a tower of strength.'

'We've helped one another, Kirsty. For a time there, I thought I would never be really useful again, and to have this job and a home, and feel that I'm really playing my part and not just being tolerated . . .'

'Tolerated? What would the school do without you?' Bob not only took the senior class but coached a French club, and the football team that Sergeant Kinloch had finally been able to put together. The sight of her old friend running swiftly down the side of the field, his good arm waving enthusiastically, warmed Kirsty's heart often. He had been a source of reliability right from the start and had even, fortuitously, been on the premises when Matthew Matthews brought the news of the Colonel's death.

It had been Bob, not Matt, who had comforted her. He had sent a boy upstairs for Jessie, and had sat beside her holding her in the circle of his one good arm until Jessie had appeared.

'I'm sorry,' Matt had said somewhat stiffly as he stood awkwardly looking down at them. 'I don't know you, do I?'

'Mrs Cameron hired me to take the third class,' Bob had answered easily, 'but we have known one another . . .' He had broken off and looked down at Kirsty in amazement, 'Good gracious, Kirsty, for half our lives.'

'How good that you were here today,' Matt said seriously. 'The Colonel meant a great deal to Mrs Cameron.'

At that Kirsty had stood up out of the shelter of Bob's arm and looked at the lawyer challengingly. 'Yes, he did, a very great deal.'

'I'm sorry, Kirsty. I have wanted to come back often to apologize . . .'

'This isn't the time or the place, Matt, and what you thought really doesn't matter.'

He moved as if to continue speaking but just then Jessie arrived.

'Matt, you here? Kirsty, what's happened, what's wrong?'

When the sad news had been broken to her, it was the ever practical Jessie who remembered what Kirsty had completely forgotten. 'But Jamie-John? What difference will this make to him?'

'Jamie-John?' Bob asked.

'My son, Bob. The Colonel was his grandfather.'

And now, two years later, Bob was more a part of Kirsty's life than he had ever been. She avoided thinking about how much he had come to mean to her. He was friendly, but always there seemed to be some barrier between them. Was it that she was the head teacher of the school, or was it something to do with his disability? She didn't know, and couldn't ask. All she knew was that, every day, more and more, she depended on him. If he was ill she worried – inordinately, she told herself, and tried to assure herself that she was concerned only for the smooth running of the school. There were now four permanent teachers: Meg had charge of the babies, but would change this year to the middle class because Kirsty did not want Jamie-John to be taught by his own mother; Kirsty herself, who would take the four youngest children; Bob, who had charge of the senior class, and Mrs Irene Pacholek, the widow of a Polish soldier. Irene had the second oldest group; this class included her own daughter, Olga, who had been the school's first girl. At the new term there would be six girls of all ages. Miss Purdy was too frail now for much teaching, but her sitting room was always open to the children and usually Kirsty would find one or two there whenever she herself went to call.

Now she stood up as she heard Sergeant Kinloch running down the stairs outside. That meant he was off to ring the bell for the end of playtime.

'Having the babes next year, Kirsty, will give you more time for administration. You've hardly touched that tea, and you always did enjoy a nice cup of tea.'

Kirsty walked with Bob to the door and realized again how many memories they shared: classes in the gloomy old school, hot buttered baps and mugs of strong, sweet tea in the janitor's room. Mr McGillivray had died last year and she had given the school a half-holiday so that she and Bob could attend the funeral. Miss McNeil had been there, and Mrs Buchanan, and Kirsty had had to steel herself to speak to them, so frightening were the memories that the sight of them conjured up.

'Well, you landed in a honeypot, didn't you, Miss Robertson, or . . . it's Mrs Something or other – not Cargill, though, one of your other . . . friends.'

Miss McNeil had lost none of her charm.

'I heard you were running that school for orphans at the castle, Kirsty.' Mrs Buchanan steered the conversation. 'Well done! Are you a political activist too, like Miss McNeil here?'

'I did intend to get involved, Mrs Buchanan, but the school and my son take all my time.'

And then she was able to chat quite naturally about Jamie-John, and the awkward meeting was over and they could make their way to the High Street to have tea before their train.

Now Jamie-John was almost nine and, had the Colonel lived, she might have been looking at a different prep school for him, for it was unlikely that the breadth of experience provided by the Aberannoch Castle School would have been enough for entry to Eton. She looked at her son as he raced with his classmates to the lines. Was it only her maternal pride or did he really stand out from the others? There was just something about the set of his head, about the directness of his look, an assurance, that set him apart.

That's because his mother is the head teacher, she told herself, not because he is special.

At lunchtime she climbed the stairs to Miss Purdy's room to share the communication from Sir John.

'Will her being on the Board bring back all the unpleasantness of her allegations, Kirsty?'

'No, it shouldn't. I doubt that we'll ever see her ladyship. She didn't like the castle when it was hers to live in, and I can hardly see her popping up here to worry about the welfare of penniless orphans. But never mind Lady Sybill. How are you today?'

'Better than anyone my age has any right to be, but I have been thinking that I'm not really earning my keep these days. I should be put out to grass like an old horse.'

'You are out to grass, my dear,' Kirsty said affectionately, 'sitting here, night after night, listening to the boys and now the girls . . .'

Miss Purdy became almost animated. 'Oh, I do enjoy having girls around. It puts me in mind of my niece, the one who has my house. Did you know that Olga Pacholek is smitten with Dougie Taylor?'

'Olga is only nine!' Kirsty was scandalized.

'And Dougie is eleven and breaking her little heart, which reminds me. Are you still seeing that nice Mr Matthews?'

'I'm having dinner with him on Friday evening.'

'That's nice,' said Miss Purdy complacently. 'There's nothing like having dinner with one man to make another man jealous.'

Kirsty felt a blush creep up her neck and she moved over to the window, ostensibly to watch the children in the walled garden. Olga Pacholek was indeed following Dougie Taylor around. How did the old woman, who never moved from her room and only rarely from her chair, know so much of what was going on around her? She decided to ignore her remark, which had been thrown like a bone to a dog. This dog was refusing to pick it up.

She thought about it later though. Since the Colonel's death, Matt had been seen more and more often at the school. He had apologized to Kirsty for all his suspicions. Yes, he admitted, it had occurred to him that the Colonel was Jamie-John's father, and he had wondered too if Jamie Cameron had had reason to believe that he himself was the child's father.

'But the more I got to know you, Kirsty, and the more fond of you I became, the less I believed that,' he had said.

'My husband knew the truth about Jamie.' She would say no more. She would not explain that she and Jamie had never lived together as man and wife. She would not

tell anyone that real love for her husband had been growing strong and sure when he had been cut down.

She was obliged to see Matt, she told herself. He was the
school's lawyer, Sir John Banniman's local representative.
She could forgive him his suspicions, could even understand them. The meetings to discuss school matters – like
Bob's contract, or later Irene Pacholek's – were held in the
beautifully furnished panelled drawing room of the castle.
Kirsty was glad that the room had never been changed.
She could sometimes feel the Colonel's presence there.
No, she did not believe that a friendly ghost visited her:
it was just that some aura seemed to remain there, some
strength of feeling. The same feeling existed, from another
source, in Jamie-John's bedroom and in the Dell.

'You wish you could feel their presence, Kirsty, and so
you do,' her practical side told her.

'Matt . . . Mr Matthews is here, Mummy.' Jamie-John burst
into the room and then he stopped stock-still to look at
her. 'You do look nice. Why are you putting on your best
frock? Can I ask him for a run in the car?'

'Thank you. I'm going out to dinner. No, lamb. Mr
Matthews and I are driving all the way to Montrose for
dinner, and it's time you were in bed.'

To her surprise Kirsty saw her young son glare mutin-
ously at her, his hands on his hips. Unconsciously she

smiled. Because he was so thin, it was hard to even find his hip bones.

'A carpenter's dream, oor Jamie-John,' laughed Mr Seaton, the school's custodian. 'A right two b'four, J-J, and no' a knot in sicht.'

But Jamie-John was not amused. 'Why are you going out to dinner with him? Grannie made us a nice dinner.'

'Come on, lamb. Is Mr Matthews in the drawing room? We'll go and say "Hello" and then I'll pop you into bed. Grannie will read you a story tonight.'

'Grannie reads soppy stories. I'm going to Mr Cargill's flat.' He turned and made to run off towards the stable wing and she caught his arm.

'No,' she said firmly. 'It's bedtime, Jamie-John, and if you don't want one of Grannie's nice stories then you can go to sleep without.'

He went with her unwillingly and, for the first time in his life, turned his head away deliberately when she bent to kiss him.

She said nothing except, 'Good night, Jamie-John,' and went downstairs to meet Matt.

He rose as she entered the room, a growing smile on his face. 'My, you look good enough to eat, Mrs Cameron,' he said, 'but there's a tiny frown. Anything I can do?'

'It's nothing, Matt,' said Kirsty firmly and thrust her son's aggressive behaviour to the back of her mind.

As always, she enjoyed the drive up the coast to the old town of Montrose. Tonight the sea lay on her right like a placid pond and the old castles that dotted the rugged coastline stood out proudly. The wheat and barley were ripening in the fields. Everything in the world was lovely – except Lady Sybill's unwelcome advent and Jamie-John's out-of-character behaviour. She did not know that she sighed.

Matt reached out and lightly covered her hand. 'What's wrong, Kirsty?'

She could hardly tell him the truth, if there was a truth there yet, that she was feeling herself more and more drawn to a man who avoided every opportunity that was given him to take their relationship a stage further.

'It's having Lady Sybill on the Board, I suppose. And then there was Jamie-John. He seemed jealous of our outing and he's usually such a sunny person.'

Matt avoided talk of Kirsty's son. 'Lady Sybill shouldn't cause any embarrassment. I doubt we'll even see her in Scotland.'

There he was wrong.

Lady Sybill Granville-Baker had actively campaigned to be given a position on the school Board of Governors. Her husband's death had not, as one would have thought, made everything easy for her. Colonel Granville-Baker had taken several days to die, and it was his wife who had sat hour after hour beside the battered wreck of what had once been a strong and good man. He had regained consciousness two days after the accident and she had even hoped that he might recover. The doctors muttered things like 'massive internal injuries'. She heard them speak of irreparable damage to the spleen, to the spinal column.

'Hugo is very strong,' she reminded their own doctor, 'and very, very determined.'

He shook his head. 'Quite frankly, Sybill, I wish he had gone immediately. He's suffering intense pain.'

'He's completely rational.'

It had not lasted, however. The Colonel had lapsed into unconsciousness and his wife had hardly been aware of the moment when his last tenuous hold on life was released. She had been unprepared for the violence of her grief. When their son had died there had been no guilt, but grief compounded by guilt was almost insupportable. She sat for hours looking through snapshots of the young Hugo.

'This is morbid, Sybill,' her friends and family told her. 'You must build a new life for yourself. You're still young.'

Build a life? On what? No child, no husband. She refused to give her faithful Arthur any hope that they would marry soon, and she had lost all interest in pleasant dalliance.

'You need some outside interest,' said her family, but Lady Sybill sat surrounded by photographs of her husband and then of her son, and to these mementoes she added school reports and letters, and always and always her husband's few last halting words tumbled around in her head.

The other members of the Trust were surprised to discover that their new member intended to be quite active. They had expected only her name and its connections with her nephew, one of England's premier earls.

'I am going to Scotland. In August it's really quite fashionable.' There was the difficulty of finding a suitable hotel. Really, the Scots were still so very, very uncivilized. One was eventually found, however, and in mid-August, just as the school was in a perfect turmoil, Lady Sybill Granville-Baker was announced. Kirsty thanked whatever good fairy had been in the castle that morning that it was Jessie who answered the imperious ringing of the doorbell. She had shown Lady Sybill into the library and gone to find Kirsty. Alice would have led Lady Sybill right to the school floor, where Kirsty in an apron and mob cap worked with the cleaners at getting a new classroom ready.

'Why did I choose this tatty old frock this morning?' Kirsty sighed as she pulled off her apron and cap and hurried downstairs to meet her illustrious but unwelcome guest.

Lady Sybill was standing before the fireplace and she turned when Kirsty entered.

'I always did wonder why Hugo left this portrait,' she said as she moved forward to greet Kirsty, but she went on as if she did not expect an answer. 'I think my late husband would have wished me to continue his interest in the school, Mrs Cameron. Perhaps I should have telephoned? You are on the telephone?'

'Yes, Lady Sybill, but I am quite happy to show you round. The Trust has found six girls this year, and therefore we need another dormitory and a fourth classroom.'

'No children are here at the moment then?'

'Little Olga Pacholek is here – her mother is a new teacher and is helping me with classrooms – and my own son. They're playing somewhere in the gardens.'

'Then if I'm not interrupting too terribly much, I should like to see the school.'

Kirsty tried to cleanse from her mind all memory of the last time she had seen Lady Sybill. 'This is a normal inspection tour,' she told herself. 'She has said nothing about Jamie-John, and perhaps that reference to a valuable family portrait shows that she knows about Jamie-John . . . and perhaps it doesn't.'

They toured the classrooms, dormitories, dining rooms, kitchens and bathrooms, and Kirsty took a malicious and unworthy pleasure in noting the unsuitability of Lady Sybill's shoes for so much walking.

'Would you like to see the play area in the gardens, Lady Sybill? We have our own football team now and we even play against other schools. We always lose because our team members are all different ages, but the boys enjoy the challenge.'

'Another day, perhaps, Mrs Cameron. I would like that coffee you promised.'

They went to the library where Jessie had set up a small table and a tray.

'Goodness. Was it only my personal things that the Colonel removed?' asked Lady Sybill, looking in astonishment at the silver coffee service.

'The silver belongs to the Trust, Lady Sybill,' answered Kirsty easily, 'and is only used to entertain honoured guests. The cloth, of course, was embroidered by my mother. Her Majesty was kind enough to admire it.'

'We were all conscious of Mrs Robertson's undoubted skill,' said Lady Sybill, neatly allying herself with the wife of the Sovereign. 'But I really must go and let you return to your endeavours.' She rose gracefully.

'I'll never be able to slide out of a chair like that,' thought Kirsty as she rang the bell for Alice to bring her ladyship's furs.

There was no response to the bell.

'Same girl, I take it, Mrs Cameron,' said Lady Sybill, but there was a smile of genuine amusement and not malice on her face.

'She really has improved,' said Kirsty as she went to the door to see what was keeping the maid.

Jamie-John and Olga were in the narrow hallway and each was draped in expensive fox tails. They minced along towards one another – Olga in a pair of high heels that Kirsty recognized as being her own – bowed grandly to each other and then tossed the furs around their small necks with gay abandon. Alice was vainly trying to separate them from the furs but, since she was laughing more than she was scolding, the children were paying little attention to her.

'Jamie-John Cameron!' said Kirsty in her most severe headmistress voice and the children stood transfixed and gazed at the adults.

'Let me show you, Olga. It is Olga, isn't it? said Lady Sybill and she took the furs from the children and draped one elegantly around the neck of her exquisitely cut frock. 'One to wear, and one to drag,' and she walked off down the hallway to the stairs with the second fox tail trailing along behind her.

Kirsty was as surprised as the children, and her guest had almost reached the front door before she caught up with her to show her out.

'Don't be too cross, Mrs Cameron,' said Lady Sybill as Kirsty apologized profusely. 'Children are all the same, aren't they? I'll come back to see the football ground. We must think about cricket. I think boys like cricket, don't they?'

The chauffeur opened the door for her and Kirsty stood and watched until the car was out of sight.

31

Bob Cargill had decided that it would be eminently sensible for Kirsty Cameron to marry Matthew Matthews. He knew, from the guarded way that Kirsty spoke about the lawyer, that something had happened between them, but he was, he told himself, really happy to see how they were becoming friends again after the Colonel's death. Sometimes he thought he saw a special warmth in Kirsty's eyes when she was looking not at Matt but at him. He ignored the looks. In the hospital in France, he had told himself that there were certain things he no longer had the right to expect: a woman's love was one of them. This had been confirmed for him by his long-time girlfriend's reaction to his emaciated appearance.

'You should hae married Jean afore ye want tae the university,' his father had said, but oh no, how much worse it would have been to return from hell to find that one's very wife could not picture the future with a one-armed man.

The teaching job had been a godsend. There were hundreds, if not thousands of returning heroes applying for the vacant positions, or the posts that had been propped up by retired teachers or even, in a few desperate areas, by married women. A not-too-pretty half-qualified French teacher with one arm and a primary qualification would not, he felt, be high on any education committee's list of 'must haves'. He had read about the opening of the Aberannoch Castle School and had carefully calculated that, should the school be successful, there would probably be a position within the year. He had donned his best suit – not much, but at least clean and well pressed, and his mother had had it hanging out on the drying green to make sure no fishy smell adhered to it – and had set off for Aberannoch.

He had not recognized Kirsty at once. After all, when he last saw her she had been a buxom eighteen-year-old, and the Mrs Cameron who agreed to see him was a slender, sophisticated head teacher. She had known him at once, though, and he had seen in her eyes not distaste, but pity, and even the pity had gone as the months had passed. He had learned that she had married, had had a child and had lost her husband in the early days of the war. He had not known or even thought about Jamie-John's parentage until the day she had told him that the Colonel who had gifted the castle and its contents to the Trust was her child's grandfather. His first reaction to the news had been 'poor wee Kirsty' and he saw no reason to change his attitude. Two men dead that she had loved, and now the Colonel. More than anything in the world, Bob wanted Kirsty to be happy, and he never once stopped to wonder why her happiness was important to him. She needed a happy marriage: Jamie-John needed a father and Matt Matthews was the ideal candidate. And so when Jamie-John, in his pyjamas, came stomping over to his rooms to complain that his mother was going out to dinner with Mr Matthews when she could have had a perfectly good dinner in their flat with Grannie, he set himself to becoming Matt's champion. He even appealed to the small boy's baser instincts: Matt Matthews had a car, he reminded him.

'Lady Sybill's got a car, Bob,' Jamie told him on the morning after Lady Sybill's visit. 'It's only rented so it's not too super, but I bet she has a Rolls in London. I'll ask her when she comes today.'

They were walking together through the castle to the schoolroom floor where Bob was helping with the setting up of the new classroom, and Bob quickened his steps. Was Kirsty all right after her meeting with Lady Sybill? She was standing on a ladder putting a flowerpot on a shelf and again he felt his inadequacy: he could not hold onto the ladder and carry a plant pot at the same time.

She did not appear to be stressed but greeted them sunnily.

'I hear you had a visitor,' he said.

'*Pas devant les enfants,*' smiled Kirsty, who had sat in on Bob's French group.

'I know what that means, Mummy,' said Jamie-John scornfully. 'Olga and me were naughty, Mummy says, Mr Cargill.' He would not presume to be too familiar in front of his mother. 'Lady Sybill was nice, and she dragged her fur on the carpet, and Olga and me would never do anything like that.'

'His French grammar is fine, Kirsty,' laughed Bob as the child darted away.

'He's becoming a real handful,' sighed Kirsty.

But Jamie-John was about to get much worse.

Lady Sybill returned to the castle to see the sports facilities. She was charming. No, she would not dream of taking Mrs Cameron away from her work. After all, she did know her way around the grounds, and Jamie-John and ... what was her name? ... little Olga could easily point out features to her.

'We would be honoured if you would like to stay to lunch, Lady Sybill,' said Kirsty, knowing that she lied. She never wanted to see Lady Sybill again, and the thought of sitting down to eat a meal with her was anathema.

'How quaint,' smiled Lady Sybill, 'school dinner.'

For the next few weeks everything that either Jamie-John or Olga saw or heard was pronounced 'quaint'. After three weeks even Jessie no longer found them amusing.

'Try to be patient, Mother,' sighed Kirsty. 'At least we've seen the last of Lady Sybill for this year, and the children will forget.'

Jamie-John was not allowed to forget, however. Two weeks after school started a box arrived from a prestigious London toyshop, with a note from Lady Sybill to say that she hoped the small gift would make the return to school less painful. An ecstatic Jamie-John set out an entire battalion of lead guardsmen on the library floor.

'It's the regiment Lady Sybill's son was in, Mummy,' smiled Jamie-John. 'He was ever so brave and he was slain by the Hun. All my other soldiers are Huns now, and I'm going to kill them all.'

He set out his Black Watch soldiers and Kirsty watched in torment as he proceeded to mow down Jamie's regiment.

She tried to smile. 'You can't make them the Hun, sweetheart. The Black Watch is your . . . father's regiment.'

Had he noticed her slight hesitation? He seemed to look at her steadily out of those heartbreaking blue eyes for a long moment.

'It's only play,' he said and flattened the Black Watch with the palm of his hand.

Before she could stop herself Kirsty had dealt him a stinging blow on his bare leg. She could see the marks of her fingers on the skin as he hopped around screaming more in fright and anger – she hoped – than pain.

'Put your soldiers away, Jamie-John. You have been very naughty, and may not play with your lovely present again today. Besides, you must write and say thank you to Lady Sybill.'

Sullenly and almost insolently he put the guardsmen away in their box. Each one had to lie exactly as he wanted, and Kirsty itched to take them away and do it herself.

I mustn't lose control, I mustn't lose control, she kept saying to herself. They're only toy soldiers, not real men, and he doesn't know what he's doing. Oh, Lady Sybill, leave my son alone!

Jamie-John put himself to bed that night. Kirsty had been working on the end-of-the-month accounts to send to Sir John, and had not noticed the time. When the clock chimed nine, she jumped up and hurried off to find her son, but he was already in bed. She looked down at him and her heart swelled with love and sorrow as she knelt down beside the bed.

'I should never have slapped him. He's only a boy,' she whispered.

A lead soldier on the little table by the bed caught her eye. It was a model of a private in the Black Watch, positioned so as to guard the sleeping child.

'Oh, Jamie-John,' Kirsty almost sobbed and moved to pull up the blankets over the child. She lifted his arm to put it under the covers, and saw that his fist was tightly closed around a red-jacketed guardsman.

Kirsty looked down at the child for a moment and then went off to her sitting room to see her mother. It was Jessie who voiced her worry.

'Do you think that woman has told Jamie-John?'

'I'm not sure. I'm not even sure about what she knows herself. The Colonel said he would take care of everything, and the accident happened as he left her house. She must know, but why has she said nothing to me?'

'She wanted to have a look at Jamie-John before deciding to acknowledge him.'

'I don't want her to acknowledge him,' said Kirsty almost viciously. 'I want nothing from her.'

'Fine words, Kirsty, but what of the child? His grandfather promised to educate him.'

'He'll do well enough here with us, Mother, and I think I'll manage the High School in Dundee if he's able.' Kirsty got up from her chair and walked to the window. The trees and the garden always soothed her. 'What does Lady Sybill want with my son?' she asked them, but she received no answer.

The autumn term went on and the girls settled in and seemed to add a necessary dimension to the life of the school. Kirsty found herself looking forward to winter. Winter meant large heating bills, but it also meant that there was less likelihood of Lady Sybill making the journey north.

She came in October, a glorious month when Angus was clothed in its finest russets and golds and when local children were off school for the tatties. Kirsty's children had no need to supplement their income by harvesting the potato crop for the nearby farmers, but they too were given a week's holiday, which most of them spent walking or picnicking in the area. Kirsty yielded to Matt's entreaties and went off motoring up the coast. They picnicked in the shadow of an ancient castle; it was Kirsty's second picnic with a man.

She giggled almost hysterically when Matt's modest hamper yielded not the wine and delicacies she had been almost dreading but homely man-sized sandwiches and bottles of milk.

'Are the sandwiches too big?' Matt asked anxiously. 'I just can't get Mrs Dodd to cater for a woman.'

'You have no idea how perfect they are, Matt,' laughed Kirsty, and she meant it. She admitted to herself that she had come on the drive prepared to allow the romance of ruined castles and sheltered headlands to weave their web over her. Bob was as far away as ever, and Matt was here and available, and oh, dear God, before she was an old woman she wanted more of love and life than one afternoon in a flowery glade. But there had to be more than sex, and that would be all there was today if she allowed the afternoon to go as she had almost planned that it should.

They ate their picnic and tidied up the basket, then wandered along the edge of the sea under the cliff on which the castle stood.

'I wonder how many couples that old place has watched over the centuries?' she mused aloud.

'I sincerely hope it hasn't watched any,' said Matt. 'I was just about to steal a kiss, my very dear Mrs Cameron, and now you have me worrying that I might be seen.'

'By seagulls only, Matt, but let's not give them anything to look at.'

'A kiss, for God's sake, only a kiss. Oh, Kirsty, you must like me a little or you wouldn't be here with me.' He reached out and grasped her arms. 'Why *did* you come to this godforsaken place with me?'

'For a picnic, Matt,' said Kirsty, trying hard not to struggle, for the face in front of her was not Matt's well-known friendly countenance but the twisted one of Mr Buchanan.

'I hoped there might be more,' said Matt, and he almost flung her from him.

'So did I, Matt. Oh, God, we had this same conversation years ago. We should have stuck to the rules we set then. I like you, Matt. You're kind and generous and I wish I could love you . . . but I can't.'

'We'd best get back,' he said stiffly. 'It's finished, Kirsty. I don't know what you want from life, but I hope you get it. I want a wife and children before it's too late.'

They packed the car and started back to Aberannoch in silence. When they arrived there was a car parked outside the huge wooden gates that led to the inner courtyard.

'Lady Sybill,' said Kirsty in a voice that was almost a groan.

'I won't come in to pay my respects,' said Matt curtly. 'No doubt if she wants me she'll send for me. I plan to hand the Trust business over to one of my associates, Kirsty. Goodbye.'

'Goodbye, Matt,' whispered Kirsty, then she stood and watched as the car reversed and drove back down the driveway.

'I couldn't marry Matt so that he could protect me from Lady Sybill,' Kirsty told herself, but before the winter was over she was more than once to wish she had done just that.

She found Lady Sybill in the library, standing with sherry glass in hand before the painting of the Regency belle.

'All her descendants have those wonderful eyes,' she said by way of greeting. 'Not that there are too many – descendants, I mean.'

'Good evening, Lady Sybill. I'm sorry I wasn't here to greet you. Did you want anything in particular?' asked Kirsty, 'Like my son,' she finished to herself.

'Well, yes, I did, I suppose. Cards on the table, Mrs Cameron. Jamie-John is Hugh's child. I found it very difficult to believe: my son and . . . you. I don't mean to be insulting, but Hugh was a very popular young man and he had lots of girlfriends . . . from his own class. I expected to announce his engagement . . .'

She turned to look into the fire and Kirsty said nothing but watched her.

'My husband was going to change his will. Did you know that?' She turned swiftly to look at Kirsty who had turned red with embarrassment.

'Colonel Granville-Baker wanted to assume responsibility for Jamie-John's education. I had no idea . . .'

'He was on his way to his solicitor's offices when he was run down, Mrs Cameron.'

Kirsty said nothing. It was all too much.

'He wanted your son to have everything. Quite something, Mrs Cameron, but of course his will stands as he originally wrote it.'

'Why are you telling me all this?' asked Kirsty. There was a taste in her mouth like vomit and a feeling in the pit of her stomach like disaster about to happen.

'I could arrange for Jamie-John to have everything that his grandfather wanted him to have . . .' Lady Sybill stopped and looked at Kirsty expectantly, but Kirsty was determined to say nothing.

'All I ask in return is a very small . . . untruth. Change your name, legally – my lawyers have drafted documents – and allow me to tell my friends that you and Hugh were married. That he didn't tell his father and me because he was sure we would disapprove and – very nobly – you remained quiet when he was killed, and later you married Cameron because Hugh had all the legal documents. Simple!'

'Obscene. I don't want your money, Lady Sybill, and neither does my son.'

Swiftly Lady Sybill stood up and all pretence was gone, the surface charm scraped away. 'I have no intention of giving a gold digger like you a penny of my money, Mrs Cameron. But the Colonel would have given the boy his, and he's a surprisingly nice little chap.'

Kirsty stood up. The interview was at an end. How *dare* she? How dare she? So Jamie-John was *surprisingly nice*, was he?

'Good day, Lady Sybill.'

Lady Sybill looked at her admiringly. 'Really, Mrs Cameron. You might be a lady . . . almost. I'll leave for tonight.' She picked up the fox capes that were draped over the chair beside her and disposed them neatly around her neck and shoulders. 'Hugo was worth nearly a million pounds, and it could all belong to your little boy. What price a name?'

She swept out, but Kirsty stayed in the room looking into the young, smooth face with the glorious eyes: Jamie-John's great-grandmother. Would she have wanted an illegitimate child to inherit her money?

'God, I'm getting fanciful.'

She left the fire and hurried across the room to the windows that looked down on the driveway. Lady Sybill was just about to enter her car, and Jamie-John in a torn yellow sweater and a too-long Cameron kilt was talking animatedly to her. Kirsty saw her hold the door open and the child disappear into the car.

'Oh, God, oh no,' Kirsty moaned and ran from the window to the stairs. She pushed past two of the boys almost without seeing them and, regardless of her dignity, ran down the stone staircase, her heels nipped by desperation. She threw the doors open as if they were made of balsa wood and flew across the courtyard in the wake of the speeding car.

Jamie-John was sauntering back along the driveway and when she reached him Kirsty threw her arms around him and hugged him until he pushed her away angrily.

'Oh, do stop, Mummy. You're breaking my plane. Look at it! Lady Sybill brought it. Bob . . . Mr Cargill says he flew in one like it in the war.'

Kirsty's heart was still beating furiously and she chided herself. Stupid. Lady Sybill would never kidnap Jamie. She would not need to stoop to such an action.

'I drove to the end of the driveway and Lady Sybill's chauffeur let me hold the wheel for a bit, the straight bit through the rhododendrons.'

She bit her tongue to stop herself from speaking. He was too small to reach the controls of a car – how could Lady Sybill be so foolhardy?

'Lady Sybill's nice, Mummy. She likes me, she says I remind her of her boy.'

'Yes, dear,' Kirsty managed to say calmly. 'She thinks all little boys are alike. They like cricket, was what she said.'

'No,' said Jamie, darting away from her, his plane held up in the air. 'I'm different. I'm special.'

Kirsty sat by her sleeping son's bed for some time that night. Had she the right to stop him from inheriting nearly a million pounds? Dear God, it was impossible to contemplate that amount of money, but it would have been Jamie-John's had his grandfather been able to reach his solicitor. And all she had to do was live a little lie. After all, hadn't she been living a lie for years? She could change her name, and Jamie-John's, to Granville-Baker and then pretend, no, allow people to believe that she and Hugh had been secretly married. Such a little thing to do for Jamie-John. She got up wearily and quietly left the sleeping child.

Although it was late and already quite dark, she decided to walk in the garden. The sky was clear and the air was cold, so cold that she wished she had brought a jacket. A harvest moon hung low over the orchard, painting the grass silver below the trees as she wandered through them, smelling the night smells and hearing the rustling of small animals and birds. The noises of the night never failed to surprise her. It was only city folk who imagined that the country was quiet at night.

'Don't jump, Kirsty,' said a quiet voice and Bob detached himself from a tree and stepped out on the path before her. 'I would have let you walk past, but I thought you might see my cigarette and be frightened.'

'Oh, Bob,' said Kirsty, 'I'm so glad to see you.'

She stepped forward to meet him and automatically he enfolded her in his good arm and held her against him. She felt as a small ship that has been severely buffeted by the wind must feel when it reaches safe harbour.

'You're freezing,' he said and tightened his arm.

'Oh, Bob,' said Kirsty, 'I've had the most beastly day.'

He looked down at her and saw her shining eyes, her hair silvered and shimmering in the moonlight. He bent and kissed her lips . . . it was so right, so perfect. She leaned against him and slowly, tentatively, lifted her arms and put them round his neck. His arm tightened around her and his lips became more and more demanding. Sleeping feelings began to stir, to waken: it was so long, so very long since she had felt any . . . desire: yes, that was it, desire.

It was Bob who moved away first.

'A little dalliance in the moonlight?' he laughed lightly. 'Here, put my jacket around you and tell me about your awful day. I thought a picnic on the beach sounded delightful.'

'It would have been, with the right man.' Could she suggest, more subtly, that he himself was the right man? Kirsty strove to be as light as Bob had been. The moment was over because he had wished it to be over. She could not bring it back.

She told him about Lady Sybill's suggestion that she change her name and Jamie-John's.

'Am I wrong to say no? How can I look my child in the eye and know that I denied him an inheritance of nearly a million pounds?'

'Lady Sybill told you that the Colonel was going to leave that much to the boy?'

'Yes.'

'Then if she has any honour, she will make sure that he gets it without any stipulation.'

They walked slowly back towards the castle. In spite of Bob's jacket, Kirsty shivered.

'Cold?'

'No, frightened. Of what, I don't know. Lady Sybill wants my son and she'll stop at nothing to get him, but she can't take him away from me. Jamie saw to that. According to law, Jamie Cameron was his father. That's what his birth certificate says.'

'Jamie meant a great deal to you?'

Kirsty stopped and forced him to stop too and look at her. 'Bob, Jamie was an old school friend, no more. He gave me his name to save me from being ostracized and embarrassed in the village and he asked nothing, *nothing* in return. I can't sell his name. If he hadn't been killed I think we could have made our marriage work – I was going to do my best to see that it did. Do you understand me?'

He turned her back towards the castle again. 'As I said, Kirsty. He meant a great deal to you.'

32

IT WAS A FRUSTRATING WINTER. The year ended almost as it had begun with storms and high winds, and Kirsty wondered whether the East Coast was now to experience a hurricane such as had struck Glasgow and the West in January. It was snow, however, and not wind that hurled itself around Aberannoch Castle School. Blizzards swept across the country and in the romantically named 'Silver Thaw' of December 21st, there were three thousand street accidents in the City of London alone. To Jamie-John's delight, there was a white Christmas.

The new term did not begin well as several children could not return on time, and it was almost February before classes were in full swing. The antiquated heating system in the castle tried valiantly to battle with the elements but finally, on a blistering cold day in February, admitted defeat and collapsed. Kirsty and the other teachers did duty bringing in coal and keeping the huge fires burning. They had stepped back in time: back to 1910. Several of the youngsters caught colds and Kirsty and her mother nursed them devotedly. The scourge of influenza, which had wiped out more people in one year than had been killed in the war, must not be allowed to attack the children, and to that end, all the healthy pupils were kept well away from the invalids. Jamie-John was one of the healthy ones and Kirsty was so busy with feverish, fretful youngsters that she saw very little of her son. Even when she was free from duty in the sick-room there was always so much administration to do. The bigger the school grew, the more paperwork found its way onto the Colonel's beautiful desk in the library. A full-time secretary was needed and, as soon as she had time, Kirsty promised herself that she would write and tell the Trust so.

At least the weather kept Lady Sybill away – but it could not prevent her influence from breaching the castle walls. A huge parcel for Jamie-John arrived from Hamley's at Christmas, and in January a hamper from Fortnum and Mason reached them.

'Lady Sybill thinks we're starving to death in the snow,' screeched Jamie-John with delight as he danced around his mother while she unpacked exotic fruits.

'Avocado pears and mangoes are just the thing,' said Kirsty sarcastically.

'Oh, it was nice of her, Kirsty,' said Jessie. 'Be fair. And it's for all the children this time, not just Jamie-John. I wonder how you eat avocado pears?'

'And what they taste like, Grannie,' said Jamie-John.

If Kirsty hoped that the luxurious gift would soon be eaten up and forgotten, she was disappointed. The children tried to grow trees from the huge stones in the fruits, and for weeks every windowsill in classrooms and dormitories held jam jars where precariously balanced pits tried to germinate. One or two even succeeded.

The vitamin content of his share did not keep Bob from contracting influenza.

'I'm feeling a bit seedy, Kirsty,' he said one afternoon after he had taken his French class. 'I think I ought to get to Auchmithie to my mother. If this takes its usual course, I'm in for a week or two. Best stay out of the way.'

'Nonsense, Bob.' Kirsty spoke brusquely to hide the fear she experienced. He looked almost as bad as when he first came to the castle. 'By the time you get to Auchmithie, you'll be really ill. You must stay here. Mother and I will manage your meals, and I'll ring the doctor and ask him to come to see you.'

He was already too weak to protest. The doctor promised to visit the invalid some time in the morning after his surgery, and Kirsty was forced to stay away and allow her mother to attend Bob in his rooms.

'I'm going to stay with him, Kirsty,' announced Jessie when she eventually emerged from the sick-room. 'He's already running a fever and I'll try to get it down.'

'I'll help,' began Kirsty. No need to hide from Jessie. 'Mother, I have to see him, to know he's all right.'

'No. You have nearly thirty children to consider and you'll have Bob's class as well as your own for a day or two – if you can even get a supply teacher to come out here. I'll take care of him as if he were Jamie-John, Kirsty.'

Kirsty wanted to protest. Bob was not strong; he had been gassed. Influenza was a killer. 'You're right, of course,' she said, 'but I'll come over first thing in the morning with some tea. Are there plenty of logs and coals in his room? If only the heating system worked.'

'Stop fussing, Kirsty. I'm taking sensible precautions. Bob's not very strong – he reminds me of your father, always overdoing it.'

It was two weeks before Bob was well enough to return to class, and at the end of that time Kirsty was almost totally exhausted. She had not realized just how much her mother contributed to the life of the school, and for a few days had found herself doing not only her own and Bob's work but Jessie's as well.

'This is ridiculous, Kirsty,' said Meg one day when she found the headmistress trying to coach rugby in the school gymnasium. 'You'll make yourself ill, and then where would we be? I'll go home at afternoon playtime and get some clothes. Ask Irene to take the whole school out to look for signs that winter's over.'

'It'll be dark by afternoon playtime . . .'

'Then it will take them longer!'

'Very funny, Meg. What about Will?'

'He won't mind. In fact, I may bring him too, if that's alright with you. He can't fish in this weather and he's bored to tears at home.'

'Jamie-John will be thrilled. Oh, you're a good friend, Meg, and a godsend if you can really move in till Bob's well.'

The first thing Meg did when she returned was to banish Jessie from the sick-room for a few hours.

'How sick do you have to get before you realize you're wasting precious time, Bob Cargill?' were Meg's bracing words to the invalid. 'I'll send Will in to keep you company. Don't worry. He doesn't talk much.'

Will's quiet presence in the sick-room freed Jessie to return to her duties as Matron, and gradually the school got back to normal. Bob was still very weak, and Kirsty watched him anxiously to make sure that he was not throwing himself head first into too many activities. The weather made outside sports an impossibility, but Bob and Will started a chess club which nearly all of the oldest boys and girls joined. Jamie-John wanted to join too.

'Och, let the lad join, Kirsty. He's bright enough. I just didn't think chess would appeal to the really wee ones.'

'We said twelve and over, Bob, and we have to stick to it. We can't change rules for my son. He can wait till next year.'

'Lady Sybill's going to send me a real ivory chess set,' announced Jamie-John when Kirsty went in to tuck him up that night.

Kirsty stood stock-still, fear clutching at her stomach, and looked at her son. 'What did you say, Jamie-John?'

'I said, Lady Sybill is . . .'

'I know what you said,' Kirsty interrupted illogically. 'When did you speak to Lady Sybill?'

'I telephoned her at tea-time. She was really pleased, she told me to ring her any time I wanted, but I know you don't like me to talk to her. Why not, Mummy? She's nice and she likes me. She says I remind her of her own boy.'

So she hadn't told him. At least that was something.

'That's nice, Jamie-John, but you're not Lady Sybill's boy, you're mine, and the chess club rule was, "children twelve and over", and you'll be twelve in May. That isn't long to wait.'

'I'll wait to join your silly little chess club, but meantime I'll teach myself to play chess. Lady Sybill might even bring the set. She says she's coming up as soon as the weather gets better. She's bringing her own car – it's a Daimler. She has a chauffeur too, and she'll take me for a drive.'

'What about the other children, Jamie-John?'

'They won't mind. They all know I'm special, Mummy,' he said in such a matter-of-fact tone that Kirsty ached to box his ears. 'They know you're my mother, and there's grannie and Auntie Meg and I call Mr Cargill "Bob" when I'm not in class, and I live in the castle all year. Of *course* I'm different.'

Kirsty fled, and her feet found their way to Bob's rooms.

'I'm sorry to burst in on you like this. It's Jamie-John,' and she told him her worry that her son was changing, was being spoiled, being bought by Lady Sybill and her wealth.

'Here, sit down and I'll make a cup of tea. A chess set isn't the end of the world.'

'It's the beginning, Bob. Every time I deny him something, he'll ring Lady Sybill and she'll buy it for him to spite me.'

'Has she told him she's his grandmother?'

'I don't think so.'

Bob thought hard for a long moment. 'Kirsty, isn't it possible that he already knows? He sees that portrait almost every day.'

'He's grown up with that, he doesn't look at it.'

'He must be aware of it. Be realistic, Kirsty. He's almost twelve and he's bright. He may not want to know it, but possibly he's faced the fact and decided, subconsciously, to use the situation to his advantage.'

She cried out almost as if she had been slapped. 'He couldn't be that devious, not my Jamie-John.' She turned to face him; her lovely face was so ravaged by fear and grief that he acted spontaneously. His arm went around her and he pressed her slight form to his. He sought her lips and she offered herself up to him willingly, hungrily. At last he drew away. 'Oh God, Kirsty, I never meant . . .'

'That's what they all say,' she laughed weakly. 'Oh, Bob, please stop apologizing for loving me. You do love me, don't you? I'm not making an absolute complete fool of myself?'

His answer was to kiss her again, a kiss that fused their very souls together. This time, shaken by the violence of their emotion, it was Kirsty who drew back first. She stood up and smoothed her skirt.

'It mustn't be a mistake, Bob, not this time. I came . . . oh, God, I probably came to hear you say you loved me. No one, not Hugh, not Jamie, no one has ever used the words . . .'

'I love you, Kirsty,' he said, so simply that she had to believe him. 'I've probably loved you since you were sixteen years old, but you don't want to hear me say it tonight. Jamie-John – tell him, Kirsty. Tell him before Sybill does. Tell him the way it was, the way you want him to hear it. He'll be able to live with the truth, you'll see.'

Simple. Just tell him the truth! How difficult in fact it was to find the words that would tell a twelve-year-old boy the circumstances of his birth. Kirsty went over explanations in her mind several times, and she rehearsed them with Bob when they stole a moment or two alone together.

'First explain his birth, Kirsty, and then we can really plan for the next big thing you'll have to explain – if there is anything to tell him about.'

'Oh, there is, Bob, there is,' breathed Kirsty from the comfort of his one good arm, but when she came to explain to Jamie-John, the clever words faded away like mist in the morning. And then the thaw came, and the spring and, eventually, Lady Sybill.

'You have had the winter to think, Mrs Cameron. I'm sure you have come to the right conclusion.'

'Yes, I have.'

Lady Sybill smiled in triumph. 'There, that wasn't too terribly hard, was it? A million pounds and whatever I choose to leave him. We'll set up a Trust, of course, to administer until he's . . . what would you suggest? Twenty-five, thirty? It will pay for a decent school . . .'

'I'm sorry, Lady Sybill. I haven't made my meaning clear. I have no intention of changing my son's name to Granville-Baker, or pretending that Hugh and I were married. Hugh loved me. I do know that, and I hope we would have been married, but it wasn't to be and I won't negate what Jamie Cameron did for both of us . . . for money.' She put as much loathing as she could into her voice. 'Can't you just love him because he's your grandson?'

There was no chance for Lady Sybill to answer what had probably been a rhetorical question, for at that moment the door burst open and Olga Pacholek almost fell into the room.

'Mr Cargill says you're to come, Mrs Cameron. Jamie-John's away for a run in Lady Sybill's car.'

Kirsty started up out of her seat in alarm and turned to face the door, but Lady Sybill remained calm.

'And why shouldn't he, my dear? My chauffeur . . .'

'. . . is having his tea in the kitchen,' Olga finished for her.

*

Jamie-John hadn't really meant to drive the huge car. He'd been showing off to Olga, who thought everything he did was absolutely wonderful, and since his mother didn't seem to think he was so special these days it really was quite nice to have someone admire everything he did.

'Lady Sybill won't mind,' he had told Olga. 'You'll see.'

'Why not?' Olga asked, but he shied away from that difficult question; he didn't really know why not, and he didn't want to know. It was one of those horrible grown-up things that always made his mother look sad.

'I'll tell your mother,' Olga had yelled after him. 'She'll murder you!'

That threat had made Jamie-John release the brake. He had only wanted to start up the car, but what could a boy do? For a second he caught a glimpse of Olga's terrified face as the huge monster slid away under his hands, and then he was too busy trying to handle it to think of much else. The driveway was nice and straight and flat and after a few yards he began to feel that this driving thing was easy. The car did all the work, all the driver had to do was steer. Jamie-John Cameron relaxed, sat up straight and looked around him. Then he sobered suddenly, for an incredible realization had just come to him. What on earth was he going to do when he reached the gates? He had no idea at all of how to stop. And then he saw the woodland path that led into the Dell, and he pulled on the wheel with all his might to turn the car off the road. His mother was going to be furious, but she would be even angrier if he was out on a public road. In the castle grounds he would be all right, surely?

The car was going faster ... the road to the Dell ran downhill. Jamie-John had been to the Dell a million times, it was one of his favourite places to sit when he needed time and space to be alone. The Dell was quiet and peaceful, and once he'd even thought it was like being in church: it had that lovely calm feeling. But he had never noticed that the slope into the Dell was quite steep. The car had taken over: it was going faster and faster and faster. Desperately the child tried to steer. The tree, the tree! He had missed it – well, bumped it a bit but, oh, no, another tree ... Where had it come from? He couldn't, he couldn't. Jamie-John Cameron screamed for his mother.

Bob Cargill had run down the driveway towards the road when Olga told him about Jamie-John's escapade. He felt as weak as a newborn baby, but fear lent him strength. He reached the gates and leaned against them as he scanned the road for signs of the car. That was when he saw the smoke rising from the Dell.

'Oh, Christ, oh Christ!' he sobbed and started back up the driveway. When he reached the entrance to the Dell, he stopped and looked down. The huge car had side-swiped a tree and was on its side. Something was on fire – no flames yet, just smoke, but any minute . . . He started forward.

'Oh, thank God, chaps.'

The soldiers seemed oblivious of the flames that began to lick hungrily about their boots. They paid no heed to Bob's greeting, but gently, very gently released the child from the tangled metal and then carried him to the side of the road where they laid him down well away from the car. Bob flung himself down beside Jamie-John and pulled off his coat just as the car exploded with a 'whoosh', which reminded him only too clearly of the crash that had cost him his arm and his liberty. Instinctively he covered his head and ducked.

'I don't know where you fellows came from but . . .'

Bob was alone in the Dell as he knelt beside the child and covered the slight body with his jacket while tears of which he was unaware rolled down his face. He was still there when the others arrived.

Jamie-John was taken to the hospital in Arbroath, the same one Kirsty had visited with the children from Aberannoch all those years ago. There were no laughing children now, with arms full of meadow flowers, just Jamie-John, bruised and broken but miraculously holding tenuously to life. Kirsty sat in the waiting room with her mother and Bob, and waited and waited and made bargains with God:

Let him live and I'll never, ever scold him again.

Let him live and I'll change his name to anything Sybill wants.

Let him live and I'll do anything, anything.

A nurse brought tea and Bob gulped his down thirstily. Kirsty sat with her hands around her cup, absorbing its warmth. They did not speak, but just sat and somehow knew that they drew strength from one another. She did not ask her mother to lie down, to go home. Suddenly Jessie looked her years. 'She should be retired,' thought Kirsty. 'She's an old woman and she's still working, working, for me . . . and Jamie-John.'

'Let him live for her, if not for me. I'll do anything, anything.'

She did not know she sobbed and Bob pulled her close to him and she wept against his chest.

'Let him live and I'll give up Bob.'

She looked at him, so drawn and pale. He was exhausted, not yet well after his influenza and yet he had, he had . . .

'Bob, how did you manage . . . was he thrown from the car . . . they think his legs are broken . . . was that when he was thrown?'

'I don't know, Kirsty.' Bob stared straight ahead as if he was seeing not the polished floor of the waiting room but a burning car and a little boy. 'The mind plays strange tricks. The car . . . he must have tried to miss a tree. Maybe he pulled too hard on the steering wheel, I don't know, I can't drive. But the car had toppled over. It was on the left, on its left.'

'Then Jamie-John would have been thrown the other way, Bob.' It was Jessie who spoke, her tired eyes brimming with tears and admiration.

'I don't know, Mrs Robertson. It happened so fast, but that policeman was wrong. I wasn't the hero, it was the other chaps. The laddie was already out of the car when I got there.' He stopped talking, his mind busy. Had there indeed been 'other chaps'? Was it a trick of the smoke, the flame? Had his mind gone back to his own crash when two old German farmworkers in dirty uniforms had pulled him from his burning plane?

'What other chaps, Bob?' Kirsty was very pale but very alert.

'I thought I saw two soldiers, lads on manoeuvres maybe, who happened to be passing.'

'Mrs Cameron?' The doctor had come in. 'You can see your little boy now but only for a moment.'

They had all started up, but the doctor went on, 'And only his mother. Dad and Grannie must wait a little longer. He's a very sick little boy.'

'Will he be all right?' Kirsty was desperate.

'He's very ill, Mrs Cameron. The broken bones will heal, but there are internal injuries. Come along. Five minutes, and then I want you all to go home.'

Jamie-John was lying in a long iron bed that made his small body look even more tiny and frail. His face was very pale and there was a large ugly bruise under one eye. He was so very still as Kirsty leaned over him. Was he even breathing?

'I can't leave him, Doctor.'

'Then you must stay in the waiting room, Mrs Cameron. I'm sorry, but we're moving Jamie-John. There is more work for us to do and there's nothing you can do to help. Really, it will be better if you rest so that if . . . when he comes round . . .'

'I'll send the others home, but I must stay.'

Kirsty stayed for nearly a week, and at the end of that time Jamie-John's eyelids fluttered and he opened his eyes. Those beautiful blue eyes, Hugh's eyes, looked calmly at his mother.

'I hurt, Mummy,' he whispered.

'I know, darling,' she tried to smile back through the tears that threatened to spill over. He had come back to her. Had his father, his fathers, brought him back for her to love and cherish? She didn't know, she would never know. She kissed the child gently on his pale cheek and turned to look at the nurse who had just entered.

'There,' said the nurse triumphantly. 'Didn't Mr Harris say it would be today if at all? I'll get him.'

Mr Harris, older and greyer, was still senior consultant and Kirsty had got to know him quite well during this past week.

'Are you angry, Mummy?' whispered the little voice.

'Oh, Jamie-John, how can I be angry? I nearly lost you.' And he might never walk again, but she would not say that, not yet, not yet.

'I bet Lady Sybill's furious.'

'No. She loves you too, Jamie-John, very much. She's been to see you every day. Who do you think can afford all these wonderful toys?'

As yet Lady Sybill only knew one way of proving her love, but she'll learn, Kirsty thought.

'I think we must leave this young man alone now, Mrs Cameron.' It was Mr Harris. 'He'll exhaust himself chattering, and you need to go home.'

Kirsty stood up. Home. A hot bath. A long sleep. The school and all the children who had filled Jamie-John's room with loving messages. Her mother . . . and Bob.

'I'll go home, darling, and tell everyone. But I'll come back soon. We have so much to look forward to . . . you'll see.'

She kissed him again, but already the eyelashes were resting delicately on the child's cheeks.

'There's a little colour there, Mr Harris?'

'There will be more tomorrow. Now go home and get a decent night's sleep.'

Bob was waiting in the corridor. Somehow she was not surprised. At first he didn't see her as he contemplated the pattern on the polished linoleum. Was it the same linoleum that they had walked on with their flowers all those years ago?

He looked up anxiously as he heard the click of her heels and she smiled at him. He said nothing, but held out his good hand to her and she took it and together they walked to the door.

'I promised to give you up if he could get better, Bob.' There, she had said it. She had got her son back. Had she to give up the man she loved, loved with a mature and lasting love, in exchange for her son?

'I promised all sorts of daft things myself in a burning plane, Kirsty love, but the God who helped me through hell didn't hold me to them.'

She looked at him, long and hard. Was he right, or was she just hearing what she wanted to hear? Would God hold her to all her promises?

'I promised never to even scold him again.'

'Well, I know that's a really daft one! Read your Bible, Kirsty. Christ got righteously angry and threw the money-lenders out of the temple. Unchecked, Jamie-John will turn into even more of a spoiled brat.'

'My son is not a spoiled brat,' she said, but she was smiling as he opened the door and they stepped out into bright sunshine.

'We'll need to buy a car for the school,' said Bob. 'I've spent a fortune on taxis this week. There's never a train when you want one.'

Kirsty turned back to look at the hospital where her little son lay. 'He's still very ill, Bob. His legs . . .'

'Will get better tomorrow or the tomorrow after that.'

'Yes, Bob. Everything will work out tomorrow, everything.' She turned to him, naturally, spontaneously, in the open air for all the world to see if they chose. 'I love you, Bob Cargill, and I want to be your wife.'

He drew her close and kissed her hair, her eyes, her lips.

'What price the education code now, you strumpet?' he said and bent to kiss her again, hard, as if to seal a bargain. 'I've waited a long time to hear you say that.'

'Let's go home, Bob, to all our tomorrows.'

Acknowledgements

I'd like to thank my agent, Teresa Chris, and the editors at Bonnier Zaffre for making such a splendid publication of this book.

Welcome to the world of Eileen Ramsay!

Keep reading for more from Eileen Ramsay, to discover a recipe that features in this novel and to find out more about Eileen Ramsay's books . . .

We'd also like to welcome you to Memory Lane, a place to discuss the very best saga stories from authors you know and love with other readers, plus get recommendations for new books we think you'll enjoy. Read on and join our club!

Meet Eileen Ramsay

I wanted to be Georgette Heyer when I grew up – but failed Higher Latin because I was reading her books instead of Caesar's *The Gallic Wars*. I had written a Scottish-set Regency as part of my Master's degree at university in California and was thrilled when an agent, to whom I was introduced shortly after returning to Scotland, sold the book to an American publisher. The publisher did not ask for another and the agent said: 'Write a saga, write about what you know.'

I thought about what I knew, and made a list: teaching, music, dance, motherhood, travel and love.

I thought of how important education is important to me. I have been both student and teacher on both sides of the Atlantic, I want a good education for everyone. I remembered Friday afternoons when we wrote compositions, which I loved, and the days when the teacher read to us, a few pages of a classic novel that I then checked out of the local library.

Once, I remember when we were waiting for exam results. The teacher separated the girls and the boys and told each group what the future might hold. Later the boys told us about marvellous possibilities, airline pilots, astronauts, engineers, lawyers, surgeons . . . the exciting list went on. Breathless with anticipation, the girls heard: 'Well, you can always be nurses or teachers.' Poor patients if I were the nurse! I became a teacher and I loved it.

I thought of my life, spending a great deal of time in Edinburgh with the U.S. Airforce, and in California with the U.S. marines. I thought of the evening when my soldier father returned from the war and I remembered being terrified when this tall strong stranger threw me up into the air. Before his twenty-first birthday, our older son took after his grandfather to became an army officer and went immediately on active service for some years. The anxieties my characters feel about their loved ones going into battle is something I know all too well.

The landscape of my childhood is huge source of inspiration for me. I grew up in the village of Dumfriesshire, a coal-mining area, there were still acres of fine farmlands and woods where thousands of primroses rioted every spring, and there were streams running into the mighty River Nith that were deep enough for us to swim in and shallow enough so that parents did not worry.

I then turned my attention to Angus, where I live. I reside in a house that is in the midst of beautiful farmland, looking across fields to the sea. Not our fields but belonging to farmers who made us welcome from the start, even though we had very large dogs and gave our sons Jacob sheep and hens as pets. Our hens laid eggs everywhere and the ones I couldn't find always hatched and became chickens that scratched up our neighbour's seeds. The Jacobs could jump everything but the paddock wall and often we had phone calls from patient neighbours who never berated us when they found one or two really lovely sheep eating their flowers.

Our sons are now grown and their children love to visit us – we no longer have sheep or hens and the children are content to note the miracles of the changing seasons, 'from Granny's window.'

Teaching, music, dance, motherhood, travel and love – they're pretty good things to write about, I reckon.

Simple Scottish Stovies

Stovies is a traditional Scottish dish made of potatoes, onions and, usually, leftover roast meat with beef dripping. During hard times, Stovies were a popular way to reduce waste and save food, using every scrap available. On New Year's Eve, Kirsty's mother brings a pot of Stovies to the castle kitchens, probably made from the ends of Christmas dinner. Nowadays, it's the perfect recipe to use up any leftovers from a Sunday roast. There is no one correct way to make Stovies, in fact, many Scottish families have their own recipe, invoking nostalgia and memories of childhood.

Serves 4-6

Ingredients:

- 30g lard or butter, or dripping saved from a roast
- 1 onion, finely chopped
- 400g swede, peeled and cut into cubes
- 2 large carrots, peeled and chopped into cubes
- 1 celery stick, finely chopped
- 500g leftover roast meat (or see below for more ideas!)
- 700g potatoes, peeled and cut into cubes
- 500ml beef stock
- Oatcakes or crusty bread, to serve

Method:

1. Heat the lard, butter or dripping in a medium sized saucepan. Add the onion and fry for 10 minutes over a low heat until softened.
2. Add the swede, carrot and celery and fry for 5 minutes.
3. Stir in the meat, if using leftover roast meat, then the potatoes.
4. Pour over the stock and season generously, bring to the boil, then turn the heat down to a simmer.
5. Cook covered for 1 hour 30 minutes or until the vegetables have softened and the potatoes have broken down completely.
6. Serve with oatcakes or crusty bread and enjoy!

Variations:

- Add tinned corned beef instead of leftover meat. Add this to the pan 20 minutes before the end of cooking.
- Slice up some sausages and add them to the frying onions.
- Go vegetarian by omitting the meat and swapping the dripping for olive oil or butter and vegetable stock.

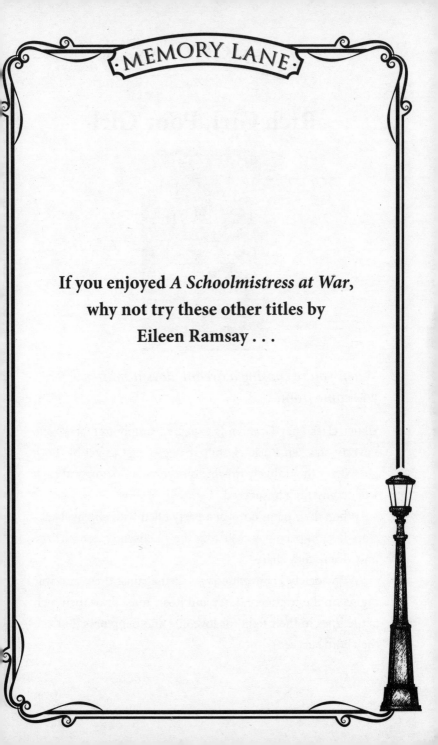

·MEMORY LANE·

If you enjoyed *A Schoolmistress at War*,
why not try these other titles by
Eileen Ramsay . . .

Rich Girl, Poor Girl

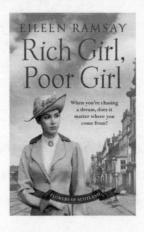

When you're chasing a dream, does it matter where you come from?

Upper-class Lucy Graham is expected simply to marry well. Poverty-stricken Rosie Nesbitt struggles just to get by. Both girls share the unlikely dream to become a doctor, and each will do anything to succeed.

When their paths cross at a party filled with eligible bachelors it soon becomes clear that their chosen career isn't the only desire they share.

With society's conventions stacked against them and war raging on the continent, Lucy and Rosie must draw their own battle lines in their fight for love, life and happiness. But can they both succeed?

The Crofter's Daughter

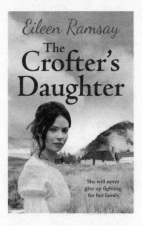

'When I'm the farmer,' began Mairi, and then she stopped, for she would never be the farmer. She was a girl.

Ever since she was nine years old, Mairi McGloughlin has known she wants to be a farmer, but by the law of the land it's her scholarly brother Ian who will someday inherit.

The next best thing might be to marry a farmer, and charming, confident Jack could be the perfect answer. But then there's Robin, her brother's best friend, more a man of books than of the land – and yet there's something about him . . .

But with the outbreak of the Great War, their choices change completely and neither Mairi, Ian or Robin can hope to escape unscathed.

As the world around them changes, only the land and love remain constant. But can it be enough to see them through?

The Glasgow Girl at War

Growing up in a convent in Glasgow, Ferelith Gallagher dreams of bigger and better things. With no money behind her, and no family to speak of, she travels to Edinburgh to study to be a lawyer – a brave choice for a woman in the 1930s. And when she falls in love with a young fellow student, she thinks she's finally found a home.

But after a brief and disastrous marriage, Ferelith swears she is through with love, and buries herself in her studies, striving to become the first female senior advocate in Scottish history. But when she finally meets a man she knows she could be happy with, Ferelith finds herself torn between love and her career.

When war breaks out, she knows life will never be the same again . . .

·MEMORY LANE·

Wartime Tales from Memory Lane

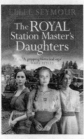

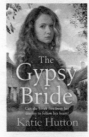

Discover new stories from the best saga authors

Available now